THE
SWEETEST
THING

Emma Blair

BANTAM BOOKS

TORONTO · NEW YORK · LONDON · SYDNEY · AUCKLAND

THE SWEETEST THING

All of the characters in this book are fictitious,
and any resemblance to actual persons, living or dead,
is purely coincidental.

A BANTAM BOOK 0 553 40373 7

Originally published in Great Britain by Bantam Press,
a division of Transworld Publishers Ltd

PRINTING HISTORY
Bantam Press edition published 1993
Bantam Books edition published 1994

Copyright © Emma Blair 1993

The right of Emma Blair to be identified as the author of this
work has been asserted in accordance with sections 77 and 78
of the Copyright Designs and Patents Act 1988.

Conditions of Sale

1. This book is sold subject to the condition that it shall not, by way of trade
or otherwise, be lent, re-sold, hired out or otherwise circulated in any form
of binding or cover other than that in which it is published and without a
similar condition including this condition being imposed on the subsequent
purchaser.

2. This book is sold subject to the Standard Conditions of Sale of Net
Books and may not be re-sold in the UK below the net price fixed by the
publishers for the book.

Set in Ehrhardt 10/11pt by Falcon Graphic Art Ltd.

Bantam Books are published by Transworld Publishers Ltd,
61–63 Uxbridge Road, Ealing, London W5 5SA,
in Australia by Transworld Publishers (Australia) Pty Ltd,
15–25 Helles Avenue, Moorebank, NSW 2170,
and in New Zealand by Transworld Publishers (NZ) Ltd,
3 William Pickering Drive, Albany, Auckland.

Made and printed in Great Britain by
Cox & Wyman Ltd, Reading, Berks.

To Eddy Boyd, good friend,
mentor and a true one-off.
Thanks for the memories!

Chapter One

Cully was dead.

Meg Stewart stared at her husband, a combination of shock, fear and cold horror gripping her heart. His eyes were open, his face contorted. The long scar on his cheek, a wound he'd received in the Great War, had gone strangely colourless, almost vanishing altogether.

Meg couldn't believe it. Cully, her Cully, was dead; there could be no mistake. Throwing back her head, she started to scream, a long-drawn-out agonized scream that tore at her throat.

'Meg, wake up for God's sake!' The voice came from a long way off. 'Meg, wake up!'

The scream ended in a gasp as she found herself sitting upright in bed staring at Cully's familiar features. His forehead was creased, his gaze filled with anxious concern.

'You've had a nightmare, lass,' he consoled. 'That's all, a horrible nightmare.'

With a sob she threw herself into his arms, taking comfort and solace from his reassuring smell. She sobbed again and buried her face against his chest.

'There, there,' he murmured, stroking her hair. 'This isn't like you at all, girl.'

A nightmare. It had seemed so very real, she thought, and shuddered. She could have sworn she'd actually been there, witnessing it all, experiencing the profundity of his loss.

'Oh, Cully,' she whispered.

'I'm here, Meg. Nothing to worry about now. It's all over. Finished.'

She shuddered again, feeling sweat trickling down her back. Her mind was still reeling, her nerves raw.

'I dreamt you were dead,' she said.

'Dead. Me!' He laughed – a laugh that warmed the coldness in her. 'I've never been more alive, and that's a fact.'

'It was so real, so terribly real.'

'Aye,' he sympathized, his voice now low and understanding, 'nightmares can be like that. I remember ...' He trailed off, momentarily lost in inner reflection.

Meg glanced up at him, noting the grim line of his jaw. 'You talking about the war?'

He sucked in a deep breath and slowly nodded. The war had been a time of nightmares: nightmares that didn't confine themselves to sleep, but could steal upon you in an instant, day as well as night; nightmares straight from hell itself.

'Your hair's wet,' he commented.

She reached up and touched her hair. He was right; it was soaked through, curled and clinging to her in places. She realized then her breathing was short and sharp, her chest rising and falling in rhythm.

'You were dead. Lying there with your eyes open ...' She paused, and shuddered yet again. 'It was ghastly.'

'I would have thought you might have been pleased to be rid of me,' he teased.

'Oh, Cully,' she husked in reply. 'Never in a million years. You must know that.'

He did, only too well. 'Do I?' he further teased, trying to cheer her up and dispel the after-effects of the nightmare.

'Of course you do.'

'I have my doubts sometimes,' he said, tongue in cheek.

She realized from his expression, the half-smile playing round his mouth, what he was doing and why he was doing it. He was such a good man, she thought; she'd never have found better.

She peered at the bedside clock and saw that it had just gone three o'clock. Then she listened, wondering if her screaming had wakened the children, but all she heard was silence. Perhaps her screaming hadn't been as loud as she'd imagined.

'Would you like a cup of tea?' he asked.

'You'd have to light the range.'

'That doesn't matter. It would keep going till morning.'

A cup of tea would be lovely; but she decided against it as it would be too much trouble and an unnecessary expense. Why waste coal over a cup of tea?

'Well?' he prompted.

'No, thanks.'

'Are you sure?'

She nodded.

'How are you now?'

'More or less recovered.'

He gazed at her. 'You look awfully young for some reason. Perhaps you should have nightmares more often.'

'No, thank you,' she replied quickly.

He drew her closer and continued stroking her hair. She closed her eyes in appreciation, snuggling into him.

'I should get back to sleep. I have a tough day ahead,' he said after a while.

'Mmm.'

'Tired?'

'So so,' she lied. She'd pretend she was so that he would settle again; otherwise he would try to stay awake to keep her company. Cully was like that.

The same hand that had been stroking her hair now moved to her face, gently caressing her nose and cheeks. She sighed with contentment.

'I wonder what brought the nightmare on?' he mused. 'Maybe something you ate?'

'I did have some cheese yesterday, but that was early on.'

'Doubt it was that, then.'

It began to rain, soft drops pattering against the window-panes. Quickly the rain grew intense until it was hammering down.

'I'd better close the window,' he said.

That meant he would have to get out of bed, which was

9

the last thing she wanted. 'Leave it. The rain won't do any harm,' she told him.

'The curtains and the sill will get wet.'

'Let them.'

The curtains started to billow and flap. Their bedroom darkened as a cloud obscured the moon. Somewhere in the distance a fox barked.

'How do you feel now?' Cully asked.

'Like we should lie down again.'

'The horrors have passed, then?'

'Completely,' she fibbed. A residue remained, making her skin prickle in patches and her insides ache dully.

'Dead, was I?' he said, tone light and joking.

'As mutton,' she replied in the same vein.

'Dear me. Where did this take place?'

She thought back. 'I can't remember. It was all sort of hazy round the edges. But ever so real.'

'And how did I die?'

She couldn't recall that, either, and said so.

'An accident at the quarry?' Men had been killed in the past at his workplace. Why, only the previous year one poor unfortunate had lost both legs in an explosion and had expired from shock and loss of blood. Keith had been a young man, only twenty-two, engaged to a smashing lass.

'I don't think so,' she replied hesitantly. 'But, then, as I said, everything was hazy at the edges. All I could see was you.'

'It'll take more than a nightmare to get rid of me, I promise you,' he assured her.

'I hope so.'

She could feel the hardness of his thigh pressing up against her own. His whole body, though slight in build, was as hard as the stone he daily dug – a complete contrast to her rounded female softness.

He listened to her breathing, which had now returned to normal, and then to the rain still hammering against the panes. Weariness crept over him, and he knew he would pay for this interlude in the morning.

Meg forced herself to relax, moulding herself against him, which she knew he liked. There was little she didn't know about her husband after sixteen years of marriage. Sixteen gloriously happy years that had given her three marvellous children and a great deal of joy.

'What are you thinking about?' he queried quietly.

'Tomorrow's laundrying.'

He laughed. 'Trust you.'

'Well, you asked.'

'You're all right again. No need to worry about you.'

'Go to sleep, Cully.'

'Aye,' he murmured in reply, desperate now to catch a few more hours' sleep.

Shortly after that he began to snore, which made her smile. She was still wide awake when the rain stopped and dawn broke. She dropped off then, but only for a little while, because all too soon the alarm was ringing and it was time to get up.

Meg put a match to the range and watched it crackle alight. She warmed her hands at the blossoming flames before turning her attention to making breakfast.

When the tea was ready she took a cup through to Cully, who was sitting on the side of the bed scratching his chest.

'How are you this morning?' he enquired, blinking at her.

'Fine. You?'

He yawned. 'I could've done with a bit longer between the sheets. But never mind; there we are.'

She kissed him on a stubbly cheek, then went to rouse the children.

'Time to get up!' she called, poking her head into Rory's room. Aged fifteen, he was her eldest.

Rory groaned and pulled a pillow over his head.

'I won't tell you again,' she declared, as she always did, moving into the adjoining bedroom where the twins slept.

Rowan and Ishbel shared a double bed; Rowan was lying straight whereas Ishbel was in the foetal position.

11

How beautiful Rowan was, Meg thought. She had pale golden hair and smooth creamy skin. Her mouth, a delicious claret colour, was puckered in sleep.

Ishbel, on the other hand, was startlingly different. Whereas Rowan was tall and elegant, she was short and dark. Her complexion was pale, her eyes black as night. The twins were two years younger than Rory and still at school.

'Oh, Mum!' Rowan protested when Meg shook her.

'The porridge is on. If you don't hurry, Rory and your dad will scoff the lot.'

'I don't care,' murmured Rowan, who didn't have a large appetite at the best of times.

'And there's toast. You'll certainly want some of that.'

Ishbel made a low noise and squirmed underneath the covers.

'Toast and gooseberry jam – your favourite,' Meg went on to Rowan. 'Now, come on, get up, you two.' And with that Meg swept from their bedroom.

Cully was standing shaving at the sink when she arrived back in the kitchen. Meg bustled on with the breakfast, stirring the porridge repeatedly to remove any lumps. The children always complained vociferously if any remained when it was served up.

'Go get the milk, there's a good lad,' she asked Rory when he appeared.

'I'm starving,' he declared.

'Tell me something new,' she jibed in reply.

He disappeared, returning a few minutes later carrying the metal milk-can, which he set on the table. He peered into it, then fished something out which he flicked away. 'Drowned fly,' he announced.

'What was that?' queried Rowan coming into the room followed by Ishbel.

'Drowned fly,' Rory repeated.

Rowan pulled a face.

'Won't harm anyone,' Meg stated, forestalling any objections there might be about the matter, as Rowan was a particularly fussy girl.

Cully glanced at Rowan and smiled. 'Get a good night's sleep, darling?' he enquired cheerfully.

Her reply was a grunt.

'Little Miss Charming as usual,' muttered Ishbel.

'Watch it, you!' cautioned Rowan, rounding on her.

Ishbel sniffed. 'I'm not scared of you, and never think I am.'

Rowan towered over her dark-haired twin. 'Well, you should be, Titch.'

'Who are you calling Titch?' Ishbel howled. She balled a fist and hit Rowan on the arm.

'Hey!' Rowan objected. 'Just what do you think you're doing?'

'Trying to teach you some manners, Prune Face.'

The two girls glowered at each other. Before they had a chance to say any more, Cully intervened.

'Shut ... *up*!' he said with emphasis. 'Not another word from either of you. Is that clear?'

'But she ...' Rowan persisted.

'I said shut up. I don't want to start the day off with indigestion. Any more nonsense and you'll regret it.'

Rowan glared at her father, then at Ishbel. 'Daddy's favourite,' she accused in a tight whisper.

Ishbel was outraged, knowing only too well the boot was on the other foot.

'Sit down, all of you,' Meg instructed, ladling porridge into bowls.

Cully wiped his face on a towel, then snapped his braces into place. He was smiling inwardly. Prune Face indeed! Nothing could have been further from the truth. Rowan didn't have a single crease or crumple to mar her perfect features.

Rory fell to as soon as a bowl was placed in front of him, watched by Cully who began sprinkling salt over his porridge.

'This is the stuff to give the troops,' Cully enthused. 'This will stick to your ribs.'

'Dad, you've said that a million times,' Ishbel told him.

'So what if I have? It's true.'

'Nothing wrong with porridge. Best breakfast you can have,' Meg stated.

'I never said there was,' Ishbel retorted. 'Only that Dad . . .' She trailed off and shrugged. 'Forget it.'

Rory finished his in double-quick time and asked if there was any more. Meg told him to help himself.

'What do you have at school today?' Cully asked the girls.

'Lessons,' Rowan answered.

Cully hesitated, spoon halfway to his mouth. 'Don't be insolent, young lady.'

'I wasn't being—'

'Yes, you were,' he snapped.

Rowan turned on the charm, positively radiating it. 'Honestly I wasn't, Dad. It's just that I don't know exactly what lessons we have today. Do you, Ishbel?'

'History, maths and geography,' Ishbel answered, prodding her porridge, thinking she might have detected a detested lump.

'Good, good,' Cully approved. While he was a great believer in education, he'd never done very well at school himself, simply not having an academic brain. He was clever enough in his own way; but certain subjects, particularly maths, had been beyond him.

'I got a star in history last week,' Rowan stated.

'We know. You've told us often enough,' Ishbel retorted caustically.

'When was the last time you had one?'

Ishbel stuffed her mouth full of porridge and didn't answer. It always galled her that Rowan was brighter than her.

'Now, don't go putting your sister down. There's no need for that,' Meg chided.

'I've got a football match after work tonight,' Rory announced. He was daft on football.

'Who are you playing?' Cully enquired.

'Just a knock-up among ourselves, Dad.'

Cully nodded. If it had been something more serious,

he might have tried to get along to watch. He adored supporting the Shielers, as the village team was called.

'You'd better watch the time,' Meg warned, glancing at the ornate brass clock on the mantelpiece.

They hurriedly finished off their breakfast before she saw them all off at the door. Cully and Rory left together, Rory still munching on a slice of toast loaded with gooseberry jam, and soon after that they were followed by the twins.

When they were gone she returned to the kitchen and surveyed the debris on the table, wishing wholeheartedly it wasn't laundry day. She toyed with the idea of postponing it till later in the week, then decided against it. She'd best get it over and done with as planned; otherwise her entire week would be awry.

With a sigh she began collecting up the dirty dishes.

Meg picked up the large framed photograph that stood on the mantelpiece beside the brass clock and dusted it. It was one of her and Cully taken at their wedding. How much younger they looked, she thought, filled with warmth and affection.

She'd put on a little weight since then, but that was only to be expected after three children. She still had a good shape, though, and Cully never complained about it. She was just perfect, he always said. Something to get hold of, which was how he liked it.

Silly man, she thought, staring at his face as it had been then – a fine face without the scar that had been inflicted by a German bayonet. She shuddered to think of those awful harrowing years when Cully had been over in France. So many fine upstanding men had gone from Glenshields and never come back. While others who had had done so without eyes or limbs, or coughing their guts up from gas-poisoning.

Cully had been one of the lucky ones, though the war had certainly deeply affected him. He'd left an outgoing devil-may-care chap, always on the lookout for a good laugh, quite different from the man who'd returned. The Cully who'd come home had been quiet, reserved and withdrawn, with a look in what had been sparkling eyes that had given her the shivers.

He still had that look. She occasionally noticed it, usually when he was sitting reflectively by himself, and when she did it still upset her. She'd thought he'd talk about his experiences after the war. He made the odd reference, but that was all. To speak about what had happened distressed him beyond belief.

'Poor Cully,' she whispered in sympathy.

She dusted the photo again and replaced it beside a smaller one of him in uniform. How grand he'd looked in the kilt, she thought. Quite the soldier laddie. She remembered well the day it had been taken, a sunny day like this with a blue sky above and the sun cracking down. A week later he'd embarked for France, and that had been the last she'd seen of him for over a year.

He'd had Blighty leave three times, and on each occasion the change in him had been both marked and frightening.

'Damn the Germans,' she muttered darkly and angrily. 'Damn them all to perdition.'

She started from her reverie when the front door banged shut, then moments later her mother Fee was in the room beaming at her. Fee and her father, who, at fifty-eight, still had some years to go before retirement, lived at the other end of Glenshields.

Fee waggled a paper bag at Meg. 'I thought we might have a wee cup of tea. I've brought some scones and a cake,' she announced.

Meg was delighted to see her mother, with whom she got on extremely well. 'Your own, I hope, and not bought?'

Fee pulled an offended face. 'Of course.'

'Then, I'll put the kettle on.'

Fee placed the bag on the table and glanced sideways at Meg. 'I've got a lovely bit of gossip,' she stated gleefully.

'Mum!' Meg exclaimed. Fee was a terrible one for gossiping.

'You don't approve, eh?' Fee teased.

'You know I don't.'

Fee plonked herself down at the table and crossed her fleshy arms over an ample bosom. 'Well, if that's the case, I won't tell you,' she replied, pretending to be in a huff.

'Suit yourself,' Meg said, knowing this was a game. Her mother could no more have withheld gossip than sprout wings and fly.

'I will,' Fee declared stoutly.

Meg fetched some plates. 'Chocolate cake. Yummy,' Meg smiled approvingly, tearing open the bag.

'I know you like it.'

'With cherries on top. A real treat.'

'I would have brought some cream, but they were fresh out at the dairy.'

'Never mind,' Meg answered.

'So how is everyone?'

'Fine. And Dad?'

'The same. He never changes, the old bugger.'

'You mentioned he had a touch of lumbago last time you called by?'

'That's cleared up now, thank God,' replied Fee. 'There's nothing worse than men for moaning and groaning when they have a few aches and pains. Honestly, you'd think it was the end of the world to hear them.'

'And Mrs McLaren?' Mrs McLaren was Fee's next-door neighbour with whom she was as thick as thieves.

'Very well. In the pink, as they say.'

'I'm glad to hear it,' Meg nodded.

A silence ensued which Meg did nothing to break. She could see Fee was bursting with her gossip and wouldn't be able to contain herself much longer. She smiled when Fee suddenly launched into some juicy titbit which in turn led to another and another. When her mother finally left Meg knew every rumour currently doing the rounds in Glenshields. Whether there was even a particle of truth in any of it was quite another matter.

'Hurry up or I'll leave you,' Rowan said crossly to Ishbel,

who was lagging behind on their way home from school.

'I'm coming. Don't get so het up!' Ishbel retorted, hastening to Rowan's side.

'Honestly, you can be as slow as treacle, you.'

'Not me!'

Rowan raised an imperious eyebrow.

'It's just that you walk so fast.'

'No, I don't. It's you that's slow.'

Ishbel stuck out her tongue.

'I sometimes wonder what I did to get landed with the likes of you as a twin,' Rowan said, resuming walking.

'You got lucky, that's what. It's me who should be doing the wondering. You're a real pain at times, Rowan Stewart.'

'Not as much of a one as you.'

'Will you slow down? You're almost running!' Ishbel complained.

'It's simply that I've got long legs whereas yours are short and stumpy.'

Ishbel could have sloshed her. How she envied Rowan's long shapely legs. They made her almost drool with jealousy.

'They're *not* short and stumpy!' she hissed.

'They are,' Rowan laughed. She enjoyed nothing more than annoying her twin, which at times she found ridiculously easy to do. Mind you, Ishbel was quite capable of retaliating, so it evened out, she supposed.

Ishbel hated her legs. Not that there was anything wrong with them. They certainly weren't stumpy, but they simply weren't a patch on Rowan's.

'What's wrong with you now?' Rowan demanded, seeing her sister's expression.

'Nothing.'

'Don't give me that. I know you too well.'

'Nothing, I tell you,' Ishbel snapped. It never ceased to amaze her that she and Rowan were twins; they were so different – not only in looks but also in character. She would have given anything to be born the pretty one. Rowan had everything; it just wasn't fair.

'I'd love to stop off and buy some chocolate,' Rowan mused.

'You can't. You've no money.'

'Have *you*?' Rowan asked hopefully.

Ishbel hadn't, but wasn't going to admit it.

'Well, have you?'

'I'm not saying.' Ishbel grinned impishly. 'Perhaps I'm saving.'

'For what?'

'A special treat.'

'What sort of special treat?'

'That's for me to know,' Ishbel replied loftily.

'But we should share everything.'

Ishbel barked out a scathing laugh. 'Since when did you believe in sharing everything with *me*?'

'I always do.'

Ishbel wagged a finger at her. 'Liar!'

'Well, more often than not.'

'You're hysterical, you are. A real comedian.'

'*Comedienne*, you mean,' Rowan corrected.

'Whatever,' Ishbel snapped back, furious with herself for using the wrong word. Trust brainy Rowan to know the right one. 'I wonder what's for tea?' she mused, changing the subject.

'Don't try that. How much? We could buy a bar of chocolate and split it, half each.'

'We could buy a bar, and I could give you a square.'

'One rotten square!' Rowan exploded. Her desire for chocolate was so great she could almost taste it.

'One,' Ishbel repeated. Then waspishly, with a slight tinge of malevolence, she added: 'Or even half a one.'

'You're a pig!' Rowan spat. 'Where did you get the money from anyway?'

Ishbel tapped the side of her nose.

At this point, a young man on a bicycle sporting a wicker carrier-basket pedalled in their direction. He smiled when he saw them.

'Fat Boy Carstairs,' Rowan murmured.

'Don't be cruel. He can't help being fat,' Ishbel chided softly. Iain Carstairs worked for the village grocer and was a contemporary of their brother Rory.

Iain pulled his bike to a stop alongside them. 'Hello, you two,' he said, eyes fixed firmly on Rowan.

'Hello,' replied Ishbel.

'Out delivering, then,' said Rowan pleasantly.

'That's it,' Iain confirmed, his pink cheeks becoming even pinker, which Rowan noted with wry amusement.

'We're on our way home from school,' Ishbel explained unnecessarily, for he must have realized that. She was only too aware that he hadn't even glanced at her yet.

'What have you been up to?' Rowan asked him. 'Anything exciting?' She couldn't imagine Iain ever doing anything interesting.

Iain shook his head. 'Just the usual.'

'Which is?'

He shrugged. 'I don't know. The usual.'

Rowan was teasing him, Ishbel thought, noting that Iain was beginning to look uncomfortable.

Iain was cursing himself. He always felt so tongue-tied and out of his depth in Rowan's company. He could chatter endlessly to other lassies, but not her. She completely put him off.

'So what are you delivering this time?' Ishbel enquired.

'Bacon, cheese and a dozen eggs to the Rattrays in Loch Street. And a pound of sausages to the McGills in Floral Wynd.'

'That is interesting,' Rowan said, face expressionless.

Iain frowned, uncertain whether she was teasing him or not. 'Aye, well, it's my job,' he replied.

Rowan could be such a bitch, Ishbel thought.

'Well, we must be on our way, Fat Boy,' Rowan smiled.

Iain blushed scarlet. 'Goodbye,' he mumbled, and hastily cycled off.

Ishbel waved to him, then rounded on Rowan. 'There was no need for that at all.'

'Need for what?' Rowan queried innocently.

'Calling him Fat Boy.'

'That's his nickname, isn't it?'

'Maybe, but there was no need for you to use it. You might have been more polite.'

Rowan didn't reply.

'You know he thinks you're marvellous.'

'Does he?' Rowan replied, her tone again innocent.

'That's obvious.'

'He's fat and boring. A complete nothing,' Rowan stated.

'He can't help being born like that. You just be grateful you weren't.'

Rowan shuddered at the thought.

'I've got sixpence and you're not having a penny of it,' Ishbel lied and rushed off down the road.

Sixpence! Rowan thought. You could buy a lot of chocolate for sixpence. She started after her sister. But for once, longer legs or not, Rowan couldn't catch up with Ishbel, who ran like the wind.

Cully finished his tea, sighed, and pushed his plate aside. 'That was grand,' he stated.

'Why the sigh?' Meg queried.

'What sigh?'

'You did, Dad, honestly,' Rowan told him.

'Did I indeed?' he mused, and shook his head. 'Wasn't aware of it.'

'Can I be excused?' Rory asked, pushing his plate aside as well. 'I must be off.'

'Where is it tonight?' Meg enquired.

'I'm going to Fraser's to help him with his motorbike,' Rory replied enthusiastically. Fraser was a close friend of his who'd recently bought a secondhand machine which needed a complete overhaul to make it roadworthy.

'Well, don't be too late. Work in the morning,' Meg said as Rory rose from the table.

'See you later, Mum,' Rory smiled, and dashed from the room.

21

'Like some blinking whirling dervish,' Cully complained, rising and moving over to his easy chair.

'Another cup of tea?' Meg asked him.

'Please,' he muttered, shaking out the evening paper.

'Can I also be excused?' Rowan asked.

'And me,' Ishbel added.

'Aye, away, the pair of you,' Meg replied. 'Let your father and I have some peace for a while.'

The twins swiftly absented themselves.

Meg stood, the last to leave the table, and began collecting up the dirty dishes. Sometimes she made the twins help her with the chores, but this evening she preferred to be alone with Cully.

'So how was the quarry?' she enquired.

Cully grunted.

'Oh, that's very illuminating!' she commented sarcastically.

He glanced at her. 'Bloody tiring, if you must know. The foreman was in a right old mood today. He's a proper slave-driver, and no mistake.'

'As bad as that?'

'Worse,' he grumbled, turning to the sports pages.

He did look beat, she thought, and slightly peaky. Maybe he needed a tonic. She made a mental note to speak to the chemist.

As she did the dishes Meg thought of Rowan and Ishbel, both of whom required new shoes. It just never stopped, she thought. But new shoes they'd have. She wasn't going to have them walking around with their soles flapping as was the case with some in the village. That was awful. But, there again, money was tight all round, even for those with a regular job. God alone knew what it must be like for those parents where the father was unemployed.

She smiled to herself. She could never criticize Cully on that score. He was a good provider. He'd never had a day's idleness since their marriage, and there weren't all that many in Glenshields who could make such a boast.

She turned to look at him, and smiled again. His

'Perhaps you should stay home and forget the service?' Meg suggested to Cully.

He was tempted, but decided against it. 'No. I'll go,' he replied through gritted teeth.

'Are you sure?'

He nodded. 'This will pass after I've had that powder.'

'Hot or cold milk?' Meg queried.

'Doesn't matter. Either.'

Cold milk would be quicker, Meg thought, pouring some into a glass. She dropped in the powder, then stirred the mixture until it had dissolved. When she handed the glass to Cully he threw its contents down his throat.

'Fetch the bibles, will you?' Meg requested of Ishbel.

'Why me? Why not—?'

'Fetch them!' Meg commanded angrily, interrupting her daughter.

Rowan smirked at Ishbel as Ishbel left the kitchen to fetch the bibles from the sitting-room where they were kept along with other family treasures. Ishbel gave her twin a filthy look in return.

Rory pushed Cully's now empty plate away and belched. 'Beg pardon,' he apologized.

Meg glared at him.

'You're the best cook in the world, Mum,' Rory declared, trying to make up for the belch.

Meg ignored the compliment, only too well aware of why it had been paid. Honestly, did they think she was simple or something?

'Ahh!' groaned Cully as the fiercest pain yet stabbed his insides. This attack was murder.

Meg worried a fingernail. Maybe she should insist that Cully stay behind. He would be mortified if he started groaning like this during the service. 'Cully, don't you think . . . ?'

'I'm going,' he stated with determination. He wasn't about to let an attack of indigestion get the better of him. He was made of sterner stuff than that. He'd endured far worse discomfort after all – his mind briefly flicking back

27

to the war when he'd had, among other things, enteritis of a particularly violent nature.

'Suit yourself,' Meg told him with a shrug.

'Can I do anything for you, Dad?' Rowan asked.

He smiled at her. 'No, but thanks for offering. That's kind of you, lass.'

'You can help me remove and pile these dishes. We'll do them afterwards,' Meg informed Rowan, having glanced at the clock to note that time was getting on.

'You, too,' Meg informed Rory.

He didn't normally assist with the dishes but knew better than to argue after that belch. Bad manners were something neither Meg nor Cully could abide.

Ishbel returned with the bibles, and now it was her turn to smirk at the busy Rowan.

'What's for sweet later?' she asked Meg.

Meg's expression became one of wry amusement. 'You seem to have recovered quickly?'

Ishbel blushed; she'd forgotten all about pleading to be out of sorts. 'I was just curious, that's all,' she stammered in reply.

'Ha!' muttered Rowan scathingly.

'I'll get my coat,' Ishbel said, and hurriedly left the kitchen.

Cully produced a handful of change and began counting out the collection – threepence for him and Meg, a penny each for the girls. As Rory worked he was responsible for his own contribution.

'We should be making a move,' Meg declared when the dishes were stacked.

'Right, then,' mumbled Cully, lurching to his feet.

'Is that powder having any effect yet?' Meg queried anxiously.

'Give it a chance, woman. I've hardly swallowed the damn thing.'

'Well, there's no need to be ratty,' she snapped back, and was instantly sorry she'd done so.

He grasped hold of the mantelpiece to steady himself,

thinking this was the worst bout of indigestion he'd ever suffered. 'So what *is* for afters?' he joked.

'Rhubarb and custard.'

'I can hardly wait,' he commented drily.

'Fool!' Meg laughed.

'I love rhubarb and custard,' Rory said.

'You love anything that fills your belly,' Ishbel jibed. 'A bottomless pit. That's what Granny Fee called you once.'

'Watch your cheek!' Rory told her, wagging a finger in front of her face.

Ishbel pretended to try to bite his finger. 'Watch your own.'

Cully winced, and clutched again at his middle. Damn this indigestion. What a curse it was.

When everyone was ready Cully and Meg, arm in arm, led the way to church. Ishbel and Rowan followed directly behind, with Rory bringing up the rear.

'It's a fine day,' commented Cully, gazing up at the sky.

'We're having a good run of weather,' Meg replied, hoping the winter wasn't going to be too awful. She loathed the biting winds that came to their part of Renfrewshire during the winter, winds that brought tears to her eyes and made her teeth chatter. As for snow, she hated that most of all.

' 'Morning,' said Peter Drummond, tipping his hat to Meg. Peter and Lena were also members of the congregation and lived close to the Stewarts.

' 'Morning,' Meg and Cully responded.

'The pain's going off a bit now,' Cully announced to Meg as the church came in sight.

'The powder must be working.'

'Thank God for that.'

Cully wiped a slick of sweat from his brow and flicked it away.

'Use your handkerchief,' Meg admonished.

He patted a breast pocket where a clean handkerchief had nestled undisturbed for weeks. 'Forgot all about it,' he explained.

The atmosphere inside the church was so cool and serene that Meg felt herself instantly relax. She took her

29

seat in their regular pew and then heard Cully quieten Rowan and Ishbel, who were giggling at a crude remark Rowan had made about Fat Boy Carstairs whom they'd spotted. Rowan and Ishbel immediately shut up, although Ishbel had to strain not to burst out giggling again when Rowan dug her in the ribs.

Children! Meg thought. There were times when she despaired and couldn't wait for them to grow up and leave home – but only times.

Fifteen minutes later, with the service in full flow, Cully was in agony. The pains had returned with a vengeance, far worse than they'd previously been. He wished he'd brought a powder with him that he could've chewed straight from the packet.

Meg glanced at him, noting how pale he'd become. His hanky had been out frequently to wipe away the sweat that kept beading his forehead. Dark blue circles had appeared under his eyes.

'Do you want to leave?' she whispered as they finished singing 'Onward, Christian Soldiers'.

'Don't be stupid!' he hissed in reply.

'You look dreadful.'

'Thanks,' he muttered through clenched teeth.

'It's not a sin to leave if you're ill,' she said.

'I'm not ill. It's indigestion, that's all.'

He stifled a groan that caused a couple further along the pew to look quizzically in their direction.

Meg tried to focus on what the minister was saying, but her attention kept being drawn back to Cully. They should never have come, she berated herself. She should have insisted Cully and she had stayed at home. The children would have been quite capable, though they'd have protested like stink, of attending on their own.

Cully writhed, feeling as though a grenade had exploded in his stomach. His feet began to drum on the floor.

'Cully?' Meg whispered urgently, now thoroughly alarmed.

He tried to answer, but couldn't. His senses were swirling,

30

while his body seemed to be coming apart. It was as though a million tiny red-hot fingers were frantically plucking it to bits.

The minister's deep sonorous voice droned on from the pulpit. Was it Meg's imagination or was he staring at Cully in surprise and consternation?

Cully slipped off the pew, his knees making a heavy jarring thump as they hit the floor.

'Dad?' queried Rowan.

Cully tried to pull himself back up, but it was beyond him. He was making a spectacle of himself, he thought. How embarrassing – and in church, too! He'd never live this down.

The entire family was staring at him in concern, Rory thinking he should do something, but not knowing what. A muttering had arisen from those of the congregation in the immediate vicinity.

The minister concluded a short prayer, then signalled to Jack Armstrong sitting in the pew adjacent, who rose and crossed to the Stewarts. Jack was an elder.

'What's wrong, Cully?' Jack enquired.

Again Cully attempted to answer, but found himself unable. Everything was going round and round while his lips were drawn back in a wolfish snarl. Unbelievably the pains he was experiencing had become even more intense.

Rowan took his arm. 'Dad, do you want to go outside?'

'Cully?' Meg whispered.

Cully groaned, a groan that was pitiful to hear. Then he started to whimper.

'The man's not well,' Jack stated to parishioners craning to see what was happening.

Cully fell sideways against Meg's legs where he tried to draw himself into a foetal position, but failed owing to the narrowness of the space he was in.

'Dad?' said Rory, pushing past a wide-eyed Ishbel and Rowan. 'Dad?'

Cully could hear Rory's voice, but not see him. A red haze had descended, obscuring his vision. His whimpering was louder now, and more pronounced, his feet jerking as though they had a life of their own.

The minister, realizing something was dreadfully amiss, left his position and came striding forward. Several other parishioners also left their seats with the intention of offering aid. A general hubbub had broken out in the church, people talking excitedly and animatedly.

'Give him air,' pleaded a distraught Rory, gesturing back those attempting to crowd round. He was still at a loss about what to do.

'What is it, Meg?' the minister queried on reaching them.

'Indigestion,' Meg replied.

The minister looked down at the severely distressed Cully. 'That's more than indigestion,' he pronounced.

Dr Parker appeared. 'Let me examine the patient,' he said.

'Shall we move him out into the aisle?' Jack suggested.

It was agreed this was the thing to do, and so Cully was manhandled out of the space between the pews.

Cully's hand rose to flap in the air. 'Meg! Meg!'

'I'm here, darling,' she answered, kneeling beside him. Her brain had gone numb with shock at this unexpected turn of events.

'Indigestion, you say?' murmured Parker, opening Cully's shirt. Cully shrieked when he felt his abdomen.

'We'll need an ambulance,' Parker declared authoritatively.

'Leave that to me,' said Jack, and hurried off.

Rowan and Ishbel were still sitting where they'd been, gazing in horror at their father. Ishbel started to cry, hot tears that rolled down her flushed face. Rowan, to the contrary, was dry-eyed and ashen.

'Appendicitis, I suspect,' said Parker.

Other elders were moving among the congregation, asking for quiet and explaining to those at the rear what was going on.

Meg took Cully's damp handkerchief from his breast pocket and wiped his face. His eyes were hard with pain, and slightly crossed. The scar on his cheek glowed as though from within.

'You're not to worry, Cully. An ambulance is on its way,' Meg crooned, hardly aware of what she was saying.

A dribble of spittle ran from Cully's mouth to his chin. Meg quickly wiped it away.

Suddenly Cully went absolutely still, and a long-drawn-out sigh escaped him. At the end of the sigh his eyelids drooped slightly, but remained open.

'Oh, my God!' someone whispered.

Parker felt for Cully's pulse, then bit his lip. He turned to Meg, his expression one of profound regret. 'He's gone, I'm afraid.'

Meg didn't understand. 'Gone?'

'Dead.'

That single word was like an arrow through her heart. 'No, he can't be,' she protested. 'You're wrong. There's some mistake.'

Parker felt for the pulse again. 'No mistake, I'm sorry to say.'

Meg stared at Cully, who gazed back at her through now sightless eyes. His face was contorted, the long scar on his cheek strangely colourless where it had been so vivid only moments before.

'Oh, my dad,' Ishbel sobbed, shaking all over.

Rory stood with his mouth wide open, face rigid with shock.

Rowan was motionless, her normally creamy white skin now grey and mottled.

The minister put an arm round Meg's shoulders. 'You'll have to be brave, Mrs Stewart,' he said, attempting to comfort her.

'Dead,' Meg repeated and, as she did, something inside her snapped. Throwing back her head, she started to scream. A horrendous agonized scream that tore at her throat and reverberated throughout the church.

Meg slowly stirred her tea, then carefully replaced the

spoon in her saucer. The funeral had been earlier; after which relatives, friends and neighbours had come to the house.

Rory sat staring at a plate of ham sandwiches, leftovers from the meal given to those who'd called. He hadn't eaten a thing all day, nor could he now. His appetite had totally deserted him.

'I still can't ... believe it,' he husked.

Ishbel and Rowan were also sitting round the table. Neither they nor their mother replied.

A silence ensued, all caught up in their own thoughts. Finally it was broken when Ishbel said: 'Granny Alice was in a terrible state.' Granny Alice was Cully's widowed mother, his father having died some years previously.

'Understandable,' Meg responded in a hollow tone. Alice had given birth to three children, all boys. The oldest, Luke, had been killed on the Western Front; now only the middle son, James, remained. Cully had been the baby.

Meg thought of her own family: her mother Fee and father Lex couldn't have been more sympathetic, while her sister Georgina and her husband Michael had rallied round.

Rory slowly pushed his plate away. 'Anyone for more tea?' he asked.

Meg shook her head, as did Ishbel and Rowan.

Rory studied his cup whose contents had grown cold. He could see his father, hear him. At any moment now he expected the kitchen door to open and there would be Cully. Only Cully, his dad, would never come through that door again. He swallowed a lump that felt the size of a football. He wanted to cry but refrained, reminding himself he was the man of the house now.

'Seems funny to think ...,' Meg began and trailed off. She removed a wisp of hair that had fallen over her eyes and hooked it behind an ear.

'It was all so sudden,' Ishbel said quietly.

Rowan nodded.

'So completely unexpected,' Meg added.

'Completely,' Rory echoed.

'What's to become of us, Mum?' Rowan asked.

Meg had no answer to Rowan's query. She hadn't thought that far ahead. Her thoughts were still jumbled. She couldn't conceive of life without Cully. Nor could she fully comprehend that he'd gone.

'Mrs Simpson was very nice to me,' Ishbel said. She was a neighbour from several doors up.

'Everyone was,' Rowan qualified. 'They couldn't have been kinder.'

'The minister spoke well at the service, I thought,' Meg said, and all her children nodded their agreement.

'Very well,' Meg went on dully, thinking of the words that had summed up Cully's life and character – a fine upstanding man, he'd been called, responsible, sober, well liked. A man who'd fought for king and country.

Meg clasped her bloodless hands together. When she'd set the table she'd routinely laid out a place for Cully. Then, realizing what she'd done, she removed it again.

She looked at Cully's seat at the table, now empty, and at his favourite easy chair where no-one had dared sit while he was home.

'Can I have my dad's watch?' Rory suddenly requested. 'I'd like that.'

'His watch?' Meg frowned.

Rory nodded. 'And the chain that goes with it.'

'Of course, son. They're yours by right. Your dad would have wanted you to have them.'

Rory swallowed hard, the lump still large in his throat.

'I'll sort them out for you,' Meg added.

'Thanks, Mum.'

'Can I have something of his?' Ishbel asked. 'It doesn't matter what. Just something.'

'And me,' said Rowan.

Meg nodded. 'I'll see to it.'

'Uncle Vincent was a real brick today,' Rory murmured. Vincent McQueen was one of Cully's cousins; he was a

35

horse dealer by profession with the reputation of a charming rogue.

'He told me how much I'd grown since he last saw me,' Rowan smiled thinly.

Meg remembered Vincent speaking to her, but couldn't recall what he'd said. A lot of the conversations she'd had that day had gone in one ear and out the other.

They all looked at one another when there was a knock on the front door.

'Someone to pay their respects, no doubt,' Meg declared. 'Rory, will you answer it?'

'Of course, Mum,' Rory replied, quickly rising.

Rory vanished from the room, to return almost immediately with a small pepper-and-salt-haired man holding his hat.

'Mr Monteith!' exclaimed Meg, getting to her feet. Monteith was the owner of the quarry where Cully had worked.

'A sad day, Mrs Stewart. A very sad day indeed,' commiserated Monteith, his thick bushy eyebrows drooping in mournful sympathy.

Meg inclined her head in acknowledgement.

Rowan and Ishbel had also risen out of respect, for Monteith was an important person in the village. He and his wife lived in a large house on its outskirts.

'I came to the service,' Monteith stated. 'You might have seen me there.'

'I did. I'm sorry I didn't have a chance to talk to you.'

Monteith held up a hand. 'Didn't expect you to, Mrs Stewart, not under the circumstances. And I did arrive later than intended, had trouble with the car. Then afterwards I just slipped away.' The real truth was he'd slipped away because he had business elsewhere.

'It's kind of you to stop by like this,' Meg said. Then: 'But what am I thinking of? Rory, pour Mr Monteith a dram.' There were whisky and other drinks left over from earlier.

'Don't put yourself out,' Monteith objected half-heartedly. 'There's no call for that.'

'We're not putting ourselves out. Rory!'

Rory hastened to obey, pouring Monteith a liberal measure into the best glass he could find.

'Water?' Rory asked.

Monteith shook his head. 'Never spoil it, lad. That's my motto. I prefer it as it comes.'

Monteith accepted the glass Rory handed him. 'Aren't you joining me, Mrs Stewart?'

'No, thank you. I . . .' That might be impolite, Meg suddenly thought. If Cully had been present, he would certainly have had one with his boss, and been proud to do so. 'Maybe just a little one, then. And plenty of water for me, if you don't mind.'

'A woman's prerogative,' Monteith smiled benevolently. He waited till Meg had her drink, then toasted: 'Slainthe!'

'Slainthe,' Meg responded, and had a sip.

'Now the reason for my visit,' explained Monteith, puffing out his chest. 'I didn't simply drop in to offer my condolences; there's more to it than that. You've already been paid what Cully was owed, I believe?'

Meg nodded. Cully's final pay-packet had been delivered to the door.

'Well, of course I don't have any obligations to you and yours, Cully dying as he did. It might have been different if . . .' Monteith hesitated, drew in a deep breath, then continued: 'No, I felt a gesture was due on my behalf, Cully being a long and trusted employee. And hard-working – mustn't forget that. No, a gesture was required, I thought.'

He hadn't had any intention of giving Meg money, but his wife Sybil had been insistent. They'd had an argument about it, and in the end he'd capitulated for the sake of peace and quiet. Besides, he'd rationalized, it would look good. Cully had left three children, after all – even if one of them was working. What he didn't know was that Sybil had insisted because of a small kindness Cully had once done her which she'd never forgotten.

'A gesture,' Meg repeated, not yet grasping his intention.

'Money,' Monteith stated bluntly, and waited for a delighted reaction.

'Oh, I couldn't possibly . . .'

'Nonsense,' Monteith interjected with a frown. 'Of course you can. I'm sure, as matters must stand, it will be most welcome.'

'I can't deny that, Mr Monteith. And it's not that I wish to appear ungrateful. It's just that . . . Well, I don't know that I should.'

'Pride can be a sin, Mrs Stewart,' Monteith pontificated. 'False pride even more so. I'm certain Cully wouldn't have disapproved.'

Meg was doubtful about that, for Cully had been a great believer in a man standing on his own two feet and being beholden to no-one. The very idea of charity had been anathema to him.

Monteith produced his wallet and began counting out five-pound notes. 'Fifty, I thought, should ease the situation,' he said. Sybil had told him to give a hundred, but during the drive to the Stewarts' he'd convinced himself that was far too extravagant. Even fifty was over-generous in his book.

'Fifty pounds,' Meg murmured, eyes opening wide. What an awful lot of money.

'Here you are, with my blessing,' Monteith declared, trying to press it on her.

Meg resisted the wad of notes, eyeing it as though it were a snake he'd suddenly magicked into his hand.

'I don't know,' she prevaricated.

'Of course you do, woman,' he urged, beginning to get exasperated. For two pins he'd have stuck the cash back into his wallet and left. Silly bitch, didn't she recognize a windfall when it presented itself?

'Accept it, Mum,' Rory said quietly.

Meg glanced at her son, who nodded.

She remained undecided, part of her desperately wanting the money. If only she had time to think.

Monteith resolved the matter by placing, almost banging, the notes on the table. 'There we are; that's that,' he declared.

Meg's resistance crumbled; it would come in so handy after all. 'I don't know what to say . . .'

'Nothing,' Monteith stated, draining his glass which he now put beside the cash.

'Will you have another?' she asked.

He would have liked to, but wanted to leave more. What he'd just done rankled. It was fifty pounds down the plughole as far as he was concerned. But it would look good, he reminded himself.

'Must be off, I'm afraid,' he replied.

'Rory will see you to the door.'

Monteith shook hands with Meg. 'Don't hesitate to get in touch if there's ever anything further I can do,' he said, not meaning it. To all intents and purposes, he was now finished with the Stewart family.

'I can't thank you enough,' Meg stammered, her gaze drawn back to the wad of notes.

Monteith held up a hand. 'My Christian duty. And Cully deserved a decent token of appreciation.'

He said his goodbyes, then took his leave, Rory duly escorting him out.

When Monteith was gone Meg picked up the wad and stared at it. She'd never held so much money before. A veritable fortune.

'That was kind of him,' said Rowan.

'Yes,' agreed Meg softly.

Rory returned. 'Are you all right, Mum?'

'Somewhat stunned, that's all.'

'It is a lot,' stated Rory.

'A godsend,' murmured Meg.

'Shall I put the kettle on and make a fresh pot of tea?' Ishbel queried.

Meg laid the fifty pounds back on the table. 'No, I'll do that.'

'And we'll clear up and do the dishes,' said Rowan.

On an impulse Meg kissed both her daughters on the cheek. 'Thank you, darlings.'

When he got home Monteith lied to Sybil, telling her he'd given Meg a hundred as she'd wished.

He thought it unlikely Sybil would ever find out he hadn't. If she did ... Well, that was a bridge he'd cross when he came to it.

Ishbel drew down her nightie, then perched on the edge of the bed, watching Rowan undress. Rowan's face was drawn and strained, as was her own when she'd looked in the mirror. It seemed to her they'd both aged years since the death of their father.

Rowan suddenly stopped what she was doing and cradled her head in her hands.

'Rowan?'

'I'll be fine in a moment,' came the muffled reply.

'We're going to have to be brave for Mum's sake,' Ishbel said in a cracked voice.

Rowan glanced up, sucked in a breath and swept the hair from her face. 'Yes.'

Ishbel, her forehead creased, regarded Rowan thoughtfully. 'Nothing's ever going to be the same again, is it?'

'No,' Rowan agreed.

Ishbel sighed, intertwined her fingers, placed them in her lap and stared at them. She could feel her heart thumping like a big drum being frantically beaten.

When Rowan had pulled on her nightie she came and sat beside Ishbel. 'I'm going to miss my dad,' Rowan whispered.

'Me, too.'

'I feel so guilty about all the times he had to tell me off.'

'He was a terrific dad,' Ishbel declared.

'The best.'

'They don't come any better.'

'They don't,' Rowan agreed.

'Poor Mum.'

'Poor all of us,' Rowan elaborated.

There was a silence, then Ishbel said: 'It didn't look

like him in the coffin. It was him, and yet somehow not him.'

Rowan nodded. 'That's what I thought.'

'It wasn't my dad in there.'

'It was what was left of him.'

There was another silence, broken only when Ishbel rose and crossed to the gas-mantle which she turned out, plunging the bedroom into total darkness. She groped her way back to the bed where she found Rowan already huddled under the covers.

'Perhaps we'll wake up in the morning and find this is all a horrible dream,' Rowan said miserably.

'It isn't, and we won't.'

'I'm glad we sleep together. I couldn't bear to be on my own during this time,' Rowan went on.

Ishbel was also pleased.

'There were lots of people at the service and graveside. Everyone came,' Rowan said. 'Dad would have been pleased.'

'He'd have been more pleased not to be dead,' Ishbel replied.

Rowan sobbed, and stuck a fist into her mouth. 'Oh, my dad!' she murmured.

Ishbel took Rowan into her arms, pulling her twin tightly against her. A few moments later Rowan encircled Ishbel with her arms so that the two of them were now in each other's embrace.

'It's funny,' muttered Ishbel.

'What is?'

'Everything.'

'You mean funny ha ha?'

'No. Funny peculiar.'

Rowan silently agreed. Who would have imagined their dad would be taken from them so suddenly? To her he'd seemed immortal. Someone who'd be there for ever.

'I wonder how Mum is,' Ishbel murmured.

'She's bearing up extremely well. Considering. We must be good and stop squabbling.'

'I'll try if you will,' Ishbel promised.

'I'll try too.'

'It's a pact, then.'

'A pact,' Rowan agreed.

Ishbel closed her eyes, and soon her heart slowed to its normal rhythm, while her breathing became measured.

Rowan sensed Ishbel fall asleep, and was filled with a great tenderness for her twin whom she loved dearly.

'Dad,' she whispered, seeing him again in his coffin. It had been merely the shell of her father, the remains, but not the soul.

Then she, too, fell asleep, and when she woke in the morning found herself still wrapped in Ishbel's arms.

Meg stared at the medals awarded to Cully after the war. Although he'd been extremely proud of them, he'd kept them at the bottom of a drawer, only bringing them out once a year for Armistice Day when he dusted them off.

She gently touched each medal in turn, recalling the reason for its being awarded. He'd been such a brave man, her Cully; but, then, so had nearly all those who'd gone off to fight in the Great War, that hell on earth which had decimated the cream of the country's manhood.

She laid the medals back in their place, then quietly closed the drawer, Cully's drawer, still full of his underwear and other miscellaneous items.

On top of the chest lay a single piece of paper, his death certificate. Meg picked it up with a trembling hand. Calum Henry Stewart, it stated, for Calum had been his real name which he'd never liked. And at the bottom the year of his death: 1925. Thirty-six, she thought. That was how old he'd been when struck down by peritonitis brought on by a ruptured appendix. Thirty-six! No age at all. They could have had another twenty or thirty years together; more, if they'd been fortunate.

Meg replaced the certificate on top of the chest and smoothed it out even though it wasn't creased or wrinkled.

42

She started when there was a tap on her bedroom door.

'Come in!' she called out.

It was Rory. 'Just to let you know I've seen to the fire, locked up, and turned out the gas-mantles.' These were jobs he'd requested to do because they were ones his father had always done.

'Thank you, son. You're a smashing lad.'

'I listened at the twins' door, and there wasn't a sound. I think they must have dropped off.'

Meg nodded. That was good. 'Now you'd better get to your own bed. I'm just off to mine.'

'Is there anything else that needs doing, Mum?'

She reached up and touched his cheek. 'Not for now.'

'I'll away through, then.'

'Good night, son.'

She kissed his other cheek. 'I'll give you your usual shout.' Rory was working next day.

'Mum?'

'What?'

He hesitated. 'You won't forget the watch and chain?'

'I won't forget. I'll put them in your room some time tomorrow.'

'Thanks, Mum,' he answered, a catch in his voice.

'Come here,' she said, and hugged him. She could feel how close he was to tears.

'Oh, Mum!' he husked.

'I know, son. I know,' she crooned, stroking the back of his head.

He broke abruptly away from her and fled the room, leaving the door open behind him.

Meg closed the door and leaned against it. She was tired through and through. When she'd felt like this in the past there had always been Cully to comfort and bolster her. Something he'd never do again. Anger rose in her at her predicament. It was all so grossly unfair! She knew if Cully had been present he'd have smiled and told her life never was.

She thought of the nightmare she'd had in which Cully

had died, and shivered. Had God been forewarning her, preparing her for what was about to happen? She didn't know. It was a mystery. But the nightmare certainly had occurred, and then gone on to become a hideous reality.

She changed into her nightdress, extinguished the gasmantle and got into bed where she shivered again, but this time from cold. Cully would have warmed her if he'd been there, but he wasn't.

She reached out and touched his place, which was as cold as she was herself. Tears welled into her eyes to go tumbling down her cheeks. She'd never experienced such loneliness – loneliness, heartbreak and profound despair.

'Oh, Cully!' she whispered. But there was no reply; only silence.

Burying her face in her pillow, she continued to weep.

Chapter Two

The Reverend David Dykes strode purposefully down the cobbled street, casting a baleful eye left and right as he went. He was a tall slim man with a long thin nose which looked as though it had been stuck on his face as an afterthought.

The Reverend Dykes had arrived in Glenshields that day, transferred from a small parish where he'd been incumbent for a number of years. He didn't view his move to Glenshields as a promotion, even though he'd be tending a larger flock.

A female laughed raucously, which caused him to pause and frown. A sinful laugh, he thought, there could be no doubt about it. He shuddered to think what the woman might be up to. That laugh, filled with riotous abandon, might have sprung from all manner of evil doings.

Dykes continued on his way, out to get the feel and smell of his new domain. So far he was unimpressed.

The long nose twitched like a scenting animal's when he caught the repugnant odour of alcohol. The source of the alcohol soon became evident when he rounded a corner to discover a pub.

He stopped outside to glare at it. The reek of beer and spirits assailing his nostrils caused his lips to curve downwards in disapproval.

He crossed to the nearest window and gazed in. The sight that greeted him was just as he'd imagined. Men and women in various stages of intoxication.

And what was that in the corner? A game of dominoes. Played for money? he wondered. Didn't they know that gambling was loved by the devil, Satan himself? He'd soon put a stop to that. But not now, not yet, he cautioned himself, not on his first night in the village. But he would certainly have something to say on the subject from the pulpit this coming Sunday.

He thought of the outgoing minister, the Reverend McNab: old and slack, in his opinion. From now on there would be a new rule in Glenshields, as the villagers would soon discover.

He turned from the pub and, glowering into the night, went on his way, eventually returning to the manse where, being unmarried, he'd be living on his own.

The manse's iron-hinged and studded door banged shut behind him, the sound echoing ominously down the gravel path and beyond. A cat, hearing the noise, mewed and slunk into the undergrowth.

That night the Reverend Dykes dined on porridge and cheese, washed down with cold water from the sink pump.

When he later went to bed, after poring over the Bible and other religious tracts, he prayed for strength to steer the inhabitants of Glenshields into the paths of goodness and righteousness.

'A steak and kidney pie and some bottled fruit for you,' said Fee, unpacking articles from a wicker basket and laying them on Meg's kitchen table.

'That's very kind, Mum. You shouldn't have!'

Fee waved a dismissive hand. 'Don't mention it, lass. Simply trying to help, that's all. So how are you?'

Meg shrugged.

'Ay, losing a man is hard, right enough,' Fee sympathized. 'But you're not the first it's happened to, remember that.'

'Shall I put the kettle on?'

'I should hope so! I'm gasping for a cup of tea and a sit-down.' And with that Fee settled herself in an easy chair, taking care to avoid the one which had been Cully's.

Meg filled the kettle and placed it on the range.

'You've lost weight again,' Fee commented. 'You must

eat. Wasting away to a shadow isn't doing anyone any good, least of all yourself. It certainly isn't what Cully would have wanted.'

'I just don't have an appetite any more.'

'Then, force yourself if you have to. You'll end up ill if you're not careful, and then where will you be? You've got children to think about if nothing else.'

'I'll try harder,' Meg promised.

'You'd better! And you can start with that steak and kidney pie. It'll melt in your mouth; you have my word on that.'

'You were always a marvellous cook, Mum.'

Fee puffed out her chest. 'I'm not bad, I'll grant you. At least so your father says; and you know how sniffy he can be about his food.'

Meg put a biscuit-tin on the table, then busied herself with the cups and saucers.

'On a plate,' Fee further scolded, referring to the biscuits. 'Because you're grieving is no excuse for letting your standards drop. Do as I taught you, lass; that's the way.'

Meg returned to the tin with a fancy patterned plate on to which she spilled some biscuits. 'That satisfy you?'

Fee made a harumphing sound, while looking to see if there were any custard creams. They were her favourites.

'Any luck finding a job yet?' Fee enquired, for Meg had soon realized after Cully's death that she would have to bring money into the house herself to make ends meet. Rory's wage was nowhere near enough to cover their living costs.

Meg shook her head. 'I've tried everywhere, but there's simply nothing going.'

'What about the dairy?'

'I spoke to Mr Murray, who said he'd bear me in mind for the future.'

Fee pursed her mouth. 'Pity.'

'And there's Christmas getting closer and closer.'

'You still have the fifty pounds Mr Monteith gave you,' Fee said.

'What remains of it, you mean. Heaven knows, I try to be careful. But every week sees it slowly being whittled away.'

She'd limit herself to one biscuit, Fee decided, worried for her daughter and family. 'The trouble is there's so little employment round here for women,' she commiserated.

'Don't I know it!'

'But something is bound to come up eventually. Has to!'

'I hope so. I really do.' Meg ran a hand through her hair. 'I'm prepared to do anything at all that will bring money into the house. Scrub floors – whatever.'

Fee reflected on her own situation. She and Lex didn't have any savings, though they did have a small insurance policy. They survived from pay-day to pay-day like everyone else. She doubted there could be many in the village had savings put by. Life was a weekly struggle, with the odd small luxury thrown in here and there to make it bearable.

'It's a pity Cully didn't have the foresight to take out an insurance policy,' Fee said, thinking of Lex's.

'I did mention it on occasion, but that would merely have been something else to lay out. And, barring an accident at the quarry, who would have thought that Cully would die so young?'

'A tragedy,' Fee murmured.

'I don't suppose you've heard anything on the work front?' Meg asked, knowing the answer. If there had been any such news, Fee would have imparted it by now.

'I've kept my ear to the ground as promised, but nothing,' Fee replied, shaking her head.

Meg sighed, thinking of the rent that had to be paid every week.

Fee decided to change the subject. 'I gather the new minister has been giving the church big licks.' Neither she nor Lex was a regular churchgoer, only attending once in a while when the mood took them or it was an important religious occasion.

They fell to discussing the Reverend Dykes, who'd become the talk of the village since his arrival.

*   *   *

Meg finished ironing one of Rory's shirts and draped it over the back of a chair. She was reaching for a pillowcase when there was a rap on the front door.

Now, who was that? she wondered, laying the iron aside and smoothing down her apron.

'Mrs Monteith!' Meg exclaimed when she answered the door.

Sybil Monteith smiled at Meg. 'Excuse me calling unexpectedly. Do you have a moment?'

'Of course!' Meg stammered, thinking she must look a right mess. Thank God she still had some biscuits left in the tin to offer her grand guest.

Meg ushered Sybil into the sitting-room, whipping off her apron in the process, and scraping back wisps of hair that had fallen over her face.

'I'll put the kettle on,' she declared.

'No, please don't bother. I shan't be long.'

Meg stood awkwardly as Sybil continued to smile at her. 'Won't you have a seat?' she offered.

'Why, thank you. My legs are painful today. Arthritis, you know.'

'I heard you were a sufferer,' Meg sympathized.

'Some days it takes me all my time to get up in the morning. But there we are. Mustn't grumble. We all have our crosses to bear.'

Meg nodded.

'Speaking of which, I was so sad to learn about Mr Stewart. Such a gentleman,' Sybil said quietly.

'Thank you. And thank you also for the money you and Mr Monteith gave us. Fifty pounds was most magnanimous of you.'

Sybil's eyes widened slightly. Fifty pounds! Meg had been quite specific about the amount. This was something she'd take up with Hugh later that evening. Trust him to renege on the amount they'd agreed; he'd always been tight-fisted. She should have guessed he'd go back on his word.

'I'm told you're on the lookout for work,' Sybil went on.

'That's correct,' Meg confirmed, looking aghast.

Sybil gave a low laugh. 'Don't look so surprised, Mrs Stewart. You know what village gossip is like. Nothing's secret.'

That was true enough, Meg thought. 'If I'm surprised, it's because you've got to hear, Mrs Monteith. I didn't think tittle-tattle would have reached you out at your house.'

'You mean you thought I was above listening to such things?' Sybil teased in reply.

Meg blushed; that was exactly what had gone through her mind. She had no idea how Sybil occupied her time, but had never dreamt she'd be interested in village goings-on.

'I hear all sorts,' Sybil said. 'You'd be amazed. We employ village folk as servants after all, and they do talk.'

'I suppose so,' Meg acknowledged.

'The point is you're looking for work, and I came here today wondering if I could help.'

'Help?' Meg queried slowly, hope blossoming in her. 'How do you mean?'

'Not in service, I must say straight off; we have no openings there. But I'm reliably assured that you're extremely handy with a needle and thread. Is that so?'

'It's true I make a lot of our clothes and other requirements. Save a deal of money that way.'

'Indeed. Do you have anything of yours I could see?'

'I made this dress I'm wearing now,' Meg informed her. 'May I?'

'Of course.' Meg went over to stand directly in front of Sybil, who gathered up a handful of material and scrutinized the stitching.

'Very neat,' she complimented Meg.

'Thank you.'

'Can you follow a pattern and cut out?'

'Yes,' Meg nodded. Could this be the answer to her prayers?

'What about finer fabrics and cloths – have you worked with those?'

'Only to a limited extent,' Meg answered truthfully, feeling hope fade just as suddenly as it had sprung up. 'I've never had much call in that direction, you understand.'

'Quite,' said Sybil.

'But it wouldn't worry me, not in the least. I'm extremely careful with whatever I make.' Meg paused, then added: 'The materials I'm used to using are worth a great deal to the likes of me, so I've learnt to be meticulous and not make mistakes.'

Sybil's expression was one of approval. 'Are you limited to plain stitching or can you also do fancy?'

'I prefer fancy; it's more interesting,' Meg replied, hope resurging.

'H'm!' murmured Sybil thoughtfully. 'I've always employed Mrs Moore in the village; but I'm afraid her eyesight isn't what it used to be, which is why I'm considering a new seamstress.'

'I see,' Meg said, knowing Mrs Moore to be somewhere in her seventies.

'I'll tell you what: we'll give it a try, shall we? How do you feel about that?'

'Delighted!' Meg exclaimed.

'And, if I'm happy with what you do initially, we'll take it from there.'

Meg's face radiated her happiness and relief at this possible solution to her financial problems. 'If I do satisfy your requirements, Mrs Monteith, how much work would there be?' she enquired.

'A considerable amount. Certainly enough to keep you busy.'

Meg could have shouted and danced with glee. 'When would you like me to start?'

'Are you free tomorrow?'

'Completely.'

'Then, come to the house and I'll show you what I want doing in the first instance. And we'll also take that opportunity to discuss remuneration.'

'What time?' Meg asked quickly.

Sybil was pleased to see Meg's enthusiasm. 'Shall we say around nine o'clock?'

'I'll be there on the dot,' Meg promised.

Later, when the twins arrived home from school, Meg greeted them both with a big kiss and excitedly told them about Mrs Monteith's visit.

Next morning, true to her word, having trudged there on foot, Meg presented herself on the Monteith doorstep at nine o'clock sharp.

It was going to be a good Christmas for them after all, Meg reflected as she sat in front of the range. Her initial efforts for Sybil Monteith had proved a big success, and now she was being given enough work on a weekly basis, coupled with Rory's wage, for the household to get by. Sybil now gave her not only mending but also new items to be made, from articles of clothing to curtains.

Meg leant forward, opened the door to the fire and poked the coals within, sparking them into new life. It was bitterly cold outside, but so far snow had failed to materialize.

Meg closed the fire door and warmed her hands in front of it. When they were satisfactory she toasted her feet in their place.

A beaming Ishbel suddenly burst into the kitchen. 'Uncle Vincent's here!' she announced.

'Vincent!' Meg exclaimed, rising to her feet. She hadn't seen Cully's cousin since the funeral.

'How are you, girl?' said Vincent, smiling broadly as he entered the room.

'Fine. It's lovely to see you.'

Vincent came over and kissed Meg on the cheek, then thrust a bottle into her hand. 'A Christmas present which I'm hoping you'll open now,' he said.

Meg stared down at the whisky he'd brought. 'This is very extravagant of you,' she told him.

'It's Christmas Eve after all. Time for a few drams to get us into shape for the real holiday.' The 'real holiday' he was referring to was Hogmanay, *the* celebration of the year in Scotland. Christmas was basically for children, men working through it till Hogmanay which was the start of a four-day binge. It was a tradition that dated from pagan times.

'Rowan, get some glasses, please,' Meg called out to her other daughter. 'And you, Vincent, sit yourself in front of the fire.'

Vincent lowered himself into what had been Cully's easy chair. 'So how are you bearing up, Meg?'

She shrugged. 'It's difficult, of course. But I have managed to land myself a little job, which is a great relief.'

'Oh, ay?'

As she poured Vincent a whisky she explained about working for Mrs Monteith.

'You were lucky there, then.'

'I consider myself to be so. Would you like some water with this?'

'Half and half would be lovely. Are you having one yourself?'

Why not? she thought. It was a festive occasion after all. She poured herself a small measure and liberally topped it up with water.

Vincent smiled at Rowan and Ishbel, flashing gleaming white teeth of which he was inordinately proud. He smiled a great deal for the express purpose of showing off his teeth.

Vincent was a smallish man with dark hair and extraordinarily high cheekbones. He was well built with broad shoulders and a slim waist.

Meg handed Vincent his drink and sat opposite him. 'When you've finished that, how about a bite to eat? I've got a pot of soup you might like, and what's left of the boiled chicken we had for tea.'

'Not for me, Meg, but thank you,' Vincent replied, holding up a hand. 'I've already eaten.'

'Are you sure?' Meg probed, wondering if he was simply being polite.

'Cross my heart and hope to die,' he declared, making such exaggerated gestures that Rowan and Ishbel, who'd also sat down, laughed.

'So what brings you to Glenshields?' Meg enquired. Vincent lived in a village ten miles away.

'Business, you know,' he answered, sampling the whisky.

'Buying, selling or both?'

'There were a few horses that I wanted to look at; which is what I've been doing this afternoon.'

And drinking, too, Meg thought, having caught the whiff of alcohol on his breath when he'd kissed her. A slight slur to his speech was also a giveaway. 'What do you think of them?'

He pulled a face. 'We haggled a bit, but the man selling wouldn't come down enough. I told him straight before I left that he'd never shift them at those prices.'

'So it was a wasted journey?'

'Not when it allows me to visit you and your family,' Vincent replied smoothly.

Meg laughed at his charm, while he treated her to another of his smiles. 'Away with you!' she chided.

'Oh, I almost forgot,' he said, digging in a pocket to produce a paper bag. 'You pair aren't too old for sweets, I take it?' he queried, addressing the girls.

'No fears!' exclaimed Rowan, jumping to her feet.

'Some boilings and caramels,' Vincent explained, eyes twinkling with good humour.

'Love them,' declared Rowan, accepting the bag. 'Thank you very much, Uncle Vincent.'

'To be shared equally,' Meg instructed, forestalling any argument as Ishbel bore down on her sister.

'*Equally*,' Ishbel repeated, reaching Rowan's side and glowering at her. 'We'll count them together.'

Vincent chuckled, enjoying this interplay.

Reluctantly Rowan tipped the sweets on to the table, and together she and Ishbel began counting them out, each eyeing the other watchfully.

'Another dram?' Meg asked.

Vincent regarded his almost-empty glass. 'I shouldn't really,' he replied, but there was no conviction in his voice.

'Of course you should!' she insisted.

Vincent immediately capitulated. 'Take it, then, that you've twisted my arm. And you?'

'I'm nowhere near ready yet.'

'Would you like one, Mum?' Ishbel asked Meg, referring to the sweets.

'I was just about to offer,' Rowan chipped in.

'Not for me, thanks. Maybe later.'

'I doubt there'll be any later,' Vincent observed drolly.

'I'll put a couple on the mantelpiece for you,' Ishbel declared to Meg, and promptly did just that.

'Me, too,' added Rowan, following suit.

'If I'd known you like sweets, I'd also have brought you a box of chocolates,' Vincent informed Meg.

'Oh, there's no need for that. I can take or leave them.'

'Preferably take them,' said Rowan. 'You love sweets, Mum, admit it.'

'Ay, well,' muttered a slightly flustered Meg, 'the occasional treat doesn't do any harm. Or hurt the figure.'

'Nothing wrong with your figure, Meg!' stated Vincent. 'You'd never know you'd had three children.'

Meg blushed brightly. 'That's very kind of you.'

The compliment pleased Meg, though she knew it was not strictly true. Her waist certainly wasn't what it had once been. Still, she thought, considering she'd had three children she wasn't in bad condition.

'I'll tell you what Mum really adores, and that's ice-cream,' Rowan confided.

'Really!' Vincent exclaimed.

'Isn't that right, Mum?' Ishbel laughed.

'I can't deny I enjoy some from time to time,' Meg admitted.

'She'd guzzle it all day long, given the chance,' Rowan said.

'Nonsense!' Meg admonished her.

'Ice-cream and jelly?' Vincent teased.

'No, just ice-cream,' Meg replied. 'It's always been a weakness of mine.'

'Nothing wrong in a weakness,' Vincent replied, looking into his refilled glass. 'We all have them. It's human nature after all.'

'I quite agree,' Meg declared spiritedly.

Rowan popped another caramel into her mouth. 'These are yummy,' she cooed.

'Scrumptious,' Ishbel agreed.

'Look who's talking about having weaknesses,' Meg accused, her turn now to tease.

Vincent pushed himself further back into his chair and allowed the warmth from the range to wash over him. It was good to be among a real family again, he thought. Something he'd missed. If only ... He mentally trailed off, sighed, and drank more whisky, wishing he could have stayed where he was for the night instead of having to go home.

'Where's Rory?' he asked.

'Out with his friend Fraser. He won't be back till later.'

'A good boy, that. You should be proud of him.'

'I'm proud of all my children,' Meg answered quickly.

'And so you should be,' Vincent declared, glancing briefly at Rowan and Ishbel. 'Damn right. They're a credit to you.' He hesitated, then added: 'And Cully.'

A moment's silence fell on the room, only broken when Meg said, a slight tremor in her voice: 'Cully would have been the first to agree with that.'

Vincent changed the subject, and soon had the three females laughing as he recounted a tale about a convoluted, not strictly honest deal he'd recently been involved in.

When he left, he gave Rowan and Ishbel each a shilling, telling them not to spend it all at once.

Despite the cold, they huddled in the open doorway as he climbed into his old and battered car, all three waving enthusiastically as he drove away.

*　　　*　　　*

'I don't want to go to a boring football match,' Rowan complained.

'Nor me,' said Ishbel.

Meg paused, considering how she should deal with this. 'Well, of course you don't have to,' she replied eventually.

Rowan's face lit up. 'Then, I won't.'

'Me, neither,' added Ishbel, already making other plans for her Saturday afternoon.

'But you do realize it is a very important match for Rory? We really should be there to give him our support.'

'There will be plenty at the match to cheer him on,' Ishbel argued.

'True enough. But we, as his family, should also be present to lend encouragement. And, as I said, it is a very important match. The villages championship no less.'

The villages concerned were those in the area who fielded a football team – about a dozen in all. It was a great honour, and considered extremely prestigious, to win this championship. Rivalry among the teams concerned was fierce. It was the first time in years that Glenshields had made it to the final.

'So what if it's important? It isn't to me,' objected Rowan.

'But it is to Rory, and he's your brother,' Meg countered.

Ishbel was now looking uncomfortable, having begun to feel as though she was letting Rory down. He'd always been so good to her after all. 'I don't know,' she muttered.

'Don't know what?' Rowan demanded.

'Perhaps we should go.'

Rowan glared at her twin. 'Do as you think fit. But I don't want to be bored witless at a football match. I just don't see the sense in kicking a stupid bladder from one end of a pitch to the other. It's pointless.'

'We could go for a short while?' Ishbel suggested.

Rowan glared again at her twin. 'You go for a short while; I've got better things to do.'

'As have I!'

'Then, what are you talking about?'

'Like Mum says, maybe we should for Rory's sake,' Ishbel muttered. 'He is our brother after all.'

'So what?' Rowan exclaimed angrily, horribly aware Ishbel was right and she wrong. It didn't help to know that if the positions had been reversed Rory would have been happy to go along and support her.

'Well, I'm definitely going,' Meg said, a statement greeted by silence. 'And so, too, would your father if he'd been alive.'

Rowan's truculence and rebellion vanished instantly. Her father! She hadn't connected him with the argument. Nothing would have kept Cully away from the final, especially when Rory was playing. If he'd had two broken legs, he'd have arranged to be carried there. A combined sense of guilt and shame enveloped her. In this new light she felt attending the match was the least she could do for her father's memory.

'Rowan?' Ishbel queried in a small voice.

'I'll go if you will.'

'We'll both go, then.'

'That's settled,' Meg said briskly. She allowed herself a smile. She'd known they'd come round; it had only been a matter of putting it to them the right way.

'Up the Shielers!' yelled Meg.

'Right up them,' Ishbel whispered to Rowan, and sniggered. Rowan, thinking it was funny, joined in.

Meg watched anxiously as Rory tackled an opponent, robbed him of the ball and headed for the opposing goal. He dribbled past another player, then lost the ball to a challenger.

'Bad luck, son!' Meg called out. The score was one up for the Shielers, the game just into the second half.

Meg shivered, and banged her hands together. When they got home they'd have a nice pot of tea and some toast, she thought. As a treat she'd also open a jar of jam she'd made from the small strawberry crop they'd had in the summer.

'Rory's doing well,' Ishbel commented.

Rowan nodded her agreement. Now she was actually

here she found she was enjoying herself, though she'd never have admitted it – not even to Ishbel.

A cry went up from the crowd when the Glenshields centre forward struck a shot which was scrambled away by the Craigkip goalkeeper. A back collected the ball and booted it up the park out of harm's way.

The back paused to watch the ball bounce and be trapped by a Craigkip winger. Seconds later the winger, having been unsuccessfully tackled twice, beat the Glenshields goalie to level the score. Loud applause broke out from the visiting supporters, while a groan went up from those belonging to Glenshields.

The back looked towards the crowd, and his eyes met Rowan's. He involuntarily smiled; which she returned. Then he was running to take up his restart position.

What an attractive face, Rowan found herself thinking. Despite the cold she found herself suddenly glowing all over.

'They were fortunate,' Meg said.

'We'll soon get back on top,' Ishbel stated, and the Glenshields supporters who'd overheard the remark agreed.

Rowan didn't comment, however. She was still staring at the player who'd smiled at her. He had good strong legs, she noted, and a chunky muscular build.

For the rest of the match she found her gaze returning to him time and again.

'Cheer up. It isn't the end of the world,' Meg consoled a morose Rory, handing him a plate of toast and jam. Glenshields had lost, two–one.

'It feels like it,' Rory replied dully.

'It was a good game, though,' Ishbel declared.

'Never mind. You played well, son. No-one could say otherwise.'

'But to lose the final,' Rory said through gritted teeth, and shook his head. He'd been convinced they'd win; to have lost was a bitter disappointment.

'There's always next year,' Meg went on, trying to cheer him up.

Rory's expression told her what he thought of that.

'Do you know all the Craigkip players?' Rowan asked casually.

'Some,' he muttered, picking up a slice of toast. 'Why?'

'Oh, just curious, that's all.'

In his mind Rory was going over the game, recalling incidents and high points. Despite the score, Glenshields was still the better team, he decided. It was simply rotten luck that they'd lost.

'Who's for more tea?' Meg asked.

'Please, Mum!' Ishbel enthused.

Meg picked up the empty pot and set about refilling it. She began to hum a tune that had recently become popular.

'Who was their left back?' Rowan enquired, her tone again casual.

Rory, his thoughts interrupted, stared at her blankly. 'Eh?'

'Craigkip's left back. Who was he?'

Ishbel's interest was instantly aroused. Now, why should Rowan want to know that?

'Left back?' Rory mused. 'That would be Gray Hamilton.'

'Gray!' Rowan exclaimed softly. 'An unusual name.'

'I've heard it before,' commented Meg. 'Though, as you say, it isn't exactly run-of-the-mill.'

Gray Hamilton, Rowan thought, the glow she'd experienced at the match returning. She liked that. It was different.

She noted Ishbel eyeing her speculatively, and decided not to probe further. She'd do so when she could get Rory on his own.

'Anyone home?' a male voice called out.

Meg straightened from the task of scrubbing the kitchen linoleum, pleased for the chance of a break. 'In here!' she shouted in reply.

A smiling Vincent popped his head round the door. 'I just came straight in – hope that was all right?'

'Of course. Mind where you put your feet.'

'Busy, I see.'

'Not my favourite job, I can assure you. Still, it has to be done.' Meg came to her feet. 'I'll put the kettle on.'

'Not yet,' he said, adding mysteriously; 'I've brought you a surprise.'

She was taken aback. 'A surprise? For me?'

'For you. Now, close your eyes and hold out your hands.'

Her expression furrowed, for she'd heard tales that Vincent could be something of a practical joker. 'It's nothing nasty, is it?'

'Like what?' he teased.

'I don't know. A handful of worms perhaps?'

He roared with laughter. 'I promise you it's not that. Nor is it nasty. It's a *nice* surprise. Word of honour.'

She still wasn't sure whether or not she believed him. 'I'll bounce this scrubbing-brush off your head if it isn't,' she threatened.

'No need for that, Meg. Take my word.'

He sounded sincere enough, she thought. Or was she merely being gullible? 'Do I have to close my eyes?'

'Absolutely essential,' he further teased.

She regarded him dubiously. 'Vincent McQueen, I'm warning you!'

'Have faith, Meg, have faith.'

She laid the scrubbing-brush aside and did as instructed. If the so-called surprise was slimy, she knew she'd scream.

'Ahh!' she exhaled. It was not slimy, but cold. She snapped her eyes open again to find herself staring at a white tub. 'What is it?'

'Genuine Italian ice-cream,' he beamed.

Relief flooded through her. 'Ice-cream!'

'A pint of the stuff, which I hereby entitle you to gorge yourself on.'

'Oh, Vincent, you shouldn't have gone to the trouble,' she chided him.

'Take the lid off and have a look. Have you ever had the real article before?'

She shook her head.

'I only hope it hasn't melted. I brought it as fast as that old car of mine would travel – which isn't saying much.'

She prised the lid off the tub to find the contents still basically firm, though a trifle melted on top.

'I wrapped it in newspaper to try to keep it frozen,' he explained.

She kissed him on the cheek. 'Thank you, Vincent. But where did you get Italian ice-cream from?'

He tapped the side of his nose. 'That's for me to know and you to wonder at. Well, aren't you going to try it?'

'Of course!'

She placed the tub on the table and hurried to get some bowls. 'You'll join me, I take it?'

'It's all for you, Meg.'

'I insist. Unless you don't care for ice-cream, that is?'

'All right, I will join you. Just so you don't feel bad.'

'You mean making a pig of myself?'

'Exactly!' he laughed.

Vincent sat at the table and clasped his hands behind his head as Meg busied herself spooning ice-cream into bowls. 'I could have had raspberry topping put on it but didn't know whether or not you liked it.'

'I like any sort of topping,' she replied wistfully.

'I'll remember next time.'

She smiled at him, then hesitated. 'Maybe I should keep some for the children?'

'It'll never last that long.'

'Quite right! It wouldn't,' she answered, conscience assuaged.

She handed him a bowl, then sat in front of hers, her mouth drooling. 'This is really spoiling me,' she declared.

'What else are women for?'

Talk about flannel – he was a charmer, right enough.

'Mmm!' she crooned. 'It's smoother and creamier than I'm used to.'

'Sort of slips down the throat?'

She nodded her agreement.

He watched in fascination as her tongue darted out to lick at a spoonful.

'This certainly hits the spot,' she murmured.

'I told you it was a nice surprise,' he smiled.

'Couldn't be nicer. Thank you again, Vincent. I just hope it wasn't too expensive.'

'Don't worry about the cost. I pulled off a trick this morning that would pay for a barrowload of tubs.'

'Trick?' she queried, frowning.

'Deal,' he explained.

'Is that why you're back round here?'

'Yes,' he lied. The truth was he'd decided on the spur of the moment to journey through to Glenshields as he'd been thinking a lot about Meg since his last visit. He'd travelled by a roundabout route in order to pick up the ice-cream from a shop he knew sold it.

'I took a chance coming during a weekday. I thought you might be tied up by your seamstress job,' he said.

'You picked the right time. I'll be getting stuck into that later.' When she saw him glance round the kitchen she added, 'I keep what I'm working on – materials, threads, etcetera – in the sitting-room. Otherwise Rory and the twins would be falling over everything, getting it in a muddle.'

'Good idea,' he approved.

Meg sighed. 'This is lovely, and completely unexpected. And it's good to see you.'

She had a most sensual mouth, he thought, the lower lip fuller than the upper. He could have happily sat for hours watching them consume ice-cream.

Meg became aware that he was studying her intently, and a prickle jigged up her spine. She found her mood changing to one of . . . what? She couldn't put a finger on it. She wasn't embarrassed in any way. Somehow more aware, she decided.

She glanced briefly at him, noting his extremely high cheekbones. He was rather handsome in a raffish offbeat way. His eyes bright and . . . *shrewd* more than intelligent. She'd never thought of Vincent being attractive before. In fact she'd never thought all that much about Vincent. He'd simply been one of Cully's cousins who'd invariably been good company and easy to be with.

'Penny for them?' he asked quietly.

She shook her head. 'Nothing.'

'You've suddenly gone all quiet.'

'Have I?' she answered, feigning innocence.

Vincent pushed his bowl away, but she was taking far longer over her ice-cream, savouring every last morsel. 'Do you mind if I smoke?'

'Not at all.'

He lit up, and blew a cloud of thick blue smoke at the ceiling. 'That's better,' he declared.

'Were you buying or selling this morning?' she asked to break the halt that had occurred in their conversation.

'Selling.'

'And you did well?'

'As I mentioned, very well. A profitable deal.'

She twirled what remained of her ice-cream round the inside of her bowl, reluctant to finish it off. 'It must be lonely for you in that cottage by yourself,' she said.

An expression of pain came over his face. 'It can be. I try to keep myself busy, but of course I can't do that all the time. Winter evenings are the worst, which is why I tend to spend most of them in the pub for the conversation and camaraderie.'

Meg thought of his wife, Faye, who'd died in childbirth, together with their first child. She had been a vivacious woman full of sparkle and wit. How long ago was it now? Three years? Four? Four, she decided, which was a long time for a man like Vincent to remain on his own.

Vincent drew heavily, almost savagely, on his cigarette. He was remembering Faye and the joy it had been for him to come home to her every night. Her death had been shattering, compounded by the demise of the baby.

Meg stared at Vincent, feeling sorry for him. She suddenly realized that he was possibly a far more sensitive soul than she'd previously given him credit for. Her heart went out to him, understanding in the light of her own recent loss how he must have suffered, and still was.

'Have you . . . met anyone else?' she asked softly.

He shook his head. 'There have been a few women, I won't deny that. But nothing serious. Nobody I would contemplate marrying, if that's what you mean.'

'Cully and I should have visited you more.' In fact, after Faye's funeral, Cully had called in several times on his own, but never she and Cully together.

'Now you've lost your husband,' Vincent stated. He puffed again on his cigarette. 'You never know what's round the corner, do you? Life is full of surprises.'

'Ups and downs,' she qualified.

'With far more downs than ups, it seems to me.'

'Oh, I don't know!'

He suddenly smiled. 'At least you've got your children. That was denied me.'

Meg didn't know how she'd have got through the period since Cully's death without them. If she'd been on her own as Vincent had been . . . She shuddered. How much more awful things would have been. A totally black abyss of self-pity and despair, devoid of the beams of light that were Rory, Rowan and Ishbel. She viewed them as a drowning person might a lifebelt, for wasn't that precisely what they'd been – lifebelts to her sorrow?

'I envy you your children, you know,' he stated.

She could well understand that.

He watched smoke from his cigarette curl upwards, his expression introverted as he contemplated what might have been.

'You're still a relatively young man, Vincent. Who knows what may still come about?' She wasn't certain how old he was: several years younger than Cully, she seemed to recall.

'Who knows?' he repeated wistfully.

She gazed down at the remains of her ice-cream, not wanting it any more. She forced herself to eat it, though, out of politeness.

'That was grand!' she proclaimed.

'And I must go,' he said, stubbing out his cigarette and rising.

'I thought we might have a cup of tea?'

'Another time perhaps, Meg.'

She rose also. 'I'll see you to the door.'

'No need for that. You've got your scrubbing to get on with. I've held you back long enough.'

The scrubbing! She'd forgotten about that. Still, it would soon be finished and then she could go through to the sitting-room and immerse herself in her sewing.

Her eyes flicked to the brass clock on the mantelpiece. It was a few hours yet before the twins would arrive back demanding their tea. She could get quite a bit done in that time.

'Take care now, Meg,' he said, coming to her and pecking her on the cheek.

The bright and breezy mood he'd had when he arrived had now been replaced by one of dejection. Meg found herself feeling guilty at having broached the subject of loneliness which had sparked the change in him.

'Call in again if you're near,' she said, forcing a smile on to her face.

'I will.'

'And the ice-cream was gorgeous. Rowan and Ishbel will be pea green when I tell them about it.'

'Pretend you scoffed the lot. That will make them even more jealous.'

Meg laughed. 'They probably wouldn't talk to me for days if I said that.'

'Goodbye, then.'

'Goodbye, Vincent. And thanks yet again.'

He gave her a salute, turned abruptly and vanished from the kitchen.

'Oh dear!' she exclaimed softly.

She put the bowls into the sink, threw the empty tub into the rubbish-bin and got back on to her knees where, with a heavy heart, she resumed scrubbing.

'What's your poison?' Vincent asked as they entered the pub. It was a Saturday night, and he'd again appeared unexpectedly, this time asking Meg out for a drink. The twins, who'd been at home, had urged her to go, saying it would do her good.

'A shandy,' Meg replied.

'Half-pint or pint?' he teased.

'*Half*-pint!' she exclaimed, shocked at the suggestion that she, a woman, would have a pint. It just wasn't done.

'How about a dram to go with it?'

'Not for me, thank you.'

'I'm going to have one, so why not you?'

'Just a half-pint of shandy,' she stated firmly.

They were fortunate to find a free table where she sat while he went up to the bar. She gazed about her, nodding to various people whom she knew. Tongues would be wagging at her appearance with an unknown man, she thought, but at the earliest opportunity she'd make it known that Vincent was Cully's cousin.

Vincent returned with the drinks.

'Slainthe!' he toasted, raising his pint.

'Cheerio!'

He looked around. 'Not a bad little pub, this. Did you and Cully often come here?'

Meg shook her head. 'He would drop in from time to time, but rarely the two of us together. We might on a special occasion, but that was about it.'

'He wasn't much of a drinker as I recall?'

'He enjoyed the odd tipple,' Meg explained. 'But more so at home than in the pub.'

'Ah, well, he knew which side his bread was buttered on, where the best company was.'

Meg flushed slightly, knowing he meant her. Vincent certainly wasn't backward in coming forward when it came to handing out compliments. It wasn't something she found disagreeable.

'Want to hear a funny story?' Vincent asked.

'It's not dirty, is it?'

'No, no,' he replied, shaking his head. 'Not in the least. Though I know some that would have you in fits.' He paused, then added: 'If you like that sort of thing, that is.'

'Which I don't,' she stated emphatically.

He made a mental note to remember that. 'Dirty stories and jokes are par for the course in my game. Part of the general chit-chat, so to speak.'

She could well believe that.

He went on: 'This is a real story, one that actually happened.' He sipped his whisky. 'Ready?'

She nodded.

'I sold a man his own horse last week.' And, having said that, a huge smile of glee lit up Vincent's face.

'His own horse?'

'His *own* horse. Silly sod.'

'How did you do that?' she asked, intrigued.

'I bought this knackered old nag, which was in a real sorry state, from him a while ago. Well, I fed it up, had it groomed and given a fancy clip, had its mane and tail plaited, then sold it back to him at a fair.'

Vincent guffawed. 'How about that, then! Made a tidy profit, too.'

'Didn't he recognize it?'

'Thought it a different animal entirely. Wait till he finds out that underneath it's still the same knackered old nag it always was. He'll be livid.'

Meg was appalled. 'But that's . . . not right.'

'Of course it is.'

'You cheated him.'

'No, I didn't,' Vincent protested. 'He examined it and was impressed by what he saw. It's his own fault if he didn't recognize the beast.'

'But you cheated him.'

'No, I didn't.'

'Yes, you did.'

Vincent sighed. 'You'd never make a dealer, Meg. I can see you're far too honest.'

'But you lied.'

'I did nothing of the sort. Simply kept my mouth shut, that's all. I sold him the beast as it stood, which he was happy to buy.'

'You lied by default, then.'

'Ah! You could say that. There, again, that's what dealing's often about. It was his own greed that really sunk him. He was so busy falling over himself thinking he'd found a bargain – trying to do me, in other words – that he got done himself.'

Vincent laughed. 'I enjoyed that little transaction tremendously. Fair made my day.'

Despite herself Meg couldn't help but have a sneaking admiration for his coup. Sell a man his own horse! It did have a certain appeal about it.

'Do you do many things like that?' she enquired.

'You mean' – he made circular movements over the table – 'a touch of the sleight-of-hand? Now and then, when the opportunity presents itself.'

'I think you're a crook, Vincent McQueen.'

'A crook? Me?' His expression became one of pretended outrage. 'Never!'

'A devious man.'

'Doesn't everyone try to be in business? Whether it's horses or those posh stockbroking chaps. The game's the same whoever you are. Buy and sell at a profit – that's all that matters.'

'But buy and sell honestly,' she persisted.

'Honestly! If I stuck totally to that, I'd soon starve. Anyway, it's a matter of definition. What I did was honest enough by my book, which is all that counts.'

'It must be an interesting life,' she said.

'It has its advantages. You're in the open air, not stuck in some shop or factory, getting round and about, meeting all kinds. There are worse jobs than being a horse trader.'

'And you're your own boss. That's something,' she commented.

'Damn right. I couldn't work for someone else now. Too long doing things my way.'

The pub door opened, and a group of men breezed in, looking as though they'd already had a few. They were greeted jocularly by Charlie Dow, the owner.

'You seem to have been around this area quite a bit of late,' Meg commented to Vincent.

He gave her a strange look. 'It falls out that way sometimes. And it gives me the chance of keeping in regular touch with you.'

She smiled at him; which he returned, flashing his gleaming teeth at her. There might have been something of the gypsy in him, she thought. A gold ear-ring and bandana would have suited him perfectly. But as far as she knew he was true-blue Scots like herself.

They talked about the children for a while, as he showed great interest in them. When she spoke Meg's eyes shone with the love she had for her offspring. Vincent didn't fail to note that, which ratcheted her even higher in his estimation.

They'd been in the pub for just under an hour when the door suddenly flew open to reveal the Reverend David Dykes standing framed. His dark intense gaze swept the interior, disapproval and condemnation oozing from his every pore.

The pub fell silent, conversations halted in mid-sentence. Guilt and apprehension crept on to faces that only seconds previously had been wreathed in laughter and merriment.

Dykes took several paces into the pub, the long black cloak he wore billowing slightly as he moved. He looked more like a devil than like a representative of the Almighty, Meg thought, her skin creeping.

Charlie Dow stood nervously behind the bar, the hand holding an empty pint pot white with tension. 'Evening, Minister,' he said at last.

Dykes didn't reply, but his lips thinned even further in censure.

The atmosphere had become strained in the extreme, and it was as though each and every customer was holding his or her breath. Then, as suddenly as he'd appeared, Dykes left the pub again, the door silently closing behind him.

Charlie Dow swore quietly. 'Bloody man,' he muttered, a hum filling the pub as low and muted conversations were resumed.

'That was impressive,' a wondering Vincent said to Meg.

'He's the new vicar. A real fire-and-brimstone type. He puts the fear of God into me and just about everyone else, from what I can gather.'

'I'm not surprised. He certainly has presence.'

'He has that all right. He is a tremendous orator. When he's in the pulpit he's spellbinding.'

'I can imagine.'

Meg sipped her drink. 'He apparently thinks pubs are dens of vice and iniquity. If it was up to him, he'd close this place down tomorrow.'

'Let's just be thankful it isn't up to him,' Vincent replied, and laughed.

'He's a complete contrast to the old minister, who enjoyed a dram with the best of them. You couldn't have found a nicer, more sympathetic man than Mr McNab.'

Vincent stared at the door through which Dykes had come and gone like some terrifying genie temporarily released from a bottle. Not someone to be on the wrong side of, he thought.

'Sorry about the interruption, folks,' Charlie Dow apologized, bustling up to their table.

'Hardly your fault,' Meg answered.

'None the less.' Charlie pulled a face. 'He's taken to doing that. Never says a word. Just shows up, glares at everyone, scaring the bejesus out of them, then vanishes.'

'Is it spoiling your trade?' Vincent enquired.

'Not so far. Though I can see it might.'

'He doesn't exactly approve of your business, does he?' Vincent commented in a dry tone.

Charlie laughed bitterly. 'You can say that again. I know it's fanciful, but I keep half-expecting him to turn up with a blazing torch and set the place alight.' Charlie shivered. 'He gives me the creeps and no mistake.'

They exchanged a few more words, then Charlie moved on, trying to jolly the atmosphere back to what it had been before the minister's appearance.

But Charlie failed, a pall of gloom continuing to hang over the pub for the rest of the evening.

'I don't understand why Mum had to come with him,' Rory said scathingly. They were at a spring dance in the village hall. Rory was referring to Vincent, now on the floor with Meg.

'Why not?' Ishbel demanded.

'He's seeing an awful lot of her recently. It isn't right,' Rory retorted.

'Oh, get away with you. There's nothing wrong with that.'

'Yes, there is,' Rory muttered through clenched teeth.

'Stop moaning. You're always moaning,' Rowan complained vaguely, scanning the crowd, sizing up the other frocks to see if there were any prettier than the mulberry-coloured one she was wearing. She decided at last there weren't; which cheered her immeasurably.

'I'm not moaning,' Rory told her, taking offence at her using that word with regard to him.

'If it gives Mum a bit of enjoyment to come to the dance with Vincent, then so what? He's family after all.'

'He's holding Mum a bit tight for family. Look at them! He's wound round her like a snake round a tree.'

Ishbel laughed. 'Hardly that. You're exaggerating.'

'I'm doing nothing of the sort,' Rory protested.

'Vincent's holding her perfectly normally,' Ishbel replied. 'They're no different from any other couple.'

Rory was seething inside. He hated watching his mother dancing with a man other than his father. It didn't help that part of him knew he was being ridiculous, which, if anything, made him even more angry.

'If you're so bothered, go and dance yourself. That'll take your mind off things,' Ishbel suggested.

'There's Morag Scofield. She's always been a fancy of yours,' Rowan said.

'Don't talk nonsense!' Rory retorted. But it was true. He'd long had a soft spot for Morag, though she'd never shown much interest in him.

'She's just arrived with her brother,' Rowan went on, pointing out the pair in question.

Rory spotted Morag whom he thought looked gorgeous. What had she done to her hair, which was swept back in some way? She looked very grown up, quite a woman of the world.

'I'd ask her up before someone else does,' Rowan advised.

'Get in there quickly,' Ishbel added.

Should he or shouldn't he? The night was young after all; plenty of time left. Perhaps he should wait till he'd had a few preliminary dances – they might bolster his confidence.

Rowan could see his indecision, guessed the cause and found it amusing. She personally found Morag boring and not really much of a looker, either. She liked what she had done with her hair, though, and wondered where she had got that idea from.

'Get on with it, slowcoach!' Ishbel hissed to Rory.

'Do you think I should?'

'Nothing ventured, nothing gained.'

'He who hesitates is lost,' a mockingly smiling Rowan added.

His sisters' clichés irritated Rory. But they were right. And wasn't that Conor Meldrum, the stupid big oaf, eyeing Morag?

Rory made up his mind. She could only refuse, which would mortify him. Squaring his shoulders, he marched towards Morag, now in conversation with a girlfriend.

'You're a good dancer,' Meg complimented Vincent as they moved effortlessly together.

'Not nearly as good as you. You have natural rhythm.'

Meg was delighted. 'Do you think so?'

'Most definitely.'

'You're a charmer through and through, Vincent McQueen,' she gently chided.

'Maybe so. But in this case I'm merely stating a fact, nothing more.'

That delighted her even further. Vincent was certainly a far better dancer than Cully whom she'd often accused of having two left feet. Anything more complicated than a waltz had filled him with a combination of deep dismay and trepidation. She smiled in recollection, remembering his look of fierce concentration when in action, and the one of relief that had invariably followed as he'd come off the floor.

'And you smell exquisite,' Vincent went on, a roguish twinkle in his eye.

'Thank you again.'

'Better than a field full of flowers. Or a summer sunrise.'

She stared at him, thinking him quite the poet. It was the first time in her life anyone had ever waxed so eloquently about her.

'What's the name of your perfume?'

'To be honest, I forget,' she confessed. 'It's something I've had for years.'

'Cully buy it for you?'

'It was a present,' she replied, not admitting that it was a present she'd bought herself. The idea of Cully going into a chemist's and asking for perfume was just too absurd for words. The only thing more absurd would be him buying lingerie. Meg burst out laughing.

'What's so funny?'

'Nothing,' she answered, smothering her laughter.

'Is it me?'

'No, Vincent,' she assured him. 'Definitely not you. I swear. Just a thought that passed through my mind. Totally unimportant.'

They halted and clapped when the dance came to an

end. 'Do you want to stay up or have a breather?' Vincent queried. 'Or maybe you'd prefer the opportunity of letting someone else give you a twirl?'

'Don't be silly,' she retorted. 'And, yes, I would like to stay up, thank you very much.'

'Your every wish is my command,' he stated, and bowed low from the waist, which made Meg laugh.

'Idiot!'

'Have you just found out?' he teased in reply.

She was having fun, Meg thought, feeling all bubbly inside. The night was proving a huge success. She was glad she'd come, although initially she had had reservations about doing so.

'Faye used to love dancing,' he said suddenly.

'Really?'

He began reminiscing about Faye, in a light-hearted way. And when he'd done that Meg told him about some of the dances she and Cully had been to, and what a trial Cully had found them.

'Another glass of fruit punch, Minister?' Jack Armstrong asked obsequiously in a different part of the hall.

The Reverend David Dykes glanced at the toadying church elder, whom he held in no regard whatever. 'That would be very nice, thank you,' he replied.

Jack took the minister's empty glass from him and scuttled off to have it refilled.

'It's a pity the Monteiths couldn't come,' Mrs Armstrong gushed.

'Yes,' smiled Dykes without looking at her, his eyes wandering over the gathering. He, too, had had reservations about attending, but had been persuaded to do so with the assurances that everything would be 'proper' and the drinks sold strictly non-alcoholic. A pastor's place was with his flock, he reminded himself, and there were many regular churchgoers at the dance.

'Sybil is such a lovely woman, so refined and genteel,' Mrs Armstrong went on, using Sybil's Christian name which she'd never have dared do had Sybil been present.

'A credit to the village,' Dykes answered.

'Oh, indeed! They both are.'

Dykes watched a young blonde sway by in the arms of a lusty adolescent. An attractive girl, he thought, if in an obvious way. He racked his memory trying to place her, for the face was vaguely familiar. One of the Stewart lassies, he now recalled, whose father had died shortly before his arrival in Glenshields.

He'd never before noticed how sensual she was, extremely well developed with legs that would—

Dykes swallowed, and turned his attention to the plump Mrs Armstrong gazing avidly up at him. She had a face like a turnip, he thought as she burbled on about a church activity she was organizing. He noticed tiny pearls of sweat on her rather hairy upper lip; which confirmed how much she disgusted him.

'Good evening, Minister. How nice to see you here.'

The speaker was Mr Barr the newsagent, who had his wife by his side, the pair of them grinning inanely.

'Good evening,' Dykes replied politely, and launched into a brief conversation with them.

Rowan wasn't at all impressed with her current partner, who was prattling on. There was also a whiff of bad breath about him which made her nose wrinkle whenever she caught it. She couldn't wait for that particular dance to finish so she could ditch him.

'Terrific band,' enthused her partner.

Rowan's reply was to smile weakly and glance away. She caught her breath when she saw Gray Hamilton, the Craigkip left back. He was standing with a group of people, some of whom she recognized as other members of the Craigkip football team.

'Did you hear me, Rowan?'

'I beg your pardon?' She couldn't for the life of her remember her partner's name.

He repeated himself: something about his work. She still didn't take in what he said, her mind focused on Gray Hamilton. 'How interesting,' she muttered, hoping that was an acceptable reply. It must have been, for he continued chattering.

Was Gray accompanied by a female? she wondered, gazing over at him again. She couldn't make out whether he was or not. With a bit of luck he wasn't.

Thankfully the number ended soon after that, and while everyone was applauding she hastily excused herself and hurried from the floor.

'How did it go?' Ishbel asked her as she reached her sister's side.

'What?'

'You and Romeo.'

Rowan failed to detect the sarcastic note in Ishbel's voice. 'Oh, it was all right.'

'Just all right?' Again the sarcastic tone.

'Not my type. I can't stand them when their breath smells.'

'Nasty!' exclaimed Ishbel, now sympathetic.

Where had Gray got to? Rowan wondered. His previous companions were still where they'd been, but of him there was no sign.

Then she spied him off to one side with his arm round a brunette's waist. As she watched he whispered something in the girl's ear, making the girl laugh.

Perhaps just a friend, she thought. After all, she had loads of lads present who might do the same with her. She desperately wished he'd look in her direction.

'There's Iain Carstairs smiling at you,' Ishbel said.

'Eh?'

'Fat Boy. He's smiling at you.'

'Bugger him!'

Ishbel acknowledged Iain instead, who waved at her. 'Mum would murder you if she heard you use language like that,' she admonished Rowan.

'Bugger her, too.'

Ishbel stared at her sister in astonishment. 'What did you say?'

Rowan was instantly contrite. 'Sorry. I didn't mean that. I've got something on my mind.'

'Oh, really?' Ishbel queried, intrigued. 'Well, come on, give.'

'It's a secret.'

That made Ishbel even more intrigued. 'What's going on in that head of yours, Rowan Stewart?'

'Wouldn't you like to know?' Rowan teased back.

Rory strolled up to them. 'I see Mum's still out there with Vincent. They haven't been off,' he grumbled.

'Are you still worrying about that?' Ishbel retorted. Then, when she didn't get a reply: 'How did you get on with Morag?'

'Fine,' he answered evasively.

'Does that mean she wouldn't stay up?'

'Excuse me, I have to go to the toilet. I'm bursting.' And with that Rory hurried away.

'She wasn't interested,' Ishbel surmised to Rowan.

Rowan's gaze was riveted on Gray, now escorting the brunette on to the floor. He was a walking dream, she thought. It was a new experience for her to be so taken by a chap, and even more surprisingly one she'd never even spoken to.

'Hello, Rowan, how are things?' asked Chick Strathearn, joining her and Ishbel.

'Fine,' she smiled in reply.

He gave a small appreciative whistle. 'Don't you look fabulous tonight! The belle of the ball without a doubt.'

Rowan preened. 'That's very kind of you.'

'A real heart-stopper and no mistake.'

Ishbel forced herself to smile also, but inside was sick with jealousy.

Chick extended an arm to Rowan. 'How about tripping the light fantastic with me?'

Considering what he'd said, she could hardly turn down his invitation, though she wished it was Gray Hamilton who'd asked her. 'Of course, Chick,' she replied, slipping her arm through his.

Ishbel watched them walk away, Chick talking animatedly and Rowan laughing. How many lads was that who'd asked Rowan up? She'd lost count. And here she was still without a single request. There were times when she could have scratched Rowan's eyes out. A wallflower, that's what she was here, a blinking wallflower. Why, oh, why couldn't she have been born beautiful like Rowan? They were twins after all. She'd have done anything to have swapped bodies with Rowan. Misery washed over her. If there had been a cat present, she'd have kicked the damn thing out of sheer foul temper and pique.

Rory let himself into the gents' toilet where he found a huddle of males drinking from bottles, the air thick with cigarette smoke and the pungent smell of whisky.

'Rory!' exclaimed a workmate. 'Welcome to the snug.'

A few of the men laughed to hear that. 'Effing minister,' another swore. 'We've got to come in here for a bevy because of him.'

'Would you like a swig?' the workmate asked Rory, proffering his bottle.

Why not? Rory thought. He might only be going on sixteen, but a little whisky was nothing new to him. Why, even his dad had given him a dram in the past.

His dad! His heart sank at the memory of Cully whom he missed dreadfully, far more than he would have ever imagined. He'd known he was fond of his dad, but until Cully's death hadn't realized just how deeply he had loved the man. As he loved his mother, now out there having a right old time with Vincent. He wished Vincent would disappear in a puff of smoke and never come back.

'Have another if you want,' urged the workmate.

Rory had several more swigs and then returned to the main part of the hall.

Rowan found herself dancing alongside Gray and the brunette who, she now noted with satisfaction, wasn't nearly so pretty close up. On the contrary: if anything, the brunette was rather plain. Without being obvious about it, she tried to catch Gray's eye, but failed, as he was being too attentive to the brunette. Then the chance of establishing any sort of contact was lost as she and Chick moved off in one direction, Gray and the brunette in another.

Iain Carstairs wandered over to Ishbel. 'The evening's a big success, don't you think?' he said.

She nodded, thinking he was the last person she wanted to talk to.

'I see Rowan's dancing with Chick,' he went on.

'Full marks for observation,' she replied tartly.

He coloured. 'Sorry. Perhaps you want to be alone?'

His stricken expression made her feel sorry for him, and annoyed with her own rudeness. There had been no call for it. 'Not at all. Are you enjoying yourself?'

He shrugged. 'So, so.'

She wouldn't have gone even that far.

'Have you been dancing yourself?' he enquired.

'I've been up lots,' she replied.

'Rowan's looking smashing tonight, don't you think?'

She could have sloshed him. 'The belle of the ball, according to Chick.'

Iain gazed hungrily at Rowan. 'I wouldn't disagree with him.'

Cinderella to my ugly sister, Ishbel thought bitterly. 'Have you asked her to dance yet?' she smiled maliciously, knowing full well he hadn't.

'Not so far. But I intend to,' Iain mumbled.

He wouldn't have the nerve in case Rowan refused him, Ishbel thought, which Rowan probably would have done.

'I don't suppose . . . ,' Iain started and trailed off.

'Suppose what?' she prompted.

'Would you care to get up?'

Why not? No-one else had offered. 'I think it's nearing the end of the number,' she prevaricated.

'Oh!' he exhaled, taking that as a refusal.

Her heart went out to him. It was hardly his fault he was fat, and he was a nice lad for all that. When he relaxed he was quite amusing. 'But we could have the next one?'

His face lit up. 'That would be lovely, Ishbel.'

By now Rowan had firmly established that Gray was with the brunette, which she found hugely disappointing.

But maybe she could still meet him and cast a spell over him. She'd always managed that in the past. She continued dancing with Chick, waiting her chance.

The Reverend David Dykes wanted to get away from there, but judged it too soon yet to take himself home. He was finding it all so . . . depressing. He paused as he raised his glass to his mouth, watching Rowan glide by. What a bottom she had, he thought, and wondered what it was like unclothed. A vision flashed into his mind which made him start and spill his fruit punch.

'Minister, are you all right?' queried Mrs Armstrong in alarm, while Jack gazed anxiously on. Several other church regulars were also present.

'Dear me!' exclaimed Dykes, wiping himself down.

'You seemed to . . . *jerk*,' said Mrs Smith.

'A sudden stabbing fibrositic pain,' lied Dykes, coming out with the first plausible excuse he could think of.

'I didn't know you had fibrositis?' queried Mr Smith.

'From time to time,' Dykes smiled. 'Nothing serious.'

'I myself suffer,' stated Mrs Armstrong, and immediately launched into an account of previous bouts.

Bored to distraction, Dykes was forced to listen patiently. Another half-hour, he promised himself, no more.

'It was a terrific pass,' enthused Sandy McKee, one of the Craigkip players.

'Terrific,' agreed Tom Durie, their centre forward. 'All I had to do was collect the ball and bang it between the posts.'

Rory, who was part of the company, tried to concentrate. The whisky he'd had earlier had gone to his head, causing him to slur a little when he spoke.

'We'll beat you when we play you next year, just wait and see,' Rory declared.

'Some hope!' retorted Alex Fisher, another of the Craigkip contingent.

Rory became aware of someone nudging his elbow and turned to find Rowan there. 'I wondered where you'd got to,' she smiled.

He made a vague gesture encompassing the group. 'Some of the Craigkip lads paying us a friendly visit. We're talking football.'

'Boring,' a girl winked at Rowan.

'I'm searching for Mum,' Rowan lied to Rory. 'Have you seen her?'

'Not for a while.'

Rowan pulled a disappointed face.

'Why, do you want her for something?'

'Just to see how she is.'

Rowan looked over at Gray, who was with the brunette. 'I thoroughly enjoyed the game between the Shielers and Craigkip,' she said.

'It was a cracker, eh?' beamed Sandy.

'Very exciting,' she nodded.

'This is my sister Rowan,' Rory explained.

Rowan noted she was getting appreciative glances from several of the chaps present. 'Introduce me to your friends,' she prompted.

Sandy McKee was the first to shake hands with her, followed by his partner, a girl called Liz. Finally it was Gray's turn.

'Gray Hamilton,' Rory said.

'Pleased to meet you,' Rowan purred in her sexiest voice.

'And to meet you, Rowan.'

She held on to his hand longer than she had the others, meantime gazing directly into his eyes. 'You played well in the villages championship,' she told him.

He smiled to hear that – a smile which curled the corners of his mouth delightfully upwards and made her heart contract.

'And this is . . . ,' Rory faltered, not knowing the name of Gray's companion.

'Sonia Millar,' the brunette stated.

'How do you do?' said Rowan.

'Nice to meet you,' Sonia replied sincerely.

Was it a long-standing relationship or a relatively new one? Rowan wondered as she shook hands with Sonia.

Sonia, sensing something she didn't understand, frowned.

Rowan stayed on chatting; but to her annoyance didn't receive any particular attention from Gray, who started up another conversation with a Glenshields player.

'Would you like to dance, Rowan?' Alex Fisher asked eventually.

That put her in an awkward position. She didn't want to dance with Alex, but she didn't want simply to walk away, either. It was galling that Gray was showing no interest in her whatever.

'Thank you,' she replied.

To her consternation Gray and Sonia left while she was still on the floor with Alex.

The figure moved through a mist, tantalizing areas of flesh being revealed only to be quickly obscured again. The face, surrounded by a halo of pale golden hair, was indistinct. Though he couldn't identify the face, he felt he knew to whom it belonged.

Curvaceous flesh he yearned to reach out and touch, the thought of which made him shake all over. And there, something he'd never actually seen before. A doorway that horribly fascinated him yet repelled him at the same time. A place of evil and awful sin.

'No-o-o!' he murmured, trying to resist these images tempting him beyond all reason, images conjured up by Satan himself.

Erotic sensations coursed through him, making him writhe in protest. These sensations terrified him but at the same time were so sweetly seductive.

The mist continued to swirl, parting briefly to reveal a pair of rounded breasts, promising him pleasures he'd never known.

With a yell the Reverend David Dykes sat up in bed, eyes starting from his head. He stared into the gloom of his bedroom and panted, trying to recover his breath.

'God Almighty,' he groaned, placing a hand on his chest which he discovered to be slick with sweat.

He was boiling hot, the bedsheets soaking. He threw back the covers in an attempt to cool down.

'Filth,' he muttered. 'Filth!' He felt profound guilt that his dreams should have been so inhabited – dreams, he hastily reminded himself, over which he had no conscious control.

'The devil's work,' he declared vehemently. He was being tempted, as Christ had been in the wilderness. This was an attempt by Satan to bring him low, cast him down from the pillar built of his belief and prayers.

The Stewart lassie, he thought. That was who it had been. The one who'd caught his attention earlier at the dance. Her youth was so enticing – and yet so dangerous. He closed his eyes, and saw again the young flesh that had enticed his sleep. Undulating flesh moving closer and closer and . . .

He sobbed, then went still.

'Our Father, who art in heaven . . .' he began. And as he prayed he wept, telling himself over and over God must have had a reason for denying him so much. He must believe in God's purpose, no matter how hard it was to bear.

'Thy will be done . . .'

His voice droned on, and the tears continued to fall.

'Will you stop fidgeting!' Ishbel complained.

'I'm not fidgeting,' Rowan replied.

'Yes, you are.'

'Go back to sleep,' Rowan said.

'How can I when you keep moving?'

'I won't any more. Now, go back to sleep.'

'I sometimes hate being in bed with you,' Ishbel yawned.

Rowan lay staring at the ceiling, and continued to think about Gray, his beautiful smile and lovely eyes.

'Is there something bothering you?' Ishbel mumbled.

'No,' Rowan lied. 'Nothing at all.' She normally confided in Ishbel, but for some reason didn't want to this time – at least, not yet.

She pictured Gray as he'd been at the dance, and went over in her head the few words they'd exchanged. At least Sonia wasn't a long-standing girlfriend but a new acquisition; she'd gleaned that from Alex.

Sonia wasn't a patch on her, she assured herself. Sonia was a mouse, nothing more; no competition at all. And yet the fact remained Gray had seemed to prefer Sonia.

If only he'd shown a flicker of interest in her. She wasn't used to this. Usually they fell over themselves for her attention. But not Gray; he'd been different. She might have had a face like a gargoyle and a figure to match, for all he'd cared.

Now that she came to think about it, her resentment fading, she liked the fact that he was different, that he wasn't instantly smitten by her charms. It was a challenge which appealed.

Beside Rowan, Ishbel started gently to snore. It was ages before she, too, fell asleep.

Vincent lit a gas-mantle which cast a warm yellow light throughout his kitchen. He was tired, for it had been a long day and a late night. Thank goodness he could have a lie-in next morning as it was Sunday. *That* morning, he corrected himself.

He crossed to a cupboard where he kept a bottle of rum and poured a hefty tot into a far from clean glass. He topped the rum up at the sink pump, the sink piled high with dirty dishes.

He looked round the kitchen, thinking what a contrast it was to Meg's neat and spotless one. He smiled, remembering the meal she'd given him before the dance.

It had been a marvellous meal, and plenty of it. She insisted on heaping his plate twice. You came to appreciate a good meal when you cooked for yourself, particularly if you cooked as badly as he did.

He glanced again about the kitchen, thinking how cold and cheerless it was, unlived in and neglected. As for his bedroom, that was worse. His bed had remained unchanged for months now. He kept meaning to do something about it but always forgot.

There was simply no comparison between Meg's house and his. Hers was a joy to be in, his too wretched for words.

He had another sip of rum, smiling as he recalled how attractive Meg had looked that evening. Mind you, he'd always found her attractive, ever since they'd first met.

He glanced around yet again, his expression one of wrinkled distaste. This was no way to live, no way at all.

'It's a great day for a fair,' Meg said, glancing up at the cloudless blue sky across which several flights of birds were flying.

'How's that toffee apple?' Vincent asked.

'Delicious.' She offered it to him. 'Want a bite?'

He shook his head. 'I don't trust those things. Saw a chap snap a tooth on one once. He was in agony till he got the stump removed.'

'Coward,' Meg teased.

'Maybe so. But you can keep your toffee apple.'

'You don't know what you're missing.' And with that she had another bite.

Vincent stopped to stare at several horses tethered to posts stuck into the ground.

'Afternoon, Vincent,' said a man, appearing from behind the horses.

'Afternoon, Sammy. How are you?'

'Couldn't be better,' Sammy replied. He was a middle-aged man whose hair had once been red but had now turned yellow. His cheeks were thin and pinched, his eyes liverish.

Vincent studied the horse nearest him, then ran a hand over its haunch. The horse snickered to his touch.

'Fine beast,' commented Sammy.

Vincent didn't reply.

'Can give you a good price on him.'

Vincent patted the haunch. 'Not for me, thanks.'

'How about the others here? This mare is a bobby dazzler. A real gem.'

The horse in question was tan with white stockings. She also had a white blaze down the centre of her forehead.

'Seems familiar,' murmured Vincent, gazing at her.

'Not this beauty. She comes from England and was only recently brought north of the border.'

'Why is she being sold?'

'Ah!' exclaimed Sammy sadly. 'Her previous owner died, and his stock was sold off cheaply, which is why I'm able to sell her on at a very reasonable price.'

Vincent grunted, and scratched the blaze.

'She is gorgeous,' Meg said.

'Wouldn't argue there,' Vincent agreed.

'And she seems to have a sweet temperament.'

'She do indeed, madam,' said Sammy, nodding.

Vincent's lips thinned into a smile. 'What's her name?'

'Perdita.'

'Perdita,' Vincent mused. Then drolly: 'Very posh.'

'Give her a good look over, Vincent. You won't find a better beast at the fair or my name isn't Sammy Campbell.'

'And the previous owner died, you say?' Vincent repeated.

'Heart attack. Not all that old, either, I understand. I should ask more for her, but I need a quick sale for other commitments I have coming up. A profit is a profit after all.'

'Of course,' said Vincent.

'Are you interested, then? Shall we talk money?'

Vincent gazed at Sammy for a few moments, then shook his head. 'I don't think so.'

'She's a buy, Vincent. Don't you even want to hear what I'm asking?'

'She's simply not what I'm looking for, no matter how reasonable the price. Thank you very much, Sammy. See you around.'

Sammy's face fell in disappointment. 'Your loss, pal, not mine.'

Vincent took Meg's arm and strolled off. His face

cracked into a huge smile as soon as they were a little way away. Meg stared at him in puzzlement, wondering what was so funny.

'Perdita, my arse!' Vincent laughed.

'You mean it isn't that?'

'Her real name's Dixie, and the only thing that beast is good for is the glue factory.'

Meg winced at the thought of such a horrible fate for so beautiful an animal. 'How so?'

'Sammy's path doesn't often cross with mine, which is probably why he thought he could get away with it. But I saw that beast a few months back up near Inverness, where Sammy comes from, and a part of the country I rarely visit. I know for a fact that she's not only nappy but a crib-biter and wind-sucker.'

'What on earth are those?' Meg queried, intrigued.

'Well, a nappy horse is one which, when being ridden, will suddenly stop and refuse to budge. If you do succeed in getting it to move along, it'll only halt again a little further on,' Vincent explained.

'I see.'

'So therefore the horse is useless as a riding animal.'

'And crib-biting?'

'Exactly that. It bites its crib when feeding, and in this instance sucks in wind at the same time. Nasty vices which would hardly endear it to an owner.'

'Which all adds up to the horse not being worth nearly as much as it would otherwise?'

'Exactly,' Vincent nodded.

'What a crook!' Meg exclaimed, referring to Sammy. 'Lucky for you you'd run into the horse before.'

'Lucky indeed,' Vincent said. 'Otherwise I could easily have been taken in.'

Meg glanced at him. 'If you had, no doubt you wouldn't have suffered any qualms about selling the horse to someone else. Doing precisely the same as your friend Sammy: selling it on without disclosing its faults?'

'Business is business,' Vincent declared. 'If caught out,

the only thing to do is try to turn the situation to your own advantage.'

'I think you dealers are all as bad as each other,' Meg commented caustically.

'I'll tell you this. If you ever shake hands with a horse dealer, make sure you count your fingers afterwards,' Vincent laughed again, this time louder than previously, thinking he'd cracked a great joke.

'I'll remember,' Meg smiled.

They looked at some more horses. Then Vincent asked Meg if she'd care to visit the tea-tent, which she thought was an excellent idea. A cup of tea and a sit-down were just what she needed; her feet were beginning to ache after all the walking around.

On entering the tent Meg secured a table while Vincent joined the queue. She was having a wonderful day, Meg reflected, thoroughly enjoying the excitement and buzz generated by the fair. She also had to admit she was enjoying Vincent's company even more than usual, as he was in a particularly light-hearted, ebullient mood.

She exclaimed in delight when he rejoined her carrying a tray bearing a varied selection of fancy cakes. 'You're spoiling me,' she said.

'You're worth it,' he answered.

An éclair oozing cream caught her eye. 'I think I'll start on that,' she stated, pointing at it.

'Help yourself.'

Her expression became one of ecstasy as she sank her teeth into the chocolate-covered delicacy. 'Mmm!' she murmured. 'Sheer heaven.'

Vincent picked out a hard flat cake for himself which he cut into sections. 'I thought I'd take this opportunity to talk to you,' he declared quietly.

'About what?'

He spooned sugar into his tea and slowly stirred. 'We get on well, you and I. Right?'

She nodded.

'*Extremely well* in fact.'

Meg wiped traces of cream from the corners of her mouth, wondering what this was leading up to. He'd suddenly become very serious.

'Wouldn't you agree?' he prompted.

'Yes,' she replied.

He pushed the pieces of cake round his plate, then began forming them into shapes and patterns. 'The last thing I want is to offend you,' he said after a lengthy pause.

Meg laid what remained of the éclair back on her plate. 'What is it, Vincent?'

He took out his packet of cigarettes, and lit up, the pieces of cake now forgotten. 'I like you very much, Meg. You must realize that.'

She nodded. 'And I like you.'

'I mean, it's more than just *like*.'

Comprehension began to dawn. 'Go on, Vincent,' she said softly.

'Well ... I'm on my own, and so are you now. It seems to me we could ... maybe get together?'

'Get together?'

He drew in a deep breath. 'On a permanent basis, that is.'

She leant back in her chair to study him, completely taken by surprise. She'd had no idea his mind was running this way. 'Are you proposing?' she asked.

'I've always had a soft spot for you, Meg. Right from the word go. But there was Cully, and then Faye for me. Now they're both gone, which leaves you and me alone. It seems a waste when it could be ... different.'

Meg was stunned, and completely thrown by this unexpected turn of events. 'Cully isn't long dead,' she managed at last.

'I know that. And perhaps I'm jumping the gun. Maybe it would have been better if I'd let things go for a bit longer before speaking to you.'

He searched her face, his own full of anxious concern. 'I wouldn't be trying to replace Cully; that's impossible. But life goes on, and somehow we have to cope with it. Make the best of the hand fate has dealt us.'

'I really don't know what to say,' she replied, shaking her head.

Vincent dropped his gaze to stare into his teacup. 'Loneliness is a terrible thing,' he said quietly. 'I can vouch for that; I've had four years of it after all. It shrivels you up inside, saps the juices. You don't seem to belong anywhere any more. There's no-one to share with, to laugh with, to worry about. No-one to worry about you. Oh, you have friends of course, but that's hardly the same as a caring partner. Every night ultimately ends in an empty house with only yourself for company.'

'I'm more fortunate than you,' she said in a quiet tone that matched his. 'I have the children.'

He smiled thinly. 'For now, Meg. But how long before they fly the nest? They're hardly babies after all. Before you know where you are it'll be time for them to move on and lead their own lives.'

That was true enough, Meg thought. The day would come when Rory, Rowan and Ishbel left home. Then she'd be in the same predicament as Vincent. They'd naturally visit, bring their own children in due course. But between visits there would be the awful loneliness that Vincent had mentioned.

'I'm not talking about love, Meg. I can't expect that. Though, as I said, I do have very strong feelings towards you. But there's companionship to consider, and friendship.'

She was confused, bewildered. It had never crossed her mind she might marry again. For her Cully had been the one and only, and yet what Vincent said made sense.

'I'll have to think,' she stated lamely.

'Of course. Take as long as you need. There's no rush after all. Just let me know when you've made a decision.'

She stared at the tempting remains of the éclair, but her appetite had vanished. 'It's certainly turned out to be some visit to the fair,' she said eventually.

He decided not to pursue his suit any further for the moment; best let matters rest as they were. 'So what would you like to do next?' he asked.

'Whatever.'

'How about we try the amusement-stalls? Who knows – we might even win a goldfish.'

She laughed. 'The last thing I need is a goldfish!'

'Then, we'll go for a doll. Game?'

'Game,' she agreed.

When they left the fair Meg was carrying a Kewpie doll Vincent had won for her at the coconut-shy.

'He what?' Fee queried.

'Proposed to me.'

'Well, I'll be . . .' Fee broke off, momentarily lost for words.

'It surprised me also, I can tell you.'

'You didn't turn him down, I hope?'

'No, I said I would think about it.'

Fee shifted her ample weight in the chair. Meg and Vincent McQueen – now, there was a turn-up for the book. Her thoughts began to race, considering the pros and cons. She tried to recall everything she'd ever heard about Vincent.

'Was there any indication he was leading up to this?' Fee probed.

'Not that I was aware of. Perhaps I was just being slow, that's all.'

'Tell me exactly what he said,' Fee instructed, listening intently while Meg spoke, occasionally prompting when she wanted something specific clarified.

'Well,' Fee breathed when Meg stopped speaking.

'What am I to do, Mum? I can't help feeling it would be wrong. That I'd be betraying Cully's memory.'

'It is only a relatively short time since his death, that's true,' Fee mused.

'Not even a year, Mum.'

'But that's as may be. Would you feel any different five years from now, or ten? The question is what's your opinion of Vincent as a possible husband?'

'I don't love him, but—'

'But what?' Fee interjected eagerly.

'He is good company, and fun. As he says, we get on very well together.'

'He has the reputation of something of a rogue.'

'They're all rogues in his line of work, from what I understand. It's that kind of business.'

Fee could well believe that. 'Are you attracted to him, lass?'

'Do you mean . . . physically?'

'If you marry, you'll have to sleep with him, you know.'

Meg blushed and hastily glanced away. She found this sort of thing difficult to talk about with her mother. 'I don't find him unattractive,' she replied in a small voice.

'So that wouldn't bother you?' Then, when Fee got no reply: 'Or would it?'

'I really don't know, Mum. There's only ever been Cully. The thought of another man is strange and, to be honest, upsetting. I somehow can't imagine myself and another man like that.'

'He must be attracted to you; otherwise he would hardly have proposed.'

'I suppose,' Meg mused. 'As I mentioned, he did say he'd always had a soft spot for me.'

'So he's not just talking companionship and friendship,' Fee commented drily and gave a low laugh. 'Your dad was a terror in that respect. Thank God he's quietened a lot of late. Age does have its compensations.'

Meg was intrigued; Fee had never previously referred to her intimate life with Lex. She'd wondered of course, but hadn't dared broach the subject which she considered none of her business. And up until now Fee hadn't been forthcoming.

'Don't look so shocked,' Fee mocked. 'You didn't arrive here by stork after all. The usual processes had to be gone through for you to put in an appearance.'

'He's clearly very lonely,' Meg stated.

'As you will be when the children have gone. He's right about that, make no mistake.'

Meg sat at the table facing Fee and wrung her hands. 'But what if the children object?' she queried.

'It's your life we're discussing here, not theirs,' Fee argued. 'Or, to put that another way, in this instance it's you you've got to consider, not them. As we've just said, it won't be long till they're up and away. How will you feel then at having lost such an opportunity? If, indeed, that's what you decide.'

Fee was right, Meg thought. For once she had to think of herself, put herself first. It would be stupid and short-sighted to do otherwise. The thing was, though, could she? Her children were so dear to her it would crucify her to hurt them, no matter how important the reason.

There, again, it was possible the children wouldn't object, that they'd understand her personal happiness was at stake. They might even be pleased for her.

'You're a fine-looking woman, Meg,' Fee went on. 'But hardly a spring chicken any more. This sort of chance may never come again, so in my opinion you should seize it while you can.'

She was thirty-six, Meg thought, or would be in a few months' time. Not exactly decrepit, but no spring chicken, either, as Fee had put it. 'I could ask Vincent to wait,' she said.

'Why?'

'For decency's sake. For all manner of reasons. Perhaps if we hung on till the children were married—'

'And run the risk of losing him?' Fee interjected. 'Who's to say he won't find someone more amenable in the mean time?'

'That's a risk I might be willing to take.'

'Then, more fool you, that's all I can say,' Fee retorted.

Meg muttered, running a hand despairingly through her hair. 'This isn't easy.'

'Nothing ever is, in my experience anyway. Certainly not for us women, and that's a fact.'

Fee regarded Meg levelly. 'If Cully was here, in this

room now, and you asked him what he thought, I believe he'd tell you to go ahead.'

'Do you really think so, Mum?'

'I do.'

'But Cully loved me.'

'Which is precisely why he'd tell you to go ahead. Loving someone is wanting the best for them. And in the present circumstances marrying Vincent would surely be that. As you said yourself, Vincent is good company and fun. What more can you ask out of a second marriage? Love? You were lucky to find that once; plenty don't, I can tell you.'

Meg wished with all her heart that Cully had been there; she'd never needed him more to give her advice. Why, oh, why had he been taken from her when he had? It simply wasn't fair.

She glanced across at his favourite chair and could see him smiling at her. Then she shuddered, recalling his last moments in the church where he'd died in agony.

'Are you all right, lass?' Fee asked anxiously.

'I'm fine, Mum. Memories, that's all.'

'Cully?'

Meg nodded.

'Ay, well, those will always be with you. The good and the bad.'

'With Cully they were nearly all good,' Meg said softly. 'That's one of the reasons I miss him so much. He was so strong and such a comfort. Losing him was like losing part of myself.'

'I understand,' Fee commiserated.

'And now . . .' Meg trailed off and shrugged.

'Now there's tomorrow to think of. And a decision to make.'

'A hard decision,' Meg qualified.

'Just don't make it until you're certain, that's all. In the mean time I'm always available whenever you want.'

Meg rose, went round to Fee and kissed her on the cheek. 'I hope I'm as good a mother to mine as you've been to me,' she declared.

Fee smiled. 'That's one of the nicest things you've ever said to me.'

They continued to discuss Vincent's proposal, thrashing the matter through.

'You're looking awfully pale this evening,' Rowan commented to Meg. 'Are you sickening for something?'

If Meg was, Ishbel hoped she didn't catch it. 'I've been thinking so, too,' she said.

'Tasty stew, this. Is there any more in the pot?' Rory asked.

'You might show some concern,' Ishbel snapped at him.

'About what?'

'Mum. We've just been saying she seems awfully pale.'

Rory peered at Meg. 'I can't see that she's pale.'

Ishbel snorted. 'You're about as observant as a blind man.'

'Don't be cheeky to your elders!' Rory retorted.

'Elders – you?' Ishbel laughed derisorily.

Meg crossed to the range to fetch the pot of rabbit stew bubbling there. Knowing Rory's appetite, she'd padded it out well with vegetables.

'You're shaking,' Rory noted in surprise as she ladled a generous amount on to his plate.

'Am I?'

'Like a leaf.' Rory's brow furrowed. Now that he came to study her, Meg *was* pale. Had she been overdoing things with the work she did for Mrs Monteith? For there had been more and more of that lately, Mrs Monteith kindly soliciting all manner of sewing from her many friends.

'Maybe a cold or the flu coming on,' Ishbel suggested.

Or a woman's complaint, Rowan thought, though she didn't voice that because of Rory's presence.

Meg sighed. The time had clearly come to state her piece. 'I have some news,' she said, returning the pot to the range.

'News?' Rowan queried.

Meg crossed and sat at the table, from where she glanced at her children in turn. She attempted a smile, which came out rather lopsided. 'Vincent McQueen has asked me to marry him,' she announced.

Ishbel dropped a knife which bounced then landed clattering to the floor, while Rowan's mouth sagged in shock and amazement. Rory's expression was one of incredulity.

'You're joking?' he said after a few seconds of strained silence.

Meg shook her head. 'I've never been more serious. Vincent wants me to be his wife.'

'Do you' – Rowan swallowed hard – 'love him?'

'That doesn't come into it.'

'Well, it should!' Rory exploded. 'What about Dad? Have you forgotten him already?'

'Don't be silly, son,' Meg admonished quietly.

Rory threw down his cutlery and lumbered to his feet. 'It's ridiculous, quite out of the question!'

'I haven't accepted yet,' Meg stated. 'I wanted to talk it over first.'

'You mean you're actually considering marrying him?' Rory demanded.

'I'd hardly bring it up if I wasn't,' she pointed out.

'Jesus Christ!' he swore.

'Language,' Meg rebuked sharply. 'I won't have swearing in the house.'

The twins looked at one another, then at Meg, both seeing her in an entirely new light.

'I didn't like the way he's been mooching round here all these months. I knew no good would come of it,' Rory raged.

'He hasn't been mooching,' Meg corrected.

'Pretending to try to help. Pretending he was a friend,' Rory went on, a gleam of tears in his eyes.

This was even worse than Meg had feared. She hadn't anticipated such a violent reaction from Rory. She'd known he'd probably be upset, but he was beside himself.

'You must refuse him,' Rory declared, thumping the table with a fist.

'Hey!' exclaimed Rowan as some gravy splashed on to her dress. 'Watch what you're doing.'

'Shut up!' Rory snarled.

'Don't speak to your sister like that,' Meg told him.

'I'll speak to her any way I like,' Rory thundered in reply.

'You will do nothing of the sort.'

Rory glared at his mother, the lower part of his face quivering with anger. If Vincent had been present, he'd have hit the swine. Stuck a knife into him.

Rowan went over to the sink where she pumped water into a bowl and began dabbing at the stain.

'Dad's hardly cold in his grave and here you are contemplating marriage,' Rory spat at his mother. 'I think it's disgraceful. How could you?'

'Cully would have approved—'

'Liar!' Rory shrieked. 'My dad wouldn't have done any such thing.'

Meg glanced at her hands whose shaking had worsened. Her thoughts were in turmoil, and there were tight bands of anxiety across her chest.

'This isn't coming out,' Rowan complained at the sink.

Meg rose. 'Let me see it.'

'I'll put the kettle on for hot water,' Ishbel said, rising also.

'Sit still, the pair of you,' Rory commanded.

Meg hesitated.

'Since when did you start giving orders here?' Ishbel replied.

'Since now.'

'Well, you're not giving them to me. Or to Mum, either. So put that in your pipe and smoke it.'

'For two peas I'd . . .'

'You'd what?' Ishbel interjected, black eyes sparking.

For a moment it seemed that Rory might lash out at his sister, but in the event he didn't. Turning, he stormed from the kitchen.

Rory went straight to his bedroom where he slammed the door behind him, the noise reverberating throughout the house. He then flung himself across his bed.

'That was some bombshell,' Ishbel said to Meg.

'You can say that again,' Rowan added.

'Is it such a bad idea?' Meg asked.

'I don't know,' Ishbel answered quietly. 'You obviously don't think so.'

'I like Vincent and ... well, hopefully I have a lot of time left ahead of me.'

Ishbel finished filling the kettle, which she took to the range. 'I'll make some tea,' she declared.

'That's what I need,' Meg said, examining the stain on Rowan's dress.

Meg straightened, knowing she could get the stain out easily enough. 'In the mean time, why don't you two tell me what you think of Vincent?'

Rory was now sitting on the edge of his bed staring at Cully's watch and chain. Still filled with anger, he couldn't believe the conversation that had just taken place. It was inconceivable that his mother should remarry. He found the concept obscene, and hurtful in the extreme.

It was horrendous enough that his dad had died. But for a new man to take his place! The thought made him want to throw up.

He didn't emerge from his room again till the following morning where he sat grim-faced and unspeaking through breakfast.

He still hadn't uttered a word when he left for work.

Scotland was the most beautiful country, Meg thought, gazing out of the window of the hired car taking her to the register office. The greens and purples of the landscape were magnificent, highlighted as they were from time to time by outcrops of stone and granite. They passed a small loch shimmering silver in the autumn sunlight. They'd been fortunate with the weather, she reflected, for although it was the end of September it was still warm enough to be summer.

'Nervous, Mum?' Rowan asked beside her.

'I'd be lying if I said I wasn't.'

Rowan patted Meg's hand reassuringly. 'It'll be all right. There's nothing to worry about.'

'Your dress is gorgeous. It makes you look ten years younger,' Ishbel said to Meg.

Meg had made her own dress especially for the occasion. Vincent had offered to take her to Glasgow to buy one there, but she'd declined, having recently seen something in a magazine she'd decided to copy. It was a tunic style that had been all the rage a few years previously in Paris. It was Egyptian blue with a rose embroidered in crimson, green and dull gold threads across the bodice. Her hat was wide-brimmed, tied round with a length of material that matched the dress.

Meg had also made the girls' dresses, printed knee-length frocks, Rowan's an overall rose colour, Ishbel's yellow. Both had ties at the waist.

Rowan's hat was a medium-brimmed straw that drooped over her face, Ishbel's a yellow cloche encircled with a black cotton band.

'Ten? Fifteen, you mean!' Ishbel exaggerated, feeling extremely smart in her own outfit.

Meg smoothed down the front of her dress, very pleased with how it had turned out. She was also delighted by the fact that all three dresses had cost a great deal less than if she'd bought them in the shops.

She leant forward to look at a scowling Rory sitting at the far side of the car. 'Rory?'

He glanced at her.

'Now, don't forget your promise to be on your best behaviour.'

He didn't reply.

'Rory?' This time her tone was sharper.

'I won't forget,' he answered sullenly.

Meg sat back in her seat and gazed at the passing countryside. It had been quite a battle for her to get Rory to attend the wedding. But in the end, after a great deal of persuasion and threats, he'd agreed. She prayed that he'd keep his word.

She thought of the forthcoming ceremony and reception afterwards. Her entire family would be present, and a contingent from Vincent's side. Her sister Georgina was to be a witness, as was Vincent's brother John.

Nervous? She was certainly that, though not as bad as she'd thought she'd be. A large sherry before leaving the house had helped in that respect.

'What's the time?' she asked.

Rory told her, consulting Cully's watch which he'd brought along with him like some sort of talisman.

In less than an hour she'd be Mrs Vincent McQueen, Meg thought. How odd that would be after years of being Mrs Cully Stewart – odd and disconcerting. But no doubt she'd soon get used to it, and the sooner the better.

She prayed again that Rory would behave himself and that there wouldn't be any sort of outburst or display of ill temperament from him.

Vincent laughed as the champagne cork popped to go flying across the room. He hastily grabbed a glass as the wine fizzed and bubbled.

'To us!' he toasted when both glasses were full and he'd handed one to Meg.

'To us,' she repeated, and sipped.

'Happy?' he asked.

She smiled and nodded.

'Me, too. Couldn't be more so. Thank you for marrying me, Meg. I know we've done the right thing.'

Meg glanced round the hotel bedroom which would be their base during their four-day honeymoon. Despite herself, she couldn't help her eyes lingering on the double bed that dominated the room, a bed turned down earlier by the maid.

'I thought it went off marvellously,' Vincent enthused.

'Everyone seemed to have a good time,' she agreed, thanking God that Rory had kept his word. There had been a couple of tense moments, but these had passed without incident.

'A penny for them?' Vincent asked, flashing her a broad smile.

'That this room must be costing the earth.'

He laughed again. 'Why not? You're worth the best. And, anyway, I hate cheapskates.'

'Are you sure you can afford all this?'

'If I can't, we'll just have to sneak out the back way before I'm presented with the bill.'

She looked horrified. 'You are joking, Vincent?'

'Of course I am. How's the champagne by the way? It's vintage, not like the ordinary stuff served up at the reception.'

She frankly couldn't tell the difference, and really would have preferred a cup of tea. 'Delicious,' she replied.

He came closer and kissed her on the lips. 'Why don't you get changed and I'll do the same? You can use the bathroom first.'

She appreciated his thoughtfulness. She'd been apprehensive about undressing in front of him, knowing how guilty she would have felt with pictures of Cully flashing through her mind. Cully was the only man who'd seen her naked.

'All right, then,' she responded.

She laid her glass aside and crossed to where her suitcase lay on a wooden trestle, Vincent's case lying alongside on another. Opening the case, she took out a brand-new nightdress.

'Don't be too long,' Vincent said lightly as she entered the *en suite* bathroom carrying her nightdress and champagne.

Inside the bathroom she leant against the door and drew in a deep breath. She could hear him moving about in the bedroom as he began preparing for bed.

She had a gulp of champagne to steady herself, placed the nightie on the side of the washbasin and started to undress.

She thought it an incredible luxury, and expense, that Vincent had booked a double room with *en suite*. In her experience only toffs did that sort of thing. Whatever else could be said about Vincent, he couldn't be accused of not having flair or of being tight-fisted.

102

She peered in the mirror at her face, wondering whether or not to take off the little make-up she was wearing. She decided to leave it on – something she would normally never have dreamt of doing.

The nightdress was pale pink and gathered below the bust to fall away to floor length. She'd also made this herself; it was identical to one a friend of Mrs Monteith's had asked her to run up. It was reminiscent of the Roman style.

When she was ready she dabbed some perfume behind her ears and on her wrists, the same perfume Vincent had once commented on and admired. Before leaving the sanctuary of the bathroom she had another swig of champagne.

She found Vincent already in bed, the champagne and ice-bucket on the table beside him. She was startled to see that his top half was bare.

He held out a hand to her. 'Come and have a refill,' he said.

'Not for me. This is enough.'

'Nonsense. Tonight's very special after all.'

He topped up her glass as she slid between the cool sheets. 'Thank you,' she said, accepting the glass back from him.

'Don't worry, I won't bite,' he teased, completely at ease, which Meg most certainly wasn't.

'I didn't think you would,' she replied in a tense voice.

'No?'

She sipped her champagne, though not really wanting it, more for something to do than anything else.

'Now, then, Mrs McQueen,' he smiled. 'How about a big kiss and I'll tell you how beautiful you are.'

He waited till she'd got rid of her glass, then pulled her to him. She'd insist he put the lights out first, she thought as their lips met. She wasn't doing anything with them on.

Shortly afterwards the lights were duly extinguished.

Meg glanced at Vincent sleeping beside her. She was

103

relieved now that was over, and that she'd actually enjoyed the experience – once she'd relaxed, that is.

He'd been quite different from Cully in all manner of ways. But the main difference had been the length of time he'd taken. He'd gone on and on till she'd begun to think he'd never finish, far longer than Cully. Nor had he been as gentle as Cully. In fact he'd been somewhat rough at points – something she didn't find totally unpleasant. But all in all she felt it had been a success, for her as well as for him.

She was just drifting off when a hand reached out to encompass one of her breasts.

'Are you awake?' Vincent asked.

'Mmm!'

'Good.'

He drew himself across, seeking her mouth with his own. His other hand came into play: touching, feeling, probing.

She really wasn't interested any more. But how could she turn his advances down on their wedding night?

When it was over he rolled over on to his back and reached for his cigarettes. 'Do you mind?' he asked, lighting up.

'No.'

'Filthy habit, smoking in bed, but I like it.'

When he put the cigarette out she hoped he would snuggle up and cuddle her. But he didn't, remaining on his own side of the bed.

She was woken with the sun streaming in the window and he climbing on top of her.

'Good morning,' he smiled.

Instinctively she arched her buttocks to receive his thrust.

Chapter Three

'I'm going for a walk. Would you like to come?' Rowan asked Ishbel. It was a Sunday morning, and the family wasn't long back from church.

Ishbel considered the proposal, then shook her head. 'I won't, if you don't mind. I'd rather stay home.'

'Suit yourself.'

Outside Rowan glanced up at the overcast sky and wondered if it was going to rain. A patch of blue on the horizon gave her hope that it wouldn't.

She made her way through the village, stopping off for a brief chat with a friend *en route*, then took a road leading to a small hamlet several miles distant. It was one of her favourite strolls.

She'd hardly left Glenshields behind her when she spotted a figure sitting on a stone bridge gazing down at the river. Every so often the figure would throw a pebble into the water.

She was quite close to the river before, with a shock and a thrill tingling through her, she recognized who it was. After all the times she'd tried to contrive a meeting, and failed. Now she'd stumbled on him purely by chance.

'Hello,' she said, halting on the bridge.

Gray Hamilton turned to frown quizzically at her.

'We were introduced at the Glenshields spring dance. I'm Rowan, Rory Stewart's sister,' she reminded him.

'Oh, yes. Hello yourself.'

'You're a long way from Craigkip?'

'I'm going to visit an aunt who lives in Drumden.' Drumden was the hamlet further along the road.

'Who's that?'

'Mrs Taylor.'

'Oh, I know her! She's nice.'

'I've always thought so, too; which is why I call in from time to time.'

'Her husband's in the merchant navy, isn't he?'

'That's right, a steward on the big liners. He's been all over the world, lucky sod. Brought me a boomerang from Australia once when I was young. I didn't half have some fun with that, I can tell you.'

'Could you make it come back?'

'Took a while, but I managed it in the end. There's a knack involved.'

Gray threw his last pebble into the river where it landed with a soft *plop*, after which he dusted off his hands by rubbing them together briskly.

'How's the football doing?' Rowan asked.

'Fine.'

'Got a game next Saturday?'

'Away to Larkfield. We'll walk it.'

She laughed. 'There's nothing like being confident!'

'Why not? They're a rotten team.'

A lock of hair had fallen over his forehead which she wanted to reach out and push back for him. She thought again how lovely his eyes were, the sort a girl could drown in.

'If you're on your way to Drumden, we could walk together?' she suggested boldly.

'Is that where you're off to?'

'A Sunday constitutional. I often do it.'

He swung down from the bridge to stand beside her. 'Let's go, then.'

'So what happened to Sonia Millar?' she asked after a few paces.

He glanced at her in surprise. 'We broke up soon after that dance. How did you know?'

'Somebody mentioned it,' she replied casually. She'd also heard he'd been out with various others since.

'Oh, really!'

'It seems you're quite the ladies' man.'

He laughed. 'Hardly that. But I've no intention of getting serious, if that's what you mean.'

You will when you meet the right one, she thought. Then you'll get serious enough.

'And what about you? Are you courting?' he enquired.

'Not at the moment. But I have plenty buzzing around with offers.'

'None of whom interests you?'

'If he did, I'd be going out with him.'

He glanced at her again, his curiosity roused. 'Have you left school yet?'

'Last summer. My twin sister and I now work with my mother, who's teaching us to be seamstresses.' She then went on to explain about their having trouble finding jobs, and how it had been Meg's brainwave that they assist her at home.

'What about you?' Rowan asked.

'A similar situation to your own. I'm employed by my dad, who's a builder.'

'So that's something we have in common,' Rowan smiled.

'It must be fascinating having a twin,' Gray commented, intrigued.

'We're not identical, by the way. Ishbel and I don't look at all alike. In fact we're complete opposites, she being small, dark and elfin.'

'Elfin!'

'That's what my dad used to say, though not unkindly. It's simply a quality she has about her. Do you have any brothers or sisters?'

'A younger sister called Lily.'

'Do you get on?'

Gray pulled a face. 'All right. Better now than we did when we were children. Then we were always at it hammer and tongs.'

'I know what you mean,' Rowan remarked drily, thinking of the battles she and Ishbel had had in the past, and still did on occasion.

'What about you and Rory?'

'I've never had any trouble with him,' Rowan replied. 'We're extremely fond of each other and rarely have words. I'm fond of Ishbel, too, of course, but she and I certainly have our run-ins.'

They continued chatting, quite at ease, until they arrived at Drumden where they stopped outside the Taylors' house.

'It's been nice talking to you,' Gray said.

She stared him straight in those lovely eyes of his. 'And talking to you.'

'No doubt I'll see you around.'

Bugger! she thought, and smiled. 'No doubt.'

'Give my regards to Rory. Who are they playing Saturday?'

'I've no idea,' she replied truthfully. 'Good luck against Larkfield. Though from what you've told me you'll hardly need it.'

A silence fell between them during which they went on staring at one another. Come on, do something! she mentally urged him.

'I was wondering . . . ,' he said slowly. 'Have you anything on Saturday evening?'

Her heart leapt. Was he going to ask her out? Please, please God he was. Normally she would have responded coyly to such a question, but not in this instance. 'I'm totally free,' she answered.

'Would you fancy going to the pictures?'

Again she would normally have asked what was showing, but not now. If it had been a film she'd already seen a million times, it still wouldn't have mattered. She marvelled that any lad should have such an effect on her. But, then, Gray Hamilton wasn't just any lad. At least, not to her. There was something about him she found irresistible, like a moth to light, or a wasp to jam.

'You mean with you?' she queried throatily.

'Yes.'

She could have shrieked with joy, and knew her face was reflecting her elation. This was a dream come true. Not trusting herself to speak, she nodded instead.

'I'll pick you up at six-thirty. Is that all right?'

'Perfectly.'

'I hope you don't mind going in a van? I'll borrow my dad's.'

'Where shall we meet?'

The arrangement was made, then he said goodbye.

'Till Saturday,' she replied.

'I'll look forward to it.'

'Me, too.' That was the understatement of the year, she thought. The decade. The century!

When she returned to Glenshields she felt as though she was walking on air.

'What's wrong?' Vincent demanded.

'I don't want to, that's all,' Meg answered, having been roused from a deep sleep by Vincent making overtures. 'You can get too much of a good thing, you know.'

She wriggled when his hand slid between her thighs. 'I mean it, Vincent.'

He was perplexed, as this was the first time she'd ever refused him. 'I don't understand,' he said.

She disengaged his hand and moved it away. 'We can't go on like this. It's every single night and morning. I need a break.'

'But why? Faye never—' He broke off and bit his lip.

That irritated Meg, though she knew his slip had been unintentional. If Faye had never complained, then she'd had more stamina than her. Or perhaps Faye had been more passionate, or simply the sort of woman who thought it wrong ever to say no.

'Let's give it a rest for now,' Meg pleaded. 'I don't feel like it, honestly I don't.'

He decided to persevere, try to persuade her to change her mind. 'Oh, come on, Meg, be nice to me.' And as he spoke his hand became active again.

Her irritation increased. She grabbed his hand and this time roughly pushed it aside. 'Vincent, enough!'

He thought of Faye whom he'd much preferred in bed.

Faye had been far more lively and inventive than Meg, who tended to be passive in her lovemaking.

'I'm sorry,' Meg apologized, seeing how hurt he was.

'It doesn't matter,' he answered. 'Doesn't matter at all.'

'Don't be cross.'

'I'm not cross,' he hissed, betraying just how angry he was.

He reached for his cigarettes and lit up. He then proceeded to blow smoke furiously at the ceiling, remembering Faye and how it had been between them.

While he thought of Faye, Meg was thinking of Cully. This sort of incident would never have happened with him, not only for the obvious reason that his demands had been less, but also because he'd been a far more understanding, sympathetic man. Also lovemaking had somehow evolved naturally with Cully, not simply taken place as a matter of course.

Vincent swung himself out of bed. 'I'm getting dressed,' he announced.

Meg glanced at the clock. The alarm wasn't due to go off for half an hour yet. A cup of tea would be wonderful before then; perhaps Vincent would bring her one.

He didn't.

'More porridge, anyone?' Meg asked at breakfast-time the same morning.

'I'll have some,' Rory answered quickly, spooning the remains of his bowl into his mouth. 'Any more toast?'

Vincent sat glowering into his teacup. He was in a filthy mood, and would have already left for work if his first appointment hadn't been local and not for a little while yet.

'Toast coming up,' Meg replied.

'I thought you'd already had two helpings of porridge,' Vincent growled to Rory.

'Are you counting or something?' Rory retorted sharply.

'Less of your cheek, boy!'

'Now, now,' Meg soothed.

'He eats more than a bloody Irish navvy,' Vincent

complained. 'I've never known anyone stuff himself like he does.'

Rory bridled. 'I pay my whack every pay-day. I'm entitled.'

Rowan and Ishbel glanced at one another. The tension that had been crackling round the table since they'd sat down had suddenly ratcheted up several notches.

Meg arrived at the table with the porridge-pot. 'Here we are, then.'

'Don't want it now,' Rory declared.

'It'll only go to waste otherwise.'

'You spoil him,' Vincent said.

'She does not,' Rory retorted before Meg could reply.

'Mummy's boy,' Vincent taunted.

'He's nothing of the sort!' Rowan burst out.

'Who asked you to put your ha'porth in?'

Ishbel could see there was every likelihood this was going to end in a flaming row, and decided to absent herself. 'I'm off to get started,' she said and, rising, left for the sitting-room.

Rory was furious. How dare this interloper, this cuckoo, criticize him in his own house? It was getting to the stage where he couldn't stand the sight of Vincent, far less be in his company.

'I'm going with Ishbel,' Rowan proclaimed, hurrying after her sister.

Meg knew only too well what this was really about: her refusal in bed. Vincent had been like a bear with a sore head ever since and quite rude to her in front of the children, which she found unforgivable. Now here he was having a go at Rory, who was simply going through that stage nearly all young men do when they eat voraciously.

'I am not spoiled,' Rory said through gritted teeth.

'Huh! Sez you,' Vincent sneered.

Meg took Rory by the arm. 'Come on, son, on your way. Your dinner piece is ready for you.'

'Go on, run away. Do as Mummy says,' Vincent mocked, beginning to enjoy himself.

'Will you be quiet!' Meg flared.

Vincent pushed his bowl away and, smirking, pulled out his cigarettes.

'I won't be—'

'That's all right, son,' Meg interjected, adopting a soothing conciliatory tone. 'Ignore him.'

Rory, despite his inclination to do otherwise, decided to take his mother's advice. He was silently fuming as he left the house clutching his midday-break sandwiches and a flask of tea.

Having escorted Rory to the front door, Meg returned to the kitchen where she stared hard at Vincent smoking unconcernedly at the table.

'That was absolutely disgraceful,' she stated in a tight voice.

'I was right, though.'

'Right!' she exploded. 'What do you mean, right?'

'He does eat more than a bloody Irish navvy.'

'That's got nothing whatever to do with you.'

'No?' Vincent replied lazily.

'No! And I won't have a repeat of what happened. Never! Do you hear?'

'Surely I'm allowed to comment?'

'Comment is one thing, being downright insulting quite another.'

'Are you saying you condone his gluttony?'

Meg was outraged. 'He is not a glutton, nor a mother's boy. Both charges are completely untrue.'

Vincent felt better now, his pent-up frustration having evaporated. 'As you will, my darling,' he replied insincerely.

Meg wanted to cry, but refused to do so. She wouldn't give Vincent the satisfaction.

'Has the paper come?' Vincent enquired.

'It's in the hallway.'

'Get it for me, there's a pet.'

'Get it yourself!'

'There's no need to talk to me like that.'

'No need . . .' She trailed off, speechless.

Vincent resisted the urge to peck her on the cheek

as he passed her *en route* to the hallway, thinking that too frivolous in the circumstances. He began humming as he left the kitchen.

Meg found her hands were shaking as she began gathering up the dirty dishes. That had been awful, simply awful. And all because she hadn't let him have his way with her in bed.

She was shaking so much she dropped several plates, breaking them. If only Cully hadn't died, they could have remained a close and harmonious family.

'I'll get the sweets,' Rowan said to Gray, the pair of them standing in the cinema foyer queue.

She went over and joined a smaller queue. When it was her turn, she decided to lash out and buy a box of chocolates. It was a special occasion after all – her first date with Gray.

She hooked an arm through his as they progressed into the auditorium where the lights were up. It surprised and disappointed her when he didn't suggest the back row, which was traditionally where courting couples went. Instead he chose seats halfway down the stalls.

When they were settled she opened the chocolates and offered them to him.

'Mmm! Delicious!' he declared on tasting the marzipan centre he'd selected.

'Have another,' she said, offering him the box again.

'I should have got those.'

'No, they're my treat.'

'Do you always buy the sweets when a chap takes you to the pictures?'

She'd never done so before, and in fact would never even have considered the prospect. But this was different; this was Gray, and she desperately wanted him to like her.

'Why? Are you complaining?'

He shook his head. 'Not at all.'

'I adore chockies, don't you?'

'Does that mean you're going to scoff the entire box?'

'I thought we might between us.'

He laughed. 'I'd be sick if I ate that many.'

Rowan felt incredibly happy, and had done so since meeting Gray earlier. She was sizzling and bubbling inside, in a state of euphoria at being with him. Again she marvelled that he had this effect on her.

Gray gazed round, wondering if there was anyone there he knew, but didn't spot any familiar faces.

Rowan wanted to touch him, for him to take her hand in his and hold it. Hopefully he would when the lights went out. Just as she hoped he would kiss her. She almost groaned in anticipation. What would it be like to be kissed by Gray? She couldn't wait to find out. It was something she'd been thinking about all week.

'Where's your twin tonight?' he enquired.

A stab of jealousy shot through her. 'Ishbel's at home. Why?'

'Just asking, that's all.'

'She's helping Mum do a few things round the house. Then she's going to settle down with a book.'

'Sounds boring.'

Rowan pulled a face. 'Not my idea of a good time on a Saturday night.'

'Me, neither.'

The lights dimmed, then went out altogether. Seconds later the curtains swished open to reveal the screen. The pianist in the pit began playing as the opening credits rolled.

'I think Constance Bennett is wonderful,' Gray whispered. The film was *The Goose Woman* starring Bennett and Louise Dresser.

Again jealousy stabbed through Rowan. 'I've seen prettier,' she whispered in reply.

'Where?'

Right here for a start, she thought, but didn't say so. She concentrated on the film instead.

Halfway through the picture she became restless. Why hadn't he taken her hand? Should she take his? No, she couldn't possibly be so forward. Girls just didn't do that sort of thing. But how she wanted to.

'Another chocky?' she whispered.

'Thanks.'

Was he always this slow? Or was it her? She prayed it wasn't the latter. Other lads she'd been to the pictures with had been quick to hold her hand. So why couldn't he?

'That was terrific,' he pronounced when the film ended.

'Would you like an ice-cream?' she smiled.

'I'll get them.'

'No, let me.'

He regarded her quizzically. 'Are you sure? Can you afford it?'

'I do earn, you know.' Her pay wasn't much, and forking out for chocolates and ice-cream would leave a considerable hole in what Meg had given her the day before, but she considered the outlay money well spent.

She went to the usherette from whom she bought two tubs of vanilla ice-cream, and on returning to her seat handed him one. They talked about the football match he'd played that afternoon, which his team had won easily as he'd predicted, then it was time for the second feature.

This was a documentary on the life of an eskimo and his family. Gray sat entranced throughout, his eyes glued to the flickering images – Rowan, to her chagrin, temporarily forgotten.

'I really enjoyed that,' Gray enthused as they left the cinema.

'I noticed,' Rowan said, a trifle caustically.

'A fascinating way to live, don't you think?'

'Fascinating,' she agreed. But her sarcasm was lost on him.

'I wouldn't mind going to the Arctic, just for a visit. And I'd give anything to paddle one of those kayaks. That must be tremendously exciting.'

'You can keep the Arctic as far as I'm concerned. Too blinking cold for my liking.' Just thinking about all that snow and ice made her shiver.

He laughed. 'Where's your sense of adventure?'

And where's your sense of romance? she nearly retorted.

'Mind you, there are lots of other places I'd rather go to first. Africa, for example, and Japan. They live in paper houses in Japan, did you know that?'

She nodded.

'That's because of the earthquakes they have there. Imagine living in a paper house!'

They reached the van, and he opened the door for her. 'Climb in,' he instructed.

The seats and surrounding area were filthy, which she now commented on, having restrained herself on the way there.

'Well, what do you expect? It is a builder's vehicle. We don't go around in smart suits carrying attaché cases, you know. Anyway, it got us to the cinema and will take us back. That's all that matters.'

She wasn't really upset, just disappointed that he hadn't held her hand or kissed her in the pictures. Maybe he really *didn't* fancy her, she thought despondently.

They drove for a little way in silence. 'How did the Shielers get on today? I forgot to ask,' he queried eventually.

Football again! Couldn't he talk about something else? 'They won.'

'Good for them.'

'According to Rory, it was a great match. Very close.'

'Do you see that house?' Gray said suddenly, pointing out of her side of the van. 'The one with the red roof.'

'Uh-huh.'

'My dad and I rebuilt part of it last summer. It's owned by people called the Ramsays. He's a bank manager.'

She looked into his face, and he smiled, a warm beam of a smile that made her stomach contract. 'You're nice,' he said.

Her despondency vanished. 'Am I?'

'Very much so.'

'You're nice yourself.'

'I love your hair.'

'Thank you,' she purred.

'It's a beautiful shade of blonde.'

She ran a hand through it. 'I'm lucky with my hair,' she stated.

'You're lucky all over.'

She melted to hear that. 'You're not so bad-looking yourself.'

'This is beginning to sound like a mutual admiration society,' he said and laughed.

They continued laughing and joking until he drew up outside her front door where he switched off the engine.

'Thank you for tonight. It was tremendous,' she said.

He sat gazing at her, not replying.

'It was kind of you to ask me.'

'Kind? Hardly that.'

She mentally willed him to ask her out again. 'I'd better go in,' she said finally, reaching for the door-handle.

'Rowan?'

She turned to him, and somehow found herself in his arms, where she'd wanted to be all night. She sighed as his lips met and pressed against her own. At last he was kissing her!

His maleness and personal presence washed over and through her, invading and capturing every fibre of her being. Her senses were reeling when the kiss ended.

Wow! she thought. No-one had ever kissed her like that before. It added a whole new dimension to kissing, making the kisses she'd received in the past pale by comparison. She closed her eyes, hoping he would do it again. And he did.

After that kiss he stroked the tip of her nose, which she found delightful, then her cheek. Reaching up, she curled a hand round his neck.

'Can I see you again?'

'Please,' she murmured in reply, thinking she'd surely died and gone to paradise. She could have remained locked in his embrace for the rest of the night, and all the ncxt day, too. She'd never known such an incredible feeling of peace and contentment.

117

'There's a small problem there, though, I'm afraid.'
Now he kissed the tip of her nose, and each side of it.

'What's that?'

'Dad and I are doing a job that's going to take us away for a month.'

'A month?' she repeated. That was an eternity.

'Nothing I can do about it, I'm afraid. We start Monday morning and will live in digs till the job's completed.'

'And where is this job?' she frowned.

'Miles away, hence the staying-over. It's too far to travel there and back every day.'

'What about weekends?'

'We might manage some of those, but I can't say for certain. It all depends how it goes.'

Damnation! she thought. After this to lose him again. But only for a while, she told herself. The month would pass, though, undoubtedly, agonizingly slowly. A month, four long weeks, twenty-eight interminable days, till his return.

'I'm sorry,' he said.

Not half as much as I am, she thought. 'Do you often work away from home?'

Gray shook his head. 'Dad doesn't really like doing it, but if there's nothing else around at the time he feels he has to.'

'That's understandable,' she replied huskily.

'Do you want me to walk you to the door?'

'Don't bother.'

He kissed her again, this the longest kiss ever. She was breathless, her heart pounding wildly, when they finally surfaced for air.

'I'll be in touch,' he promised.

'You'd better.'

He laughed softly and pecked her on the lips. Sheer nectar, she thought. The taste of him was far better than any chocolates; his breath, hot on her face, a perfumed aphrodisiac.

'Take care in the mean time, Rowan.'

'And you.'

She lingered on. 'One last kiss?' she pleaded.

His tongue probed her mouth, to which she eagerly responded.

She left the van to stand by her front door watching him drive away. It might have been a first date, but she knew she was in love – head over heels.

She was back in the van, he kissing her, her hands fluttering, touching, caressing him, while his hands were doing the same to her.

'Rowan, stop day-dreaming!' Meg admonished. 'What's up with you, girl? You looked miles away.'

Rowan snapped herself out of her reverie. 'Sorry, Mum,' she mumbled.

'What a stupid grin you had on your face. Like you were half-witted or something,' Ishbel teased.

'Shut up, you!'

'Well, you did.'

'What were you thinking about?' Ishbel persisted.

'Nothing.'

'That'll be right.'

Rowan glared at her sister. 'I said shut up and meant it.'

'That's enough, you two,' Meg warned, rising from the sewing machine she'd recently acquired and crossing to Rowan. 'Let me see that.'

Rowan handed over the cream blouse she'd been stitching, aware that her mind had been wandering all morning. She'd found it almost impossible to concentrate for thinking about Gray.

'This is dreadful, quite unacceptable,' Meg stated, grim-lipped. 'These stitches are all over the place.'

'Hah!' Ishbel jeered, for which she received another glare from Rowan.

'Unpick the lot and do them again,' Meg instructed, returning the blouse to Rowan.

'Unpick the lot?'

Meg made a series of quick gestures. 'This, this, this and this. And unpick carefully, understand?'

Rowan nodded.

'Honestly, Rowan, I don't know what's come over you today. But you'd better buck up your ideas. You're supposed to be helping, not hindering.'

'Sorry, Mum,' Rowan apologized again.

'Ishbel, put the kettle on. It's time for a cup of tea anyway.'

'Let Rowan do it. I'm in the middle of a tricky bit.'

'*You* put it on as you're told,' Meg said with emphasis.

'But . . .'

'No buts,' Meg interjected, exerting her authority. 'Just get on with it.'

Ishbel, feeling hard done by – after all, there was nothing wrong with her work – flounced from the sitting-room.

'If you need help, say,' Meg stated quietly to Rowan.

'I'll be all right now, I promise you.' Rowan bent over her blouse and began the task of unpicking.

Meg regarded Rowan thoughtfully, then mentally shrugged. An off day, she decided. Youngsters could find prolonged concentration difficult after all. Still, this was unusual for Rowan, who didn't normally suffer from being distracted.

Rowan swallowed hard, and forced the temptation of dwelling on Gray from her mind. Later, when her time was her own, she'd conjure him back again.

'Right, then, I'm off for a pint,' Vincent declared. 'Are you coming, Meg?'

Meg glanced at the brass clock on the mantelpiece. 'I won't bother. I'm tired.'

'Don't be daft. It's Friday night.'

'Maybe that's why I'm tired,' she replied drily. 'It's been a hard week.'

'Then, all the more reason to let off a little steam and enjoy yourself.'

'You go, Vincent. I'm happy to stay at home.'

He was about to argue with that, then changed his

mind. 'Just don't say you weren't invited, that's all.'

'I'd much rather stay in, honestly.'

He picked up his cigarettes. 'Well, if you change your mind, you can always come along and join me.'

'I wish someone would offer to take me out,' Ishbel complained from where she was sitting. 'I wouldn't need to be asked twice, I can tell you.'

Meg smiled sympathetically at her. 'Your day will come, lass. Just wait and see.'

'But *when*? That's what I want to know.'

'I'm away, then. Ta ra,' Vincent said, and left the kitchen.

'Don't feel the need to hurry back!' Meg called after him. 'Hang on till the bell if you like.'

Rowan gave her mother a strange look, thinking that was an odd thing for her to say. She couldn't remember Meg ever saying the same to her dad.

Meg listened with satisfaction as the front door clicked shut. She was pleased it was Friday night and he was going to the pub. With a bit of luck, and without her company to restrain him, he might drink a skinful and be incapable when he returned. What a relief that would be. Honestly, it was unbelievable that a man could be so regular in his demands. It was so exhausting.

Rowan was thinking of Gray and the fact that there was only one week remaining until he returned. She'd hoped he might write, and was disappointed he hadn't. Even a few lines would have been something. It had struck her he probably didn't know her address, but if he'd been keen enough surely he'd have had ways of finding it out.

Oh, well, she sighed mentally. No doubt he wasn't the writing sort. Still, it would have been nice if he'd made the effort.

'I've never seen you look so smug and happy as you have recently,' Ishbel commented with a smile.

Smug? Rowan wasn't sure she liked that applied to herself. But, now she came to think about it, it might well be true. *Self-satisfied* was a description she would have preferred. As for happy, there was no denying that. Her happiness was marred only by her temporary separation from Gray, a separation shortly to end.

'You have been a bit different lately,' Meg said, settling herself into what had been Cully's chair.

'I wasn't aware of it.'

'I think you're up to something,' Ishbel probed.

'Me! I'm afraid not.'

'What do you know that I don't?' Ishbel continued.

Rowan hadn't yet told them about Gray, enjoying keeping their relationship to herself. Time enough to tell the family about him when the relationship was more firmly established. She'd only been out with him once after all. She didn't want to appear soft by waxing lyrical after only one date, particularly a date that had left her knowing she was in love.

In love, she thought, a thrill running through her. What a wonderful feeling it was, exciting and gloriously exhilarating. There were times she wanted to shout it to the world, but for now preferred to keep it her secret, deriving even more pleasure and satisfaction from it that way.

Meg's ploy worked. When Vincent later stumbled home all he was interested in was sleep. And next morning he had a raging hangover.

It was a ploy Meg determined to use again whenever possible. And after that it was rare for her to accompany Vincent to the pub.

The Reverend David Dykes was in full flood, his voice booming out to every last corner of the church, his finger jabbing the air as he made point after point.

'Fornication is a sin against God and man, and will – mark my words – be punished in the next world if not in this. Hellfire and eternal damnation await the fornicators, those transgressors of the flesh who choose to ignore God's holy laws and commandments. Intercourse outside the blessed state of matrimony is giving yourself over to the evil works of Satan; it is allying yourself with his cause, and against the Lord God Almighty. There is no forgiveness for those who sin in this way; you have voluntarily removed yourself from God's light and cast yourself into the deep pit of dreadful despair where you will writhe in agony till the end of time itself. The sins of the flesh are particularly iniquitous, for by committing them you desecrate the pure vessel of your body, defiling it by lust and unbridled passion. I say to you . . .'

Meg gazed about her, at the many faces transfixed and mesmerized by the minister's sermon. Some of these had paled white as milk, while one nearby was covered in a faint sheen of sweat. She couldn't help but wonder to how many present the sermon applied.

'He's on form today,' Vincent whispered to Meg.

'Shhh!'

'Old John Knox himself would have approved.'

'I said shhh!'

Fornication . . . hellfire . . . sins of the flesh . . . lust . . . These words were repeated again and again throughout the sermon, and each time Dykes spoke them he shook from an inner passion of his own.

Nor were various members of the congregation the only ones sweating; Dykes was, too, while his eyes burnt with an intensity awesome to behold.

'Rowan! Rowan!!'

Rowan stopped and turned. For a moment she didn't recognize the figure rushing towards her. Then, when she did, her face lit up.

'Beth, how are you?' Beth Porter had lived in the village until several years previously when her family had moved away. This was the first time Rowan had seen her since.

Beth came to a halt beside Rowan. 'You look fabulous, Ro. Even prettier than I remembered.'

'You've had your hair cut,' Rowan observed. 'The bob suits you'

'Think so?'

'Definitely. Makes you appear very sophisticated.'

Beth laughed. 'That was the intention. I did toy with the idea of getting an Eton crop, but settled for a bob instead.'

Rowan grasped Beth's shoulders. 'How are you, and what are you up to?'

'I'm well as can be. And working in an office. It's the bee's knees.'

'You've lost weight,' Rowan commented.

'I have slimmed down. Tony said he wanted me thinner.'

'And who's Tony?'

Beth extracted herself from Rowan's grasp and waggled her left hand. 'My fiancé, that's all.'

'You're engaged,' Rowan squealed.

'Since last week.'

'Congratulations.'

'What do you think of the ring?' Beth said, putting on a posh accent and pretending to be all hoity-toity. She flashed the ring in Rowan's face.

'It's a beauty,' Rowan observed.

'Cost an absolute mint, I can tell you.'

Rowan examined the ring more closely. Atop an eighteen-carat gold hoop was a large diamond surrounded by a circle of smaller ones. The large diamond sparkled in the winter sunlight, throwing off shafts of pale yellow fire. 'Magnificent,' Rowan breathed, imagining it on her own wedding finger.

'For various reasons we won't be getting married for several years yet, but when we do it'll be a big church affair with all the trimmings.'

Rowan was green with envy. 'Tell me about Tony.'

'He's studying to be an accountant – terribly safe and respectable, just like him. He's absolutely wild about me, worships the ground I walk on. I'm incredibly lucky.'

Rowan thought so, too. 'Is he rich?'

'Well, let me put it this way. They own two houses, one in Edinburgh and the other by the seaside.'

Rowan's eyes grew wide. 'Two houses! You *have* fallen on your feet, Beth.'

'Haven't I just!' Beth gave a tinkling laugh.

They continued talking, bringing one another up to date on their news. Rowan didn't say anything about Gray, though she did hint, and wouldn't be drawn further, that she had recently met someone 'extremely' interesting who was just as mad about her as Tony was about Beth.

When they parted all Rowan could think about was Beth's engagement ring. She could see it on her own finger, given to her by Gray of course.

Engaged to Gray, that was what she wanted, she decided. She would move heaven and earth to bring it about as soon as possible.

Engaged, and married – that had become her ambition. It was a crystallization of everything that had been running through her mind since her date with Gray.

Meg flexed both sets of fingers and winced. Being troubled with arthritis was a new experience for her, something that had only happened within the last few weeks. She hoped it wouldn't get any worse, or flare up in any other part of her body.

'Why don't you come to the dance with me tonight?' Ishbel asked Rowan. 'It might stop you being so boot-faced.'

'I am not boot-faced!' Rowan retorted, knowing full well she was. It was six weeks now since Gray had gone off on his job, and there still had been no word. She could only assume that the job had taken longer than anticipated.

'Boot-faced,' Ishbel repeated. 'A dance is just the ticket to jolly you up.'

'I'm not going,' Rowan replied emphatically.

'Oh, come on, be a sport!'

'No,' Rowan stated.

'Well, why not?'

Rowan became exasperated. 'You just won't take no for an answer, will you?'

'I'm very persistent,' Ishbel smiled. 'Besides, I need you there for support.'

That roused Rowan's curiosity. 'Support for what?'

'Something . . . someone . . .' Ishbel replied, becoming suddenly coy.

'Someone?' Rowan prompted.

'I haven't met yet.'

'Oh!' exclaimed Rowan softly, disappointed.

'But want to.'

Rowan smiled as the penny dropped. 'And he's going to the dance?'

'Exactly.'

'And it's your intention to get yourself introduced?'

'By hook or by crook,' Ishbel laughed.

'Who is he and what's he like?'

'Come to the dance and maybe you'll find out.'

Now it was Rowan's turn to laugh. 'Devious cow!'

'That's me.'

'And what if I do come along and he prefers me to you?'

Ishbel's face fell. 'You wouldn't let that happen, Ro, would you?' she queried in an anxious voice.

Rowan felt guilty at teasing Ishbel in such a way, for she loved her twin and would never knowingly have hurt her – not where the matter was important, that is.

'Of course I wouldn't, silly,' Rowan replied.

'So will you come to the dance and give me your support?'

'I'll come and give you all the support you need,' Rowan answered magnanimously.

'Thanks, sis.'

'And you're right: I *have* been boot-faced.'

'Why? Is there a reason?'

'Isn't there always?' Rowan replied, but refused to elaborate.

'Good crowd here,' Ishbel commented, glancing about.

'Spotted your chap yet?'

'Give me a chance!'

Rowan grinned, for they'd only walked into the hall moments before.

'There's a friend of yours,' gestured Ishbel.

'Who?'

'Iain Carstairs.'

'Fat Boy,' Rowan groaned. 'I hope he doesn't ask me up. That would be embarrassing.'

'There's no fear of that. He knows full well you'd refuse. No compassion, that's your trouble.'

'And you have, I suppose?'

'I'm brimming over with it.'

'Hello, Rowan. Hello, Ishbel.'

They were greeted by Margie Bremner whom the twins knew well. They were animatedly discussing another girl's dress, which all three of them agreed looked ghastly, when they were joined by a smiling Chick Strathearn.

'I thought I'd come over and give you the benefit of my scintillating conversation,' he said.

The three girls hooted with laughter.

'You must be joking!' Margie Bremner exclaimed.

'Joking? Me? Certainly not,' Chick replied, assuming an air of wounded innocence.

'You're quite the comedian,' commented Ishbel.

'Well, I made you laugh.'

Ishbel conceded that point. 'True enough.'

'Are you dancing, Rowan?' he asked.

Rowan saw that Ishbel wanted her to stay where she was. 'Maybe later, Chick. I don't want to just yet.'

'Suit yourself,' he said with a shrug. 'Either of you other ladies care to grace the floor with me?'

'I will,' responded Margie quickly. 'That's if you don't mind, Ishbel?'

'Go ahead,' Ishbel told her, then returned to perusing the crowd.

'Are you sure he's going to be here?' Rowan queried.

'So I was led to believe. But it's early yet. Maybe he's still to arrive.'

'What's his name?'

'Andrew, which is virtually all I do know about him. I'll tell you the rest when I find out.'

'*If* you find out,' Rowan muttered.

'What was that?'

127

'*When* you find out,' Rowan smiled.

'There he is!' an excited Ishbel declared a few minutes later. 'He's with a friend.'

'Which one is he?'

Ishbel surreptitiously pointed him out.

Rowan saw a tall lad with freckles and limp red hair – not her sort, but clearly Ishbel thought differently. 'So how are you going to approach this?'

Ishbel shrugged. 'I don't know.'

'There are two of them and two of us, which must help. Come on.'

Ishbel trotted after Rowan, now busily carving her way through the throng. On nearing Andrew and his friend Rowan slowed to a saunter, eventually halting some feet away from them. Then, with Ishbel by her side, edged her way unobtrusively closer.

'What next?' Ishbel whispered.

'Leave it to me. Just try to take advantage of the situation as it develops, all right?'

Ishbel nodded.

Honestly, the things she did for her sister, Rowan thought. What she was about to do was quite out of character. There, again, thinking of Gray, perhaps not so out of character as would have once been true.

Rowan appeared to stumble and fall against Andrew's friend, who grabbed her. 'I'm awfully sorry,' Rowan stammered. 'My ankle went over.'

'Is it twisted?' the friend asked in concern.

She pretended to try it. 'Doesn't appear to be, thank goodness.'

'That's a relief.'

She smiled at him. 'You *are* kind. Thank you very much.'

The friend thought her a real smasher, and could hardly believe his luck that she'd literally fallen right into his arms. 'Would you care to dance?' he asked.

'How kind.'

The friend held out an arm, which Rowan took. 'See you when I get back,' she said to Ishbel standing beside Andrew.

128

' 'Bye,' Ishbel smiled.

As Rowan and the friend walked away Rowan glanced round to see Ishbel and Andrew now deep in conversation. She smiled in self-congratulation; her plan had worked. A few minutes later she smiled again when Ishbel and Andrew joined them on the dance-floor.

That smile went cold and died on her face when she spotted a couple nearby. The man was Gray, the female nestling cosily in his arms Sonia Millar.

Gray was back without getting in touch as he'd promised. And, to make matters worse, here he was out with that bitch Sonia. She felt a complete fool. To think she'd been mooning around waiting to hear from him, and all the time he'd been doing the dirty on her!

Tears welled up in her eyes, while her chest heaved. She had to get out of there, she told herself, and fast.

'What is it?' the boy queried.

Rowan shook her head, unable to speak for the moment.

'Is it your ankle?'

She glanced again at Gray, who was obviously enjoying himself. He and Sonia seemed to have eyes only for one another.

'No,' she answered tightly.

'Do you want to sit down?'

She fumbled for the scrap of hanky she had tucked up one sleeve and used that to dab away her tears. She prayed Gray wouldn't see her; that was the last thing she wanted.

'Will you take me to the cloakroom?' she asked the chap.

'Are you going?'

'I've suddenly come over unwell,' she explained, which was true enough, if not the full truth. 'I'm sorry we haven't had much of a dance together.'

'I'm sorry, too. But you can't help it if you're poorly.' Inwardly he was cursing. Trust him to meet such a ravishing creature and then lose her before they could get properly acquainted.

'Perhaps I can take you home?' he proposed.

'I'd rather you didn't. But thanks for asking.'

The music stopped, and the dancers applauded. Rowan seized her chance to leave the floor. The boy took her by the elbow as they made for the cloakroom.

'Don't you want to say goodbye to your pal?' the friend queried.

'She's my sister.'

'Oh!'

'And, no, I don't. Just tell her I've taken an early bus and not to worry.'

'I'll do that . . . I didn't catch your name.'

'Rowan.'

'Pretty,' he commented. 'Mine's David.'

She was at the point where she wanted to scream. She didn't care whether he was called David or Nebuchadnezzar. All she wanted was to get out of there, away from the dance and Gray, to be alone.

When she was handed her coat, David helped her on with it. She could hear him talking but couldn't take in what he was saying. Everything had somehow become hazy and jumbled. She was also finding the heat in the building stifling. It was clogging her nose, choking her, making her desperate for fresh air.

'Be sure to tell my sister,' she gasped, and fled out into the night, a puzzled David staring sadly after her.

She leant against a tree and gulped in breath after breath. Behind her the sound of the music filtered from the hall, music overlaid with noise and laughter.

The tears were coursing now, streaming down her cheeks. But she loved him, she kept thinking. She *loved* him! How could he do that to her?

She recalled the evening he'd taken her to the pictures, and the kissing in the van afterwards. She'd been in seventh heaven with his promise to get in touch when he returned. Well, he hadn't; he'd got in touch with Sonia Millar instead. Sonia who was nothing, a mouse, by comparison.

Rowan retched as sick rose suddenly in her throat. Bending over, she vomited, not once but several times.

When she was finally finished she wiped her mouth with the scrap of hanky which she then threw away.

She stared up at the night sky where a million bright stars were twinkling. And there was the moon, cold and white. She stared at the moon, and Gray's face stared back.

'Bugger!' she swore, and shook her head. It was then that she realized she'd developed a headache.

She started walking in the direction of the bus-stop and found her legs had gone all weak. Her mind was racing while her emotions were mixed up, jangled and raw.

When she reached the bus-stop she halted. How long till the next one? She had no idea, but could perhaps have a lengthy wait.

She was impatient, anxious to be elsewhere, on the move. It was as if she wanted to run away from herself, which was of course impossible.

She began the long trek home, and shortly it began to rain. Soon her hair lay plastered to her head, the rain on her face mingling with her tears.

She would never have believed she could feel so appallingly wretched. She knew it was her imagination, but she could actually smell Gray as she walked. She would have given anything to have had him there by her side, his hand in hers. Anything at all, no matter what the cost or sacrifice to herself.

She staggered on through the darkness, thinking of Gray, trying not to think of Gray, imagining all sorts. At least Ishbel would have had a good night; she was pleased about that.

The lavatory was the only place Rowan could find at home to be on her own. She was sitting there now with the tears cascading down her face as she blubbed into a handkerchief. It was three days since the dance, and she was, if anything, even worse than she'd been then.

It was as if she'd come apart at the seams. Her mind wasn't always rational, she knew that. And her emotions were seesawing wildly. One moment she was beside herself with frustrated love and longing, the next uncannily serene and peaceful. As for the tears, they kept overwhelming her, often bursting forth without warning. She'd explained them to the family by saying she'd caught a cold coming back from the dance.

Ishbel had wanted to know what she'd been playing at going off like that. Why hadn't she spoken to her before rushing away? And to walk home! That was sheer madness in such weather.

Madness! That was just the word to describe her present state: mad as a hatter. And all for a chap she'd only been out with once. Ludicrous, when you thought about it. But, then, she was now learning that there was never any sense where love was concerned. Love could strike as quickly as a bolt of lightning with devastating results.

Rowan looked up when she heard a tap on the lav door. 'Are you all right?' Meg asked anxiously. 'You've been in there quite a while.'

'Diarrhoea, Mum,' she lied.

'Oh! Can I help?'

'No.'

'Have you plenty of paper?'

Rowan smiled at her mother's practicality. 'Loads, Mum.'

'I'll put the kettle on for a cup of tea.'

A cup of tea was Meg's answer to everything, Rowan thought, though not unkindly. The universal panacea for all ills and problems. Well, it would take more than a cup of tea to cure what was bothering her.

God, how she ached inside, physically ached. She felt as if she'd been punched and pummelled by an expert. She wouldn't have been surprised to find herself covered in bruises. Only her bruises were in the mind which, metaphorically, must have been black and blue all over.

To think that a chap could do this to *her*, Rowan Stewart. If anyone had told her this would be the result of her meeting Gray, she would have laughed the idea off as complete nonsense. But nonsense it wasn't, as she was only too acutely aware.

'Gray,' she whispered the word aloud.

She would have keened like a whipped cur if she hadn't been worried that Meg might still be around to hear.

The Reverend David Dykes strode through the late-night darkness, shoulders hunched against the soft drizzle falling over Glenshields. He should go home to bed, he told himself, but knew if he did he wouldn't sleep. As he walked he recited passages from the Bible to himself, and when not doing that thought of the sermon he would deliver the following Sunday.

His lonely footsteps echoed along the road, while behind him his shadow was cast long and large by a nearby street-lamp whose gas hissed snake-like within its glass dome.

He found himself outside the Stewart house and stared first at the front door, then at each window in turn. Which window was Rowan's bedroom? he speculated. He chose one window and focused on it. Perhaps she was in there, fast asleep, only feet from where he stood.

He could see her in a nightdress, something very feminine and frilly, with her blonde hair hanging to her shoulders. She'd been in church again that Sunday, and it had taken every ounce of his willpower not to keep looking at her. How gorgeous she was, how stunningly attractive. There were times when her presence simply took his breath away.

He was certain she wasn't aware of his interest. To her he was no doubt just a stern and forbidding min-ister who didn't differentiate between her and others of his flock.

He thought of threading his fingers through the blonde hair that so fascinated him, twisting it into curls which he then laid against her neck. And above the neck he visualized that face and those haunting eyes.

A tug, and the nightdress fell to the floor, revealing her in all her splendour. Such perfect skin, smooth and silky to touch. Her breasts, large and full. He bent and took a nipple into his mouth and greedily sucked. As he sucked Rowan moaned and writhed against him.

Dykes screwed a bunched fist into his side and sobbed. Turning from the house, he began hastily striding away.

Rowan. The great temptation that had come into his life. A woman he longed for with all his heart and soul, but whom he would never possess, could never possess. If only she had been several years older, the situation could have been so different.

It was so mechanical, Meg thought as Vincent pumped inside her like a well-oiled piston. It was as though she was an object, not a person. There was no oneness as there had been with Cully.

She fought back the urge to tell him to hurry up. She knew that that only infuriated him and made him do his best to drag it out much longer.

He might be on top of her, but it was as if there was a barrier between them; which was something that had never existed with Cully. With Cully it had been true lovemaking, yet with Vincent it was simply sex. And these days she no longer enjoyed sex, but found it a chore.

Her mind wandered to the work she'd been doing that day, and to Rowan about whom she continued to be worried. What was wrong with the girl? She'd become a shadow of her former self, and so moody! Maybe she should have another word with her; but she'd already tried that on several occasions – to no avail. All she got were evasive answers and mutterings about colds.

Her mind moved on to Rory, who was another worry. He'd found an old motorbike he was trying to buy, which she wasn't at all sure about. She'd hoped he'd go off the idea of motorbikes; that dabbling and having the occasional run on Fraser's would be enough for him. But that wasn't proving to be the case. They were so dangerous, those things, deathtraps one and all. She could forbid him to buy it, of course, but experience had taught her that that would probably only make matters worse.

The trouble was he had his own savings to do with – theoretically anyway – as he pleased. She wondered what

Cully would have had to say on the subject, and how he would have handled it. Being a man, he would have had more sway and influence in this issue than she. If Cully had objected, Rory would have listened, whereas in her case Rory would just put it down to her being an over-anxious mother.

Nor was there any point in asking Vincent to help; there was no rapport at all between him and Rory, who continued to be resentful of Vincent's presence in the house.

At least Ishbel wasn't giving her any problems at the moment, she thought. Ishbel recently had been as good as gold, a real help round the house, and at work she was proving to be an excellent seamstress – far better than Rowan, who was decidedly mediocre when it came to needle and thread. Ishbel had flair and a natural understanding of what she was doing. Meg rarely had to explain things twice; while with Rowan it often took three or four times, sometimes more.

It never ceased to amaze Meg how completely different those two were. If she hadn't known they were twins, she'd never have believed it.

'Ouch!' she yelped as Vincent's body trapped her hand, sending a sharp arthritic pain shooting up her arm. 'That hurts,' she complained, trying to free her hand.

'What?'

'My hand.' She pulled and tugged, but her hand remained trapped owing to the slightly off-centre position he'd adopted. Now thoroughly entangled, it was being squeezed together. The hand itself felt as though it was in a vice, while pain after pain lanced up her arm. She prodded him till at last he twisted his body, thereby releasing it.

'Get off!' she commanded, furious.

He blinked at her. 'What is it?'

'My hand – it got caught.'

She heaved herself into a sitting position where she nursed her hand, rubbing and massaging it.

'Come on, stop making such a fuss. It can't have been that bad.'

She glared at him. 'I have arthritis in my hands. I've mentioned it in the past.'

He'd completely forgotten about that. 'Sorry. I got caught up in what I was doing.'

'Selfish,' she muttered.

He reached for his cigarettes and lit up. 'I thought you were just getting excited, that's all. Is it better now?' he asked.

'No thanks to you.'

'I said I'm sorry. What more do you want? Meg, don't be so unreasonable.'

She could have cried. There he was smoking his damn cigarette when he should have taken her into his arms and comforted her. That was what Cully would have done. But, then, she thought bitterly, Vincent was no Cully, not by a long chalk.

'You'll have to be more careful in future,' he said. 'I'm sorry. I suppose I got carried away,' he added lamely.

'You don't care, do you? Certainly not when that thing between your legs is involved.'

'Of course I care, Meg!' he protested.

In a pig's eye, she thought. 'I'm going to sleep,' she declared, turning over and presenting her back to him.

'Be like that, then,' he grumbled.

She heard him stub out his cigarette, then within a short while begin to snore.

When he approached her in the morning she told him exactly what to do with himself.

'So how long is Vincent away for this time?' Fee asked.

'A couple of days,' Meg answered, thinking what a relief it was. She so looked forward to these trips of his when he travelled to different parts of the country on business. She only wished they occurred more often.

'And how are things going between the pair of you? Everything working out all right?'

'Fine,' Meg replied vaguely.

'You don't sound too sure about that?' Fee queried,

regarding her daughter shrewdly.

'Don't I?'

Fee stirred her tea, and wondered if she should allow herself another cake. They were so fattening after all, she really should limit herself to one. With a sigh she reached into the box she'd brought and selected a chocolate fudge finger that was just too tempting to resist. 'No regrets, then?'

Meg shrugged. 'He's so very different from Cully. I suppose I find that hard.'

'Men are just like those horses he buys and sells – no two are the same. And a good thing, too, say I.'

'My experience is strictly limited in both respects,' Meg declared, which made Fee laugh.

'He's a good provider, though; there's no denying that,' Fee stated.

'So was Cully. And so am I.'

'Ay, you're doing well with that wee business of yours,' Fee acknowledged, proud of Meg's success. 'Going from strength to strength from what you tell me.'

'I enjoy having the independence.'

'Except that's not what we're talking about, lass. But you and him.'

Meg didn't reply to that.

'You mustn't dwell too much on the past,' Fee counselled. 'That's gone for ever. No matter how you might wish it otherwise.'

'So you've said before.'

'Because it's true.'

Part of Meg wanted to discuss things in detail with Fee, to unburden herself. But she found it far too personal to do so. 'Why these questions?' she asked instead.

'I'm interested of course. I want you to be happy after all.'

'It's taking me a while to adjust,' Meg confessed. 'But I expected that.'

'Adjustments are only natural.'

'As I said, he's just so very different from Cully.'

'Another horse entirely,' Fee nodded.

'You can certainly say that again.'

'He treats you all right, doesn't he?'

'Of course,' Meg replied, a shade too quickly, which wasn't lost on Fee.

'It's early days yet,' Fee went on. 'And no-one ever said it would be easy for you.'

'Early days,' Meg echoed in agreement.

'I still think you did the right thing in marrying him. I'm convinced of it.'

Was *she*? Meg wasn't sure. If, indeed, she ever had been. What she'd done was take a gamble, considered her future when the children had grown up and left home.

'It'll all work out, you'll see,' Fee stated enthusiastically.

Meg hoped so. 'How's Dad?' she asked. 'I haven't seen him for ages.'

'The same. He never changes.'

Meg thought of her mother and father's relationship, and the one that had existed between her and Cully. Would hers with Vincent ever reach such a level of happiness and contentment?

Perhaps, but she doubted it.

Vincent was in a filthy mood when he arrived home. A deal he'd set up had fallen through, which had not only lost him a handsome potential profit but money he'd laid out into the bargain. He also had the niggling feeling that something had been put over on him, the idea of which he hated. He was looking forward to a good meal and a brief visit to the pub afterwards.

He was certainly fortunate with Meg's cooking, he reflected. He couldn't fault her in that department. She kept a marvellous and varied table.

He parked his car in front of the house and got out to find Rory and Rory's friend Fraser surrounded by bits and pieces of a dismantled motorbike.

'What's all this, then?' he demanded.

'What does it look like?' Rory retorted.

Cheeky young bastard, Vincent thought. 'A mess.'

Rory shrugged and didn't answer. 'Pass me that spanner,' he said to Fraser, deliberately ignoring Vincent.

'I suppose this is the bike you've been talking about buying?' Vincent said.

'She's a beaut, Mr McQueen,' Fraser grinned.

'Watch where you put your feet!' Rory snapped at Vincent as he stepped towards the door.

Anger bubbled inside Vincent. 'Your behaviour leaves a lot to be desired.'

Rory smiled thinly and again didn't reply.

'You'll have to clear all this up, you know,' Vincent went on. 'And you can't leave patches of oil on the pavement. What if someone was to slip and break his neck?'

Rory's look told Vincent that Rory wished that he would do just that.

'We'll clean up, Mr McQueen,' Fraser promised.

'Well, see you do. I don't want the neighbours complaining.'

'None of your concern if they do,' Rory muttered in an aside.

'What's that?'

'Nothing,' Rory replied, his tone contemptuous and impertinent.

Vincent stared at Rory, who glared darkly back. 'You'd better start clearing up now. The meal will be served directly,' Vincent said.

Inside he hung up his coat and hat. That little exchange had worsened his mood. Not for the first time he wished that Rory never existed. He got on all right with the lassies, but the boy was a different story.

Walking into the kitchen, he found Meg cutting bread, Rowan and Ishbel setting the table. 'Hello,' Meg smiled. 'How did it go?'

'Don't ask,' he snarled in reply.

Rowan and Ishbel exchanged glances.

'Is there any beer in?'

'There might be a bottle in the cupboard if you look.'

The cupboard was empty. He should have bought some

before getting back, he told himself. 'What's to eat?'

'Mince and potatoes.'

His face fell. 'We had that the night before last.'

'I thought you liked mince!' Meg exclaimed.

'I do, but not all the time.'

That was a further disappointment to Vincent; he just didn't fancy mince again.

Meg crossed to the range to check the potatoes, which still weren't ready. They needed a few more minutes.

'Call Rory,' she instructed Ishbel.

'He's bought that motorbike, I see,' Vincent said.

'For a good price, he says.'

'He should have asked me to do the deal for him. Whatever he paid, I'm sure I could have got it down even more.'

'He wanted to negotiate himself. That's part of the fun,' Meg responded.

Rory breezed into the kitchen still wearing dungarees and wiping his oily hands on a rag.

'I hope you cleared up as I told you,' Vincent jibed.

Rory tossed the rag aside. 'I can't wait to get her on the road, Mum,' he enthused to Meg, ignoring Vincent.

Vincent bridled. 'Am I talking to myself or something?'

Rory stared levelly at him. 'Fraser's just finishing off now. Anything else?'

'You can't have cleared up properly in that short time.'

'Maybe I get things done faster than you.'

'I doubt it,' Vincent retorted.

'Well, I don't.'

'Enough, you two,' Meg intervened.

'And I hope you're going to take those dungarees off before you sit down,' Vincent went on.

Rory had intended to, but now decided he wouldn't. 'There's no reason for me to do so.'

'Yes, there is,' stated Vincent.

'Mum?'

'They're not that dirty,' Meg appealed to Vincent.

'That's right, go on, give in to him like you always do.'

'I don't always give in to him,' Meg protested.

'Always, without exception.'

'Don't speak to my mother like that,' Rory growled.

'She's my wife!'

'And my mother. So watch it.'

'Watch it!' Vincent laughed. 'Just who the hell do you think you are, boy?'

'Not so much of a boy,' Rory riposted.

'Christ,' Rowan whispered to Ishbel. There had been a lovely atmosphere in the house until Vincent had arrived home.

Vincent laughed again, this time derisively. 'Imagine you're grown up, do you? The big man?'

'I never said anything about being a big man.'

'You're still wet behind the ears, son.'

'I am not your son! Thank God.'

'Vincent, enough is enough,' Meg said.

Vincent rounded on her. 'Bloody mince. You can shove it, as far as I'm damn well concerned.'

It had been a hard and exhausting day for her as one of Mrs Monteith's friends for whom she was doing a job had been particularly trying to the point of exasperation.

Ishbel bit her lip, tempted to say something, and knowing it was better if she didn't as that might only exacerbate matters. In her opinion Vincent was being most unreasonable, not to mention downright insulting. She'd always had some sympathy for his position in the house, but not at this moment. He was behaving like some latter-day Genghis Khan.

Meg suddenly burst into tears, shocked and deeply upset at being shouted at in such a brutal fashion. After Mrs Monteith's friend this was the final straw.

'Now see what you've done,' Rowan chided Vincent, putting her arms round her mother.

'I'll be all right. Just give me a moment,' Meg sobbed, dabbing at her eyes with her sleeve.

Rory was both appalled and furious that his mother was

141

being treated in such a way. He marched up to Vincent and stuck his face into the older man's. 'Don't speak to my mother like that ever again,' he hissed.

Vincent pushed him away. 'Bugger off, boy.'

'Leave it, Rory,' Meg pleaded.

'I'll leave nothing of the sort. It's time this clown was taught a lesson.'

'Clown!' Vincent exploded.

'Clown,' Rory repeated.

'Why, you . . .'

Rory grabbed Vincent by his shirtfront and hauled him on to his toes, for he was taller than his step-father. Vincent was amazed at Rory's strength, which was considerably greater than he'd imagined. He winced in anticipation when Rory drew back a fist and aimed it at his face.

'No!' Meg shouted, throwing herself at Rory and Vincent, managing to get between them.

'Let me, Mum,' Rory pleaded.

'No.'

'Mummy's boy,' Vincent sneered.

'Let him go,' Meg said, attempting to pull Rory away from Vincent, who now knew he was safe.

'Let him go, Rory,' Rowan echoed, her expression reflecting her worry at this latest development.

Rory glanced at Rowan, whom he was extremely close to, then back at Vincent. Slowly he released his grip, allowing Vincent to take several steps backwards.

'That's it, son,' Meg approved.

Vincent was shaken and doing his best to conceal the fact. He'd had no idea Rory was so strong. Still, he would have had a few tricks up his sleeve. Strength wasn't everything; experience counted just as much, maybe even more. And he had plenty of that.

'You were lucky,' Vincent said to Rory.

'Don't listen to him,' Ishbel urged.

'Your mummy saved your bacon.'

Rory's lips thinned to become a white slash. How he hated Vincent and wished his mother had never set eyes on him, far less married him.

'Some day,' Rory said slowly, staring hard and meaningfully at Vincent. 'That's a promise.'

Vincent laughed. 'And cows might fly, boy.'

Rory turned to Meg. 'How are you, Mum?'

Before Meg could answer Ishbel exclaimed and dashed to the range from which she hurriedly removed a pot. Removing the lid she peered inside, then sniffed the pot's contents.

'The mince is burnt,' she announced.

Vincent threw back his head and bellowed with laughter, treating the others to a dazzling show of gleaming white teeth. Rory would quite cheerfully have shoved those teeth down his throat.

'I'm going to the pub,' Vincent said, and sauntered cockily from the room.

'Some day,' Rory repeated to himself. 'Some day.'

'Any bargains?' asked Chick Strathearn, peering at a section of the many articles on display at the white elephant stall.

'They're all bargains,' Rowan replied.

'That depends on the price.'

Rowan was enjoying herself. She always did at jumble sales, regardless of whether she was helping as she now was or browsing like Chick. 'You can try haggling if you want,' she suggested.

Chick made a face. 'Haggle! You mean like one of those Arab johnnies?'

'Exactly,' she smiled.

He picked up a pretty brooch. 'How much for this?'

'The price is on the back.'

He turned the brooch over and peered at it. 'Two and six! That's daylight robbery.'

'No, it's not. It's worth every penny.'

'Cheap old thing.'

'Old, yes; cheap not. I think that's been chucked out by mistake and could be a real find.'

Chick held the brooch up to the light and perused it with new interest.

'Is it for yourself?' Rowan teased.

'Of course!' he quipped in reply. 'Don't you think it'll go with my Sunday suit?'

'So are you interested?'

'Sixpence,' he offered.

'Sixpence! Don't be ridiculous.'

'Sevenpence, then?'

'Away and fly a kite.'

'Eightpence, and that's my final offer.'

She shook her head. 'No can do, Chick. As I said, it's a real bargain at two and six.'

'I can't afford half a crown because I'm hard up. And I want it for my aged granny.'

Rowan laughed. 'Aged granny indeed!'

'With white hair, varicose veins and a heart of gold. This will be my birthday present to her.'

'You've certainly got the chat, Chick Strathearn, and the cheek to go with it. I'll let you have the brooch for two bob, and I don't believe a word about your granny.'

'Can you wrap it?' he asked.

'I have some tissue paper – that all right?'

He nodded.

'So who is it for?'

Chick tapped his nose. 'Ask no questions, get no lies . . .'

'Shut your mouth and you'll catch no flies,' Rowan interjected, finishing off the children's rhyme for him. They both laughed.

'A lassie, is it?' Rowan further probed.

'Hardly in the way you mean.'

'Not a girlfriend, then?'

'I just said that, Rowan. But what about yourself? Who are you going out with nowadays?'

'Fat Boy Carstairs.'

He was thunderstruck. 'You're pulling my leg!'

'Am I?' she asked innocently.

'You must be. You and Fat Boy! I just don't believe it.'

144

'I'm glad. I would have biffed you if you had. I'm not that desperate.'

Chick grinned. 'I can't imagine you ever being desperate, Rowan. So who is the current lucky chap?'

'No-one. I'm fancy free.'

Rowan handed Chick his brooch wrapped in tissue paper. 'That's two shillings.'

He gave her the money. 'Are you really currently unattached?'

She nodded.

'I'm surprised, stunner like you.'

'Well, there you are, then. Life's full of surprises,' she said, counting out his change.

'Same with me – unattached, that is,' he stated, suddenly awkward.

She raised an eyebrow.

There was a moment's hiatus, then he shrugged. 'No, there isn't any point. You've always turned me down in the past.'

'I'll have to go,' Rowan smiled. She made to move away.

'Rowan?'

She turned again to him.

'How about next weekend? The pictures, say.'

'Fine.'

His face lit up in a huge smile. 'Are you serious?'

'Of course I am. Now, can I get on?'

'I'll speak to you later and make the arrangements,' he enthused.

A date with Rowan Stewart! Chick thought jubilantly as he walked away. The brooch he'd bought for his mother had been well worth the money.

'The back row all right?' Chick asked.

Rowan nodded in the darkness split by flickering light from the projection-box. She went in first, he followed, squeezing their way past those already seated.

When they were comfortable Chick opened the bag of

sweets he'd bought and offered them to Rowan, who took one.

'I love lemon sherbets,' Chick said, popping one into his mouth and proceeding to crunch.

Rowan tried not to dwell on the fact that the last time she'd been in this picture-hall had been with Gray whom she hadn't laid eyes on since that awful night of the dance.

'A good film, I'm told,' Chick whispered.

Rowan stared up at the silver screen, hoping it would be as good a film as Chick had said it was. To her delight it turned out to be a love-story that soon had her enthralled.

She hardly noticed when Chick's arm crept round her shoulders. Then shortly after that he pulled her closer to him.

The hero in the film was such a dreamboat, she thought. An attractive man with large soulful eyes and gorgeous dark wavy hair. When he smiled, which was rare, it was like a bolt from heaven.

'Rowan?' Chick husked beside her.

She turned to find him staring intently at her. She gave him a smile of encouragement.

'You're terrific,' he said.

She continued smiling. Then his lips were on hers.

There was simply no magic in the kiss, she thought, none at all. Her body and emotions were not responding at all, not like they had with Gray. Now, that had been real kissing!

Gray. The memory of him turned her sour inside. He was worth a hundred Chicks. At least, to her he was, because to her he was something very, very special.

If she could have got up and left there and then without offending Chick, she would have done. For her evening was ruined, the ghost of Gray lying over it like a wet blanket.

When she again focused on the lovers inhabiting the silver screen there was the sparkle of tears in her eyes, while her mouth was curved in a thin wry smile.

'So who is it tonight?' Meg asked Rowan, who'd just come through to the kitchen from her bedroom where she'd been getting ready to go out.

'No-one you know, Mum.'

'Someone new, then?'

'Uh-huh!'

'You're really getting round and about of late,' Vincent commented from his chair.

'You're only young once,' Rowan replied.

'But it's real musical chairs with these boyfriends of yours. It's Chick one day, Harry the next and goodness knows who the day after that,' Meg said reprovingly.

'You'll get yourself a name, my girl, if you're not careful,' Vincent warned.

'I can't help it if I'm popular.'

'So who is it tonight?' Meg queried again.

'I said, no-one you know. He's called Edgar and don't ask me where we're going; I've no idea. All I can tell you is he'll be knocking at the door any minute now.'

Ishbel entered the kitchen, she, too, having been getting ready to go out. She was still seeing Andrew. 'How do I look?' she asked.

'Too much lipstick in my opinion. You should tone it down,' Rowan counselled.

'You do seem to have rather a lot on,' Meg added.

Ishbel pulled out a compact, opened it and stared at herself in the mirror. Was Rowan giving her genuine advice or simply being bitchy? 'Too much?' she queried.

'Definitely,' Rowan nodded.

'I think she looks fine,' Vincent said.

The twins and Meg ignored him. 'Take it off and start again,' Rowan suggested.

'You're not just getting at me, are you?'

'Would I do such a thing!' Rowan exclaimed, tongue in cheek.

'In a word, yes.'

147

'Well, I'm not. Cross my heart and all that nonsense. Now, here, let me help you.'

Rowan was still engrossed with Ishbel when there was a rap on the front door. 'I'll get it. That'll be Edgar,' she said, and hurried from the room.

She returned less than a minute later. 'Where were we?'

'What about the young man?' Meg asked.

'I've told him to wait outside till I'm ready.'

'You should have invited him in!'

Rowan gave her mother a cynical smile. 'He can hang on where he is; it won't do him any harm.'

Rowan then put fresh lipstick on Ishbel, which she did expertly and, as she put it, with taste.

Rowan's heart leapt into her mouth when she spotted the familiar van parked by the side of the road. Its bonnet was raised, a figure hunched over the engine.

Her route lay past the van, but she could easily detour, she thought. Then, why the hell should she? She hadn't done anything wrong. On the contrary, he was the one at fault.

Should she stop and speak or not? If he said hello, should she sweep on past, cutting him dead? One thing she wouldn't do was speak first; her pride wouldn't allow that.

The figure glanced up, and their eyes locked. She could see how disconcerted he was by her presence.

'Hello, Gray,' she heard herself say.

'Hello, Rowan.'

'Having trouble?'

'I've broken down.'

'Tough luck.'

She was glowing all over, her skin tingling. What was it he did to have such an effect on her!

'I've rung my dad, who's coming down to give me a tow,' Gray went on. 'That's if I can't fix it in the mean time, which I don't think I can.'

She wanted to reach out and touch him, to ask why

he hadn't contacted her again, to slap that adorable face as hard as she could, to take him in her arms and hold him tight, to spit in his eye for being such a rat.

'How's Sonia?' she asked, smiling sweetly.

He studied her levelly. 'You know about that?'

'Saw you at a dance, the two of you. She was all over you like a bad dose of measles.'

Gray laughed. 'I can't remember that. And which dance was it?'

Rowan told him.

'Didn't see you there.'

'But I saw you. And her. Together.'

He opened his mouth to speak.

'You're not going to try to tell me you weren't, are you? Together, that is. It was patently obvious you were. I mean, a blind man could have seen you were a couple.'

'I wasn't going to deny anything,' he said. 'I was there with Sonia – together, as you put it. Who were you with?'

'None of your business.'

'Oh, you were there with somebody, then!'

'I didn't say that.'

'Or were you on your own?'

'I didn't say that, either.' She'd been with someone all right, her sister Ishbel, but that wasn't what he meant.

He laughed, while she stared daggers at him. She wanted to walk on, but somehow her feet wouldn't move. She stood rooted to the spot.

'I must admit I felt guilty about you,' he confessed.

'That's nice to know,' she retorted tartly.

'I promised to get in touch and didn't.'

'I noticed.'

'I fully intended to, I swear.'

'So what happened?' she demanded.

He shrugged. 'I got home and almost immediately bumped into Sonia. We sort of took up where we'd left off.'

'She's such a mouse,' Rowan said contemptuously.

'She's got a lovely personality. I have a lot of time for Sonia.'

Jealousy flared up in Rowan. Lovely personality indeed! If the bitch had been there, she'd have taken great delight in scratching her eyes out. As for personality, she could out-personality Sonia any day of the week. And she was far better looking.

'We broke up again,' Gray said.

'Really! Went off her personality, did you?'

'Miaow!' he said.

Rowan sniffed. 'I am not being catty, if that's what you're driving at.'

'Oh, yes, you are.'

'Oh, no, I'm not!'

Gray grinned. 'We're beginning to sound like a Christmas pantomime.'

She matched his grin, for he was right. She was very aware of the electricity which seemed to crackle between them.

'What are you doing this weekend?' he asked.

The breath caught in her throat. 'Why?'

'We could go out.'

'Are you sure my personality is up to it?' she jibed.

'Oh, I think you'll pass,' he replied drily.

'I mean, I wouldn't want to let you down in any way. Be deficient, that is.'

'Is it yes or no?'

'And you've definitely finished with Sonia?'

'*Definitely*,' he assured her.

'I must be mad,' she said.

'Does that mean yes?'

She nodded.

'I'll take you to a party. How's that?'

'What sort of party?'

'A fun party. Just wait and see.'

She stared him straight in the eye. 'I could have killed you for what you did,' she said.

'I'm sorry. Truly.'

She had a sudden horrible thought. 'You will turn up? You won't leave me standing somewhere like a proper Charlie?'

'I'll turn up. I promise.'

When she left Gray she was in a daze, unable to believe her luck. Chick and all the other lads she'd gone out with were completely forgotten. Only Gray existed for her.

'Cape Town is my favourite city. It's simply incredible there,' James Taylor declared. 'And the natives! They don't come any friendlier than Kaapstaders.'

'I couldn't agree with you more,' smiled Tiny Bowles, a shipmate of James's. 'Cape Town is the best and friendliest port in the whole wide world.'

Rowan was sitting on the floor between Gray's legs. The party was at the Taylors' in Drumden; they were entertaining some friends of James's for the weekend. It was a cosy affair consisting of drinking, eating and a great deal of reminiscing. Gray was in his element, lapping up the stories of faraway places.

'You know, South Africa is the only place where I've ever seen gallon jars of brandy,' James said.

'Gallon jars!' Rowan exclaimed.

'That's right. You buy them in the off-licence, or *drankwinkel* as they call it. Gallon glass jars.'

'Imagine,' mused May Taylor.

'When you say *natives*, do you mean white people or black?' Gray asked James.

'White of course.'

'Mainly British stock in Cape Town,' said George Smedhurst, a Yorkshireman. 'That's why we get on so well with them.'

'Not like the Afrikaaners or Boers,' explained Tiny. 'They're a different thing entirely.'

'Hate us,' said James.

'You can say that again,' agreed Tiny.

Gray would have given anything to have been to Cape Town, to be able to talk and recollect as his uncle and James's pals were. He felt like a child in Wonderland.

'Have you ever been to Maracaibo?' James asked George.

Maracaibo! That sounded like something out of a story-book, Gray thought. It conjured up pictures of pirates and dark-haired wenches, of Spanish galleons and pieces of eight. He listened intently, drinking in every word and syllable as James spoke about that fabled city.

And after Maracaibo they talked about the golden beaches of Brazil, and the whales that gathered once a year off the coast of Patagonia, and India where ...

A few weeks later, having seen each other regularly, Gray and Rowan were back at the Taylors' house.

'I'll do the fire if you feed the cats,' Gray said to Rowan. She'd accompanied him there as he had volunteered to look after their animals while they spent a few days with Tiny Bowles and his wife in Berwick-upon-Tweed.

Gray busied himself with the fire, which was soon made up and lit. May had asked him to light one every day they were away to keep the house dry and aired.

'There is nothing like logs. They beat coal every time,' Gray commented.

Rowan came through and joined him in front of the now roaring fire. 'I enjoyed that party the other evening,' she declared.

'Me, too. The night just seemed to fly by.'

Rowan held her hands out to the blaze and rubbed them. When she looked at Gray he was regarding her oddly. 'What is it?' she asked.

'I've just realized – we're here alone.'

She smiled. 'So we are. Just us and the cats.'

He took her into his arms. 'Far better than the pictures or the van, eh?'

'Far better.'

'There's no rush to get home, is there?'

She shook her head. 'None at all.'

'Let's sit down here in front of the fire, shall we?'

'Gray?'

'What?'

'I'm a virgin.'

'I presumed you were.'

She laid her cheek against his neck, the heat from the crackling logs washing over her. She felt completely at peace to the point of serenity. When his hand curled round a breast, she smiled.

Rowan was aghast, her expression incredulous. It was several weeks later, and they were sitting in the van. 'When?' she queried in a trembling voice.

'Tomorrow. I'll tell my folks later tonight, and then I'm away first thing in the morning.'

'Why so soon, Gray?'

'I've decided it's best to leave as quickly as possible. Less messy that way. And it also means I don't have a long-drawn-out argument with my dad, who's bound to hit the roof.'

Gray's eyes shone with excitement. 'I can't wait. It's what I've wanted to do – dreamt of doing – for years. Just to take off and see the world. Go wherever – Hong Kong, Maracaibo, Australia . . .'

'Japan and their paper houses,' she muttered.

'Exactly!' he cried. 'Why not?'

'And how long will you be away for?'

He shook his head. 'I've no idea. But quite some time. Years probably.'

Years! The word echoed round her brain, making her want to throw up.

'I must go before it's too late and I get trapped. Can you understand that?'

'Of course, Gray,' she replied quietly.

He took her hand. 'I'll be back some day.'

'Maybe,' she said, forcing herself to smile. 'There, again, you might settle down with a girl you meet. It could be you'll never come back.'

He didn't reply to that.

'Where will you start? I mean, where will you go from here?'

'Glasgow perhaps, and sign on a ship there. Or London;

there are huge docks at Tilbury. Every day ships go from there all over the world.'

'I'll miss you,' she said, thinking what an understatement that was. Miss him! She'd have cut off her right arm if that would have made him stay.

'And I'll miss you, Rowan. But I must . . .'

She silenced him by placing a finger across his lips. 'Sshh! You don't have to justify yourself any more. You've done that. This is something that's terribly important to you, and I do understand.'

'You're terrific, Ro. One of the best.'

A little later she kissed him for the last time, wished him luck, then watched him drive away.

Strangely, she didn't cry. Dead people didn't, she told herself. And that was exactly how she felt: dead through and through.

Rowan knew she couldn't put the inevitable off any longer, for her condition was starting to show. She chose a time when Vincent was out of the house.

'Mum?'

Meg glanced up from her sewing machine and smiled. 'What is it, darling?'

Rowan took a deep breath. 'I've got something to say to you.'

Meg's smile widened.

'I'm pregnant, Mum.'

The smile froze on Meg's face, while Ishbel stared at her sister in astonishment.

'Pregnant,' Rowan repeated, and burst out crying. They were the first tears she'd shed since Gray's departure three and a half months previously.

Chapter Four

'The minister,' Ishbel announced, ushering the Reverend David Dykes into the sitting-room which Meg had cleared of their work paraphernalia for the occasion.

Meg was still uncertain about enlisting the assistance of the minister, which had been Vincent's idea. But, as Vincent had argued, Dykes would have found out sooner or later and come calling anyway. This way he was there by invitation.

'You can leave us,' Meg said to Ishbel, rising to greet the stony-faced minister. Ishbel closed the sitting-room door behind her and went through to join Rory in the kitchen.

Dykes fixed his gaze on a pale Rowan, then solemnly shook hands with Meg and Vincent.

'I'm deeply and profoundly shocked,' Dykes stated. 'A terrible, terrible thing bringing shame and disgrace on to your family.'

Rowan went even paler and bit her lip.

'Will you be seated, Minister?' Vincent said.

Dykes sat and stared at Rowan. 'You have sinned in the eyes of God, child. Do you repent?'

Rowan gave an almost imperceptible nod.

'We considered getting rid of it, or trying to, but Rowan is against that,' Vincent blurted out.

'I'm glad you did no such thing, for that would be adding sin to sin,' Dykes reproved. 'The sin of murder to that of fornication.'

'If only she would tell us who the father is, we could maybe sort matters out,' Meg murmured.

'You refuse to divulge the name of the father, I understand?' Dykes said to Rowan.

'I've begged her, but she won't say,' Meg explained.

'We've both begged her,' Vincent added. 'To no avail. She's being totally unreasonable.'

'It's pointless,' Rowan whispered.

'Why?' Dykes queried. 'The young man must be held to account for the situation he has helped create. And pay for his lust and foul carnality.'

'I'm not naming anyone, and that's final,' Rowan stated stubbornly. She'd thought about it and come to the conclusion that all she would achieve would be to bring disgrace on the Hamiltons, who couldn't do anything anyway. Gray was gone, run off to sea; no-one knew where he was or when he'd be back. So what was the point in dragging his name and that of his family through the mud as well? No, she would bear this responsibility alone.

It would be different if she could get hold of Gray and explain the position to him, for she was sure he'd want to marry her. But in the circumstances that was impossible.

'Who is the young man, Rowan?' Dykes demanded.

Rowan shook her head.

'You do know who it is? I presume there wasn't more than one person involved?'

Meg was dismayed that the minister could even think such a thing.

'I know who the father is,' Rowan replied quietly. 'There's no question of others.'

Dykes's lips thinned into a bloodless slash. 'That's something, at least. We can't add the accusation of harlot to that of fornicator.'

'It happens all the time,' Vincent said reasonably. 'What we need to do is get it sorted out.'

The stony expression became even stonier. 'Happens all the time?' Dykes repeated, his tone a combination of disapproval and condemnation. '*Not* in my parish, Mr McQueen, I can assure you.'

Vincent began to wonder if he'd made a mistake inviting Dykes to call. He'd expected a hard judgemental line – the man's reputation was well known after all – but mixed with

Christian compassion. So far there had been no sign of the latter.

'Name your partner, child,' Dykes commanded Rowan.

Again she shook her head.

'You must.'

There was no must about it, she thought.

'If you'll only tell us, Rowan, we can hopefully get it all sorted out,' Meg pleaded.

'I've said, Mum, it can't be.'

'Why not?' Dykes thundered.

'It just can't be. You'll have to take my word for that.'

Dykes regarded Meg levelly. 'Have you no inkling who she's protecting, woman? Surely as her mother you must know who she's been seeing.'

'There have been a number of boyfriends lately,' Meg explained. 'I suppose it could be any one of them.'

'Perhaps the culprit will come forward when this gets out, as of course it will.'

'He won't,' Rowan stated.

'Is he a coward into the bargain?' Dykes goaded, hoping to get a reaction that way.

Rowan refused to rise to the bait.

'A coward,' Dykes repeated scornfully.

Rowan looked down at her hands, which she folded in her lap. She thought of Gray and wondered for the umpteenth time where he was and what he was doing. And, as always when she thought of him, she was filled with a dreadful physical ache.

'Are you listening, girl?' Dykes demanded.

She nodded, but continued staring at her hands.

Dykes gave a sigh of exasperation. 'How old is she?' he asked Meg.

'Fifteen.'

'Fifteen,' Dykes repeated slowly. She appeared older, but he'd found that was often the case with young women.

'Come on, Rowan, this is silly,' Vincent urged.

A silence fell over the room, only disturbed by the

heavy sound of Dykes's breathing. The silence stretched on and on.

'I'm sorry, Minister,' Meg said at last. 'It seems we've wasted your time.'

'I'd hoped you could make her see sense,' added Vincent. 'But apparently not.'

'One last chance, Rowan. Who is the child's father?' Dykes asked.

Again Rowan didn't reply, continuing to study her hands.

Dykes rose. 'I'll be on my way, Mr and Mrs McQueen. But rest assured I shall be praying for you all.'

'Thank you, Minister,' Vincent said, rising also.

'Perhaps a cup of tea before you go?' Meg offered.

'No, thank you.'

'Then, I'll see you out.'

Dykes decided to go straight from there to his church where he would pray and ponder the matter. This needed thinking about.

Dykes, sweating despite the fact that it was freezing in church, was ashamed of the images that kept crowding his mind. All too clearly he could visualize Rowan with some unknown young man, their naked bodies entwined, lost in unbridled passion. And then, to his horror, the young man's face took shape and form, to become recognizable as his own. It was he with Rowan, his mouth on hers, his hands on her flesh, burying himself inside that sumptuous body he so desperately desired.

'No!' he cried in anguish, writhing on his knees. 'Get behind me, Satan. Stop tormenting me. Get out of my mind!'

But the images persisted, causing him to be racked with envy and jealousy. Awful jealousy that ate and gnawed at him, clawed at his insides. He couldn't bear the thought that another had done what he secretly longed to do himself, a longing that filled him with burning mortification.

In a frenzy he pulled and tore at his hair, then fell prostrate.

'Help me, Lord, help me!' he pleaded.

After a while his emotional turmoil subsided, and he became rational again. An example had to be made here, he decided. This girl had fallen, but others mustn't be allowed to go the same way. They had to be saved from themselves, the fear of God put into their hearts and heads.

'An example,' he proclaimed aloud, knowing what he had to do.

The evildoer could not remain unpunished. The righteous must triumph, Satan and all his works rebuffed and cast out.

He smiled in grim satisfaction. He would prove his worth to God by ridding himself of this temptress, this instrument of the devil.

Thereby lay redemption and relief.

Ishbel snuggled up to her sister and slid an arm round Rowan's waist. 'Are you still awake?'

'Uh-huh!' Rowan replied after a few seconds' pause.

'I think he's a horrible man.'

'You mean the minister?'

'He makes my skin crawl.'

'Mine, too.'

Ishbel shivered. 'There's something about him. I don't know what, but something.'

Rowan knew exactly what Ishbel meant, and agreed wholeheartedly. 'He reminds me of a gargoyle. He has that sort of frightening quality about him.'

'Did he give you a bad time?'

'Bad enough.'

'I'm glad it wasn't me who had to face him,' Ishbel confessed.

'Anyway, it's over now.'

'I heard Mum crying after he'd gone.'

'I heard her also,' Rowan replied quietly.

'She's awfully upset.'

'I'd be surprised if she wasn't.'

'What has Rory said to you?'

'Not a lot,' Rowan answered. 'He has been rather cold and distant, though, as if I'd let him down personally.'

'He'll get over it. As will Mum in time.'

'They'll both have to. There's nothing else they can do.'

'I suppose not,' Ishbel said. Then: 'Weren't you tempted to get rid of the baby? That would have been so much easier.'

'No,' Rowan stated emphatically.

'Do you love the father?'

'I don't want to talk about him.'

'Suit yourself,' Ishbel responded, slightly miffed. She was used to being taken into Rowan's confidence.

'It's best I say nothing at all. Not even to you.'

Ishbel shifted slightly so that she was even more snugly fitted against Rowan's back. 'Can I ask you something?'

'That depends.'

'What was it like?'

'What was what like?'

Ishbel giggled. 'You know. *It*.'

Rowan considered that. 'Absolutely incredible.'

'Yes. Fine. But that doesn't explain what I'm after,' Ishbel prompted.

'You mean how did I feel while it was happening?'

Ishbel giggled again. 'I couldn't ask anyone that except you. I'd be too bashful.'

'You! Bashful! I don't believe it,' Rowan teased.

'I would, honestly.'

Rowan frowned in the darkness. 'It's hard to describe. I felt relaxed, dreamy and wildly excited at the same time. And wanted it to go on for ever.'

'Did you strip off? All the way, that is?'

'All the way,' Rowan confirmed.

'And weren't you embarrassed?'

'Not in the least. Not even afterwards when we were just lying there. It was all rather sweet really, and very innocent.'

'Hardly innocent when you ended up with a bun in the oven!' Ishbel exclaimed with a low laugh.

Rowan couldn't help but smile. 'Don't be crude!'

'Well, it's true.'

'Bun in the oven indeed,' Rowan repeated, thinking what a dreadful expression that was, so cruel, completely lacking in romance. And what had happened between her and Gray had definitely been romantic. Their lovemaking had been like a honeymoon night where everything had gone just right. It couldn't have been more perfect.

'Did you feel more of a woman when it was over?' Ishbel enquired.

'Oh, yes, very much so.'

'And was it only the once? Or did you do *it* more than that?'

'You're asking an awful lot of questions,' Rowan sighed.

'Because I'm curious. You are my sister and twin after all.'

'Only once,' Rowan confirmed.

'Then, it was rotten luck you fell pregnant.'

Rowan thought so, too, and considered it even worse luck that Gray had decamped without knowing the outcome of their liaison.

'You must love him a great deal not even to try getting rid of the baby,' Ishbel said.

Rowan didn't reply to that.

'You can take pills. I've read about those. And they also say if you—'

'Ishbel, shut up!'

'Sorry.'

Sweet and innocent, Ishbel thought, speculating who the father might be. He certainly sounded nice, quite the tender caring type.

'Now can I get some sleep? I'm tired,' Rowan said.

'I still don't understand why you won't say who it was? Surely he must—'

'Good night, Ishbel,' Rowan stated firmly.

'Good night. Sleep tight.'

Ishbel fell to wondering what her own first experience would be like, and who would it be with. Would she also think it sweet and innocent? She hoped so.

While the Stewart household slept, the Reverend David Dykes laboured over his sermon for the coming Sunday.

'I have spoken in the past about fornication; which seems to have fallen on at least some deaf ears. Today I have to tell you that there is one among us who has become pregnant because of her sin . . .'

Rowan had wanted to cry off church, but Meg had insisted she attend. She now listened, incredulous, as Dykes ranted on. Unable to believe that this was really happening, she began to shrink further and further back into the pew.

Meg was equally incredulous, wishing with all her heart the family had stayed at home. She was unaware of the fact she had started to shake all over.

Dykes, eyes sparking with zeal, continued. 'A sin that will surely mean she will burn in the everlasting fires of hell, screaming in awful torment for allowing herself to be seduced not only by a man, but also by Satan himself . . .'

Rowan winced as the minister's gaze fastened on to hers, a gaze that held her transfixed. She might have been the mesmerized prey of an advancing snake.

'Holy shit,' breathed Vincent.

Ishbel reached out and grasped Rowan's hand. If she could have scooped Rowan into her arms and run from the church, she would have done.

Rory was completely rigid, hating the minister for doing this. But the worst was still to come.

'Stand up, Rowan Stewart. Show yourself to the congregation . . .'

A murmuring broke out, eyes swivelling in Rowan's direction, necks craning, people ogling.

'Shame!' someone called out, though it wasn't clear whether the remark was directed at Rowan or at the minister.

'Stand up, I say, Jezebel! Let us all look upon a fallen woman, one who did not heed the words from this very pulpit. Stand up, fornicator!'

Rowan shook her head, her gaze still held by the

minister's. She tried to break contact, look down, away, anywhere, but couldn't.

'Stand, I say!' he shrieked, pointing a finger at her.

Meg collapsed in upon herself, now shaking almost uncontrollably. This was a nightmare come true.

'Don't,' Ishbel whispered, but Rowan didn't hear her.

'Stand, I command you in the name of the Lord God Almighty whose laws you have ignored and transgressed, in whose sight you have become less than nothing. Stand!'

Rowan felt herself rise, as though pulled by invisible wires. And as she did a great sigh went up from the congregation.

Dykes raved on and on, while Rowan stood before him like a ritual lamb at the slaughter.

The family sat round the kitchen table, all stunned into silence. Meg had stopped shaking and crying, but her face remained a battlefield on which the battle still raged.

'I'll never be able to walk down the street again,' Rowan finally whispered.

'Nonsense,' chided Ishbel. 'You aren't the first lassie in Glenshields this has happened to.'

'But the first who's ever had the finger pointed at her in church,' Rory stated. He exhaled. 'To be made to stand up like that.'

'It'll all blow over, you'll see,' Ishbel declared, trying to console Rowan. She herself was shaken to the core.

'How could he?' Meg said in a cracked voice.

'Sod!' Vincent swore.

'The neighbours who were there ... the friends ... the Monteiths,' Meg choked.

Vincent scraped his chair back and went to the cupboard where he knew there was an unopened bottle of whisky. He didn't give a damn how early it was; he needed a drink.

'Old McNab would never have done such a thing,' Meg commented. 'Privately he might have had some hard remarks to make, but he would have kept them private.'

'The man's a monster,' Ishbel declared, then added

vehemently: 'I don't care if he is the minister and God's holy representative; he's still a monster.'

Vincent poured out a hefty measure and saw it off in one swallow. 'Meg, how about you?'

She shook her head.

'It'll do you some good.'

'I'd . . . I'd vomit.'

Vincent stared at her, thinking how awful she looked. He understood what anguish she must be going through.

'I'll have a dram,' Rory said.

Vincent almost refused him, then thought better of it. 'Help yourself,' he replied, indicating the bottle.

'Oh, Rowan,' Ishbel whispered in sympathy. She loved her twin deeply and hated to see her so hurt and in such a state.

Rowan regarded Ishbel, her expression one of deepest despair and total wretchedness. 'I really thought I was going to die there and then. In fact I want to,' she stated quietly.

'Don't talk like that, Ro.'

Meg put a hand to her mouth and worried a fingernail, remembering how Cully had died in that self-same church. If only he were here now, he'd soon sort out this terrible situation.

Vincent poured himself more whisky. What a mess, he thought.

'Excuse me,' apologized Rory and left the room.

Meg stared after her son, wondering how this would affect him at work. Many of his workmates had been at the service.

'I'll get on with the meal,' she said, rising, pleased to have something to do.

'I'll help you, Mum,' Ishbel offered.

'And I'll go to bed,' Rowan declared, rising also. She wanted to be alone with her agony, the bedclothes pulled up over her head to shut out the world.

She paused in the doorway. 'I'm sorry, Mum.'

'I know, lass.'

'We must look on the bright side,' Vincent said when she'd gone. 'From now on, no matter what, it can only get better.'

He couldn't have been more wrong.

The next morning Vincent left early as he had previously planned a buying trip that would take him away from Glenshields for several days. He did volunteer to stay at home if Meg wished, but the suggestion was so half-hearted she told him not to bother.

A little later Rory set off for work, worried and apprehensive about the reception he might receive. He'd already decided his best course was to keep his mouth shut and himself well under control regarding any possible comments.

Shortly after that Meg, Rowan and Ishbel went through to the sitting-room to start work. Around midday there was a rap on the front door which Meg would normally have asked one of her daughters to answer, but in the light of recent events decided to answer herself.

'Good morning,' said a grave Constable Hart, flanked by another policeman she didn't know and the Reverend Dykes. Parked at the kerb was a police car.

Meg stared at them in consternation. What now? she wondered. 'Can I help you?'

'I think it best we come in.'

The last thing she wanted was the minister in her house, but didn't see how she could refuse – and certainly not when he was accompanied by the law.

Meg ushered them inside, resisting the impulse to glance up and down the street to see if anyone was watching, and closed the door. Both policemen removed their helmets.

'I can't begin to tell you how this grieves me,' apologized Constable Hart whom Meg had known all her life.

'Get on with it, man,' Dykes urged.

'Is Rowan home?' Hart enquired.

'Yes, she is.'

'Then, may we speak to her?'

'Come through.' Meg led them into the sitting-room.

'This is Constable Samuelson,' introduced Hart, gesturing towards his companion who gave a curt nod.

'No use beating about the bush,' declared Hart. 'We've come to arrest Rowan.'

'Oh, my God!' Meg whispered.

'On what charge?' queried Ishbel.

Rowan was standing spellbound, her eyes starting from her head.

'For having sexual intercourse under the lawful age of sixteen,' Hart answered.

'You can't do that!' Ishbel exclaimed.

'I'm afraid we can, lass. What she did, and has confessed to the minister, is against the law of the land. I can quote you chapter and verse if you like.'

'Arrest me?' Rowan whispered, finding her voice at last.

'That's right. You will appear in court before the sheriff, who will decide what to do with you. I therefore have to ask you to accompany us, Rowan.'

'Now?'

'Now,' he confirmed.

'This is ridiculous,' an aghast Meg said.

'I only wish it was, Mrs McQueen,' Hart replied sympathetically.

Meg turned to stare at the minister whose face was completely devoid of expression. 'This is all your doing, isn't it?'

'I have my duty to my flock and the community,' he replied sanctimoniously.

'Would you like to get your coat, miss?' Samuelson said to Rowan.

'What if I refuse to go?'

'We'll use force if necessary,' Samuelson spelt out. 'We, too, have our duty to perform.'

'Where are you taking her?' Meg demanded.

'Into custody,' Hart replied.

Rowan's mind was numb with shock. She was trying to think but was unable.

'Like a common criminal?' Meg breathed.

'That's what she is,' Dykes informed her.

Meg was about to spring at the minister when Ishbel, realizing her intention, grabbed her. 'No, Mum, that won't do any good. On top of all this, he'd probably have you up for assault.'

Dykes's lips twitched into a smirk which confirmed what Ishbel had said.

'Your coat, miss,' Samuelson repeated.

'I'll get it,' Rowan said, and left the room in a complete daze.

Meg took a deep breath. 'Can I come, too?' she asked Constable Hart.

'Of course.'

'And me,' said Ishbel, not wishing to be left behind.

'I take it Mr McQueen isn't home?' Hart asked of Meg.

'No, he's away on business.'

Hart nodded. 'Would you like me to try to contact him?'

Meg thought about that. 'It's impossible. He's gone down to the Borders somewhere; he didn't give me any details.'

'Then, perhaps you'd get your coat as well.'

They all trooped from the sitting-room and went out to the car where Meg, Rowan and Ishbel were forced to sit in the rear with Dykes whom they now discovered would be going with them.

Meg spotted several curious neighbours peering from behind their curtains as the car sped away.

'Wait in here, miss,' the constable instructed Rowan.

The cell was small and a bilious shade of green, the paint flaking off in places. There was a slightly raised platform on the floor at the far end and a toilet without a seat in the corner. It had a small iron-barred window facing the door.

Rowan had spent about an hour alone with her thoughts when the door was opened again. 'If you'll come with me, please, miss,' requested the same constable who'd shown her into the cell.

167

Rowan had never been so frightened in her life. She wished she was safely at home in bed with the bedclothes pulled up over her head. Anywhere but where she now was.

The room he led her to was sparse and clinical. The minimal furniture consisted of some filing-cabinets, an examination-table and a large screen. There were also several wooden chairs.

'You can sit down if you like,' the constable said before leaving her.

A few minutes later two men and an elderly woman entered the room. 'Miss Stewart?' one of the men queried.

She nodded.

'I'm Dr Brown and this is Dr McPhie,' he said, indicating the other man. 'We have to make an examination for our reports. Please go behind the screen and undress, then come and lie on this table.' He didn't introduce the woman, who assumed a position in the background.

Rowan stared at the doctors. 'Undress? How far?'

'Everything, Miss Stewart. You'll find a gown to slip into.'

Everything! 'No,' she whimpered.

'I'm afraid you have to; there's no choice involved.'

Both doctors then proceeded to a sink Rowan had previously failed to notice where they took it in turns to wash their hands.

Rowan glanced despairingly at the woman. 'Do you need some help?' the woman asked.

'No, thank you,' Rowan whispered in reply.

Her heart was pounding furiously as she went behind the screen where she found another wooden chair over which a thin cotton gown was draped.

She stood rigid for a little, biting her lip and fighting back tears, then slowly began to undo her skirt.

'Right, if you'll just get up on the table,' Brown instructed when she reappeared.

She pulled herself on to the table and lay down.

'Now open your gown,' Dr McPhie requested.

She closed her eyes as she did, horribly aware of

her nakedness and feeling totally vulnerable at being so exposed before strangers.

Each touched her breasts, after which they made brief notes.

'If you would spread your legs for us, Miss Stewart,' Dr Brown said.

Please God let this be over soon, she prayed. Please God!

'They did what?' an appalled Meg exclaimed.

Rowan repeated what she'd had to endure.

Meg wrung her hands while Ishbel gazed at Rowan in sympathy.

'It was awful,' Rowan stated unnecessarily.

Meg swept her daughter into her arms and held her tight. Humiliating as it would have been, she'd gladly have undergone the same ordeal to have spared Rowan.

'What happens now?' Rowan asked when Meg finally released her.

'You'll have to stay here tonight and go before the sheriff in the morning,' Meg answered. Constable Hart had filled her in on these details earlier.

'Stay the night . . .' Rowan trailed off, looking round the bleak and unsavoury cell.

'I never thought to bring any money with me, but Constable Hart has kindly arranged for you to be brought in a few little comforts.'

'He's taking us back in the car,' Ishbel said.

'Can you come tomorrow?' Rowan asked. 'I don't want to face the court alone.'

'A police car is picking us up early and taking us there. They want me to be present apparently,' Meg declared.

'I'll be coming, too,' Ishbel added.

They spoke for a while longer, then it was time for Meg and Ishbel to leave. It was a tearful parting, all three of them clinging to one another. Meg told Rowan not to worry; everything would be all right.

Rowan listened to the door clang shut behind her mother and sister, and the key turning in the lock. Because there was no place to sit, other than on the floor or on a raised platform, she began to pace up and down.

Rowan lay on the palliasse she'd been issued, wrapped in a single grey blanket. She was frozen.

A pale shaft of moonlight lanced through the small window to bisect the cell; otherwise she was in complete darkness. Hours passed, but she was unable to sleep. Several times she heard footsteps in the corridor outside, and at one point a noisy drunkard was locked in another cell. He shouted abuse for a bit, then fell silent. The next thing she knew the key was rattling in the lock announcing the arrival of breakfast: a greasy fried-egg sandwich and a pint mug of tea. After this she was taken along the corridor to an area containing sinks where she was given a rough towel and told to wash. The only water available was icy.

She returned to her cell feeling tired, wrung out and wretched.

A calm had settled on Rowan by the time she was taken to the court and placed in an anteroom; she had convinced herself she would be home again before the day was over. Although quite alone, she found herself smiling.

She was held in the anteroom for half an hour, then a constable came in to tell her she was now due to go before the sheriff.

As she entered the courtroom the first people she saw were Meg and Ishbel sitting to one side. She gave them a small wave, and Ishbel waved back. Meg's face was drawn and haggard; it was clear she hadn't had much sleep the previous night, either.

There were a number of officials present, including the Reverend Dykes, his face expressionless.

Her name was read out, then she was escorted to a stand, where she was questioned by the sheriff, a kind-faced man wearing pince-nez.

A complaint had been registered by Dykes, and the medical reports confirmed that she was indeed pregnant. It was a cut-and-dried case, the sheriff said, and pronounced sentence. She was to be taken from the court to a lawful place of detention where she would be held until such time as the authorities deemed right for her release.

The impact of the sentence hit Rowan like a hammer blow. Her knees buckled, and she had to hang on to the stand to stop herself from pitching to the floor. She wasn't going home at all.

Everything became confused then. She was aware of raised voices, then hands were on her arms leading her from the court. She glanced round, but all the faces she saw were a blur, with the exception of Dykes. He looked smugly triumphant.

She walked along various corridors, then out into the open. She climbed into the back of a car where she sat with a man on one side, a woman on the other.

'Stoneydyke,' the man instructed the police driver.

She came apart then, dissolving into tears and hysteria. As the car was emerging from the yard at the rear of the court she heard a loud rushing wind that seemed to engulf her. In the wind were many coloured lights flashing on and off, dazzling her, hurting the inside of her head.

'Mummy!' she shrieked, fighting the hands pinioning her to the seat.

Then she fainted.

The police car stopped in front of a building which was large and constructed of red brick topped by a slate roof. It had many windows, all barred. Through one of the windows a vacuous face stared down at the car.

'Stoneydyke,' announced the driver.

Rowan swallowed hard, hating the building on first sight. A grim edifice that reflected precisely what it was: a mental institution.

'Come on,' said the woman, getting out of her side of the car.

The main door opened, and a burly female in a matron's

uniform came marching towards them, her expression as grim as the building.

'This is your patient, Miss Bethel,' declared the man.

The matron of Stoneydyke eyed Rowan up and down. 'Do you have the document?' she asked the man, who handed her a sheet of paper he'd taken from his coat pocket.

Miss Bethel produced a fountain pen, rested the paper on the roof of the car, and signed it at the bottom.

'Transfer complete, thank you,' she stated in a hard uncompromising voice.

Bethel grasped Rowan's arm and propelled her towards the door. Inside she locked the door using a key belonging to an enormous bunch that dangled on her left hip.

'Follow me,' ordered Bethel, and strode quickly off.

From somewhere upstairs a horrendous scream rang out.

'Strip,' said Bethel, turning on the taps of the nearest bath. There were eight baths in the room, all large and free-standing. Bethel put the plug in the bath, then crossed to a cupboard from which she took out a bottle. She poured a liberal measure from it into the bath, after which she returned it to the cupboard.

'When the bath's ready, use. And make sure you give yourself a good going-over. You'll be inspected before being allowed to dress again,' Bethel informed Rowan. She then swept from the room.

The water in the bath was a milky white, its smell indicating to Rowan that Bethel had put in a disinfectant of some sort. At least the water was hot, Rowan thought.

She was still soaping herself when Bethel came back carrying a pile of clothes and a towel. 'Hurry up. Don't take all day,' Bethel snapped, laying the clothes on a chair. She scooped up those Rowan had taken off and disappeared with them.

The towel was even rougher than the one Rowan had been given at the police station. She winced as she dried herself, as the towel left her skin streaked red in places. She had just finished when Bethel reappeared.

'Let me look at you,' she said.

Still holding the towel, Rowan dropped her hands to her sides while Bethel stared at her.

She grunted. 'Turn round.'

Burning with embarrassment, Rowan did as she was asked. At least it wasn't as bad as her experience with the doctors, she told herself.

'Fine. Now get dressed, and be quick about it. You've got work to do; there are no slackers here.'

Alone once more, Rowan picked up the thick calico knickers that lay on top of the pile and put them on. They were scratchy and made her itch. There was no bra, instead a vest that was even itchier than the knickers. The rest of the clothes comprised a uniform: grey blouse, grey woollen cardigan and a long grey skirt. The socks were grey, woollen also and matted. The shoes were black and clumpy.

Bethel returned again, scrutinized Rowan closely, then instructed Rowan to follow her. As they moved swiftly along a corridor Rowan felt like a dog hurrying at the heels of its master.

They halted in another corridor that seemed to stretch on endlessly. Bethel threw open a cupboard and took out a bucket with a scrubbing-brush inside plus a mop. These she thrust at Rowan.

They went to an adjacent room where there was a sink. Bethel told Rowan to fill the bucket with water and add some powder from a canister lying by the side of the sink.

When Rowan had done this she was taken back outside and ordered to start cleaning – scrubbing first, then mopping. She was to continue on down the corridor until relieved.

'You must change your water when necessary. Understand?' Bethel said.

Rowan nodded.

'Then, get to it.'

Rowan dropped to her knees and started scrubbing what appeared to her like an already pristine floor. Bethel stayed for a few moments to watch, then strode off.

What had she landed in? Rowan wondered, filled with foreboding. She gazed about, thinking Stoneydyke positively oozed unfriendliness.

Two nurses walked past chatting animatedly to one another. They completely ignored her as they trod over the small area she'd already cleaned.

Rowan used the mop to wipe away their footprints.

Rowan had never before appreciated how good a cook her mother was. The meal she'd been doled out was mutton stew swimming in grease, lumpy mashed potatoes and vegetables that had been boiled almost to destruction. It tasted nauseating.

She had to eat, she thought, forcing a morsel of mutton into her mouth, for the baby's sake if not her own. It was like chewing on a piece of old slimy leather.

Silence reigned in the dining-hall as talking was forbidden during meal-times. The only sounds were those of cutlery being used, interspersed by the rattle and clink of crockery.

Suddenly the female opposite Rowan threw back her head and began to laugh in a demented fashion. Her laugh made the hairs on Rowan's neck prickle.

'Oh, shit, she's off again,' someone commented in a low whisper.

The laughter grew and grew in volume, while the woman began flapping her arms up and down as if she was a bird trying to take off.

Nurses came running along the aisle to congregate round the woman. 'Stop this at once, Lizzie!' one of them commanded.

Lizzie paid no heed, but continued to laugh and flap.

Rowan watched as Lizzie was bundled out of her chair and frogmarched away.

A woman who'd been beside Lizzie surreptitiously helped herself to what remained on Lizzie's plate.

'Well, that was a worthwhile trip,' Vincent announced cheerfully as he breezed into the kitchen. He stopped dead when he saw Meg's stricken expression.

'What's wrong?' he demanded.

Meg told him.

'Holy Christ!' he exclaimed softly when she'd finished.

Tears crowded Meg's eyes. 'My angel,' she choked.

He went to her, knelt down and curled an arm round her shoulders. 'There, there,' he consoled.

'My wee angel,' Meg repeated.

'I'll see what I can do. There's a lawyer I know. I'll go to him for advice first thing tomorrow.'

Meg grasped at this straw. Everything in the court had happened at such bewildering speed. All she'd really taken in was that Rowan was to be locked away. 'Do you think he can help?' she asked hopefully.

'I'm sure he can,' Vincent replied. 'I'm sure he can.'

Meg wrung her hands. 'And you'll go first thing?'

'First thing,' Vincent promised her.

'Ishbel told me I'd find you here,' Fee said.

Meg, who'd been lost in thought, turned to find her mother beside her. 'I didn't hear you.'

Fee gazed at Cully's grave and sighed. 'You don't have much luck, do you?'

Meg shook her head.

'Your dad's distraught, to say the least. He says this sort of thing has never happened in our family before. Why, oh, why did Rowan do it!'

'She's young, I suppose.'

'But you brought her up knowing better than that. At least Cully isn't around to know what's happened.'

'How is Dad?' Lex hadn't been near her since Rowan's arrest.

'Thoroughly ashamed. He says he can't look anyone straight in the eye at work any more, and that they're talking and laughing behind his back. Thank the Lord we weren't in church when the minister pointed the finger. That would have finished him off.'

'He might have shown some support since then.'

'Support!' Fee exclaimed. 'If he'd laid hold of Rowan, he'd have knocked her silly. That's the support you'd have got.'

'I'm sorry if this is proving difficult for him. But it's not exactly easy for us, either.'

Fee relented a little. 'I'm sure it isn't. Talking of which, how did Vincent take it?'

'He's gone to see a lawyer he knows for advice. He'll be back later today.'

'That's good,' Fee nodded.

'I had no idea what sort of reaction I'd get from him. It could have been anything.'

'At least he doesn't have workmates to contend with. Not in the way your father has.'

'True,' Meg acknowledged. That hadn't been the case with Rory who, thankfully, seemed to be coping with the situation.

'Now let's go home and have a cup of tea. That'll be better for you than standing round here.'

'I should be working, but . . .' Meg trailed off and shook her head.

'I understand. It's all been a terrible blow.'

Meg had a last look at the grave, then turned away. She ached all over and had hardly slept a wink in the last few nights. She was deathly tired, but knew even now if she went to bed she wouldn't sleep.

'Mrs McLaren was full of it,' Fee said as they left the graveyard. Mrs McLaren was the neighbour with whom she was very friendly. 'Wanted to know all the ins and outs, every last detail. Well, there wasn't all that much I could tell her.'

Fee paused, then queried: 'And you've still no idea who the father is?'

'None,' Meg admitted.

'Children,' Fee sighed. 'You gave me a few problems in

176

your time, but nothing like this. What came over the girl?'

'She was unlucky, too, I suppose,' Meg muttered. As unlucky as she could be.

Meg leapt to her feet the moment she heard the front door open. Ishbel rose also, but Rory remained seated. When Vincent entered the room she knew the news wasn't good. 'Well?'

He made a face. 'They've every right to put her away. That's the law.'

'And there's nothing we can do about it?'

'Having sex under the legal age of consent, and getting pregnant into the bargain, means she's classed as feeble-minded and a moral imbecile. Those were the lawyer's exact words.'

'Feeble-minded!' Meg exclaimed. There was nothing feeble-minded about Rowan.

'That's how they class her,' Vincent went on. 'If I remember correctly, he said the law under which she'd been put away was the Mental Deficiency and Lunacy Act. It was introduced into Scotland in 1913.'

Meg returned to her chair and slumped into it.

'And that's why she's been taken off to a mental institution as opposed to anywhere else,' Vincent explained.

'How long for?' Ishbel asked.

Vincent shrugged. 'They may review the case after she's turned sixteen, by which time she'll have had the baby. There's the possibility they might release her then, particularly as she has a family to return to. But my lawyer friend didn't hold out too much hope in that respect. The chances are they'll keep her in for a considerable time.'

'It's a disgrace,' Rory said vehemently.

'I agree. But the law is against her, not to mention the minister. Don't forget how powerful a figure he is.'

'It was you who called him in,' Rory accused.

'I don't deny it. But he would have found out; there was never any way round that. Not unless we'd sent Rowan off somewhere, which with hindsight we might have done. But who'd have guessed he'd have reported her to the authorities and lodged a complaint against her? Certainly not me.'

'He's a bastard!' Rory swore.

'Don't,' said Meg. 'He is the minister after all.'

'How can you defend him after what he's done!' Rory exclaimed.

'I'm not defending him personally. It's his office I'm thinking about,' Meg replied.

'I've done all I can, Meg. I'm sorry,' Vincent said to her.

'God!' she whispered, burying her head in her hands.

'I'm going out,' declared Rory, coming quickly to his feet.

'Where?' Ishbel asked.

'It doesn't matter. Anywhere. Just out.' And with that he blundered from the room.

'I miss her so much,' Ishbel whispered. 'When can we see her?'

Vincent glanced over at Ishbel. 'I don't know. We'll have to wait to find out.'

'Soon, I hope,' Ishbel said.

'Soon,' Meg repeated in a mumble from behind her hands.

Vincent could tell from Meg's breathing that she was still awake. He shifted restlessly and felt her tense. His body was clamouring for release, but he was hesitant about approaching her. It would hardly be fair in the circumstances.

He was only too aware of how upset she was; but she might accommodate him if he made a move. Life had to go on after all, he argued to himself.

He shifted again, and pulled the clothes up under his chin. What an inconvenience this was, and how long before Meg was herself again? He hated to think.

He turned towards her, and as he did she edged away from him, taking herself to the far side of the bed.

He swore mentally. 'Meg?'

There was a long pause. 'Yes?' she answered at last in a small voice.

'How are you now?'

'How do you think?'

He reached out and placed a hand on her hip. 'Is there anything I can get you?'

'What do you mean?'

'I don't know. Anything.'

'Go to sleep, Vincent.'

'I could make you some cocoa.' He loathed the idea of getting out of bed but would do it if it helped get him what he wanted.

'No, thanks.'

'Or hot milk?'

'I'm fine.'

'I can feel you all tensed up.'

'Am I keeping you awake?'

'No,' he lied.

She pulled her hips away, dislodging his hand. 'Then, go to sleep.'

He swore again mentally. 'Or how about tea?'

'Good night, Vincent.'

He rolled on to his back and sucked in a deep breath. Let it be, he counselled himself. For that night anyway.

He began thinking of the business he'd conducted while away on his trip. That had been most satisfactory and realized him an excellent profit. And there was that travelling girl he'd met. Now, there was a cracker! If only it was her in bed with him now rather than Meg.

He continued thinking about the travelling girl until eventually he dropped off.

Rowan stopped scrubbing when the scream rang out. It was a similarly horrendous scream to the one which had greeted her arrival at Stoneydyke. 'What's that?' she asked Josie scrubbing beside her.

Josie pushed herself up into a sitting position. She was enjoying being teamed with Rowan because Rowan seemed so much kinder than the others. 'Someone in the treatment room,' she explained.

Rowan recalled Barbara mentioning this treatment. 'What are they doing to her?'

'She's being given electrical shocks. They have a variety of shock treatments here.'

Rowan gulped. 'Shock treatments!'

'That's right. They strap you down, attach these wire things to your head, and then *bang*!'

Rowan stared at Josie in alarm and dismay.

'You don't half jump, I can tell you,' Josie elaborated.

'You've had it, then?'

Josie shuddered. 'Often. It's very painful. And while they're doing it to you your body jerks and chucks itself about something awful.'

'But why?' Rowan queried.

'To try to cure you of course.'

'There's nothing wrong with me, so surely I won't get it?'

A sly look came over Josie's face. 'You'll get it all right. But not until after the baby's born, for safety's sake.'

Rowan digested that piece of information. Electrical shocks, wires attached to her head. It didn't bear thinking about!

Another scream rang out, this one absolutely blood-curdling.

Josie cackled and returned to her scrubbing. 'You'd better get on,' she advised Rowan. 'If an orderly catches you day-dreaming you're likely to get his toe up your backside.'

A fearful Rowan hurriedly set to her scrubbing as well.

'Sherry, dear?' Hugh Monteith asked his wife Sybil.

'Please.'

He poured her a small measure, then himself a far larger one of malt whisky. 'There you are, my dear,' he said, handing her the sherry.

'I must drop by the McQueens' when I'm out later,' Sybil said.

Hugh glanced at her over the rim of his glass. 'The McQueens'? Whatever for?'

'To offer my sympathy, and take Meg in some curtain material I want made up.'

His expression became one of disapproval. 'I forbid it, Sybil. You'll have nothing whatsoever to do with that family. They're a disgrace.'

Sybil laid her sherry aside and regarded her husband levelly. 'If I stop taking Meg work, then I destroy her livelihood.'

'That's none of our concern.'

'Oh, but it is, Hugh. It's precisely that.'

Anger flared in him. 'I categorically forbid it, Sybil, do you hear?'

'Where's your Christian charity, dear?' she countered softly.

'Christian charity nothing!' he declared. 'We've washed our hands of that family once and for all. When that girl lost her character they lost our business as far as I'm concerned.'

'That's hardly fair, Hugh.'

'Fair! I would say it's exactly that. I can't afford to be seen employing such people. Think of my reputation.'

'Aren't you being just a teensy self-righteous?'

He knew the signs. Sybil had set her heart on something he was dead against. He guessed correctly that she'd instigated this conversation for a confrontation on the subject.

'I repeat, I forbid you to give them any more work,' he stated pompously.

'Do you know what you look like right now, darling? A strutting pigeon with its feathers all puffed up,' she teased.

He glared at her. 'You saw what happened in church when the minister spoke out against the girl.'

'I thought that deplorable. This is nineteen twenty-seven after all, not the Middle Ages.'

'It may be nineteen twenty-seven, but we're dealing with the Church of Scotland. The Government may prevail in matters temporal, but the Kirk prevails in matters moral and spiritual. And prevails with a rule of iron, as you well know.'

'That's as may be,' countered Sybil. 'But Jesus Christ

181

preached forgiveness and understanding, not condemnation and castigation.'

His face softened. 'You're a tender-hearted woman, Sybil, which I admire about you and was one of the things that drew me to you in the first place, I believe. But I do not subscribe to modern thinking; that would only bring about a weakening of the fabric of our society.'

'Poppycock!' Sybil exclaimed. 'A weakening, my foot. Besides, you believe in whatever suits you. As I've often commented on.'

'That's not true!'

'Oh, yes, it is. You're a born hypocrite, Hugh Monteith, whose business practices are as sharp as a butcher's knife.'

He drank some more whisky, remembering that he'd received several cases of it from a grateful contractor. 'I prefer to describe my business dealings as astute,' he replied.

'Well, naturally you do. Far more acceptable.'

He finished his whisky and poured himself another tot. Damn fine stuff, this, he thought, and hoped more of the same would be forthcoming. 'I'm not going against the minister,' he stated.

'Leave him to me. I can quote the Bible as well as any mealy-mouthed preacher.'

'You seem to forget, Sybil,' he said drily. 'The average man in Glenshields holds that self-same mealy-mouthed preacher in awe and veneration. Seeing him as literally the mouth and hand of the Lord God Almighty.'

She had to concede that point. But it didn't alter her resolve. She would do what she considered right, and that was an end of it. 'I believe the minister would think twice before crossing swords with us, such an important family in the area,' she said. She was convinced that Dykes was just as much a hypocrite as her husband. It was one thing to lambast poor Rowan Stewart, quite another to take on the largest employer in the village.

'Meg McQueen has enough to contend with without us adding to her troubles. Besides, by continuing to give her work, though not condoning the actions of her daughter, I might ease her troubles somewhat.'

'I'm totally against this,' Hugh stated, knowing he was fighting a losing battle. He always seemed to lose where Sybil was concerned.

'We will do the right thing, the Christian thing,' Sybil told him.

'And if I continue to put my foot down?'

The answer to that was silence.

'Very well,' he relented, the silence having taken root in his imagination. 'Do as you wish.'

She went to him and kissed him on the cheek. 'Thank you, darling. You're a true Christian.'

With a little guidance from her, she qualified mentally.

'They're ... beautiful,' Meg stammered, gazing at the large bunch of flowers Sybil Monteith had just handed her.

'From our own hothouses.'

'It's so very kind of you,' Meg beckoned Ishbel over. 'Go and put these in water straight away.'

Ishbel took the flowers and vanished from the sitting-room.

Meg brushed a stray wisp of hair away from her forehead. 'I wasn't sure that . . .'

Sybil laid a hand on Meg's arm. 'I can't say how sorry I was to learn of your misfortune. It must be extremely trying for you.'

Meg bowed her head. 'Yes,' she whispered.

'How are the villagers reacting?'

'Mixed,' Meg answered. 'Some have cut me dead, others sort of smirk when they talk to me. Others have been ... sympathetic.'

'Difficult indeed.'

'Very,' Meg agreed.

'I thought it time I dropped by to discuss your working for me.'

'I would understand perfectly if you wish to terminate our agreement,' Meg said in a low voice.

'On the contrary, I want you to know that I wish it to continue.'

'You do! I fully expected . . .'

'Of course I don't condone what happened, and I want to make that quite clear. None the less, I don't see that you should be penalized for your daughter's misdemeanours.'

'Again, you're very kind, Mrs Monteith. I can't thank you enough.'

'I can't promise that my friends will take the same view. But I can promise that I shall do everything in my power to try to persuade them to continue using your services as I shall be doing.'

This was a huge relief to Meg, who enjoyed being financially independent of Vincent. And there was Ishbel to consider; this meant that her job was secure and she wouldn't have to go hunting for another.

Meg clasped her hands together, and a spasm of pain shot over her face.

'Is something wrong?' Sybil enquired.

'Arthritis, Mrs Monteith. I get it in my hands, and it's been worse since Rowan was taken away.'

'My poor dear. I suffer from it myself, as you know. It's the most horrid and inconvenient thing.'

Meg nodded her agreement.

'There's a lot of it in this part of the country, and the climate certainly doesn't help.'

'I only hope mine doesn't spread,' Meg said, glancing down at her hands. That had been added to her list of worries recently.

'Let's hope it doesn't,' Sybil commiserated.

Meg took a deep breath. 'Now, can I get you a cup of tea, Mrs Monteith? I'd be delighted to do so.'

'And I'd be delighted if you did,' Sybil smiled.

Meg was pleased about that; it was a small way of showing her gratitude. She would send Ishbel out to buy some fancy cakes, she thought. If she'd known Mrs Monteith was going to call, she'd have baked some herself.

*   *   *

The woman was in her twenties, thin as a rake with long bony arms. She was sitting cowering in a chair, her expression one of stark terror.

'No,' she whimpered, drawing her legs up to her chest.

'What's wrong with her?' Rowan asked Barbara.

Barbara stared at the woman. 'She's been to the treatment room.'

The woman encircled her legs with her arms and began rocking back and forth. Spittle appeared at one side of her mouth, only to dribble its way down her chin.

'Are you all right, Peg?' Barbara called out.

Peg focused on Barbara. 'They ... they ...' She broke off, and turned her face away from Rowan and Barbara.

'I was worse than that the first time I had it,' Barbara said softly.

Peg gave a small animal-type cry and started to shake violently all over.

Was that how she'd react when her time came? Rowan wondered. Would she be reduced to a shaking bag of flesh? She shuddered at the prospect.

'Not very pretty,' commented Barbara.

Rowan sucked in a breath. 'No,' she agreed.

'Still, you don't have to worry for a long while yet.'

Rowan touched her middle where the growing baby was; Gray's baby. While she was carrying it she was safe, for which she silently thanked God. But the day would come when the baby would be born; then it would be her turn for the treatment room.

The thought petrified her.

Rowan paused to wipe sweat from her brow. She'd been taken off scrubbing duties and assigned to the laundry room, where she was expected to hump heavy baskets of dirty laundry once they arrived to the large coppers in which everything was boiled. The heat in the room was tremendous.

'Haven't seen you here before,' a dark-haired woman said to her.

'I'm new at this,' Rowan explained.

The woman nodded. 'Anne Allen's the name.'

'And I'm Rowan Stewart.'

Anne gazed about. 'There are worse jobs than this – toilet-cleaning for one.' She pulled a face. 'That can be awful. It's incredible the mess some of them get into.'

Rowan could imagine.

'I've seen sights in toilets that would turn the strongest of stomachs, some of it done quite intentionally. I tell you, it could make you ashamed of your own sex.'

Anne peered at Rowan. 'You don't look like one of the fruitcakes, so what are you in for?'

Rowan dropped her gaze in embarrassment. 'I'm pregnant,' she replied quietly.

'And not married, eh?'

Rowan didn't answer.

'How old are you?'

'Fifteen.'

Anne sighed. 'It was the same with me, only in my case I was fourteen. I had a lovely little boy who got adopted. You can keep the child, but they make it very difficult for you. They prefer the child to be adopted.'

'Fourteen!' Rowan exclaimed. 'So how long have you been here?'

'Twenty years.'

'Twenty . . . !' Rowan gulped. 'They've kept you in for twenty years?'

'Bastards, aren't they? When I went with the lad I hadn't a clue about the facts of life; they were a total mystery. That's the God's honest truth. We were on a picnic, and one thing led to another. How I've paid for that bit of fun.'

Rowan was stunned; Anne was the first person she'd met at Stoneydyke who was there for the same offence as her. 'But surely they should have let you out long before now?' she protested.

'They can do as they like. Once you're in here you're theirs to deal with as they wish. They can keep you locked away for ever if they choose. And there are plenty they've done that to.'

Twenty years in Stoneydyke – the idea was mind-boggling. Why, long before then she'd be as crazy as most of the inmates. And what if they incarcerated her for life!

'I often think of my little boy,' Anne said wistfully. 'Wonder about him, what he looks like, how he grew up, that sort of thing. He might even be married himself now for all I know. He had silky blond hair and a beautiful smile. I called him John after his dad!'

'What happened to the father?' Rowan asked.

Anne shrugged. 'Didn't want to know. And of course he got off scot-free; there was no being locked away for him. He said he loved me, but was lying. He took to his heels when I told him I was pregnant, and I never saw him again.'

Rowan's senses were reeling at this bombshell. 'I thought they'd let me go when I turned sixteen,' she said.

'You'll be lucky. Twenty-one maybe, but only maybe. I wouldn't pin too many hopes on it.'

Anne stared sympathetically at Rowan. 'What about your chap? Was it the same with him?'

'No, he'd gone abroad before I found out I was pregnant, and there wasn't any way of getting in touch with him. I know he'd have married me if he'd stayed.'

'And now you're here, eh?'

Rowan nodded.

'I'm sure there are worse places than Stoneydyke, but not many. It's a hellhole, and no mistake.'

Despair overwhelmed Rowan and was replaced by a sense of panic. She wanted to run screaming from the laundry room, home to Meg, to the love and security from which she'd been so abruptly wrenched.

'I'll speak to you again later,' Anne said, spotting an orderly who'd appeared at the far end of the laundry room. She hurried away.

Rowan went to fetch another basket of soiled articles to

take to the coppers. A haze of tears formed over her eyes as she bent to lift it.

Rowan sat on the broad window-sill gazing out, her view spoiled by the iron bars that crossed the window as they did every window in Stoneydyke. Somewhere a bird sang, a joyous song that under different circumstances would have brought a smile to her lips. But not now, not there. She didn't think she'd ever smile again.

They can keep you locked away for ever if they choose. Those words had been going round and round inside her head since Anne Allen had uttered them earlier. It seemed impossible that they could do such a thing for a relatively minor offence, which was how she viewed it, but Anne was living proof that they could.

Living? You could hardly call being in Stoneydyke that. It was the dreariest and hardest of existences, hour after hour of back-breaking drudgery. They drove you from morning till night with few moments like this where you could relax and catch your breath.

Locked up for ever with lunatics, and others she'd never normally dreamt of associating with, as company. And what about the baby when it came? Anne had talked about adoption, the baby taken away never to be seen, or heard of, by her again. While she languished in Stoneydyke, wondering, regretting, eaten alive by remorse and ongoing despair.

'Oh, Gray!' she whispered, picturing him in her mind. How she loved and missed him. If only he hadn't gone away when he had, this would never have occurred, for she was certain he'd have stood by her, done the right thing. If only he'd known the outcome of their sleeping together. If only . . .

The bird sang again. Or was that merely in her imagination? She wasn't sure. She was already learning that reality and fantasy could become strangely intertwined at Stoneydyke, for the sane as well as for the insane.

They can keep you locked away for ever if they choose. She felt like an animal who'd unwittingly walked into a trap, a trap from which there was no escape.

'So how's your sister? Have you heard?' enquired Bill Patterson innocently.

Rory shook his head.

'And you never discovered who the father is?'

Rory knew he was being provoked, that Bill was probing, thinking it great sport. He shook his head again.

Bill turned away and made some comment which Rory didn't catch, but which caused others to laugh.

'What was that?' Rory demanded.

'Pardon?' Bill queried, using an innocent tone.

'What did you say?'

'I simply remarked I wished it was tea-break.'

That was a blatant lie, as Rory was well aware. It had been a crack about Rowan. 'Watch it,' Rory cautioned through gritted teeth.

Bill glanced about. 'Watch what? Where?'

'Your mouth.'

'Hard to do that. Unless in a mirror.' Bill guffawed, considering himself extremely funny, and walked off, winking to several of their workmates as he went.

Rory was livid, both with Bill who was usually a nice enough bloke, and with Rowan for landing him in this predicament. He loved her, they always had been particularly close, but at the same time he would never forgive her for what she'd done. How could she have let herself and the rest of the family down so badly? He was humiliated beyond belief, both within himself and by the provocation and ridicule he had to endure.

He'd come to hate his work and home. Perhaps he should leave both and make a fresh start somewhere else. But it would be such a break leaving behind everything he'd previously held so dear. The temptation, however, was great.

He busied himself with the job in hand, forcing himself to concentrate, trying to drive all else from his mind.

*　　*　　*

'You look ... dreadful,' Meg breathed. It was three months since Rowan had been taken to Stoneydyke, and this was the first visit Meg had been allowed. Ishbel was with her.

Rowan had changed dramatically during these three months. Her face was spotted with pimples; while her hair, now cut short and ragged at the ends, was dry and listless. Her face beneath the pimples had gone a pasty shade of grey.

'The food isn't very good,' Rowan replied dully.

Ishbel stared at her twin in dismay, finding her almost unrecognizable as the golden girl of only such a short time ago. 'What have you done to your hair?' she asked.

Rowan ran a hand through it. 'Easier this way. Easier to keep. I cut it myself.'

Hacked it more like, Meg thought. And those pimples! Rowan had never been bothered with pimples in the past.

'Your tummy is naturally bigger, but other than that you've lost weight,' Ishbel commented.

'As I said, the food isn't very good. I eat what I can.'

Meg was thoroughly shaken, the transformation in Rowan so horrendous. How thin she'd become – with the exception of the baby, that was – to the point of being skeletal. Blue veins stood out on her hands and wrists, and there were dark circles under her eyes.

'I shall complain to the person in charge. A Miss Bethel, isn't it?' Meg said.

Rowan grasped her mother's arm. 'Don't do that; it would only make matters worse. They'd take it out on me afterwards, you see. They don't like complaints.'

'But . . .'

'Don't, Mum, please,' Rowan pleaded, animation coming into her face for the first time.

'All right, darling, if that's what you want.'

The animation disappeared again. 'Shall we sit down?'

The room Meg and Ishbel had been conducted to was bare with the exception of a plain wooden table round which a number of chairs had been placed. They sat facing newspaper had slipped to the floor while his head had slumped forward. As she watched him he began to snore gently, his chest rising and falling in unison with the snores. He'd complain of a sore neck when he woke, she thought. He always did after he'd dozed off in the chair.

Rory lay in the darkness thinking about Fraser's motorbike. What a smasher it was, and what a bargain. Fraser had been so lucky to find it.

Well, one day he would own a bike just like it. He could picture himself roaring through the village and other villages in the area. What a dashing figure he would cut in leather helmet and goggles, face smudged and streaked with oil as he opened up the throttle.

He was saving hard, but it would be a long time yet before he could realize his dream.

'Brooommmm!' he muttered to himself. 'Broommm, broommm, brooommmm!'

He placed his hands behind his head and continued fantasizing about Fraser's bike, and the bike he would own some day.

'Bed,' Cully said, rising abruptly from his chair. The twins had gone through a while ago, and Rory shortly after that.

Meg paused in her mending to glance at the brass clock. Somehow the last hour or two had simply flown by.

Cully opened the door to the fire, raked over the coals, then back-banked them with dross so that the fire could be easily relit in the morning. Meg rose and put away her mending. As she was doing this, Cully locked up.

In their bedroom Meg turned down the covers. She was undressing when Cully joined her.

Having shrugged into her nightdress Meg slipped between the sheets, making a face at the coldness of them; but she knew it would soon disappear once Cully was alongside her.

Cully took his time, carefully folding and draping each article of clothing over a chair. It was a habit he'd acquired in the Army.

'Good night, Cully love,' Meg whispered when he was settled on his side of the bed.

'Good night, Meg.'

A few seconds ticked by. 'Meg?'

'Yes?'

'I'm not in the least bit sleepy now.'

She knew what that meant, what he was leading up to. 'I am.'

'Oh!'

Her lips thinned and curled upwards to hear the disappointment in his voice. 'The girls need new shoes,' she said.

He didn't reply.

'Did you hear me?'

'The girls need new shoes,' he echoed.

'And I'm cold.'

There was a hesitant pause. 'Me, too.'

'It might help if you cuddled me.'

'Ay,' he answered eagerly, turning and reaching for her.

She shut her eyes as his arms curled round her bosom, and he inched closer till they were touching. How reassuring his embrace was, she thought, and how safe it made her feel. It was like a ship reaching port after a storm.

She could smell his maleness and feel the hardness of his body, which was now pressing urgently against her own.

He began to move, causing her nightdress to shift up and down.

'Cully?'

'What?'

'The new shoes. Can I get them at the weekend?'

His hand moved to find the opening at the front of her nightdress and delved inside, seeking out a breast. 'If the girls have to have them, then you'd better.'

'And Rory . . .'

24

'Quiet, woman. Enough!' he breathed firmly.

'Am I upsetting you?' she asked, tongue in cheek.

'Why don't you stop yapping and kiss me?'

'Yapping? Me?'

'Yapping,' he repeated, and covered her mouth with his.

She squirmed as his other hand snaked up the length of her thigh.

'Oh, Meg,' he whispered in her ear.

'I'm getting warmer. Maybe that's enough cuddling,' she teased.

He muttered an expletive which made her laugh.

'Maybe not,' she added as a new hardness prodded her.

It was a tender loving, the two of them rocking together as one. Then it was over.

She took his hand and squeezed it tight. 'You're lovely, Cully.'

'And so are you, lass.'

'Don't go away. Stay close.'

'If you want.'

He snuggled up again, putting an arm round her waist.

'Are you sleepy now?' she asked softly.

'Mmm!'

She smiled to hear that. 'Good.'

'And you?'

'I was to start with.'

'Good night again.'

'Good night.'

She was thinking about the price of shoes as she drifted off into the sweet all-enveloping blackness.

Cully stared at the plate of bacon, eggs, black pudding, fried bread and tomatoes that Meg had laid in front of him as his Sunday-morning treat. 'I don't think I can eat this,' he said.

Meg stared at him in astonishment. 'What's wrong with it?'

'Nothing. It's just that my stomach is giving me gyp.'

'So early!' This was unusual; he hadn't even had a drink the night before.

He nodded miserably. 'Ever since I got up this morning.'

'I'll have your breakfast if you don't want it,' Rory said hopefully.

'Greedy Guts,' jibed Rowan.

'I'm nothing of the sort. I simply don't want it to go to waste,' Rory retorted in a sanctimonious tone.

Ishbel laughed. 'That's right. I can see how concerned you are.'

'Well?' Rory asked his father.

'Help yourself,' Cully answered, pushing the plate in his son's direction.

'Is there anything else I can get you?' Meg enquired.

Cully shook his head. He rose and slumped into his easy chair.

'A powder and milk perhaps?' Meg queried. He took powders for his recurrent indigestion.

Cully nodded. 'Please.'

'I don't think I feel very well, either,' declared Ishbel.

'Too bad,' replied Meg. 'You're still going to church.'

'Oh, Mum!'

'Oh, Mum, nothing. It's kirk for you, my girl. Then, if you're still unwell when we get back, you can trot off to bed and miss dinner.'

Ishbel sniffed. There was nothing wrong with her, of course. Meg had realized she'd merely been trying to get out of church.

'Too bad,' whispered Rowan. She'd been about to try the same trick, but Ishbel had beaten her to it.

Cully clutched his middle and bent forward. 'Christ!' he muttered.

Rory finished his plateful and began wolfing down his father's. 'Can I have a piece of that fried bread?' Rowan asked him.

'Get lost.'

'The pair of you might show some consideration for your poor dad,' Meg snapped.

'Sorry,' Rory and Rowan muttered together.

'I should think so,' Meg frowned.

26

one another, Meg and Ishbel together, Rowan opposite.

'So how is it in Stoneydyke?' Meg asked.

'Difficult,' Rowan answered.

'What do you do all day long?'

Rowan related a typical day: her work in the laundry room, scrubbing duties to which she was occasionally switched back, kitchen duty – a list of her endless daily toil.

'Have you made any friends?' Ishbel enquired.

Rowan considered telling them about Anne Allen and decided not to; she'd spare them that. 'A few,' she mumbled.

'And what are they here for?' Meg asked.

'It's a mental asylum, Mum; they're here for being mad. Except me, and a few like me.'

'And you're forced to mix with these people?' Meg went on.

'I can't avoid them.'

'I hope none of them is dangerous?'

Rowan thought of Cissie. 'They have methods and means of dealing with those.'

That sounded sinister, Ishbel thought. 'But none of them has caused you any harm?'

Rowan had been looking forward to this visit. Now she found her sister and mother irritating and wished they'd go away. What did they know? How could they even begin to understand? How could she explain she wasn't the Rowan who'd come to Stoneydyke? It might only be three months in actual time, but for her it had been an eternity, a sleeping, dreaming, waking, nightmarish eternity. 'No,' she answered truthfully. Then added to herself: Not yet.

'Are you in a dormitory?' Meg asked.

Rowan nodded.

'What's it like?'

'Fine,' Rowan lied. In truth it was appalling: eighteen women who were crowded together, some who snored, others who cried out in the night, a few incontinents who caused dreadful smells. And then the wailer, who like a wolf at full moon howled at least once a week, sometimes twice, all through the night. Nor could you get her to shut up once she started. You'd have thought the staff would have done something about her, but they didn't, probably because she was harmless.

'Let's look on the bright side. They could release you when you're sixteen, which isn't that far off.'

Rowan regarded her sister impassively. When she was sixteen! There was about as much chance of that as Ishbel had of suddenly sprouting wings.

'That's true,' Meg smiled.

Rowan didn't answer.

'Rory sends his regards,' Ishbel fibbed. He hadn't at all.

'And so, too, does Vincent.' Vincent had, but only because he'd known it was expected of him.

'We all miss you,' Meg declared.

Rowan didn't answer that, either.

'How is the pregnancy coming along?' Meg enquired. 'Any problems?'

Rowan shrugged. 'Not really. I get terrible indigestion from time to time, but that's about all.'

'Will you have the baby here or in a proper hospital?' Ishbel asked.

'Here.'

'Attended by a good doctor and midwife, I hope?' Meg said.

'I'm sure they'll do their best,' Rowan replied drily. Good doctor and midwife indeed! She'd get whoever was available; good didn't come into it. Delivery procedures varied, she'd been told. One woman had simply been left to get on with it by herself.

'I hope they won't work you so hard closer to your time?' Meg said.

Fat chance, Rowan thought. She'd be grafting like stink up until the last possible moment.

'Well?' Meg prompted.

'I presume,' Rowan replied.

Ishbel stared into her twin's eyes which had been so bright and alive. Now they were dead, the spark that had once illuminated them extinguished. She could have cried.

'I brought you some treats which were taken away when I arrived. I was assured you'd get them later,' Meg said.

'Thank you. I'll look forward to them,' Rowan answered, knowing full well they'd never be handed over. Treats and gifts never were. But she wouldn't tell Meg. Let her mother believe otherwise. Why cause her unnecessary distress?

'You must try to eat more,' Ishbel urged.

'I eat enough to keep myself and the baby going,' Rowan replied. That was difficult considering half the time the slop served up wasn't fit for pigswill.

Rowan was thankful when it was finally time for Meg and Ishbel to leave. Their visit had been a complete disappointment. They'd tried hard enough, but she was no longer part of them. She didn't belong with them any more; she belonged to Stoneydyke and that hideous world.

'We'll come again as soon as we can,' Meg promised at the door.

Rowan nodded.

Meg forced herself to kiss her daughter's pimply face. 'Take care of yourself.'

Rowan almost laughed aloud to hear that.

'We all love you,' Ishbel added, kissing Rowan.

'How are the Shielers doing?' Rowan asked suddenly, which caught both Meg and Ishbel by surprise. The football season had recently started again.

'They won on Saturday,' Ishbel answered.

She fought back the temptation to enquire how Craigkip had fared; they might wonder about that. 'Goodbye, then.'

When Meg and Ishbel were gone Rowan returned to the laundry room only to learn that during her absence Anne had fallen foul of an orderly and had been punched.

He would have punched her, too, irrespective of the fact she was carrying a baby, Rowan thought. That was Stoneydyke for you.

*　　*　　*

193

Vincent was fed up with Meg, who had become morose, introspective and boring since the Rowan incident. All the fun had gone out of her; she never laughed or joked any more, and rarely left the house except to go to the Monteiths' to collect and return work.

Vincent sighed. The only thing he couldn't complain about was her cooking: there had been no drop-off in that department, thank God. And the house continued to be clean and tidy. But the woman herself! That was something else entirely.

He thought grimly of their sex life. It had deteriorated drastically of late; and, although he understood that Meg was worried, she seemed to have little time for him. He wondered if she still thought about Cully. As Rowan was his daughter, he would have been able to support Meg more readily, found the right words, offered her the kind of love she was looking for. Vincent did try, but Meg seemed so unresponsive. And when she did consent it was 'Please hurry up'. She failed to recognize his needs.

He tapped the wheel of his car in frustration, wishing things could go back to how they'd been when they'd first married. She'd been compliant enough in bed then, and a laugh to be with. Now everything had turned on its head. Meg just wasn't the same at all since Rowan had been carted off.

He promised himself he'd have his way that night. Why should he suffer? It simply wasn't fair.

His gloom lifted. He'd take her back a little something, he decided. A box of chocolates perhaps. That should go down well. Bribery and corruption! he thought, and laughed.

'Women,' he said, and shook his head.

A sudden jagged pain lanced through Rowan's insides causing her to yelp. She dropped the basket she was humping, scattering its contents over the floor. She doubled over when another crippling wave followed the first.

Anne Allen hurried across. 'Are you all right, Rowan?'

Rowan, face contorted, explained about the pains.

'Do you think you've started?'

'Too early,' Rowan mumbled in reply.

Anne put her arms round her. 'You'd better sit down.'

An orderly joined them. 'Why have you stopped working?' he demanded.

'She's got stomach cramps,' Anne said.

'Oh, ay!' the orderly exclaimed disbelievingly.

'I'll be fine in a moment,' Rowan muttered.

The orderly smiled. 'Thought you'd use that belly of yours to do a bit of malingering, is that it?'

Rowan shook her head.

'I know the tricks you lot get up to. Any excuse to skive.' Then scornfully added: 'You must think me a right mug!'

'She's not trying to have you on. Surely you can see that!' Anne protested.

The orderly stared hard at Rowan. 'Are you going into labour?'

'I don't think so. It doesn't feel like that. And it's too soon anyway.'

'So it's simply supposed stomach cramps?'

'Let her sit down for a while,' Anne pleaded.

'Not on your life. I'm not getting a name as a soft touch, or have the pair of you laughing at me behind my back. She can pick up that stuff she's dropped and get on with it.'

'I'll manage,' said Rowan, straightening. The pains appeared to have gone.

'I'll help you,' declared Anne, scooping up a few items from the floor and tossing them back into the basket.

'Leave that. You've got your own work,' the orderly told her.

'Thanks, Anne, I'll be all right,' Rowan smiled weakly.

'On your way,' the orderly instructed Anne, who reluctantly left them.

The orderly stood and watched as Rowan gathered up the remainder of the spilled laundry, then staggered off under the weight of the basket.

Heartless bugger, she thought. But, then, most of the orderlies were. They just couldn't give a damn.

To her relief, the pains didn't recur.

'Mum's devastated that she can't come, but she's flat out in bed with flu,' Ishbel said. She was alone with Rowan in the same bleak room they had met in previously.

'You should have stayed and looked after her,' Rowan answered.

'She'd have none of that. She's anxious to hear your news. She wanted you to know that life at home is much better these days. The other night Vincent brought her back a box of chocolates – you can imagine how delighted she was.'

Ishbel thought Rowan looked even worse than before. She was, unbelievably, thinner still, while the circles under her eyes were larger and darker.

'That sounds good,' Rowan replied dully, desperately trying to remember what chocolate had tasted like. 'News? I don't have any. Every day here is more or less the same. It gets so you can hardly distinguish one from another.'

'Are you eating more?'

'I try,' Rowan lied. 'But it's so unappetizing.'

'What about your work? Have they stopped you doing so much? Your time can't be far away now.'

'A couple of weeks only,' Rowan stated.

'And the work?' Ishbel persisted.

Rowan could see how concerned her sister was. 'They've cut my duties right back,' she further lied.

Ishbel sighed. 'That's something anyway.'

Silence fell between them, neither able to think of anything to say. Rowan found it curious. In the past they'd never had any trouble chatting together. Now it was as if they were strangers.

Rowan suddenly reached out and grasped Ishbel's arm. 'I want you to make me a promise.'

'Of course. Anything.'

'I've been thinking about the birth. Things do go wrong,

you know; women die. It happens. If I should die, I want you to bring up the baby. They'd want to have it adopted, you see, which I don't.'

'Don't talk nonsense. You won't die,' Ishbel protested.

'But it's possible. So promise me, Ish, please?'

Ishbel nodded. 'I promise.'

'You'd have to go straight to Miss Bethel and demand the baby. If you left it even a short while, the baby could be gone, and then there would be no getting it back.'

'I'll go to her right away, but I'm sure I won't have to.'

'Probably not. But it eases my mind to know the baby will be safe with you if anything occurred.'

Ishbel was finding this conversation frightening. She'd never considered the possibility of Rowan dying in childbirth. And yet Rowan was right; it did happen.

Now that Rowan had extracted the promise she'd have been pleased for Ishbel to leave. She removed her hand and stared past her sister into space. She was seeing their house, the bedroom she'd shared since childhood with Ishbel, the bed where they'd slept together. She visualized Meg, Rory, her dead father Cully in his chair reading a newspaper. How long till she returned there? Five years? Perhaps ten? Perhaps never.

'Rowan?'

She roused herself from her reverie to gaze at Ishbel. She would have given anything to be in Ishbel's shoes, free to walk away from Stoneydyke and do whatever she chose. If she'd had a magic wand, would she have waved it, transporting herself into Ishbel's body and Ishbel into hers? No, she couldn't have done that, inflict on Ishbel what had been inflicted on her. She loved her sister far too deeply for that. But how she envied Ishbel and everyone else who was free to go about their daily business, do as they wished.

'News?' Rowan repeated in a strange tight voice. 'I don't have any.'

'Who was the father?' Ishbel asked. 'Won't you tell even me?'

'He can't help. Never could. By the time I discovered I was pregnant it was already too late.'

197

Ishbel was baffled. 'I don't understand.'

'Too late,' Rowan repeated, and shook her head.

Another silence ensued, broken only when Ishbel said, 'Have you any messages for Mum or Rory?'

'None.'

'Or anyone else?'

'No.'

'Oh, Rowan!' Ishbel exclaimed softly, suddenly overwhelmed by emotion. How she loathed seeing her sister reduced to the pathetic creature she'd become. It was obscene!

Rowan stood. 'I'm tired, and think I'll go for a lie-down,' she said, deciding to terminate the visit. She smiled inwardly. A lie-down! That was a laugh.

At the door she again grasped Ishbel's arm. 'You won't forget your promise now?'

'I won't,' Ishbel assured her.

'It's best to be prepared in case the worst comes to the worst.'

'But it won't.'

Rowan kissed Ishbel on the cheek. 'Thanks for coming.'

'I'll be back just as soon as they allow it.'

'Tell Mum to try not to worry. I'm getting by all right.'

'I'll tell her.'

Rowan wound a finger in Ishbel's dark luxuriant hair, thinking how beautiful her own had once been. 'I had a message after all,' she said thinly.

'So you did.'

Outside in the corridor Ishbel watched Rowan walk away. In a peculiar way she'd never felt closer to her twin than she did at that moment – closer and, conversely, more apart.

Rowan was humping a basket of dirty laundry when her waters broke. 'Anne!' she shouted. 'Anne!'

Flora, who'd recently joined them in the laundry room, appeared to stare at her.

'Get Anne,' Rowan instructed, laying her basket on the floor.

Flora giggled, which enraged Rowan. 'Anne!' she shouted again. But there was no answer from her friend.

A small contraction rippled through her. 'Get Anne,' she repeated to Flora. Rowan pushed the girl aside, horribly aware of the wetness between her legs, and went in search of her friend. Another contraction rippled through Rowan, a little stronger than the first. 'Anne!' she yelled. 'Where the hell are you?'

Anne ran out from behind one of the coppers, her face streaming sweat from the heat and condensation. 'What is it, Rowan?'

'I've started,' Rowan replied.

'Right,' said Anne, putting a supporting arm round Rowan.

'I'm all wet.'

'Don't worry. We'll soon get you cleaned up.'

'Stay with me if you can.'

Anne doubted that would be allowed, but she'd try.

'I knew those stomach pains a few weeks ago weren't it,' Rowan muttered as they left the laundry room.

'Push, girl!' commanded the midwife.

Rowan shrieked, the pain beyond belief. It was as if her flesh was being torn asunder.

'Push!' the midwife repeated.

Rowan did so with all her might. Then the contraction ebbed, giving her blessed relief.

She gasped and sucked in much-needed breath. She wished her mother could have been there to give her comfort and solace. Instead she had a frozen-faced midwife without an ounce of sympathy in her. She could have been meat on a slab instead of a living human being.

The midwife grunted. 'You're doing fine. I won't be long.'

Rowan was aghast as the midwife sauntered from the room leaving her alone. Then the next contraction struck, and she was shrieking again, her tightly knotted fists drumming the bed on which she was lying.

*   *   *

'There,' said the midwife as the baby's feet slid from Rowan's body. 'It's a little girl.'

A girl, Rowan thought numbly. For some reason she'd always thought it would be a boy. She heaved, and the placenta came away.

There was the sound of a smack, followed by a lusty cry. 'Everything quite normal. All the bits and pieces where they should be,' the unsmiling midwife pronounced.

'Let me . . . have her.'

'I don't think that's wise, dear, do you?'

'Let me have her!' Rowan pleaded.

The midwife, who'd now wrapped the baby in a sheet, ignored Rowan and put the baby into a cot standing by in readiness.

She returned to attend to Rowan, and refused to speak further.

'No,' Rowan stated emphatically. 'I'm keeping the baby.' She'd fallen asleep shortly after the birth, only to wake up and find Miss Bethel gazing down at her.

'It's best the baby goes for adoption. Sign this form,' said Miss Bethel, thrusting a sheet of paper and fountain pen at Rowan.

'I won't sign. Not now or ever,' Rowan declared. God, she was tired, completely exhausted.

'It's for the best, believe me.'

'I'm keeping the baby. I told you before, and I haven't changed my mind.'

Miss Bethel's expression became even grimmer. 'It is your right of course . . .'

'I'm keeping her, and that's final,' Rowan interjected.

'You're being totally and utterly selfish.'

Rowan didn't answer.

'Do you really want her brought up here in Stoneydyke?' Miss Bethel went on.

'I want her with me.'

'Think of the child, not yourself.'

'I am.'

'I would dispute that.'

The witch could dispute all she liked, Rowan thought. She wouldn't change her mind. She was adamant about that.

'You are a most obstinate stubborn girl,' Miss Bethel hissed.

'Can I have my baby now?'

'No,' Miss Bethel said stiffly and, turning, stalked away. She hadn't given up yet, but would continue to try to persuade Rowan to sign the consent paper. Having babies and children around the institution complicated matters whereas it was her policy to keep everything as simple as possible. It made her job easier.

Left alone, it didn't take Rowan long to fall asleep again.

Miss Bethel tried on several occasions, but Rowan wouldn't relent. She insisted on keeping the child whom she'd decided to call Jessica.

When she was finally allowed to see Jessica, who'd been removed elsewhere shortly after the birth, she was already being bottle-fed, so she had no chance of feeding her herself which she'd planned. Still, it was a small price to pay for achieving victory.

As soon as Rowan was judged recovered she was returned to the dormitory and put back on full working duties. She was only allowed to visit Jessica twice a day – once in the morning and again in the evening. The rest of the time Jessica was looked after by nurses. That was the reality of a baby remaining at Stoneydyke.

Rowan sat and burst into tears, something she'd been doing regularly since Jessica's birth. She'd become profoundly depressed. It was as if a great weight had attached itself to her mind and was dragging it deeper and deeper into a bottomless abyss.

She'd despaired before Jessica was born, but this was

far worse. It was rapidly draining her will, her energy, her very life force.

'Come on, get up,' snapped an orderly who'd come to stand beside her.

Rowan glanced at him, her face awash with tears.

'What's wrong?' he demanded harshly.

'I don't know.'

'Then, get up and go about your duties.'

She rose and stumbled on her way, her thin shoulders shaking, the tears continuing to stream down her face.

What *was* wrong with her? she asked herself. The only answer she could come up with was Stoneydyke. That was what was wrong.

Rowan put Jessica to her shoulder and gently patted her on the back to wind her. Jessica was such a gorgeous child whom she was convinced looked like Gray. She crooned as she patted her, enjoying the warmth of the child against her. When the winding was over she'd change Jessica's nappy.

A young lad called Tom came running in through the open door to hide behind a free-standing cupboard. Seconds later an inmate called Helen appeared.

'Have ... have ... have ...' Helen swallowed and tried again, for she had trouble speaking. 'Have you seen boy?'

Rowan stared at Helen. 'What do you want him for?'

Helen smiled – a smile that made Rowan go ice cold inside. 'P-p-playing.'

'Are you supposed to be?'

Helen nodded. 'Nurse ... t-told me to.'

Rowan was appalled that Helen should be alone with Tom, whose mother was another inmate. Helen was known to suffer from fits during which she could smash anything she could lay her hands on.

Rowan clutched Jessica tightly to her. The thought that Helen, or someone like Helen, could be allowed to play with, or look after, Jessica filled her with horror. 'He's not here,' she lied.

Helen glanced about the room. 'I thought ... I thought he came in, boy.'

'No,' Rowan repeated.

'Playing,' Helen said, and hurried from the room.

Tom poked his head round from behind the cupboard. 'Thanks, Rowan.'

'Are you often told to play with the inmates?' she asked.

'Sometimes, when the nurses are busy. They can be fun.' He winked conspiratorially. 'Particularly the really daft ones.'

Tom emerged fully from his hiding-place, skipped to the door and peered out. ' 'Bye!' he called over his shoulder, and vanished.

'The really daft ones,' Rowan repeated, and shuddered.

Doubt assailed her. Maybe Miss Bethel was right and she should have Jessica adopted. Wouldn't that be better than her being brought up among lunatics? Until now she hadn't realized the full ramifications of having Jessica with her.

But adopted! Who knew what sort of people Jessica would be given to? They might be awful, exploit her, mistreat her. No, she couldn't take the risk. Besides, her whole instinct was to keep Jessica with her, to love her daughter, cherish her. But at what price? She was between the devil and the deep blue sea.

Helen and her like looking after Jessica! She shuddered again, and as she did so tears began to flow. She started to shake violently all over.

She didn't know what to do! If only she did. She prayed that God would give her an answer to her dilemma.

Rowan covered her ears, pressing her hands as hard as she could against them, but it didn't help. It never did.

The wailer was sitting up in bed howling at the ceiling, and would go on until it was time to get up.

It seemed to Rowan that the howling was now inside her head where it was reverberating round and round, bouncing from one part of her skull to the other.

'For Christ's sake shut up!' she yelled from beneath the

bedclothes, knowing full well that wouldn't do any good.

What had she done to deserve this? she raged inwardly. What? Slept with Gray, that was all. Slept with a man she loved. What a terrible punishment, out of all proportion, for so small a sin.

The howling continued unabated.

She stared at the meal in front of her which was the worst yet, the smell of it reminding her of animal food – and cheap animal food at that. Steeling herself, she speared a tiny piece of meat and put it in her mouth.

It tasted even worse than she'd imagined, its foulness quickly rising up to clog her nostrils.

She gagged and gagged again. Hastily she removed the meat and returned it to her plate. But the damage had been done.

Her stomach revolted, and she knew she was going to be sick. She pushed back her chair and, with one hand clamped over her mouth, fled from the dining-hall.

'Stewart!'

Rowan ceased scrubbing to look at Miss Bethel, who was her usual grim-faced self. She'd been solidly on scrubbing duty since Jessica's birth, and missed working alongside Anne.

'I have to inform you that you'll be starting treatment this coming Monday,' Bethel said.

Rowan's mouth dropped open. Treatment! The one thing she feared above all else.

'You'll be given a full medical beforehand as a matter of course, but I don't envisage any problems there.'

'Mon . . . day,' Rowan stammered.

'Monday,' Bethel confirmed, and strode swiftly off.

Rowan thought of what happened to you in the treatment room, petrified at the prospect.

Uttering an anguished sob, she collapsed over her bucket.

The toilet was filthy, excrement caking the inside of the

bowl which stank abominably. Rowan had just come from the medical where she'd been passed fit for treatment, and had now been assigned a number of toilets to clean out and disinfect.

Hell, she thought. That was Stoneydyke – hell on earth. And on Monday the roasting would begin. Her mind and body were to be roasted with jolts of electricity.

She whimpered and blinked back tears. If only she could escape, but there was no escape from Stoneydyke; no inmate ever had succeeded as the security was far too tight. Then she remembered Anne's words, *They can keep you locked away for ever if they choose.* For ever; till the end of her natural life, whenever that might be.

Whimpering again, she sank to her knees and bowed her head. Reaching up, she grasped her hair, trembled, and yanked. Clumps came away, and with them blood which spurted over her hands. She then began banging her head against the wall.

'Mum! Mum!' she cried, hot tears staining her cheeks. 'Oh, Mummy, Daddy!' As she'd done so often of late, she began to shake, while her face twisted into a terrible grimace.

She'd had enough. Enough! She couldn't take any more. But there was no escape, none. And even if she had pulled off the impossible they'd only recapture her again and drag her back. And on Monday . . . Monday . . .

Her mind, deep in the abyss, seemed to shatter and fly apart in a million glittering fragments. Pictures danced before her. Jessica, Gray, Miss Bethel, her own horrible spotty face, all whirling round and round in an ever-changing kaleidoscope. And while this was happening she could hear screaming, screaming she realized was her own.

Torture. That's what the treatment room was. Torture. They strapped you down and . . .

The screaming grew louder, piercing her eardrums, the pictures continuing to whirl – her making love to Gray, lunatics playing with Jessica, Stoneydyke . . . Stoneydyke . . . Stoneydyke . . .

Her eyes lit on a bottle of disinfectant she'd brought

into the toilet with her, and everything else ceased. The pictures, the screaming, all disappeared in a flash. Serenity settled over her as she stared at the bottle.

Her lips curled into a smile. God had been kind and given her the answer she'd prayed for. There was escape from Stoneydyke after all, an escape no security could thwart.

There was a third solution to the Jessica problem, a solution she could accept. Ishbel had given her her promise and would keep it. Ishbel would rescue Jessica and, with Meg's help, bring her up. All she had to do was remove herself to a peace more sublime than the one she was now experiencing.

She reached for the bottle and picked it up. Still smiling, she pulled out the cork.

She was doing the right thing, she was certain of that. *They can keep you locked away for ever if they choose.* Anne had proved that already by doing twenty years with no obvious sign of release. And Anne was in for the same offence as her.

She thought of Gray and Jessica as she raised the bottle to her lips. And kept on thinking of them as she swallowed again and again and again . . .

'Amen,' said the minister, concluding the graveside service.

Ishbel glanced down at Jessica, wrapped warmly in a thick woollen shawl, whom she'd rescued from Stoneydyke the moment she'd learnt of Rowan's death. Vincent had waited in the car while she'd confronted Miss Bethel, Meg too badly in shock to accompany them. An unusually compliant and silent matron had offered no resistance or argument, but had in fact seemed pleased to be rid of Jessica. The horrendous way Rowan had died had affected even her.

The entire family had now foregathered within the grounds of Stoneydyke to bury Rowan, the grave overcast by the shadow of the mental institution.

A few friends and neighbours had also managed to be

present, among them Fat Boy Carstairs. A lump had risen into Ishbel's throat when she'd spotted him.

Ishbel's mind was filled with a host of memories, all jumbled together. She and Rowan as children, laughing, playing together. The occasion she'd gashed her leg and Rowan had bandaged the gash. The argument over a hair-clasp Rowan had been given and then refused to lend her. The many secrets they'd shared in the darkness of their bedroom, the pair of them lying snuggled up in bed. The time . . .

Rory, too, was remembering other incidents, other happinesses. He stared at Stoneydyke in sheer hatred. Given a pick and a sanctioned go-ahead, he would have set about demolishing the place brick by brick.

The local minister moved over and spoke to Meg and Vincent, Meg leaning heavily on Vincent for support. As could only be expected, she looked absolutely ghastly. Since they'd received the news she'd hardly been able to string two words together without breaking down.

Rory turned to Ishbel whom he was standing beside. His face was pale, his eyes red-rimmed. 'That's that, then,' he said in a choked voice.

She nodded.

He took her arm. 'Time to go home.'

They began making their way to where the hired cars waited.

Chapter Five

'There, there, my wee lamb,' crooned Meg as she winded Jessica. 'That's a lot better now, isn't it?'

The baby replied with a contented gurgle which delighted Meg. She was still happily comforting Jessica when the kitchen door opened and Vincent came in.

'What's for tea?' he asked.

'Liver. But it'll be a while yet.'

He glanced at the brass clock on the mantelpiece. 'Why isn't it ready?'

'You can see why. Jessica needed feeding.'

He swore under his breath. 'Where's Ishbel? She could have done that.'

'Ishbel's gone to the Monteiths' to deliver something. She won't be long.'

'I'm starving!'

'Well, you'll just have to wait.'

That angered him. 'Wretched child! Everything has to wait for it. Honestly, you do nothing but dance attendance on it!'

'Jessica's not an *it*, but a *she*,' Meg retorted sharply. 'And I do not dance attendance on her; I look after her.'

'Far too much for my liking. That's supposed to be Ishbel's job. She brought her back after all.'

'I don't know why you're complaining. It doesn't affect you in any way.'

'In a pig's eye, it doesn't!' Vincent grumbled. 'I've got a blinding headache from being kept awake half the night by her crying.'

'Babies do cry,' Meg replied patiently. 'That's only normal. And you should be used to it by now; she's been with us three months.'

He muttered to himself, then took out his cigarettes and

lit up. He was genuinely ravenous as he'd eaten nothing since breakfast. 'Your son's late,' he said, looking at the clock again.

'You might call him Rory,' she admonished.

'Well, he is your son, isn't he?'

Meg began changing Jessica, who struggled and waved two podgy fists in protest.

'I hope I get a decent night's sleep tonight,' Vincent went on sourly.

'You could have a little more tolerance and sympathy,' Meg chided softly.

He bit back an angry retort. Never having had children, Vincent was finding it difficult to adjust to being woken up at least twice every night.

He lumbered to his feet. 'I'm going to get myself a slice of bread.'

Meg tickled Jessica's tummy. 'Coochee coo.'

'How long will you be?' Vincent asked Meg, taking a loaf from the bin.

'I'm being as quick as I can.'

Vincent cut a thick slice of bread, then spread butter and jam on it. He began wolfing it down.

The front door banged shut, and seconds later Rory breezed in. 'Sorry I'm late, Mum. I got held up.'

'Probably racing round on that bike of yours,' Vincent said nastily through a mouthful of bread. Rory rode his motorbike to work and back.

Rory's good mood abruptly vanished. 'Have you two had another row? I can sense it.'

'No row,' Meg replied.

'The tea isn't even on yet. She's been mucking about with that stupid baby,' Vincent declared.

'The baby isn't stupid!' Meg retorted hotly.

'I knew there was a row,' Rory commented.

'You can shut up!' Vincent told him, spraying crumbs. 'The house has never been the same since that baby came into it. She's a pain in the arse,' he groused, cutting himself another slice of bread.

Meg was furious. 'How can you say such a wicked thing!'

'There's a pain in the arse round here, and it isn't the baby,' Rory declared.

Jessica, disturbed by the argument, started to cry.

'Oh, for God's sake, that's all I need!' Vincent snarled.

Meg picked up the baby and held her to her bosom. 'Be quiet, you!' she instructed Vincent.

'I'll do no such thing!'

'Yes, you will. You're upsetting Jessica.'

'I've had enough,' declared Rory. 'I'm going out.'

'Good,' smiled Vincent.

'What about your tea?' Meg asked.

'Forget it.'

'Don't talk to your mother like that,' said Vincent.

Jessica's crying became a full-throated howl. Rory swung on his heel and marched from the kitchen; which brought a smile of grim satisfaction to Vincent's face.

'Now see what you've done,' Meg stated angrily.

'How long will tea be?'

'Make it yourself!'

Vincent's face went bright pink. 'Like hell I will!'

'Shush, shush,' Meg crooned, rocking Jessica back and forth.

Vincent threw down the bread-knife and watched it skid across the room. He blamed Jessica for all this.

'Can't you shut up that thing? I've got a headache,' he complained.

Meg gave him a contemptuous withering look and then turned her back on him. Cully would never have behaved so unreasonably, she thought wistfully.

Rory opened up the throttle to send his motorbike roaring along the quiet country lane. How he hated that man and wished his mother had never married him. He didn't even seem to make her happy. There was constant friction between them, and often terrible rows. It had subsided for a bit after Rowan's death, then flared up again. If only Vincent would pack his bags and go, but he supposed that was too much to hope for.

Everything about Vincent annoyed him – the way he looked, the way he spoke, his mannerisms, but mostly the fact that Vincent was there at all.

'Bastard,' Rory hissed through clenched teeth.

He opened the throttle up even further, enjoying the sensation when the bike bucked beneath him.

For the next few miles he repeatedly imagined Vincent on the road ahead of him and he running Vincent down.

'Wait,' whispered Meg.

Vincent paused on top of her.

'What's wrong?'

'It's Jessica. She's crying again.'

He resumed moving. 'So?'

The bedside clock told Meg there was still three-quarters of an hour until the alarm went off. 'I'd better go to her. Ishbel's been up twice already.'

'You're joking!' Vincent exclaimed, still moving.

'I'm nothing of the sort. I can't expect Ishbel to do it all when I'm here to help out. It isn't fair.'

'Not fair! What about me?' he protested, moving faster.

'Don't be so selfish.'

He swore.

'Now, stop and get off.'

She wriggled and writhed, pushing him away. Finally she succeeded in rolling over, and swiftly escaped from their bed.

He stared at her in disbelief, his face contorted with passion and frustration.

Meg reached for her dressing-gown and slipped into it, then padded out of the bedroom.

Vincent swore again. How could she do that to him? Why couldn't she just wait?

He lay back fuming, hoping she'd return before the alarm went off. But he was disappointed.

*   *   *

'Hold Jessica for a moment, will you?' Meg said to Rory, sitting by the range.

He looked up in surprise. 'Me!'

'You're capable of holding a baby, aren't you?'

'Of course, but ...' He trailed off in consternation when Jessica was thrust into his grasp.

It was the first time Rory had held Jessica; not because he was apprehensive or frightened of babies, but rather that he was ambivalent towards her. He couldn't help but feel that, if it hadn't been for Jessica, Rowan would never have been sent to Stoneydyke, and would still be alive.

Jessica gurgled happily at him, her bright blue eyes remarkably like Rowan's. He found that both disturbing and appealing.

'I won't be long,' Meg declared, vanishing from the kitchen.

He stared at Jessica, thinking of the amount of trouble and grief she'd caused. Again he wondered who the father was. If he ever found out, he'd give the bugger a hiding that he would never forget.

Rory tapped Jessica on the nose. 'Hello.'

She frothed bubbles and, reaching out, seized hold of his finger and clung to it.

'Strong little girl, aren't you?'

She blew more bubbles and waggled her feet.

His antipathy towards the child began to melt. It was hardly her fault she'd been conceived after all. She was a gorgeous creature.

'Bubba, bubba, bubba,' he crooned.

That delighted her and made her smile.

'Bubba, bubba, bubba,' he repeated.

He thought of Rowan and her agonizing end. It was a dreadful way for her to kill herself. What a state of mind she must have been in. She must have been desperate, to commit suicide in such a manner.

'And all because of you,' he said to Jessica.

His heart hardened again, and he wanted to put the baby from him, but couldn't do that until either Meg or

Ishbel reappeared. He was forced to hold on to her.

She had a lovely smell, he thought. Milky and powdery. And he was surprised how vulnerable a baby was, totally dependent on adults to look after it.

She let go of his finger and, forming a fist, bashed herself on the mouth.

'Don't do that, silly,' he chided her softly.

As if she understood, she opened her fist and placed her hand over her mouth.

If it had been up to him, he wouldn't have had the baby home but would have allowed her to be adopted. For wasn't she a constant reminder of what had happened? But Ishbel had promised Rowan, a promise Ishbel had insisted on keeping. Now, to all intents and purposes, Ishbel was Jessica's mother, and would bring the baby up as her own.

It was a brave thing for Ishbel to do, he thought. She was so young, and it would mar her matrimonial prospects. He couldn't help but admire his remaining sister for taking on the commitment.

He stroked Jessica's forehead, then ran a finger down her cheek; which she clearly enjoyed. Babies could be rather fun – if you didn't have to do the messy bits, that is. He found dirty nappies quite revolting, and was pleased he'd never been called upon to change one. He fervently hoped he never would!

'Jessica,' he murmured, tickling her under the chin.

'You two seem to be getting on all right,' commented Ishbel, who'd come into the kitchen without his hearing as he had been so engrossed with the baby and his thoughts.

'You can take her,' he quickly said, offering her to Ishbel.

'It seems a pity to disturb her when she's so contented,' Ishbel replied, tongue in cheek.

'Come on,' Rory urged.

'It would be useful if you'd look after her for a while longer.'

'Not on your life. This has been long enough.'

Ishbel accepted Jessica and cradled her in her arms. 'Has he been nice to you?' she smiled.

'Nice as pie,' Rory said.

'She is lovely, isn't she?'

'I suppose so,' he answered, pretending indifference.

'It's time for your bottle,' Ishbel said to Jessica. Then, turning to Rory, teased him: 'Perhaps you'd like to give it to her?'

Alarm flooded his face. 'No, thank you! I don't want to know about any of that business. Holding her for a minute is my limit.'

He picked up the newspaper and started reading it, effectively dismissing Ishbel and Jessica.

On the next occasion he was asked to hold Jessica he did so with less reluctance.

Meg frowned in concentration, intent on the hand sewing she was engaged in. It was a complicated piece of stitching requiring considerable skill.

'Fancy a cup of tea?' Ishbel asked.

'Bit early yet, isn't it?'

'I know, but I'm dying for one.'

Meg relaxed and sighed. Maybe she should take a break; her concentration afterwards would be all the better for it. And she needed to be particularly alert for this specific job. 'I'll put the kettle on,' she said.

She began to rise, and as she did a bobbin of thread fell from her lap to the floor. Automatically she bent to retrieve it, moving awkwardly from one motion to the other. She cried out when something went in her back.

'Mum?'

Meg staggered, clutching herself.

Ishbel jumped to her feet and crossed to Meg. 'What is it?'

Meg tried to straighten, which only made things worse. She bent over again. 'My back,' she gasped.

'You'd better sit down.'

Meg's face was screwed up in agony as she sank on to the chair. 'I'll be all right in a moment,' she said through clenched teeth.

'Maybe a muscle has gone into spasm?'

'Could be.'

'Or is it cramp?'

Meg, still bent over, shook her head. 'No, it's not that. It's as though . . . I've been stabbed.'

Stabbed! 'Where's the pain exactly?'

Meg reached round and touched a section of her back. 'There. That area.'

'Shall I rub it for you?'

'Please.'

Ishbel started to rub, but quickly stopped when Meg cried out a second time.

'This is awful,' Meg moaned.

'I think I should get you through to your bed.'

'Wait a bit. See if it goes off.'

A minute passed, and then another, but the pain remained as fierce as ever. 'Perhaps I had better lie down,' Meg conceded at last.

It took them ages to get through to the bedroom, with Ishbel supporting Meg who could only take small shuffling steps and had to pause every few feet for a breather.

Eventually they reached the bedroom where Ishbel helped Meg on to her bed. 'It's not so bad like this,' Meg announced, lying on her side in a curled position.

'I don't know what to do,' Ishbel confessed.

'Leave me and get on with the work. Hopefully this will pass off.'

'Do you think I should go for the doctor?'

'I'm sure that won't be necessary. It can't be anything serious – just one of these silly things that happen. It'll right itself, you'll see.'

'I'll put the quilt over you to keep you warm,' Ishbel then eased the quilt out from underneath Meg and draped it over her mother.

'Would you still like that cup of tea?' she asked.

Meg replied she would.

Ishbel first checked Jessica, who was sound asleep in her cot, after which she went to the kitchen where she made the tea. It was difficult for Meg to drink it, however, but eventually she managed. At Meg's insistence Ishbel returned to work and continued sewing.

Jessica woke, and had to be changed and fed. When she'd completed that Ishbel looked in on her mother whose condition remained the same.

'It's been an hour now,' Ishbel stated. 'Maybe I should run and get the doctor.'

'I don't want to trouble him over nothing.'

'It's hardly that!' Ishbel exclaimed.

'You know what I mean.'

'I'll ask Mrs Simpson to come in and care for Jessica while I go to the surgery. I shouldn't be long.' Mrs Simpson was a neighbour.

'All right, then,' Meg reluctantly agreed.

Ishbel hurried away.

Dr Nairn pulled the quilt back up over Meg whom he'd just examined. 'No doubt about it, Meg, you've got a slipped disc,' he pronounced.

'I only bent over,' she said defensively.

'That's how it happens sometimes.'

He opened his bag and took out a small brown bottle. 'I want you to take two of these pills now, and two early evening. Send Ishbel round to the dispensary and I'll give her an adequate supply. You'll need to take them for at least a week.'

'Can I get up after I've had the first two?' Meg queried.

He regarded her steadily. 'It's not as simple as that, I'm afraid, Meg. You need complete bed rest for some time to come.'

'But I've got work to do!' she protested.

'That's out of the question.'

'But, Doctor!'

'Complete bed rest, that's the only way to cure what you've got. And when I say complete, I mean exactly that. I don't suppose you have a bedpan in the house?'

'No, we haven't.'

'Then, I'll return shortly and bring one.'

Ishbel, who was holding Jessica, now asked: 'You said "some time to come". How long is that likely to be?'

'I've simply no idea, Ishbel. It varies from patient to patient. Weeks – months even.'

'Months!' Meg exclaimed, appalled.

'That's quite possible. And there's no hurrying matters. All we can do is let nature take her course.'

Meg bit her lip, thinking of the pile of work in the sitting-room.

'Will you be able to cope?' Dr Nairn asked Ishbel.

'I'll have to.'

'Good girl. And how's little Jessica?'

Ishbel smiled. 'There's nothing wrong with her, except for the occasional bout of colic.'

'She's certainly a beautiful baby.'

'That's hardly surprising considering she's Rowan's daughter.'

'Ay,' murmured Dr Nairn. He'd thought it scandalous that Rowan had been committed, and it was his private opinion, shared only with his wife, that the Reverend David Dykes had a lot to answer for.

'The first thing to do is get Meg undressed and properly into bed. Would you like me to help with that?' He laughed when he saw Meg's expression. 'I am a doctor after all.'

'None the less, I'd prefer to let Ishbel do that by herself if you don't mind,' Meg replied modestly.

'Fine. Now, if you'll take these pills, they'll ease the pain somewhat.'

He held Jessica while Ishbel went through to the kitchen to fetch a glass of water, and on Ishbel's reappearance Meg swallowed the pills.

Dear me, Meg thought as Ishbel saw Dr Nairn to the door. This was a real blow, and so unexpected. She shifted without thinking and gasped with pain. It was too soon for the pills to have had any effect.

Having put Jessica in her cot, Ishbel returned and began the business of stripping Meg and getting her into her nightclothes.

'Where's Meg?' demanded Vincent with a yawn. It had been a hard day, and he was tired. He planned a snooze in the chair after tea.

'In bed.'

'What!' he exclaimed.

Ishbel, busy making the evening meal, explained what had happened.

'Slipped disc,' Vincent frowned.

'All she did was bend over, and that was it.'

'I'll go and see her.'

Vincent found Meg lying on her back staring at the ceiling. 'How are you?' he asked.

'Bored stiff, and worried. I've got a stack of work in for some of Mrs Monteith's friends which Ishbel will now have to do on her own.'

He sat on the edge of the bed. 'Forget about the work; it's not important.'

'It is to me and Ishbel.'

'She'll manage.'

'I hope so.' Meg wasn't at all certain Ishbel would. There were various tricky bits of sewing to be done that might be beyond Ishbel's current ability.

'Ishbel said the doctor's given you some pills.'

'I've just had another two. Ishbel went to the dispensary earlier and picked up some more for me.'

'Are they helping?'

'Oh, yes. Though I'm still in pain.'

Vincent's expression was sympathetic. 'Damned inconvenient, eh?'

'Extremely.'

'And all you did was bend over?'

'That's all.'

He took her hand and patted it. 'Is there anything I can get you?'

'No, but thanks for asking. Ishbel said she'll bring my tea when it's ready. Though, to be honest, I'm not hungry.'

His eyes strayed to the bedpan sitting close by on a chair. 'And the doctor's ordered complete bed rest?'

'I'm not to get up for anything, not even the toilet.'

'Rather you than me,' he laughed.

'It's not funny!'

'Certainly not to you,' he declared, patting her hand again.

She glanced at the bedpan. 'I'm going to hate using that thing. It will be so embarrassing!'

He couldn't have agreed more and was thankful it wasn't him in the same fix. 'Let's just hope you get better soon,' he said.

'The sooner the better.'

'And there's nothing I can get you?'

'Not for the moment.'

'I'll come in and see you again after tea.'

She was touched by his genuine concern, not having known what his reaction would be.

She went back to staring at the ceiling.

Meg gave a yelp of pain which woke Vincent. 'What is it?' he asked, bleary-eyed.

'You moved.'

'I can't help that. I was asleep.'

'You keep moving, turning over and the like.'

He sat up, and in doing so made Meg wince.

'If only you would lie still,' she said.

He stared at her, yawned and scratched his stubbly chin. 'Sorry.'

'I've had an idea.'

'Oh?'

'I think you should sleep in the kitchen cavity bed. It seems the ideal solution for both of us.' A cavity bed was one set into the wall, like a tomb. They used theirs for the occasional visitor who stayed over.

That irritated him. He'd got used to sleeping with a woman again, and the thought of being alone in bed didn't appeal at all. 'I don't know,' he prevaricated.

219

'It would be for the best, Vincent. Honestly, it's sheer agony every time you twist and turn.'

'I suppose so,' he sighed, loathing the prospect.

'Thank you. You're being very understanding.'

He got out of bed and shivered. 'Right, then,' he said. 'Good night.'

Opening the curtains that hid the cavity bed, Vincent discovered the bed wasn't made up. Just his luck! he grumbled.

Ishbel sat in front of the range and gently massaged her forehead. She was dead beat. She closed her eyes for a few seconds, then snapped them open again when she realized she was in danger of nodding off.

She glanced over at the basket of ironing, thinking it was going to take her hours to get through that lot. But first there was Jessica to attend to, and the tea dishes to wash and dry. Rory normally did those, but he'd had to dash out that evening, having arranged to meet his pal Fraser.

Rory had been reasonably helpful since Meg had slipped her disc, and Vincent did try. But thank God for Granny Fee and the neighbours who'd rallied round; she didn't know what she'd have done without them.

If only she could have packed in sewing, at least temporarily; but she needed the money, because she had to pay her own way in the house, and for Jessica. There was simply no question of them living off Vincent. She could well imagine what he'd have to say if she'd suggested it. Besides, pride wouldn't have allowed her.

But it was hard going. She seemed to be at it from first thing in the morning to last thing at night. There was always something that needed to be done. Cooking, cleaning, shopping, the baby to see to, Meg ... The list went on and on and, like painting the Forth Bridge, when you got to the end you had to start all over again at the beginning.

'Ishbel!'

She came to her feet at the sound of her mother's voice, and hurried to Meg's bedroom where Meg informed her she needed to use the bedpan.

She was in the middle of dealing with that when Jessica began to cry.

'It's been a month now, a whole month,' Meg complained to Dr Nairn.

'I did warn you it could take a while.'

'But there's no improvement at all.'

'It is difficult for you, Meg, I understand that.'

'Just lying here day after day, it's driving me potty.'

'Lots of people would love the excuse to stay in bed,' he joked.

'Well, I'm not one of them. And it's not just a case of lying in bed. There's the pain. I haven't had a decent night's sleep since this started.'

'I've been reluctant to give you sleeping tablets on top of those other pills, but if you feel it's essential?'

'I think it is, Doctor.'

'Right, then,' he nodded. 'I'll give you a few to begin with, and we'll see how you get on.'

'Thank you,' she said, breathing a sigh of relief.

'As for the boredom, I'm afraid there's nothing I can do about that. You'll just have to grin and bear it.'

'I'll bear it; but I won't be grinning, I can tell you,' she answered sourly.

When Dr Nairn had taken his leave Meg went back to fretting and worrying: something she'd been doing continuously since being laid low.

If only she could occupy her mind, but even reading in that position was a problem as her arms began to ache after only a short time. Sitting up quickly became excruciating and had to be abandoned. When she ate she did so on her side.

Poor Ishbel. She was taking the brunt of all this, and was being quite cheerful about it, too. The lass was a brick.

Meg scratched her head. Her hair badly needed washing again, but what a performance that was! An added chore for Ishbel, who had more than enough on her plate.

She'd let it go at least another day, Meg decided, scratching a second time.

Vincent tied the cord of his pyjama bottoms and gazed crossly at the cavity bed where he'd been sleeping alone for the past six weeks.

How he missed Meg's body, which he'd become so used to, denied him now because of her stupid slipped disc. He ground his teeth in frustration, literally aching for the release her body would have brought.

He muttered to himself, wondering if Meg was missing him as much. She seemed so withdrawn these days; which worried him. She never told him what she was thinking about, and he could only speculate that it was about the past and the good times she had had with Cully, when they had been a happy family together, before the disasters had begun.

He smiled wryly. He had been so keen to make Meg happy. But, Christ, it wasn't easy.

What now? Ishbel thought wearily when there was a knock on the front door. It couldn't be Granny Fee or any of the neighbours as they would just have opened the door and come straight in. She laid her sewing aside and went to answer the knock.

'Good morning,' said the Reverend David Dykes.

Ishbel gaped at him. He was the last person she'd expected to find standing there. None of the family had been back to church since Rowan's arrest.

'What do you want?' she demanded, none too civilly.

'I've dropped by to enquire about Mrs McQueen. I've hesitated in coming round because of the circumstances, but have now persuaded myself it is my duty to do so. I am her pastor and spiritual guide after all.'

Ishbel swallowed hard, biting back the hard and bitter words that leapt into her mouth.

'A slipped disc,' Dykes went on. 'Most painful, I believe.'

'Most,' Ishbel agreed in a tight voice.

'May I see her?'

'Wait here,' replied Ishbel, and slammed the door in his pious face.

She took a deep breath, then headed for Meg's bedroom.

'Who is it?' Meg asked, having heard the knock.

'You'll never guess, not in a thousand years.'

Meg frowned. 'Who?'

'The minister enquiring after you.' Then added sarcastically: 'Here as your pastor and spiritual guide.'

'The minister!' Meg repeated incredulously.

'Says he hesitated at coming round in the circumstances but has persuaded himself it is his duty to do so.'

'After what he did to Rowan he has the effrontery . . . .' Meg trailed off, momentarily speechless. Fury and indignation erupted inside her.

'Shall I bring him through?'

'Bastard,' Meg hissed. 'Rotten fucking bastard.'

Ishbel was shocked to hear Meg use that particular word; she was normally so vehemently anti-swearing. How potent it sounded coming from her.

Meg glared at Ishbel, white with emotion. 'I don't want him taking one step into my house. Not one. Understand?'

'I understand,' Ishbel repeated softly.

'And, if he tries, I'll leave this bed and throw him out on his ear. So help me I will!'

'Don't get so upset, Mum. He's not worth it.'

'Upset! How can I not be?'

'It is a cheek.'

'It's more than that; it's downright wicked. Just as he is. Wicked through and through.'

'I slammed the door in his face.'

'Good. Let it stay shut. And, if he knocks again, don't answer. He can stand on the doorstep till hell freezes over for all I care.'

223

'I'll get back to work, then.'

'Bastard,' Meg whispered.

Ishbel woke thinking she'd heard sounds from Jessica's cot. But she was mistaken; the child remained fast asleep. Uttering a soft sigh, Ishbel closed her eyes, only to realize that she was thirsty. She'd go through and get herself a glass of water, she decided.

She was at the kitchen sink when suddenly she sensed a presence behind her. Turning, she found Vincent standing in the door-frame, his eyes fixed staringly on her body clad only in her nightie.

'You're up late,' he slurred.

The slur, and other tell-tale signs, told her he'd been drinking. She winced when he belched.

'I just came through for some water,' she explained, wishing she'd put on her dressing-gown.

'Water's for ducks,' he replied, and laughed, thinking that hilariously funny.

She laid the still partially filled glass by the side of the sink and headed for the door. 'Good night, then.'

He didn't budge, but continued to stand where he was. 'What's the hurry?'

'I've had my drink. Now I'm going back to bed.'

His gaze fastened on to her breasts, partially revealed by the V at the top of her nightdress. 'Stay and keep me company for a while, lass. We can talk a bit.'

'I don't want to talk. Now, please let me pass.' When she attempted to ease herself by him he put out an arm, blocking her way.

She recoiled from his breath, which stank of alcohol. 'Vincent?' she pleaded.

'Playing games, eh?' he leered.

'I'm not playing anything. I just want to go back to bed.'

A hand came up to touch her shoulder. 'You're a fine-looking girl, Ishbel. Have I ever told you that?'

She jerked away from the hand and took several paces backwards. 'Vincent, this is silly. Now, let me past.'

'Silly?' he repeated, finding that amusing. 'I don't think it's silly.'

'You're in my way.'

'Am I?' he said, pretending surprise.

'Please stand aside.

'I had a great night down the pub. Don't you want to hear about it?'

The beginnings of panic were fluttering inside her. 'You can tell me tomorrow. You can tell us all then.'

'I'll tell you now,' he declared persistently.

Ishbel folded her arms to mask her breasts. Prickles of apprehension sprang up on her back and across her shoulders. She realized her breathing had become shallow.

'You are lovely, Ishbel,' he further slurred, his eyes bright and glinting.

This was ridiculous, she told herself. 'You're being a nuisance, Vincent. Now, please get out of my way.'

'How about a kiss, eh? Just a teensy one.'

'You don't know what you're saying.'

'Oh, yes, I do.' He lurched forward. 'What about it?'

She tried to dash past, but he caught her and pulled her towards him. 'Just a kiss,' he said as she wriggled in his grasp.

She couldn't break free; his grasp was too strong. At the last moment she twisted her head away so that his lips landed on her throat.

'Vincent, let me go this instant!'

He moaned into her throat as she continued to writhe. This was becoming a nightmare, she thought frantically. And, if he did succeed in kissing her, would he stop at that? She doubted it. A hard nudge against her thigh informed her he was already aroused.

'Come on, where's the harm?' he argued.

'Let me go!' she repeated as firmly as she could, trying to keep her rising panic out of her voice.

He pushed her till she was against a wall, and there he held her pinned. His face was contorted, ugly from a combination of alcohol and passion.

'I've watched you, often watched you,' he panted, 'wondering what you'd be like, wondering how it would be.'

His face darted forward, but again she thwarted him. This time his lips landed on her cheek.

'Ishbel?' he breathed hotly.

She knew that if this didn't stop now she was going to have to scream. There was nothing else for it.

'Kiss me, beautiful. Kiss me?'

Beautiful! At any other time she would have laughed to be called that, but not on this occasion.

He clasped her right breast, squeezing it hard. She knew then she had no option, and screamed, a high shrill sound that reverberated round and round the room. She was abruptly silenced when an arm clamped itself across her windpipe. 'Shut up!' he hissed.

But, for Vincent, the damage had been done. Seconds later Rory flew into the room, coming up short at the sight which greeted him.

'What . . . ?' Rory said, then charged at Vincent, smashing the side of his head with a balled fist. Vincent gave a startled cry as he fell to the floor.

Rory pounced on Vincent, hitting him again. Vincent rolled over and managed to spring to his feet.

'I'm going to kill you,' Rory declared, fists clenched tightly in front of him.

'That'll be the day, boy,' Vincent sneered, slurring the words.

'Are you all right, Ish?' Rory queried, glancing sideways at his sister.

She nodded.

'You rat,' Rory spat at Vincent.

Vincent beckoned to Rory. 'Let's see what you can do, big man!'

'He's drunk,' Ishbel said.

Rory advanced on Vincent, who grinned in anticipation, convinced he was going to give Rory the thrashing of his life – something he considered long overdue. 'I'm going to enjoy this,' he mumbled.

Rory feinted, then lashed out at Vincent, catching him with a heavy body-blow.

Vincent grunted, and grappled with Rory. He swung several times, both swings hitting Rory's chest. Rory spun away, to go banging into a chest of drawers. An ornament that had been on the chest fell and smashed on the floor.

Vincent snatched up a chair and brought it down across Rory's shoulders, the chair breaking into two pieces. A section of wood slashed Rory's cheek, drawing blood.

Vincent laughed on seeing the blood, tossed aside the remains of the chair and fell on Rory.

Punches flew as both men staggered and careered round the room. Then Rory hit Vincent in the face, knocking him flying. Moments later Rory kicked Vincent to send him crashing against a nearby wall. He kicked him again, straight up the backside.

Vincent was labouring for breath now. This wasn't going the way he'd expected. Rory was far stronger than he'd imagined. He was no boy, but a full-grown man with a man's strength.

Bent half over, Vincent drove into Rory, which was a mistake. Rory hooked him round the neck and began hitting him on the side of the head and face. Blood spurted from Vincent's nose, spattering over both of them. Vincent struggled to break free, but couldn't. Fear began to build within him as he realized he was outmatched.

Rory hit Vincent again and again, then threw him to the floor where he grabbed Vincent's neck. Vincent clawed at the hands strangling him, but couldn't break their hold.

'Enough, Rory!' Ishbel yelled. 'Enough!' Running to her brother, she tried to pull him off.

'Stop it!' Meg shouted from the doorway where she was leaning against the frame.

His mother's voice made Rory pause. Exclaiming, he released Vincent and came unsteadily to his feet. Vincent gasped in air.

'What is going on?' Meg demanded.

'Mum, you shouldn't be up,' Ishbel said, crossing to her.

'Was I supposed to go on lying there listening to this bedlam? Now what's going on?'

Rory pointed an accusing finger at Vincent. 'I caught him trying to molest Ishbel.'

'Lies!' Vincent mumbled. He was horribly sober now, the inside of his head pounding from a combination of the after-effects of alcohol and his encounter with Rory.

Meg was staring hard at Vincent, her expression venomous. She switched her attention to Ishbel. 'Well?'

'Nothing happened, Mum. Not really.'

'It's all a misunderstanding,' Vincent declared, rising from the floor.

'No misunderstanding,' Rory hissed.

Vincent dropped his gaze.

Meg was sickened. Vincent trying to molest Ishbel. Sweet God!

'I got carried away,' Vincent mumbled apologetically.

'You're despicable,' Rory snarled.

Vincent ran a hand over his face. He was shaken by what he'd done, and by the fact that Rory had bested him.

'I think . . .' Meg broke off, and groaned with pain.

'We'll get you back to bed,' Ishbel said, putting a supporting arm round her mother.

'Meg, I—'

'Shut up!' Meg interjected, her voice a whiplash.

Vincent hung his head.

A trembling Rory went to Meg, then he and Ishbel helped her through to her bedroom.

When she was lying down again Meg forced herself to look Ishbel straight in the eyes. 'Was he going to . . . you know?'

'It got nowhere near that far, Mum. Honest.'

'But that was his intention?'

Ishbel didn't reply, for to have denied it would have been lying.

'Thank Christ you screamed when you did,' Rory said.

Meg exhaled, and closed her eyes, aware of a withering

taking place inside her. She thought of Vincent with total contempt.

'I can't stay in this house any longer. I'm leaving tonight,' Rory announced.

Meg's eyes snapped open. 'Don't say that, Rory,' she pleaded.

He fingered the bloody cut on his cheek. 'I must go, Mum. It's been in my mind for a while, and this clinches it. And tonight I'm scared of what I'll do if I stay.'

'Oh, son!' she breathed.

'Where will you go?' Ishbel queried.

'Granny Fee's.'

'At least wait until the morning,' Meg further pleaded.

He shook his head.

Ishbel suddenly remembered Jessica, completely forgotten by her during the recent drama. 'Excuse me,' she muttered, and hurriedly returned to her bedroom.

Miraculously Jessica remained fast asleep, not having been disturbed by the recent goings-on, which was a great relief to Ishbel.

She gazed down at the deeply slumbering child, and smiled. Then she rushed back to Meg, who informed her that she hadn't been able to dissuade Rory who'd gone to get dressed and pack.

'Where's Vincent?' Meg asked.

'Still in the kitchen as far as I know.' She shuddered at the memory of what had happened.

'I'm sorry,' Meg said.

'You've got nothing to be sorry about. It wasn't your fault.'

'I married the sod.'

That was true enough, Ishbel thought. 'Do you want to speak to him?'

'No,' Meg whispered.

'The baby's fine. I just checked. She slept through it all.'

'How could he . . . ?' Meg said, and trailed off. When she spoke again it was in another whisper. 'The trouble is he's very highly sexed. And with me laid up like this . . .' She trailed off a second time.

'Don't apologize for him, Mum.'

'I'm not. Simply trying to . . . explain.'

How wretched her mother looked, Ishbel thought, which was perfectly understandable. Her heart went out to Meg.

'I don't want Rory to leave,' Meg stated quietly.

'Maybe it's better that he does.' She paused, then added meaningfully: 'At least for now.'

Meg got the message.

Rory hastily packed the panniers that went on either side of his motorbike and then lay them beside the front door. He next went in search of Vincent whom he found in the kitchen standing at the sink pressing a cold flannel against his damaged nose.

A frightened Vincent glared at Rory, aware that the position of dominance had changed between them. Rory now held the upper hand. He cringed backwards against the sink when Rory stalked towards him.

'I'm leaving,' Rory said tightly. 'But before I do I want to make one thing plain to you. And you'd better believe I mean what I say. If you ever try anything like that again, or even so much as lay a finger on Ishbel, I swear by all that's holy I *will* kill you. Understand?'

Vincent didn't respond.

Rory grabbed hold of Vincent's pyjama top. 'Understand?'

'Yes,' Vincent replied weakly.

'That applies to tonight, tomorrow, next week, next year, whenever. I'll come back and do for you.'

A little of Vincent's bravado returned. 'You'd swing for it.'

'Then, I'd swing.' Rory released Vincent and, stiff-legged, strode from the kitchen.

Vincent slumped, thoroughly shaken. What a mess, he thought. He would have given anything to have been able to turn back the clock, never to have encountered Ishbel. What had he been thinking about? The drink, he blamed that. And Meg being out of action for so long. Even so, he must have been mad.

He sighed, his headache having worsened. Should he

go and have it out with Meg now, or wait till morning? Wait till morning, he decided. This needed careful consideration, and it wouldn't do any harm to let all concerned cool off for a bit.

One thing he could be sure about. Rory would carry out his promise. He was in no doubt about that at all.

'Can I come in?' Vincent asked.

Meg regarded him coldly. 'I wish to speak to you.'

'How did you sleep?'

'I didn't.'

'I didn't much, either,' he said, smiling ruefully.

'I want you to go,' she told him. 'We can't continue, not after last night.'

He crossed the room to stand by the side of her bed. 'I'm sorry, Meg, truly I am. It was the drink. I was out of my mind with it.'

'To have a go at my daughter, with me under the same roof.'

'I can't apologize enough,' he said.

'I still want you to go.'

'Give me another chance, Meg, please? I'll make it up to you, honest I will.'

'My daughter,' Meg repeated in disgust.

'It was the drink.'

'That's no real excuse.'

'I'll never get drunk again. You have my word on that.'

'It's no use, Vincent.'

'Please, Meg? Don't make me beg. What I did was wrong, I admit that. An insult to you as well as to Ishbel. But you being laid up has put an awful strain on me of late. I've been so frustrated – frustration that's been building and building until last night when it simply boiled over. And it's not entirely my fault, you know. You haven't helped matters by being so withdrawn lately.' He paused, his expression one of anxiety overlaid with genuine concern. 'Surely you can forgive me one mistake, no matter how dreadful that mistake was?'

'I could never trust you again.'

'You'll learn to, you'll see. I'll make more of an effort from now on, I swear. In fact I think we both should. A new beginning, what do you say?'

His conciliatory words were slowly melting Meg's resolve. What he had done was despicable, but he did appear genuinely sorry. He wasn't an easy man and he did like his drink, but they had had some good times together. In her heart of hearts Meg realized that she hadn't been altogether fair. These last few weeks she had been morose and withdrawn, her mind preoccupied with thoughts about how life could have been. But she had married him, and there didn't seem to be any alternative for Meg but to forgive him.

She fixed him with a stare. 'You really are sorry, Vincent?'

He looked shamefaced. 'If I could put the clocks back, Meg, I would. I don't want this to come between us.'

Meg was impressed by his sincerity. 'All right, Vincent, let's consider this a new beginning. But if anything like this happens again there will be all hell to pay.'

Vincent beamed at her and then kissed her. 'Thank you, Meg. You don't know what this means to me.'

He then went to the door, paused and looked back at her. 'Is there anything I can get you?'

She didn't answer, simply shook her head.

'I'll be off to work shortly. See you again tonight.'

'Have you apologized to Ishbel?'

'Not yet.'

'Well, I think you should. You at least owe her that.'

Vincent nodded. 'I'll do it right away. My heartfelt and sincere apologies. I can assure you, I'm not proud of last night at all.'

As the door clicked shut behind Vincent, Meg turned her head to one side and began quietly to weep.

Chapter Six

Meg threw back the bedclothes and slowly swung her feet off the bed and on to the floor. She then rose, swaying unsteadily. Well, what did she expect after five months? she asked herself. It was only natural she'd be weak.

She took a hesitant step, and another. She stopped after a few more to pick up her dressing-gown, slipped it on, then headed for the sitting-room.

'Mum!' Ishbel exclaimed in surprise when Meg appeared. 'What are you doing up?'

'I thought it high time I tried.'

'But the doctor—'

'Blow the doctor. I know how I feel, and it's time I was mobile again.'

Ishbel laid her sewing aside. 'What about the pain?'

'Not a twinge.'

Ishbel was delighted, but still uncertain Meg should be doing this without the doctor's sanction. 'Do you want to sit down?'

'Not for the moment.'

Meg gazed about the sitting-room. 'How's Jessica?'

'Fine. Having a nap.'

'Why don't we go to the kitchen and have a cup of tea, eh?'

'Can you manage that far?'

'Let's find out, shall we?'

Halfway to the kitchen Meg came up short and put a hand to her forehead.

'What is it?' Ishbel enquired anxiously.

'A bit light-headed, that's all. It'll pass.'

'Let me help you.'

Meg allowed Ishbel to hook an arm round one of hers.

'I can't tell you how sick and tired I am of that bed,' she declared.

'I can imagine.'

'Even being able to sit up and read or do some sewing doesn't stop me being bored to distraction.'

'You don't want to rush things, mind.'

'Stop fretting. I'm all right. I'd say if I wasn't.'

When they reached the kitchen Meg sat in what had been Cully's favourite chair while Ishbel got on with making tea.

'Granny Fee brought a lemon cake when she called in yesterday. Would you like a slice?'

'Mmm!' Meg murmured, thinking that would be a treat.

Meg stayed up for half an hour then, not wanting to overdo it, and as she returned to bed she told Ishbel what she planned for later that evening.

'It's been a bugger of a day,' Vincent grouched, tossing his evening paper on to the end of the table.

Ishbel glanced up from her cooking but didn't comment. She'd often wondered why Meg hadn't given Vincent his marching orders after the incident, but Meg had never volunteered an explanation and she'd never enquired as she considered it to be Meg's personal business.

Relations between her and Vincent had been strained since that night; though, to be fair to him, he'd been charm personified. She didn't trust him, however, and never would. She lived in a perpetual state of wariness where Vincent was concerned.

'What's to eat?' he asked.

'Wait and see. It's something special.'

'Special, eh? Why's that?'

'You'll find out.'

He laughed. 'Not giving much away, are you!'

She smiled enigmatically. She was preparing poached salmon, a great favourite of Meg's.

'How long till you dish up? I'm starving.'

'Shortly.'

He lit a cigarette, then frowned as he noticed that

three places had been laid. 'Are we expecting a guest?'

'Sort of.'

'What does that mean, "sort of"?'

'It's a surprise.'

'Surprise! I don't know that I like surprises.'

He went over and gazed down at Jessica in her play-pen. She was teething at the moment; which meant more night-time crying.

'Why was it a bugger of a day?' Ishbel decided to enquire out of politeness.

'A chap reneged on a deal. I hate it when they do that.'

'Why did he renege?'

Vincent shrugged. 'I suppose because he thought he could make a better deal elsewhere.'

He glanced at Ishbel out the corner of his eye. 'I was looking at that old pram of yours. Would you like me to give Jessica a new one for her birthday?' Jessica's first birthday was the following month.

Ishbel frowned. 'That's very generous of you,' she answered slowly.

'You'll accept, then?'

'Why?' she asked bluntly.

'I'm trying to make up to you and your mother, and it does seem that you need a new pram. And I'm fond of the child.'

'Are you? You never show it.'

'That's just my way. I am a man, don't forget. We're not as soft and slobbery as you women.'

'A new pram would be extremely expensive,' she stated, thinking she'd love one. The old one was really clapped out, but all she'd been able to afford.

'If you're worried about the cost, I could make it a combined birthday and Christmas present. How about that, then?'

'I don't know,' she prevaricated.

He decided to let the matter rest for now, not to press it. 'Well, let me know when you make up your mind. But it would be my pleasure, I can assure you.'

Doubt about his motives niggled at Ishbel. Perhaps he really was ashamed of what he'd done and was trying to make amends. Not that he ever could as far as she was concerned; some things were just unforgivable. None the less, a new pram would be lovely. His offer was certainly tempting, as Vincent was well aware.

Meg came into the kitchen. 'Tea smells delicious. Is it what I think?'

'Meg!' Vincent exclaimed.

'The surprise,' Ishbel informed him.

'You're up.'

'No, it's an apparition,' Meg replied caustically.

'Did the doctor—?'

'Off my own bat,' Meg interjected.

He hurried to her. 'You'd better sit down. Let me help you.'

'I don't need any help,' she declared, shrugging him off.

'Does this mean you're better?' At long last, he added mentally.

'I hope so.'

She sank into Cully's chair and sighed. 'I'm weak as a kitten, but that's bound to improve with exercise.'

'I can't tell you how delighted I am,' Vincent beamed.

'Not half as delighted as me,' Meg retorted.

He laughed and clapped his hands together. 'Shall I open a bottle of sherry to mark the occasion?' He'd brought home a bottle the previous month which he'd picked up on his travels.

'Suit yourself,' she said, thinking she'd enjoy a glass. It was a celebration after all.

'Then, I'll do so.'

Vincent was excellent company during the meal, full of bonhomie and high spirits. Afterwards, when Meg sat by the range again, he brought her a cushion which he insisted she use.

'Anything else?' he asked.

She shook her head.

'Meg?'

'What?'

'I do care, you know,' he said quietly.

She didn't reply.

To Ishbel's amazement, and Meg's, he gave Ishbel a hand with the drying-up – something he normally considered to be strictly women's work.

'I was thinking,' Vincent began hesitantly. 'As you're so much improved, how about me moving back to bed with you? It's so lonely by myself in the kitchen.'

She regarded him coldly. 'After what you did?'

'You can't go on punishing me for ever,' he reasoned.

'Who says I can't?'

Irritation flashed across his face. 'I'm trying to be patient, Meg.'

'And you'll just have to go on that way.'

'For how long?'

She didn't answer, but instead stared grimly at him.

'Oh, for Pete's sake, Meg, I—'

'Pete's sake nothing!' she interjected.

'Please? I miss you.'

'Huh!' she exclaimed in disbelief.

'I do. Honest.'

'I know what you miss, and it isn't me.'

'There is that, I won't deny it. But I also miss you, being together with you.'

'Anyway, I'm not well enough to share my bed yet,' she lied. 'So there's no question of your returning.'

'When, then?' he persisted.

'I've no idea!' she snapped. 'Now, will you drop it?'

He could see he wasn't going to get the answer and agreement he wanted. He swore mentally; yet, to be fair, she did have a lot to be grieved about.

'I think I'll go out,' he said, rising.

'To the pub?' she mocked.

'Would you like to join me?'

'No, thanks.'

'It would be nice if you did.'

237

'No,' she stated emphatically.

He went on his own to sit morosely alone in a corner.

'A fur coat!' Meg exclaimed in wonderment, pulling it from the gaily wrapped box it had come in. It was Christmas Day, and they were opening their presents.

'Mink,' Vincent informed her.

She draped it over an arm and rubbed a section. 'Gorgeous,' she purred.

'I'm glad you're pleased.'

'Who wouldn't be?' she murmured, never having thought she'd ever own a fur coat.

'It cost a mint,' Vincent stated proudly.

She was momentarily ashamed of the small gift she'd bought him: two pairs of socks and two linen handkerchiefs.

'Try it on,' Ishbel urged.

Meg did so, hugging it tightly to her, revelling in its sheer luxury and extravagance.

'You look like a queen. The queen of Glenshields,' Vincent told her.

'There aren't many fur coats in Glenshields,' Meg babbled. 'Mrs Monteith has one of course—'

'That's even nicer than hers,' Ishbel cut in.

'Do you think so?'

'Definitely.'

'Now open yours,' Vincent said to Ishbel.

As she was doing that he reflected on the meal they'd just consumed. The capon had been done to a turn, the pudding fantastic. As Christmas dinners went he'd never had better.

By God she could cook, he thought contentedly. She had a way with food, able to turn the plainest dish into something memorable. He would have had to search far and wide to find someone better in that department.

Ishbel took out a gold chain pendant sporting an aquamarine centrepiece. 'It's beautiful,' she gasped, incredulous that he'd spent so much money on her.

'Eighteen-carat,' Vincent stated.

She held it in the palm of her hand, staring at it. Then she dangled it, holding it by the clasp.

'Put it on,' Vincent said.

'How's that?' Ishbel queried a few moments later.

'Very nice. Suits you, as I knew it would,' Vincent responded.

'You're lashing out this year,' Meg commented drily.

He shrugged. 'Why not?'

It wasn't a case of why not, but why, Meg thought. And she knew exactly why.

He was about to ask for a general kiss of thanks, then decided against it. That might not go down well, with Ishbel in particular.

'Now Jessica's,' he prompted.

'I hope it's nothing expensive. You've already given her the pram,' Ishbel said.

Jessica's present turned out to be a porcelain doll that both women proclaimed to be wonderful. Dolls were a bit old for her yet, but it wouldn't be too long before she'd enjoy it.

A successful Christmas, Vincent thought with satisfaction. He didn't even mind when he discovered that Ishbel had also given him socks.

'Good night, then,' said Vincent, closing the door behind the last of their callers. It was five o'clock on New Year's morning, and they'd been celebrating Hogmanay. He returned to the kitchen to find Meg clearing away, Ishbel having already taken herself off to bed.

'A last dram, to toast each other?' he suggested.

'Not for me.'

He poured himself a small whisky and held it before him. 'To a good and prosperous new year for the pair of us. A new year and . . .' He paused. 'A fresh start. And I mean a *real* fresh start. Not as it's been. What . . . What do you say?'

Meg didn't reply.

'It's the perfect time and opportunity, Meg.'

'Is it?'

'Of course. Let's make up and be friends, eh?'

She busied herself with some glasses, taking them to the sink.

'Meg?'

She didn't want him in her bed; the thought was repugnant to her. But could she expect him to remain in the kitchen for ever? She couldn't continue saying she wasn't well enough when it was patently obvious she was. If nothing else, her resuming work full-time proved that.

He crossed to stand directly behind her, but refrained from touching her. 'I've bent over backwards to try to redeem myself, Meg. You can't deny that. Give me another chance, please?'

She turned to face him, noting his pleading and, it seemed to her, sincere expression. She relented a little. 'All right,' she nodded. 'You can come back to bed, but it's simply that. A place where you sleep and nothing else. Is that clear?'

He swallowed hard, while swearing mentally.

'I mean it, Vincent. Sleep and nothing else.'

'Fine,' he agreed.

'Go on through,' she said. 'I won't be long.'

Was she making a mistake? she wondered when he'd gone. She really didn't know.

'It's torture for me, Meg, sheer torture,' Vincent complained. It was a fortnight now since he'd been allowed back into her bed.

'That's too bad,' she replied unsympathetically.

When he reached out and laid a hand on her thigh she immediately stiffened.

'That's enough of that,' she snapped, wriggling away.

'You're being unreasonable.'

'I don't think so.'

'It's more than flesh and blood can stand. I'm desperate, Meg, desperate.'

'That's *your* problem, I'm afraid.'

'Oh, Meg!' he moaned.

'I made it plain that nothing would happen, so don't "Oh, Meg" me.'

His passion turned to anger. 'You're a bitch,' he snarled. 'A cold-hearted bitch.'

'Good night, Vincent.'

'You're unnatural, that's what you are. Bloody unnatural.'

'Hardly,' she commented drily.

'Cold-hearted, without an ounce of compassion in you.'

She didn't bother denying or defending herself against that ridiculous accusation. All she could think about was how different life had been with Cully.

'Hello, Rose. How are you?' Vincent said, flashing his teeth. He pointed at the cigarettes stacked behind the counter. 'I'll have a packet of the usual, please.'

'Haven't seen you for a while, Vincent,' Rose said, laying the packet in front of him and scooping up the money he'd laid down.

'I haven't had any call to be around here,' he explained. The newsagent's shop was in the village of Penderry, which was fifteen miles from Glenshields.

'How are things?'

'Couldn't be better.'

'I'm pleased to hear it,' she replied.

'And how about with you and Ronnie?'

Her bright expression changed to one of sadness and anger. 'You obviously haven't heard. Ronnie left me.'

'No!' Vincent exclaimed.

'Ran off with a younger female. They're somewhere in London where I believe he's got himself a job.'

'I am sorry,' Vincent commiserated. 'And frankly surprised. You and Ronnie always seemed so close.'

She shrugged. 'That's what I thought. Just shows how you can be mistaken.'

'So now you're running the shop on your own?'

'Not quite. That would be too much – on a permanent basis anyway. I've taken on a part-time assistant who helps out in the mornings, which is my busiest time.'

He took pity on her obvious distress and decided to make a gesture. He glanced at the wall clock. 'What time do you close?'

'Six.'

It was quarter to. 'Why don't I buy you a drink to cheer you up?'

She hesitated, then smiled. 'Yes, I'd like that.'

'I'll call back at six.'

'Make it a few minutes after.'

'Right,' he nodded.

He returned to his car where he sat and smoked till it was time to collect Rose.

'Gin and orange,' he said, placing the drink in front of her.

'Thank you.'

He sat and stared at her. 'Do you want to talk about it, or is it a forbidden subject?'

'I don't mind.'

'So what happened? Did you know about this younger female?' Vincent was intrigued. Ronnie just hadn't seemed the type to run off with someone. He'd been quiet and reserved, a typical family man, except he and Rose had never had children.

Rose shook her head. 'It came right out the blue. He said he was going to see one of our suppliers, which he did occasionally, and simply didn't come back. I found a letter after he'd gone telling me what he intended.'

She laughed bitterly. 'I thought it a joke to start with. That he was pulling my leg. But it was no joke.'

'I am sorry,' Vincent said softly. He'd always liked Rose and Ronnie, particularly her as she had a highly developed sense of humour and was usually fun to be with. She was a looker, too, with a large bust complemented by shapely hips and legs.

'You must have heard some news of him if you believe he's got a job?'

Vincent listened while Rose poured out her heart to him. She found him a very sympathetic listener.

She thanked him for his concern when later he dropped her off at her door, touching him lightly on the arm before going inside.

All the way home his thoughts kept returning to Rose whom he saw in a new light now that Ronnie had left her.

Later that night, as Vincent lay next to the uncompromising Meg, he thought of Rose, imagining her stripped, in bed with him instead of Meg. There would be nothing stiff and unyielding about her – quite the contrary, he was willing to bet.

He decided to call back at her shop the following day and chance his arm. What the hell? He had nothing to lose.

'A meal?' Rose said.

'Somewhere nice. Perhaps there's a hotel or restaurant you could recommend?'

'How about . . . ?' She stopped, remembering the occasions Ronnie had taken her there. No, that was out. 'The Mill Hotel isn't far away. It's under new management, and I hear the food is good.'

'Then, the Mill it is. What time shall I pick you up?'

'Seven-thirty?'

'I'll knock on the dot.'

'And I'll be waiting.'

He smiled, flashing his teeth at her. 'Seven-thirty, then.'

He hummed as he left the shop, while a quizzical and speculative Rose started planning what she'd wear. For a moment guilt stabbed at her, which she quickly banished. Regarding Ronnie, she had nothing to feel guilty about; she was the injured party after all. And it was only a meal; nothing more.

Or was it?

*   *   *

'Won't your wife mind you taking me out?' Rose enquired, tucking into the prawn cocktail she'd ordered.

'She would if I told her. But I've no intention of doing that,' Vincent replied.

'Oh?'

'She and I . . . Well, let's just say we're not on the best of terms any more.'

'I see.'

Vincent eyed Rose across the table, thinking how attractive she was. She was wearing a pale green dress that stretched tightly across her bust, emphasizing it. Her lipstick was crimson, her light brown hair parted in the middle to fall to shoulder length.

'You could say she doesn't understand me.'

Rose gave a low laugh. 'Isn't that rather a cliché?'

'I suppose so, but in my case it's true.' Or a version of the truth, he thought.

'Are you still in love with her?'

Vincent shook his head. 'Never was, or she with me. We were both alone, she a widow, me a widower. Getting together seemed a good idea at the time.'

'But it hasn't worked out.'

'She's frigid,' Vincent lied.

Rose's eyebrows shot up. 'Really!'

'Just isn't interested, which of course makes life difficult.'

'I can imagine.'

'We go through patches of getting on well enough, but only patches.'

'That's sad.'

'Now, let me ask you something. Are you still in love with Ronnie?'

Her face clouded. 'I was, but after what he's done I'm not so sure. How can you be in love with someone you could happily murder?'

'It must have been a shock.'

'I keep wondering how long it had been going on for. And what he's told her about me.'

'You mean intimate things?'

244

Rose flushed slightly, and nodded. 'I mean, he's bound to have said certain things. And I find that hard.'

'A complete betrayal,' Vincent nodded, thinking he mustn't say anything intimate about Meg. To do so could easily lose him Rose's respect.

'He can't have loved you,' Vincent went on smoothly. 'It stands to reason.'

'No,' Rose whispered.

'He must be mad. I think you're gorgeous.'

She was delighted by this flattery. 'Do you really?'

'If you were mine, I'd never dream of going off with another female, younger or whatever.'

'Maybe she's prettier?'

His expression was one of disbelief.

Rose had another spoonful of prawn cocktail, her spirits buoyant for the first time since Ronnie's departure. How that had knocked her, destroying her self-confidence, which this conversation was beginning to restore. Gorgeous! She hadn't been called that in years. Complacency had set in between her and Ronnie, she now realized. For a long time they'd been taking one another for granted. But surely that was the case with most couples who'd been married as long as they had?

'Is your wife pretty?' Rose asked.

'She's attractive, or can be when she makes the effort,' Vincent replied. 'Only I'm afraid she doesn't do that too often nowadays.'

Rose pulled a sympathetic face.

'She's tended to let herself go,' Vincent went on, lying further. 'I've mentioned it often, pleaded with her, to no avail.'

'How awful for you.'

Vincent decided to change tack a little. 'Do you think this was Ronnie's first affair, or might there have been others?'

'It's the only one I know about. As for others . . .' She shrugged. 'Who can say?'

'It's possible, I suppose,' Vincent murmured.

'And what about you? Have you ever strayed?'

Vincent considered his reply. 'Not to date. But it's become so bad between us that I must confess I'd be tempted if I met the right woman.'

He studied Rose's reaction to see what she made of that. Was it his imagination or did she show a flicker of interest? He mentally rubbed his hands. The meal was going well, he was scoring points in his favour.

Rose contemplated Vincent's last remark. Was it an overture? It could well be. Hadn't he said he thought her gorgeous? But was she ready for a new relationship? She doubted it. It was far too soon for that. There, again . . .

'Do you like jokes?' Vincent suddenly asked.

'Not smutty ones.'

'Of course not. How about this, then?'

He proceeded to tell her a stream of daft jokes that soon had her laughing and eventually brought tears to her eyes.

'Thank you for this evening,' Rose said when they reached her front door.

Should he kiss her or not? He wasn't sure. 'Would you like to do it again?'

He was certainly good company. She'd enjoyed their time together. He'd taken her out of herself, which was just what she needed. But he was married, even if it wasn't a happy marriage.

'Please?' Vincent pleaded, flashing her his most winning smile.

She relented. 'Yes,' she replied softly.

'What about Friday?'

'I'm free.'

'Seven-thirty again?'

She nodded.

'On the dot.'

'On the dot,' she agreed, smiling also.

Not, he decided. Turning he strode back to his car, leaving her staring after him.

Bugger Meg, he thought as his car sped away.

*　　*　　*

Vincent was in a particularly good humour as he strode round the horse-market. He was thinking about Rose whom he'd seen several times now. He'd progressed to kissing her good night, but hadn't yet tried anything beyond that. He was still adopting his softly softly approach, which he felt certain was the right one.

'Hello, Vincent. How are tricks?' The speaker was Dan Quilp, an old acquaintance of Vincent's whom he'd often done business with in the past.

'Fine. And yourself?'

'Oh, I'm getting by.'

'Are you buying or selling today, Dan?'

'Selling. What about you?'

'I might be buying – if I come across the right beasts at the right prices, that is.'

'I've got some beauties I can recommend.' Dan then led Vincent to where he had a string of tethered animals inside a semi-circle of horse-boxes.

'What do you think of this mare?' Dan queried, indicating a placid-looking beast. 'Her name's Snowdrop.'

Vincent made a cursory examination, but Snowdrop wasn't for him. He had several clients in mind and knew exactly what he wanted.

'Then there's this gelding,' Dan said as Vincent moved on.

The gelding was a possibility, Vincent thought, asking the price. He wouldn't haggle now, but would if he was interested enough to return.

A gust of wind snatched Vincent's hat from his head, sending it spinning to the ground. 'Damn!' he muttered, and bent to retrieve it.

It was a stupid mistake. He'd been around horses long enough to know better. But like all humans he wasn't above making mistakes.

His hand had just touched the hat when, uncharacteristically, Snowdrop suddenly bucked and viciously lashed out with her rear legs.

Vincent saw the hoofs coming and tried to dodge out of the way. But he wasn't quite quick enough, and one of the hoofs caught him a glancing blow on the side of his head.

Vincent literally saw stars as he tumbled to the ground and went rolling over. He must have blacked out, for the next thing he knew an anxious Dan was staring down at him.

'You all right?' Dan asked, brow furrowed in concern.

Vincent sat up, winced, and put a hand to his throbbing head. 'My own fault. Damn silly of me,' he muttered.

'Did she catch you badly? I heard a crack.'

'Right here,' said Vincent, pointing.

Dan peered at the spot. 'Hasn't broken the skin. You were lucky. But it's already started to bruise.'

He *was* lucky, Vincent thought, and had got off relatively lightly. He could easily have been killed or disfigured for life.

'How do you feel?'

'Like I've been kicked on the head by a horse,' Vincent retorted drily.

'Here, let me give you a hand up.'

Vincent groaned as he lurched to his feet. 'I've a good mind to buy that Snowdrop and take it straight to the knacker's yard.'

'I'll happily sell to you. And considering what's happened I'll accept a lower price than I would otherwise have done.'

'Don't tempt me.'

'You look awful,' Dan commented.

'That's hardly surprising, is it? I *feel* bloody awful. A sit-down is what I need, and a good strong cup of tea.'

'Can you manage by yourself, pal? I don't want to leave here, not for the moment anyway.'

'I'll be hunky-dory. Don't worry about it.'

'And none of them has taken your fancy?' He was referring to his horses.

'Maybe,' Vincent replied, thinking about the gelding. 'I'll possibly stop by you again later.'

Dan nodded, understanding perfectly.

'Sorry about that,' Dan called out to Vincent as Vincent walked away.

'Not your fault,' Vincent reassured him, replying over his shoulder.

He went directly to the refreshments-tent, considered ordering alcohol but decided tea would be better. He sat and had a sip; then glanced about, waving to several familiar faces.

Despite the headache he didn't abandon his visit to the market but continued on until he'd seen everything he'd wanted to. He bought three horses in the end, all of whom he arranged would be picked up from their owners later in the week.

'Vincent!' Rose exclaimed.

'Can I come in?' he croaked.

She stared at him and frowned. 'Are you drunk?'

'No, though I have had a couple of whiskies.'

'You seem . . . peculiar?'

'Well, I'm certainly not funny with it. Let me in and I'll explain.'

'Follow me.'

Vincent closed the door behind him, staggered a few steps, then had to halt and lean against a wall.

Rose hurried back to him. 'What is it?'

'I got kicked by a horse this afternoon, and I've had a blinding headache ever since. And when I say blinding I mean exactly that. I've started seeing double, which is why I came here rather than go home. You were closer.'

'Poor chap,' Rose crooned sympathetically.

'Look at the bruise I've got. Isn't it a whopper?'

He pointed to the black-and-blue swelling which she now noticed for the first time. 'That *is* nasty,' she declared. 'Perhaps I should call the doctor.'

'Let's leave him out of it for now, eh?' Like many men

249

Vincent would only consult a doctor when it was absolutely necessary, and he didn't think this was.

'How about a couple of tablets? I have the very thing through in my kitchen.'

Vincent staggered again when he tried to walk, so Rose hooked a supporting arm round his waist, and they made their way to the kitchen where Vincent immediately slumped into the most comfortable chair.

'Try these,' Rose said, handing him two tablets and a glass of water.

'Thanks,' he mumbled.

'I don't like the sound of this seeing double,' she commented.

'It's very hard to drive when you see two of everything. Quite put the wind up me, I can tell you.' Vincent hesitated. 'I hope you don't mind me coming here. As I said, you were closer than home.'

'Of course I don't mind. You did the right thing. But tell me, how did this kick happen?'

She listened intently as he related the story, impressed when he accepted total responsibility for the accident and didn't try to put blame on the horse. He rose even higher in her opinion because of that.

'So there you have it,' he said at last.

'The moral being: never bend over behind a horse.'

'Never,' he smiled.

'Listen, I've eaten, but I can easily make you something if you're hungry.'

'Surprisingly, I am. But something light.'

'Scrambled eggs? Omelette?'

'Omelette would be lovely.'

'It won't take me more than a few minutes.'

He watched her as she moved about the kitchen, reminding him of a cat – lithe, graceful and certainly in her case elegant.

'Would you like some beer to go with it?' she asked, cracking eggs into a bowl.

'Please.' A leftover from Ronnie, he thought.

250

He glanced about. The kitchen was far smaller than theirs, and quite untidy. But it was a cosy untidiness that had a warm feel about it. He wondered what the rest of the accommodation was like.

Rose paused to stare at him. 'You are white,' she said. 'It's very noticeable from here. Have those tablets started to work yet?'

'Not yet.'

'Well, they should do soon.'

When the omelette was ready she laid it on the table and set a glass of beer next to it.

Vincent rose unsteadily and made for the table. 'Gone all dizzy suddenly,' he muttered, leaning on the back of his chair and closing his eyes.

'A good night's sleep is what you want,' Rose declared.

'I'm not looking forward to the drive home. It was murder getting this far.'

Rose bit her lip as she thought about that. 'I'd suggest you stay here but ... well, there's only one bed. And what would your wife say if you didn't turn up?'

'That would be easily explained,' Vincent informed her, sitting down. 'I'm often away with my job.'

'Let's see how you are after the meal,' Rose went on, busying herself at the sink.

If the omelette was anything to go by, Rose was no great cook, Vincent thought. Meg's omelettes were simply out of this world, each and every one a mouth-watering treat.

'How is it?' Rose asked.

'Delicious,' he lied.

Whether it was the omelette, or his condition, or a combination of both, he didn't know, but all of a sudden he knew he was going to be sick. He rose, gagging, and rushed to the sink where he threw up.

'Sorry, love,' he mumbled when it was over. He felt dreadful, both physically and about what he'd just done.

Rose ran both taps to start clearing away the mess. 'That settles it: you'll have to stay here the night. You're in no fit state to drive anywhere.'

'But what about the bed?'

'You can have that. I'll sleep on a chair by the fire.'

'I'll use the couch if there's one,' Vincent suggested.

'There isn't, as I don't have a sitting-room.'

'I feel guilty about taking your bed,' Vincent said. 'I'll have the chair instead.'

'You'll do no such thing,' Rose stated firmly. 'And that's that.'

Vincent sucked in a deep breath, and immediately regretted doing so as his dizziness returned. 'Ooohh!' he groaned.

'Maybe I should go and get that doctor?'

'Not now. Let's see how I am tomorrow.'

'Suit yourself.'

Rose cleaned and disinfected the sink, then thoroughly washed her hands. 'How are you now?' she asked Vincent, still standing beside her.

'Rough.'

'Do you want to remain up or go to bed?'

'Bed, I think.'

'I've got some pyjamas of Ronnie's you can wear. Though they'll be a bit big for you.' Ronnie had been a larger man.

In the bedroom Rose looked out the pyjamas and placed them on the bed which she then turned down. She left Vincent undressing, returning later when he was in bed with a stone hot-water bottle.

He grasped her hand. 'Thanks, Rose, I appreciate this.'

She kissed him lightly on the lips. 'I hope you're better in the morning.'

'Me, too.'

'I'll put the light out.'

Gradually the dizziness subsided, and soon sleep claimed him.

Rose was freezing. When she'd said she'd sit by the fire she'd thought to keep it going all night. What she'd forgotten was that she was low on coal, and she'd just used the last of it. She pulled the blankets more tightly about her and shivered.

She thought of the bed and how warm it would be in there, particularly with someone to snuggle up to.

'Sod it!' she said aloud. She wasn't going to freeze any longer. That would just be stupid.

As he came out of a deep slumber he became aware of the body lying beside him. Meg, he thought, reaching for her. Then he remembered where he was. 'Rose?'

'Mmm?'

He moved his hand on to her breast and caressed it through her nightdress. 'I thought you were going to sleep in the chair.'

'Got too cold,' she mumbled. 'Ran out of coal.'

His hand slipped inside the top opening of her nightdress to ease out a breast. He began kissing it, slowly working his way towards the nipple.

If she was going to say no it had to be now, Rose thought. It wouldn't be fair to let this go further. But did she want to say no? If she was honest with herself, she'd missed lovemaking – not to the extent it had worried her, or concerned her physically, but missed it none the less.

'How's your headache?' she asked.

'Gone.'

'Completely?'

'Yup. It must be thanks to those tablets combined with a decent sleep.'

'And the double vision?'

There was a pause, then he answered; 'Seems back to normal.'

She wouldn't say no, she decided, but would warn him to be careful. How ironic if she was to fall pregnant by Vincent after years of failing to with Ronnie. She couldn't help but wonder if that was one of the reasons Ronnie had left her, for she'd known he'd always wanted a son and heir. Perhaps his new woman would give him one.

Vincent continued with his foreplay, thoroughly enjoying himself.

*　　*　　*

'So how was it?' Vincent asked.

Different, was what she wanted to reply. It had certainly been that. Vincent's performance was totally different from Ronnie's which, among other things, had been far, far quicker.

'Nice,' she answered instead.

'Nice! What sort of bland word is that to use?' Vincent protested, thinking he'd excelled himself.

She smiled in the darkness. He had quite a sexual ego, she now realized, and was after praise. '*Very* nice,' she teased.

'I thought *you* were fabulous.'

Did he mean that? She wasn't sure. 'You certainly have stamina,' she commented. Which he was obviously proud of, she thought to herself.

Vincent sighed with satisfaction. Things couldn't have worked out better, he reflected. That kick on the head had been a blessing in disguise, a passport into Rose's bed. Reaching out, he ran a hand up and down her thigh.

Rose leant over and switched on the bedside light so she could see the alarm clock. 'I'll have to get up shortly,' she said. 'It's an early rise when you own a newsagent's.'

'Rose, this isn't a one-off, is it? I mean, I won't have to get myself kicked by another horse to get back into your bed again, will I?'

She laughed. 'I don't know.'

He gathered her into his arms and held her close. She snuggled up to him and gave another low laugh. 'I would have thought you'd be worn out.'

'Not me! It's you. You make me this way,' he replied smoothly.

She didn't believe him, but it was flattering to hear. For some reason she thought of Ronnie, and her mood changed to one of melancholia. 'Be gentle with me,' she whispered. 'Be very gentle.'

And Vincent, to his credit, appreciating the change that had come over her, though not knowing the reason, was.

'Where have you been?' Meg demanded. Although Vincent often went away on business, he'd never remained out all night without first informing her.

'Why, were you worried?' Vincent queried sarcastically.

Meg shrugged. 'Anything could have happened.'

'I had an accident,' he explained. 'A horse kicked me, and I felt so unwell afterwards I decided to stay the night in a hotel.'

'Kicked you!'

'Here, see the bruise.'

'Looks painful,' she frowned, peering at it.

'I had a blinding headache and double vision, both of which have now cleared up. The double vision made driving extremely dangerous, which is why I decided on the hotel.'

'Quite right,' she murmured in sympathy.

'I could use a cup of tea.'

She hurried to put the kettle on. 'Being in a hotel, you'll have had breakfast?'

'I did.'

'Bacon and eggs?'

'The full works,' he lied. In fact he'd had toast and honey.

'So how did you come to be kicked by a horse?'

He told her all about it as she made them both some tea.

Meg was surprised when, after muttering 'Good night', Vincent turned over. He must have been even more badly affected by the kick than he'd let on. It was totally unlike him not to demand the usual before sleep.

As though reading her thoughts, Vincent smiled. He was saving himself for Rose whom he'd arranged to visit the following evening. For the moment he wasn't interested in Meg, not when he had the delights of a willing, co-operative and enthusiastic partner to look forward to.

'That bloody baby!' Vincent snarled, putting his hands over his ears.

'She can't help it; she's teething,' Meg explained.

'I know she's teething. It seems she's been teething for months. It's driving me out of my head.'

'Oh, come on, Vincent, stop making such a fuss.'

Meg drew back in alarm when he thrust his face into hers. 'I'll make a fuss if I want to.' He'd gone all red, while his eyes had taken on a manic glazed quality. He now started to shake all over.

'Vincent?'

Exclaiming in anger, he suddenly threw himself out of bed and marched from the bedroom.

Meg swiftly followed him into Ishbel's bedroom where Ishbel was tending to the distressed Jessica.

'Do you mind leaving?' Ishbel said to Vincent.

'Can't you shut that baby up!' he roared in reply.

'I'm doing my best.'

'Vincent, calm down,' Meg pleaded.

He rounded on her, and for a moment she thought he was going to hit her. 'Don't tell me what to do, woman.'

Jessica, upset by the commotion, yelled even more loudly.

'Sshh! Sshh!' crooned Ishbel. 'I asked you to leave,' she whispered, addressing Vincent, only too aware of how revealing her nightdress was.

'You shut her or I will,' Vincent retorted. 'A man needs his sleep.'

'And a real man would be more understanding and sympathetic,' Meg told him.

He flared his nostrils in anger. 'Are you inferring I'm not as good a man as the one who went and died on you?'

That incensed Meg. 'Don't you dare speak about Cully like that.'

'Dare! I'll dare what the hell I like. Particularly when I'm being insulted.'

'No-one insulted you.'

'You just did. You said I wasn't as good a man as your first husband.' He then added with a sneer: 'Of blessed memory.'

Meg fought back the urge to slap him. This was neither the time nor the place.

He swung on Ishbel. 'Why don't you stick a dummy in its mouth?'

'I've tried, but she keeps spitting it out. Now, will you please leave my bedroom,' Ishbel requested yet again.

'The sooner you do, the sooner Ishbel will get Jessica quietened down,' Meg reasoned.

Abruptly, Vincent turned on his heel and strode from the room.

'Would you like me to stay?' Meg queried.

'No, I'm all right by myself. You go back to bed.'

Meg hesitated. 'I'm sorry about that.'

Ishbel gave her mother a wry smile. 'He isn't half the man that Dad was.'

'No,' Meg agreed softly, and left Ishbel to it.

Meg was buttering bread when the idea came to her. Of course! It was the perfect solution.

'What are you smiling at?' Vincent demanded with a scowl.

'Am I?'

'Only idiots smile for no reason.'

'Then, I must be an idiot.'

'They'll be locking you up next.'

Ishbel could have killed him for saying that. Had he no sensitivity at all? How she'd come to loathe Vincent.

Meg continued buttering bread. Aunt Dot was the answer. If Ishbel went to stay with Dot, it would relieve the terrible atmosphere between her and Vincent that had existed since 'the incident'. It was an atmosphere so thick that at times you could almost touch it.

Yes, that was the solution, and it would also give her the opportunity to focus all her attention on Vincent; which might, hopefully, improve their relationship, which had sunk to its lowest ebb ever.

Meg decided to speak to Ishbel as soon as she could get her alone.

*   *   *

'Go and live in Glasgow?' Ishbel repeated.

'With your Aunt Dot. You remember her, don't you?'

'Of course I do. She came to Dad's funeral.'

'If Dot will agree, you and Jessica can go and stay with her. She's a nice woman; the two of you will get on well together.'

'Stay for how long, Mum?'

Meg shrugged. 'That depends. You might enjoy it so much there you won't want to come back.'

'I could never leave Glenshields! Not for ever, that is.'

'It might be the best thing,' Meg stated quietly.

'Why's that?'

'Well, the atmosphere here is so terrible. I understand exactly why you are wary of Vincent, but I'm married to him and I ought to try to preserve our relationship. If you went to Glasgow, that would give me more time to spend with him.'

Ishbel listened to her mother and realized that what she said made sense.

'Oh, Mum!' Ishbel exclaimed softly. 'I will miss you.'

'We mustn't let on why you're going away, though. The story must be that you're going to Aunt Dot because she's unwell and needs help. I'll write to her explaining everything and have her write back requesting you go and live with her. And of course, if you go, Jessica goes, too. That way both problems are resolved.'

'And what about you, Mum? That leaves you alone with him.'

'For a while anyway,' Meg stated. 'Let's just see how matters work out. If you settle well in Glasgow, then maybe Vincent and I can start again in time.'

Ishbel went over and hugged Meg. 'I feel so guilty. But I find him so difficult.'

'You're not the one at fault. He is,' Meg stated. 'So don't feel guilty.'

'I wish you'd never married him.'

'So do I, Ishbel. How I've regretted that decision, I can tell you.'

'If only Dad hadn't died,' Ishbel murmured.

'If only,' Meg agreed. What happy days those had been, and how she missed him. She would have given anything to have had him back again. He there, and Vincent gone. But unfortunately that could never be. No amount of wishful thinking or remorse would bring back the dead.

'It's Jessica we've got to think about now,' Meg said. 'We must get her out of harm's way.'

'When will you write to Aunt Dot?'

'The sooner the better. Tonight if I get the chance.'

She managed to find a moment, and posted the letter first thing the following morning.

Chapter Seven

Rory stopped to watch two men manoeuvring a large sofa from a van. Both were sweating and clearly finding the sofa extremely heavy.

'Wait a minute,' one of the men grunted, and shifted his hold on the bottom of the sofa.

'Would you like a hand?' Rory offered.

'That would be great. This bugger weighs a ton,' the man who'd adjusted his hand replied.

The sofa was really solid, Rory thought as they carried it to the front door of the house.

'Mind the step!' an anxious female voice warned. She smiled at Rory as he passed her. 'This is kind of you.'

'Don't mention it,' he muttered in reply.

They set the sofa down in the sitting-room among other pieces of furniture. There were also many cardboard boxes and a number of tea-chests scattered round the room.

'Thank God that's done,' one of the men declared, wiping his brow. 'We were keeping that sofa till last because we knew what a sod it was going to be. I can't thank you enough for helping.'

'My pleasure,' replied Rory.

'I'm Henry Cameron by the way, and this is my brother-in-law Alastair.'

Rory shook hands with Henry, then with Alastair. 'I'm Rory Stewart. I live a little further along the street with my grandparents.'

'Well, it's nice to know the neighbours are so friendly,' Henry said.

The woman who'd warned them to mind the step, and was obviously Mrs Cameron, entered the room. 'Will you have a cup of tea?' she asked Rory. 'The kettle's just coming to the boil.'

'This is Rory Stewart,' Henry introduced.

She wiped her hand on her pinny before offering it. 'Pleased to meet you. I'm Peggy.'

'How do you do?'

'As you can see, we're moving in.' She glanced around. 'What a mess, eh!'

'You'll soon get things sorted out, Peggy,' Henry said.

'You mean *we* will,' she corrected.

Henry pulled a face at Rory. 'Women nowadays! I don't know what the world's coming to.'

'Hello,' said a new female voice.

Rory turned to find himself facing an auburn-haired girl whom he judged to be a bit younger than he was. She had pale green eyes with gold flecks in them, and a pointy nose which was curiously attractive.

'This is our daughter, Mary Louise,' Henry beamed.

They shook hands, and he found hers hot in his. 'I'm Rory,' he said.

'He helped your dad and Uncle Alastair with the sofa,' Peggy explained.

'Do you live near by?'

He repeated about staying in the street with his grand-parents. Mary Louise looked as though she would have liked to ask why his grandparents and not his parents, but she didn't. Nor did Rory volunteer the information.

'Now, how about that tea?' Peggy enthused.

Should he or not? He hadn't been going to, but that was before he'd met Mary Louise. 'A cup would be lovely,' he replied.

'Good!' declared Peggy, rubbing her hands together. 'And I've got some nice scones in to go with it. How about that?'

'Better still,' Rory said.

He was disappointed when Mary Louise left the room with her mother, the pair of them heading for the kitchen. But she soon returned carrying a tray.

'So what brings you to Glenshields?' Rory enquired of Henry.

During the general chit-chat that followed Rory's gaze kept returning again and again to Mary Louise, something a bemused Peggy didn't fail to note or comment on later to her daughter when Rory had gone.

'I got the job. Start Monday,' Ishbel announced to Aunt Dot.

'Oh, that is good news!' Aunt Dot answered in delight. Ishbel had arrived in Glasgow four weeks earlier and ever since had been looking for work. Now her efforts had been rewarded, and she'd been taken on by the Blue Bonnet Distillery.

'It's good money, too,' Ishbel went on. 'Better than many of the jobs I went up for.'

'And not that far away, either, which is handy.' Aunt Dot was Cully's mother's younger sister who'd lost her husband eight years previously. She'd lived on her own since then – existing on a small pension – until Ishbel and Jessica had come to stay; which, she kept repeatedly saying, had given her a new lease of life. Meg had been right about her and Ishbel getting on well together, and she absolutely adored Jessica, never having had any children herself.

'I can walk there and back, which will save tram fares,' Ishbel said thriftily.

'Weather permitting,' Aunt Dot qualified.

'How's Jessica, by the way?'

'Fast asleep. Away through and have a look.'

The flat Aunt Dot lived in consisted of a kitchen and bedroom, with a shared toilet on the tenement half-landing. There was no bathroom, so if a proper bath was wanted, as opposed to an all-over wash at the sink, you had to go to the local bath-house, which Aunt Dot did once a week, usually on a Friday.

Ishbel went to the bedroom where Jessica was tucked up in the large bed that had once been Aunt Dot's, and which Ishbel and Jessica now shared. Aunt Dot had insisted on using the cavity bed in the kitchen, which she assured Ishbel was extremely comfortable.

Ishbel smiled down at her niece, thinking how like Rowan she was. She had the same gold-blonde hair and creamy complexion. 'Little darling,' she whispered.

Jessica stirred, but didn't wake – though she would do shortly when she'd want to be fed.

Ishbel crossed to the window and stared out over Glasgow. How ugly and dirty it was, yet it had a certain charm she found appealing. Everything seemed grey and soot-encrusted. She often experienced the urge to rush out and go mad with a scrubbing-brush, as if she could single-handedly clean the city, restore it to the pristine sandstone it had once been.

She thought of Glenshields, which she missed dreadfully. Although it had only been a month since she'd left, it seemed far longer. She made a mental note that she must write to Meg later and tell her mother about the job.

Meg wrote faithfully every few days, so Ishbel was quite up to date on all the Glenshields news.

Ishbel watched a tram shake and rattle its way down the street, two little boys running alongside, each with an iron hoop he was propelling with his hand. One boy had bare feet, the other a huge revealing rip in the backside of his shorts. It was a poor area Aunt Dot lived in, but the folk were cheerful enough despite that.

'Penny for them?' Aunt Dot asked as she came into the room to stand beside Ishbel.

Ishbel smiled. 'I'm thinking of Glenshields.'

'Do you regret leaving there?'

'It is a big wrench, I can't deny that. I was so happy there until ... until it all started to go wrong. First my dad, then Rowan, then Vincent marrying Mum.'

'It must have been hard for you,' Aunt Dot sympathized.

'Harder on my mum in many ways. She's the one who's really suffered.'

'Ay,' Aunt Dot agreed softly. 'And no-one deserved it less. I've always thought very highly of your mother – a real gem.'

'And then there's Jessica. What's to become of her?'

'You mean, in Glasgow?'

Ishbel again glanced out of the window. The two little boys with iron hoops were now coming back up the street, retracing their steps. 'There is that.'

'Glasgow's not such a bad place, believe me. It has many, many good points. I know, I've lived here long enough. Besides, don't forget the possible alternative for you and Jessica.'

Ishbel sighed. Aunt Dot was right, but that didn't make it any easier.

'You've taken on a big responsibility in Jessica, lass.'

'I did what Rowan wanted. How could I not have done?'

'At least she's not your child. That isn't a stigma you'll have to bear.'

'She's becoming to feel like mine.'

'That's only natural,' Aunt Dot smiled.

'I love that wee girl very much.'

'You can't give her anything better than that. Love is the greatest gift of all.'

Ishbel looked at Aunt Dot whom she'd become very close to in the past month. Despite the age difference they'd become good friends and confidantes. She thought yet again that it had been inspirational of Meg to send her to Dot.

'It's what my mum misses,' Ishbel stated flatly.

Aunt Dot's eyes misted over. Having lost her own Ben, she knew only too well the truth of that. 'Life's a funny old thing,' she said. 'Most of the time there's no sense to it. And it can be cruel – oh, ever so cruel. I suppose you just have to believe He has a reason for everything, even if we can't see or understand what that reason is.'

'I can't think of any reason for what happened to Rowan. A nicer, warmer-hearted girl you'd go a long way to meet. Reduced to killing herself in that awful fashion because of one rotten mistake.'

'As I said, life can be cruel,' Aunt Dot repeated.

'That was cruelty beyond belief.'

264

'And the young man never came forward?'

Ishbel shook her head.

'Then, I hope what happened to her preys on his mind for ever more. Surely he must have heard?'

'Of course he would have heard,' Ishbel said bitterly. 'Heard about her pregnancy, heard about her being sent to Stoneydyke, heard about her death.'

There was a murmuring from the bed, and Ishbel turned to find Jessica sitting up. 'You're awake at last, my angel.'

Jessica started whimpering.

'Are you hungry, pet?' Ishbel asked.

'Hungry,' the baby repeated enthusiastically.

'Then, myself and Aunt Dot will get you something right away. Won't we?'

'With pleasure,' Aunt Dot replied.

They both went to Jessica and sat on either side of her. 'Did you have a good sleep, precious?' Aunt Dot asked.

Jessica nodded.

'And what would you like to eat?' Ishbel enquired.

Jessica thought about that. 'Eggs.'

'Then, eggs it is,' Aunt Dot declared.

And the three of them trotted through to the kitchen.

Rory hadn't been to a dance in ages, and wished he hadn't bothered with this one. He'd been talked into coming by his pal Fraser.

'What's wrong with you?' Fraser demanded, somewhat tipsy from the beer he'd consumed earlier.

'Boring,' Rory muttered.

Fraser glanced about. 'I don't think so.'

'Depends on your sense of priorities, I suppose,' Rory replied caustically.

'There's a fair bit of talent here.'

'Mostly old faces.'

'Maybe you're just getting past it,' Fraser jibed.

Rory refused to rise to the bait. 'Maybe.'

'Hello, you pair. How are things?' asked Chick Strathearn.

'Rory says he's bored,' stated Fraser.

Chick raised an eyebrow. 'Oh, really!'

Rory wished Chick would go away. Chick had been one of Rowan's boyfriends and possibly Jessica's father. He'd spoken to Chick about it at the time, but Chick had flatly denied any responsibility. Rory hadn't been sure whether he believed him then, and still wasn't certain. If he ever found out it was Chick who'd done the dirty on Rowan, then God help Chick Strathearn.

'I've got a half-bottle in my pocket. Would a swig from that unbore you?' Chick offered.

'No, thanks.'

'I wouldn't mind a swig,' Fraser said.

'But you aren't bored.'

'I can very easily become so.'

Chick laughed. 'All right, come on, then. A quick trip to the lav.'

Rory watched them walk away, and wondered if he should leave. He was contemplating it when he spotted Mary Louise Cameron whom he hadn't seen since the day he'd helped her family with the sofa. Conor Meldrum was with her, the stupid big oaf, and from what he could make out was chatting her up.

He considered asking her for a dance, and decided he would. He'd been rather taken with her when they'd met.

The current number finished, and there was a hiatus during which Rory wondered whether she'd stay up. He was delighted to see her come off the floor, leaving a perplexed Conor staring after her.

Before Rory was halfway to Mary Louise she was surrounded by a number of chaps, all clearly with the same intention as himself. He stopped and stayed where he was, not wishing to join the mêlée round her. Eventually, after some laughing and joking, she accepted the invitation of a lad Rory had never seen before. He'd have to be faster next time, Rory thought. Then the same routine happened again, and she was instantly beset by chaps clamouring for a dance.

Well, mused Rory, Mary Louise was certainly proving to be popular. Look at them, like flies round a honey-pot.

Later that evening Rory was standing by himself as Fraser was dancing with a girl they'd gone to school with. Suddenly Mary Louise was only a few feet away, and miraculously alone.

She glanced at him, their eyes met, and she smiled. This was his chance, the moment when he should have moved in. But instead of doing so he found himself blushing, overcome with shyness. She was still smiling at him when he turned away.

Fool! he thought. What an idiot she must think he was! He sighed and shortly sneaked a look in her direction to discover three hopefuls, including Chick Strathearn, vying for a dance.

He didn't know why, for he certainly wasn't enjoying himself, but he stayed for the last waltz. As everyone was leaving he caught sight of Mary Louise being helped into her coat by Ewan Kirkpatrick whom he knew well. Ewan was obviously walking her home.

He kept his eyes averted as he passed Mary Louise, then hurried on ahead so he wouldn't encounter Ewan and Mary Louise on the road.

Rory was weary, as it had been a particularly hard day at work. After tea he'd have a snooze in front of the fire, he promised himself.

He eased off on the motorbike's accelerator as he swung into the street where he lived with his grandparents, and suddenly there was Mary Louise ahead of him, standing on the pavement about to cross.

She glanced at him, recognized him behind his goggles, and gave him a cheery wave.

He instinctively waved back, which was quite the wrong thing to do at that precise moment. He lost control and the bike wobbled dangerously beneath him.

'Damn!' he muttered, grabbing the handlebars again, steadying the bike and himself.

How embarrassing, he thought as he continued on down the street. He'd wobbled there like a rank beginner, and right in front of Mary Louise! He felt his neck and cheeks burn as he imagined her laughing at him, thinking him an even bigger idiot than he must have appeared at the dance.

His neck and cheeks were still burning when he parked the bike and went inside.

Vincent smiled wolfishly at Rose beneath him, her entire body convulsed with pleasure. Then he, too, climaxed, giving a long-drawn-out groan that washed over her naked form.

Vincent sucked in a deep breath, rolled over on to his back and reached for his cigarettes.

Rose opened her eyes and sighed contentedly. Sex with Vincent just got better and better. He was simply incredible.

'Well?' he demanded, lighting up.

'Well, what?'

'Well, how was it?'

She brought herself on to an elbow and stared at him. 'Why do you always want praise? You know it was good for me.'

He shrugged. 'I just like a bit of confirmation, that's all.'

It was something about him she was beginning to find irritating. He might have been a small boy who needed his head patted every time he did a job round the house. It was a matter she would have liked never to discuss, preferring to have let it simply exist between them.

'I was thinking,' he mused. 'Wouldn't it be lovely to go away for a few days together?'

She became intrigued. 'Away where?'

'Wherever. Within reason, that is. I mean, we can't exactly get to China and back in a few days.'

She laughed, thinking he was being quite amusing and whimsical. Well, if he could be whimsical, so, too, could she. 'Perhaps not China, but we could go to Moscow.'

'Mos—' He broke off and eyed her. 'Is that so?'

'Oh, yes. Easily.'

He knew she was teasing him. 'And how would we manage that?'

'In your car.'

'My car, eh?'

'Nothing would be simpler.'

He blew a perfect smoke ring, aiming it at one of her nipples. It missed, disintegrating high up against the same breast. 'Are we talking about Moscow, Russia?'

'No,' she smiled. 'There's a village of the same name not far from Kilmarnock. I passed through there once.'

'Very funny,' he said.

'You could still truthfully say you'd been to Moscow.'

'Outside Kilmarnock,' he murmured thoughtfully. 'Never heard of it.'

'Well, you have now.'

'Does that mean you'll go there with me? A long weekend perhaps?'

'I'm afraid that's impossible, Vincent. I have the shop to run, don't forget. I can't just close it down for a couple of days and swan off. That's not on.'

'If there was a nice hotel thereabouts, we could have a really good time. We'd have the best room available – in fact the best of everything available. Money would be no object.'

She closed her eyes, lay back and thought about it. A few days' break would have been wonderful. There, again, did she want to spend that amount of time with Vincent? She enjoyed going to bed with him, and he could be entertaining company, but she had the feeling he would pall in anything other than small doses.

'It's very kind of you, Vincent,' she said, opening her eyes again and smiling at him. 'But quite out of the question.'

'What about your part-time assistant? Couldn't she do the job for a weekend?'

'No, it's not as simple as that. I doubt she'd cope.'

'Well, what about someone else?'

'There isn't anyone.'

'Surely . . .'

'It's just not on, Vincent. I'm sorry.'

He drew heavily on his cigarette. 'Pity.'

'Yes.'

'It would have been lovely.'

Rose slipped from the bed. 'I'm going to have a bath.'

'Can I join you?'

She didn't really want him to; but she had turned down his offer of a weekend, which had disappointed him. 'If you like.'

He was out of bed in a flash, which made her laugh. 'Lead on, McDuff.'

'Go back to bed and I'll call you when it's ready.'

He gathered her into his arms and kissed her deeply. 'You're terrific, Rose. I can't tell you how much I look forward to seeing you.'

'And I look forward to seeing you.'

'Let me bring you a present next time I come. What do you fancy?'

'A present?'

'Anything at all.'

'Anything?' she teased.

'You know what I mean.'

'*Within reason*,' she said, tongue firmly in cheek, echoing his earlier limitation.

'Exactly.'

'Tell you what,' she said eventually. 'Why don't you just surprise me.'

'Then, that's what I'll do.'

She regarded him fondly. He could be such a sweetie at times. Though there was a darker side to him, which she'd only occasionally glimpsed, that she wasn't so sure about.

'I'll run the bath,' she said and, breaking away, padded towards the bathroom, putting on a Paisley-patterned dressing-gown *en route*.

Vincent climbed back into bed and began thinking about what he'd buy her.

*   *   *

Rory slipped the small spanner over the nut and tightened it. He was frowning in concentration, his mind firmly on the job in hand.

'Hello.'

He blinked and glanced up to find Mary Louise staring at him. 'Hello,' he mumbled in reply.

'What are you doing?'

'Frying an egg,' he quipped.

'Yes, I can see that,' she said sarcastically, making him blush a little.

'Sorry,' he apologized.

'I'll try again. What are you doing?'

He waved a hand at the partially disassembled motorbike. 'I've been having various problems which I've hopefully fixed. Now I'm putting all the bits and pieces back together again.'

Mary Louise took in his dirty overalls and oil-streaked face. 'Messy business.'

'You can say that again.'

'You like motorbikes, then?'

He beamed. 'Love them.'

'I've watched you zoom up and down the street. You look quite the daredevil.'

Was she taking the mickey? he wondered, remembering how he had wobbled the previous week. 'Do I?' he muttered.

'How fast does it go?'

He told her.

She whistled. 'That's really moving, eh!'

'It gives you a tremendous feeling when you're going flat out. I can't describe it other than to say it's the most exciting thing I've ever experienced. The machine becomes part of you and . . .' He trailed off, lost for words.

'I think I understand,' she nodded.

'I'm hoping to buy a bigger, better bike soon,' he informed her. 'Then I'll be able to go even faster.'

'Which will be even more exciting,' she teased.

He ignored that. 'How are you settling in?'

271

'Fine. We all like it here.'

'And how's your dad's job going?' Henry Cameron had come to Glenshields to take up a post as gardener to the Monteiths. Their previous gardener had retired.

'He's enjoying it. He gets on well with everyone there.'

'So it was a good move?'

'He thinks so.'

'And what about you?'

'I also think so. There's a nice feel about Glenshields. We've all been accepted and seem to fit in without any problem.'

'Mmm!' he murmured, thinking of the dance.

'Do you always work on your bike outside your house?' she queried.

'There's nowhere else.'

'I suppose not.'

Silence fell between them. 'Well, then . . . ,' she said, as if to move away. Changing her mind, she suddenly asked, 'Tell me something. Why did you cut me dead at that dance?'

He coloured. 'Did I?'

'You know you did. You were aware of doing it.'

Christ! he thought. He picked up an old rag and wiped his hands. 'I'm sorry if I offended you.'

She didn't answer that, but stared quizzically at him.

'The truth?' he queried.

She nodded.

'I'm shy,' he stammered.

So that was it. The possibility had crossed her mind. 'Are you now?'

'Not all the time, but in certain instances. I had intended asking you up, but got put off by the hordes surrounding you.'

She laughed. 'Hardly hordes!'

'Well, that's what it looked like to me.'

Hordes. She liked that description. It was very flattering. It also told her more about Rory than he realized: that he was interested, for example. 'If you'd asked, I would have been delighted to dance with you.'

He bit back a smart reply. Mary Louise was being gracious; he should accept that. 'I'm pleased to hear it,' he muttered, pretending to study the motorbike frame.

Shyness in other lads would have put her off, but somehow it didn't with Rory; with him she found it rather appealing. It enhanced his attractiveness.

'I'd better let you get on,' she said.

'Yes.'

'You've still got a lot to do.'

He nodded, and wiped his hands again on the rag.

'You know, I've never been on a motorbike,' she stated.

'No?'

'Never.'

He considered that.

Oh, come on! she thought. Don't be so slow.

'Would you . . . ?' He swallowed. 'Would you like a ride some time?'

'I'm sure I'd enjoy it,' she enthused.

'Er . . . '

'Not now,' she smiled. 'How about . . . this Sunday?'

'Afternoon?'

'Suits me.'

'I'll knock on your door. About two?'

'Two-thirty,' she said. There was no reason why he couldn't have knocked at two; she simply wanted the last word in that respect.

'Two-thirty it is, then.'

'I have a pair of slacks – shall I wear those?'

'They would be ideal,' he nodded.

'Till then.'

He waved to her as she walked away and stopped abruptly when he realized he was waving to her back.

Two-thirty Sunday, he and Mary Louise, he thought bemused. When he tried tightening the nut he found his hand was shaking ever so slightly.

Meg grimaced with pain as she tried to keep on sewing, but it was proving impossible. Her hands were afire and

273

clumsy in the extreme. And she was being so slow!

She stopped and laid her work aside. This was useless. There was only one thing for it, and that was another visit to the doctor.

Meg rose and pulled a face as pain lanced up her back and across her shoulders. She could have done with Ishbel being there to help her. How she missed her and the baby, particularly in the evenings with Vincent often being out.

At least they were doing well in Glasgow, which not only pleased her but was also a great relief. Perhaps she could travel through and see them soon. She'd enjoy that. But she'd have to choose a time when her arthritis would allow her to make the trip.

Meg glanced out of the window, wondering about the weather. It was a raw autumnal day, with a sharp wind blowing. She'd wear her fur coat, she decided, keep herself wrapped up warm against the elements.

She made a cup of tea first, then went to the wardrobe where she kept the mink – only to find it wasn't there.

Meg frowned. Had she put it somewhere else? She thought about that. No, of course she hadn't. She always kept it in this wardrobe. So where was it?

She searched every wardrobe and cupboard in the house, thinking Vincent might have moved it for some reason. But of the mink there was no sign. It had vanished.

Burglars? It couldn't be that as nothing else had been taken. As she put on her day-to-day coat she made a mental note to speak to Vincent about the mink later. This really was puzzling.

'I had to go to the doctor's today. My arthritis has been acting up again,' Meg informed Vincent, who'd just arrived home and thrown himself into a chair.

'Oh, yes?'

'He gave me some new pills, which I've taken.'

'Any good?'

She gazed down at her hands, which were tightened into claws. 'Not so far.'

'Mmm!' he said, shaking out his newspaper. Then he had a sudden thought. 'Does that mean there's a problem with tea?'

'No, I've managed all right. Though it's only sardines on toast, I'm afraid.'

'Oh!' he muttered, clearly disappointed.

'I'm sorry, but it's the best I can do.'

She gave him a hard stare. 'I went to get my fur coat today and couldn't find it. Do you know anything about that?'

He went very still. 'I sold it,' he said after a while.

'Sold it!'

He lowered his paper and looked at her. 'I needed the money, so I sold it.'

'You never told me you were short of money.'

'It's none of your business.'

Anger flared up in her. 'Of course it's my business. I am your wife after all, and it was my fur coat.'

'Which I bought for you.'

'That's irrelevant. It was my coat.'

'I bought it and I sold it again. That's all there is to it.'

'You might at least have said something.'

'I should have done. I forgot,' he murmured.

'And how come we're short of money?'

'It's been a lean period for me,' he lied. On the contrary, business was flourishing.

'You've never mentioned it.'

'Well, I'm mentioning it now.'

Meg let out an exasperated sigh. 'I thought perhaps we'd had burglars.'

'No, it was me,' he declared, burying himself again in his newspaper.

'Honestly, Vincent, you—'

'Enough!' he suddenly shouted. 'Leave it alone, will you? Now, where's my tea?'

Meg sucked in a deep breath, then another. She was furious. It wasn't his selling the coat that upset her, but the cavalier fashion in which he'd done it. Any normal husband would have at least had the courtesy to speak to his wife before selling her prized fur coat. But not Vincent. As far as he was concerned, he could do as he liked without a word of explanation.

'You're a disgrace,' she said quietly.

He glanced up at her. 'And you're not worth a monkey's toss. So I guess that about makes us equal.'

'Don't speak to me like that,' she said venomously. A monkey's toss! If Cully had been there and heard her called that, he would have knocked Vincent flying. But, then, if Cully had been there, Vincent wouldn't. Chalk and cheese, that was the difference between her two husbands, one a born gentleman, the other a born rat.

Meg turned to get on with the meal, and while she was busying herself Vincent smiled behind his newspaper. He hadn't sold her coat but given it to Rose: the surprise present he'd promised her.

Naturally Rose had been thrilled to bits.

Rory pulled the motorbike off the dirt road and brought it to a halt. From their vantage-point they had a splendid view of the valley nestling below.

'If you get down, I'll put the bike on its stand,' he said over his shoulder to Mary Louise.

When he'd arranged the bike he joined her, standing slightly apart, staring out over the valley. 'It's a gorgeous view,' she declared.

'I think so, too. I often come up here.'

She glanced sideways at him. 'With girls?'

'Oh, all the time!' he replied drily, tongue in cheek.

'What's the valley called?'

'Strathdhu.'

'But that means "black valley"!' she exclaimed in surprise. 'And it isn't black at all.'

'Somebody must have thought so to give it that name.'

'Maybe it appears dark at certain times of the year,' she mused.

'Maybe,' he mused also. 'So tell me, how did you like your first ever ride on a motorbike?'

'I loved every moment of it. You were right; it is very exciting.'

'I'm glad. I'd have been upset if you hadn't enjoyed it.'

'Would you?'

'Of course.'

She reached out and touched his cheek. 'You're a very nice lad, Rory – and I don't want that to sound condescending, either. I like you a lot.'

'And I like you,' he husked in reply.

Mary Louise looked back down the valley. 'I think Scotland must be one of the most beautiful countries in the world.'

'I couldn't agree more. Although, I have to admit, I haven't been anywhere else.'

'Would you like to travel?'

He thought about it. 'A bit perhaps. I certainly want to see England some time.'

'I'd love to visit Cornwall myself. They say parts of it are very similar to Scotland.' She sighed. 'I simply adore hills and heather, don't you?'

He nodded.

'It's the sheer ruggedness of Scotland that appeals to me. It has a great natural wild beauty.'

'Just like yourself,' he declared, and couldn't believe he'd said such a thing.

She stared at him in astonishment. 'Why, thank you.'

He was horribly aware that he was blushing. 'I hope it isn't going to rain,' he said, staring up at the cloudless sky. They both knew there wasn't a hope of that.

'I heard about your sister,' Mary Louise stated softly. 'It's a sad appalling story.'

His embarrassment disappeared. 'Yes.'

'Your family must have been distraught.'

'We were. Rowan and I were particularly close. Real pals, considering we were brother and sister. I miss her dreadfully.' He gazed grimly out over the valley, remembering he'd brought Rowan up here once on Fraser's bike. She, too, had thought it a gorgeous view.

'For what it's worth, I'm sorry.'

'Thank you,' he whispered in reply.

'And your other sister has gone off to Glasgow, I understand?'

'To help an aunt of ours who isn't well,' he said. That was the story he'd been told, which he believed.

'She took the baby with her.'

'Jessica,' Rory smiled. 'She's a real poppet. It was lovely having her round the house.'

'Would it be intrusive of me to ask why you left home to stay with your grandparents?'

He shrugged. 'Simple really. I can't stand my step-father, nor can he stand me. It was best I went.'

Mary Louise gave him a sympathetic smile. 'My life seems quite tame by comparison. A pond with hardly a ripple on it. But it won't always be like that.'

There was something in her voice which intrigued him. 'How do you mean?'

'Oh,' she said vaguely, 'I have plans.'

'What sort of plans? If I'm not being intrusive now.'

'Are you really interested?'

He nodded.

'I want to get on, get ahead. Achieve something.'

'Like what?'

'I don't know yet. But I'm quite determined about it. I want a better lifestyle than the one I was born into.'

'But you don't even have a job,' he laughed, though not unkindly.

'That's true; and it's not for lack of trying, either, I can assure you.' A glint came into her eyes. 'Still, as they say, there's more than one way to skin a cat.'

He wasn't sure he understood what she meant by that.

'Are you ambitious?' she suddenly asked.

'I don't know. I don't think so. I'm happy just to get by.'

She snorted.

'I take it that was the wrong reply?'

'It was the honest one, though. I hate people who lie.'

'I've never really thought about ambition,' Rory mused. 'It's just never entered into my scheme of things.'

'Then, maybe you *should* think about it.' She eyed him speculatively. 'I'll bet there's all sorts you could do if you put your mind to it. It seems to me all you need is the proper motivation.'

'And what would that be?'

'The right woman for one. With the right woman behind you who knows what you could achieve – the moon even.'

He laughed again. 'What would I want with the moon!'

'I don't mean literally. I was referring to money, position, power.'

'Well, I'm certainly not against money; that's for sure. I never seem to have enough of the stuff.'

'Imagine being so rich you never had to worry about it ever again,' she breathed. 'Wouldn't that be wonderful?'

'Wonderful,' he agreed.

'And it's possible. Sometimes it only boils down to a case of hard work and a belief in yourself.'

'Where did you get these ideas from, Mary Louise? I've never heard any other girl speak the way you do.'

'I don't know,' she said. 'Out of my own head, I suppose. It just seems common sense to me.'

'If you could be anything, who or what would you like to be?' he asked.

'Ahhh!' she exhaled. 'Now, there's a question. With regards to *who*, someone stinking filthy rich—'

'So rich you never had to worry about money ever again,' he interjected with a smile, paraphrasing her earlier words.

'Exactly! As to *what* – the same, I suppose. The Duchess of something or other, say.'

'Why not the Queen herself?' he teased.

'I wouldn't turn it down.'

'You're a caution, Mary Louise,' he further laughed.

'Because I want to get on? I don't see anything wrong with that. In fact I consider it admirable. Too many people are content just to sit and let life roll over them. Well, not me. You can bet on that.'

'You're so different,' he stated quietly.

She frowned. 'And so are you, Rory. Though I can't quite put my finger on why.'

That thrilled him. 'Am I?'

'Yes. There's a quality about you that ... stands out. At least, that's how it seems to me.'

'I'm flattered.'

'You should be. It takes something special to make a chap stand out from the herd.'

'And I have that something special?'

'Now, don't get too big-headed. But, yes, I believe you do. I think I recognized it the first time we met.'

'Well,' he said, lost for words.

'Shall we get back?'

He took a deep breath. 'Can I kiss you first?'

'I thought you'd never ask.'

'You're very sure of yourself, aren't you?'

'In many ways, yes. In others, no.'

He encircled her waist with his arms and gazed into her eyes. 'I'm glad we came up here and talked as we have.' He paused, then said; 'From now on I shall call you "Duchess" – at least, in private. That's going to be my nickname for you.'

'Duchess!'

'Duchess,' he repeated.

She was about to protest when he silenced her by covering her mouth with his own. When the kiss was over they were both strangely silent as, hand in hand, they walked to the motorbike and climbed aboard.

The silence between them remained unbroken when they roared away.

'Damnation!' Meg muttered, staring helplessly at the claws her hands had become. They were now so bad she couldn't even thread a needle.

She tried to lay the needle down, but was so clumsy she only succeeded in dropping it to the floor.

She was filled with self-pity and anger that this had happened to her. She'd always been so healthy when younger, her body able to do anything required of it. Now she was reduced to being a woman who couldn't even thread a needle.

She stared at the pile of work she had in from Mrs Monteith, wondering what to do about it. Should she hold on to it in the hope that her hands would ease sufficiently for her to cope, or take it back to Mrs Monteith and explain the situation? If she did return it, Mrs Monteith might well find someone else, which would mean her being out of a job. But if her hands continued as they were – and all they ever seemed to do was get worse – then she was out of a job anyway.

'Damnation!' she repeated.

She held her hands out in front of her and stared at them. How ugly they'd become and, above all, useless.

Hot tears ran down her cheeks. What had she done to deserve all this? Cully, Rowan, Vincent, arthritis. What had she done? It must have been something dreadful if it was in relation to the price she was paying.

She wiped away her tears. 'Get hold of yourself, girl,' she said aloud, knowing how close she was to completely breaking down.

She'd make a cup of tea, she decided, and smiled wryly. Wasn't a cup of tea the answer to everything? Well, it certainly seemed so in her case.

And after the tea she'd go out and buy a bar of chocolate. Now, that really would cheer her up. A *large* bar of chocolate, which she'd eat all by herself, every last square.

She went in search of a hanky before putting the kettle on.

'Is Vincent home?' Fee enquired as Meg ushered her and Lex into the kitchen.

'No, he's away on a trip.'

Fee exchanged glances with Lex. She'd known that, but was double-checking.

'How are you, Dad?' Meg asked.

'So so, lass. Could be better, could be worse. And what about yourself?'

'I'm fine – apart from my arthritis, that is.'

'Still bad, is it?' Lex sympathized.

Meg showed him her hands. 'Worse than ever.'

'What does the doctor say?'

Meg shrugged. 'There's no cure. I'll just have to live with it, that's all.'

'And work?'

'Haven't done any for ages. Mrs Monteith hasn't said, but I think she's found another seamstress.'

'Rotten luck,' Lex commiserated.

'I've had my fair share of that recently, and no mistake.'

'And I'm afraid we're bringing you some more,' Fee stated quietly.

Meg stared at her mother. 'In what way?'

'You tell her, Lex. It was you who found out.'

Lex sat and ran his fingers through his hair. 'Maybe you, too, had better sit down,' he suggested to Meg.

Meg sat facing him, wondering what this was all about. Her parents were clearly perturbed.

'Go on,' Fee urged Lex.

'It's about Vincent,' he said.

'What about him?'

'I have a friend who lives in Penderry, just across from the newsagent's there. The shop was run by a man and his wife, until the man ran off leaving the wife on her own. Quite a pretty woman apparently, called Rose.'

Lex stopped and cleared his throat. He was hating this, finding it difficult in the extreme. But it was his duty as Meg's father, he reminded himself. He went on. 'Well, it seems Vincent's car has been parked all night outside that shop on a number of occasions. Several times my friend has seen him leave there early in the morning.'

'Oh!' Meg murmured.

'I wasn't sure we were right to come and tell you,' Fee said nervously. 'But your dad insisted.'

282

'No, you were right,' Meg replied dully. Vincent and another woman! That explained why he'd been away from home more often of late, and why his demands in bed had fallen off considerably.

'What are you going to do?' Fee asked.

Meg put a hand to her forehead and rubbed it. 'I don't know yet. I'll have to think.'

'Throw the bugger out. That's what I'd do in your shoes,' Lex declared vehemently.

'And live on what, Dad? I've no money of my own coming in any more. Thanks to my arthritis, I'm now totally reliant on Vincent.'

'You can come and stay with us!'

'We haven't got the room,' Fee reminded him. 'Not unless Meg shares with Rory, and neither would want to do that.'

'Rory could move out?' Lex proposed.

Meg shook her head. 'Let him remain where he is. I'm happy for him to be there.'

'What about Ishbel coming back?' Fee queried.

'No,' Meg replied instantly.

'Why not?' Fee frowned.

'That would only lead to other problems, which I don't want to go into.'

Fee was mystified, but took the hint from Meg's tone and didn't enquire further.

'Of course there may be a reason other than the obvious for Vincent staying overnight at the Penderry newsagent's,' Lex said.

Fee barked out a scornful laugh. 'He's a man, isn't he?'

'It'll be the obvious, take my word for it,' Meg said softly.

'It's disgraceful,' Fee declared. 'I mean, you haven't been married that long!'

Long enough to make it seem like a lifetime, Meg thought. 'You say she's called Rose?'

Lex nodded.

'Right, then,' Meg said, and sighed.

'I'm sorry,' Lex smiled ruefully.

'So am I,' Fee added.

'You did the right thing in telling me,' Meg repeated, feeling curiously hollow inside.

'Is there anything we can do?' Fee queried.

Meg shook her head.

'All you have to do is say and I'll come running,' Lex stated.

'I know that, Dad.'

Fee moved across to Meg, pulled her upright and took her into her arms. In those arms Meg imagined herself a child again, young, carefree, without a worry in the world.

If only that could have been the case. When Fee released Meg she came back to harsh reality, the harsh reality of, among other things, an unfaithful husband.

'How's your tea?' Meg asked Vincent, staring at him across the table.

'All right.'

She looked down at her own meal, which remained untouched. It was a waste of good food, she thought, disliking the idea of waste in any form. 'So how was your trip?'

He shrugged. 'Fine.'

'Do any deals?'

'A couple.'

'Make any money?'

'Some.'

'Go anywhere near Penderry?'

His fork stopped halfway to his mouth. 'Pardon?'

'I said, go anywhere near Penderry?'

He glanced at her, noticing that her face was impassive. Her eyes, however, were glinting. 'Why Penderry in particular?' he queried.

'So you could stop off with Rose.'

He went very cold inside, while sweat broke out on his shoulders and under his arms. How in the hell had she found out about Rose?

'Rose?' he repeated innocently.

'Don't play silly beggars with me, Vincent,' she retorted

284

icily. 'Rose who owns the newsagent's and whose husband ran off with someone else. Rose whom you've been sleeping with.'

He took a deep breath, then laid his knife and fork alongside one another on the plate in front of him. 'Who told you?' he asked.

'That doesn't matter. All that does is I know about you and her.'

She'd caught him totally unprepared; he imagined his secret was safe. He tried to put his thoughts in order.

'Attractive, I believe,' Meg said bitterly.

'Extremely.'

'How did you meet her?'

'I've been calling in the shop, off and on, for a long time to buy cigarettes.'

'Ah!' Meg exclaimed softly. 'So you knew the husband?'

'Yes.'

'And when he decamped you saw your opportunity.'

He winced at the bluntness of that. And yet wasn't it true? That was exactly how it had been. He pushed his plate away and got up.

'Where are you going?'

'To get my cigarettes.'

'Don't you want your sweet?'

'Screw the sweet!'

She smiled thinly. 'It's apple crumble – one of your favourites.'

That floored him. Why should she make him one of his favourites knowing what she did. 'I'm not hungry any more,' he muttered, lighting up.

'Can't say I'm surprised. A guilty conscience does that to you.'

'I do not have a guilty conscience.'

He'd gone quite white, she thought. 'Then, you should have.'

He remembered there was some whisky in the house, went over to the cupboard where it was kept, and took the bottle out. He splashed a liberal measure into a glass and drank it off.

'Why?' she asked.

'Why what?'

'Why the need?'

He stared at her, incredulous. 'Why the need? For Christ's sake, Meg! You've been a disaster. You're forever putting me off or pushing me away.'

'That's not entirely true.'

'It is. And when you do consent you're simply not enthusiastic. It's just . . .' He halted, and drew heavily on his cigarette. 'It's just that you don't seem to want me and there are other women who do.'

'Such as Rose.'

'Such as bloody Rose!' he yelled. 'She appreciates me. Oh, yes, she appreciates me all right.'

Meg swallowed hard. Was she at fault? Was there something wrong with her? She couldn't believe that to be so. 'That must be nice for you,' she replied.

'Nice! What has nice got to do with it!'

Meg stood and began gathering up the dishes. 'You'll stop seeing her of course.'

Vincent glared at Meg. 'I'll do what I damn well want.'

Meg gazed defiantly back at him. 'Not in this instance, you won't. You'll stop seeing this Rose as from now.'

'And if I don't?'

'Then, you'll have to face the consequences.'

'What consequences? How pathetic! God alone knows what I ever saw in you. I must have been stark raving mad.'

She wouldn't cry, she told herself. Not here, not now. That was something she'd promised herself before initiating this confrontation.

He poured what remained of the whisky into his glass and knocked it back. All he could think of was Rose, and what a pleasure it was to be with her and how awful it was to be with Meg.

'Christ!' he screamed, and threw his empty glass across the room. It shattered against the wall.

Meg blinked and instinctively cowered as shards of glass flew all around. Later she would find several pieces entangled in her hair.

Even though it had been a small amount, and he'd just eaten, the whisky had gone straight to Vincent's head.

Meg stared down at the glass littering the floor. 'I'll have to clear that up now.'

'So what?'

'It was completely unnecessary.'

He watched her take out a broom and pan, noting the difficulty she had in manipulating both as she swept up the glass. Instead of feeling sympathy, he felt contempt. A cripple, he suddenly realized, that's what she was on the way to becoming.

'You will stop seeing her,' Meg stated again when she was finished with the glass.

'Oh, fuck you,' he spat. 'I'm off,' he stated, and strode from the kitchen.

She slumped down at the table and put her head in her hands. Despair welled up inside her, while her body and hands ached. She found herself thinking about Rowan, and wished she had the guts to do what her daughter had done. But there was Rory to think about, and Ishbel. She mustn't do anything silly because of them. They'd already lost a sister through suicide. Who knew what the effects would be on them of losing a mother the same way? No, tempting as it was, that just wasn't on.

A few minutes later Vincent reappeared carrying a suitcase. 'I'm leaving you,' he announced.

Good riddance to bad rubbish, she thought.

'Well?'

'Goodbye. I hope you're happy with her,' Meg replied.

That infuriated him. 'I'll be far happier with her than I ever was with you, that's for certain.'

'Just go,' she said.

'With pleasure.'

As he left the house he slammed the front door behind him.

Now what was she going to do? Meg wondered.

'Coming!' Rose yelled in reply to the knocking. She quickly wrapped her newly washed hair in a towel, then slipped into her dressing-down.

'Ta ra!' Vincent beamed when she opened the door. He was holding his suitcase in one hand, a bottle of whisky in the other.

Rose frowned. 'What's this?'

'It's your lucky day. I've left Meg and have come to stay with you.'

Stay with ... Her heart sank. 'Have you, indeed?' she said quietly.

'And this bottle's to celebrate.'

Vincent kissed Rose as he brushed past her. 'I'll pour us out a drink right away, shall I?'

She managed a weak unconvincing smile. 'Please.'

Her thoughts were whirling. He might have telephoned to warn her instead of just arriving on her doorstep like this. A telephone call would at least have given her time to think things over. It was very presumptuous of him to do what he'd done.

'Cheers!' he said, handing her a glass.

'Cheers.'

'Malt,' he informed her. 'Nothing but the best. I wanted champagne, but the off-licence didn't have any. Said it was rare for them to be asked for that.'

'What happened between you and your wife?' Rose asked slowly, eyeing Vincent over the rim of her glass.

'We had a fight.'

'Must have been a big one.'

'It was,' he smiled.

'Can I ask what it was about?'

'You,' he stated.

'Me!'

'Meg somehow found out about you. I've no idea how; she wouldn't say.'

Rose laid her glass aside and pulled her dressing-gown

288

more tightly about herself. 'And so you left. Or did she throw you out?'

'I left. Packed my suitcase, and that was that.'

'And came straight here.'

'I must confess I did stop off at a pub first. And the off-licence of course.'

'You didn't think of going anywhere else?'

He stared at her, puzzled, and now a little unsure. 'Should I have done? I mean . . . I thought . . .'

Rose sighed. 'Wait here till I get dressed.'

'I'll come with you if you like.'

'No. Wait here.' She wanted to be alone so she could think.

She took her time about dressing and brushing her hair. It was almost half an hour before she returned to Vincent, who by then had consumed about a third of the whisky.

'I was beginning to think you'd died,' he commented drily.

Rose picked up her drink and sipped it. 'I don't want you staying here,' she stated.

His face fell. 'Why not?'

'I just don't, that's all.'

'You must have a reason, Rose.'

She regarded him levelly. 'I enjoy your company, Vincent; you're good to be with. But I don't think I could live with you.'

'But Rose . . .'

'In fact I'm certain about that,' she interjected.

His shoulders drooped. It had never crossed his mind that she wouldn't want him there. He'd fully expected her to jump for joy when he announced the news.

'You and I are great together,' he said lamely.

She could see how much she'd hurt him, which she hadn't wanted to do at all, for she was extremely fond of Vincent. 'We have our moments,' she smiled.

'More than moments surely?'

She didn't answer that.

He went to her and put his hands on her shoulders. 'Please reconsider, Rose. Please?'

She broke away.

289

'At least let's give it a try?' he further pleaded.

Rose shook her head. 'It wouldn't work, Vincent. I'm convinced of that. You're very sweet, but . . .' She shrugged. 'I don't love you, I'm afraid.'

'You might learn to?'

'No,' she said softly. 'And don't tell me that you love me, for I know you don't.'

'I believe I could, though,' he declared in desperation.

'Not real love, Vincent. That happens spontaneously or not at all.'

Suddenly he knew what this was really all about, why she wouldn't let him move in. 'You're still in love with Ronnie, aren't you?'

She turned away so he couldn't see her face.

'Rose?'

'Yes,' she whispered in reply.

'And you don't want me here in case he comes back to you?'

She took a deep breath. 'Yes,' she admitted.

'And what if he doesn't? What if you never clap eyes on him again? Just think what you'll have thrown away.'

'I can't help how I feel, Vincent. I shouldn't love him, not after what he did, but I do. I love him now and always will. That's how it is.'

'I'll be good to you, Rose, I swear. You wouldn't want for anything.'

'I'm sure,' she replied, warmth in her voice.

'Only that's not enough?'

She shook her head. 'Meeting up as we were, going out together and to bed was fine. But in a way it was me getting back at Ronnie.' That would hurt him even further, but she'd decided honesty was the best policy. 'I'm sorry if that's hard.'

'Hard! It couldn't be harder.'

'I am sorry, Vincent, truly I am.'

He was outraged to think he'd been so used. Bloody women, he inwardly fumed. You couldn't trust any of them. They were all double-dealing connivers.

'Let me at least stay the night?' he said.

'No,' she stated emphatically. 'If I allowed that, I'd never get rid of you. So you'll just have to take that suitcase and go elsewhere.'

'But I've walked out on Meg, burnt my bridges.'

'You should have spoken to me first before leaving her. It's hardly my fault you took so much for granted.'

'But you gave every indication . . .' He trailed off, now more furious with himself than with her. She was right: he had taken things for granted.

'I'll have a little drop more of that whisky if you don't mind,' she requested.

'Help yourself.'

Her lips twisted into a cynical smile. 'Like that now, is it?'

'Well, what do you expect?'

She could appreciate how bitterly disappointed he was, and resolved to end their relationship that evening. Going to the bottle, she poured a small amount into her glass.

'What will you do?' she asked.

'How the hell do I know? A hotel, I suppose.'

'It wouldn't work between us, believe me,' she said softly.

'Not with you still in love with Ronnie, it wouldn't. I suppose every time we've been in bed together it's him you've been thinking of?'

She averted her gaze.

He drew himself up to his full height. 'At least I'm better at it than him. You've said so.'

Better? Technically, yes. But there had been no emotional involvement between them as there had been between her and Ronnie. With Vincent it was purely physical, which she found sad as it meant he was missing so much. He could play the instrument beautifully, except his playing lacked heart and soul, consisting purely of technique.

'I think you'd better leave now,' she said.

'I'm leaving all right, don't worry about that. I've never been so humiliated in my life.'

His ego had taken an awfully large dent, she thought, a

small part of her finding that amusing. It was such a large ego after all.

'I *am* better, aren't I?' he queried harshly, eyes starting from his head.

'Far better,' she smiled.

He made a harumphing sound. 'I'll be on my way, then.'

'Vincent?'

He stopped *en route* to his suitcase and turned to face her.

'Take care, eh?'

'You're making a mistake,' he said, a tinge of self-pity in his tone.

She knew she wasn't. 'Don't forget the whisky.'

'Keep it. It was a present for you after all.'

'You might want a drink later.'

'Then, I'll buy another bottle.'

And with that he picked up his suitcase and swept from the room.

She'd miss him, no doubt about it. Then she smiled again, thinking she'd miss him the way she'd miss a favourite dog. In a peculiar way their relationship had been rather like that.

Vincent blew a smoke ring, watching it float lazily upwards eventually to break against the hotel bedroom ceiling. The question now was: what next?

Did he want to live by himself again? Do his own cooking, cleaning, washing, ironing and all the rest of it? The answer was a resounding no.

It had come as a profound shock when Rose had rejected him, and as for her still being in love with Ronnie, and thinking about Ronnie when she was in bed with him, that was dreadful! He swallowed hard, aware that his ears were burning with embarrassment.

But, if not Rose, who? He was certain he could get someone else in time, but meanwhile what? He couldn't go on staying in a hotel – far too expensive. Besides, he didn't like hotels all that much. He found them impersonal and generally depressing.

He could soon rent a cottage; no problem there. But that meant living by himself, which he didn't want. He'd backed himself into a corner right enough.

He stubbed out his cigarette, wishing he'd bought a second bottle of whisky. Worse still, he was hungry, and it was too late to get the hotel to make him anything. If he'd been at home, he'd have soon organized a sandwich. Or, if Meg hadn't already gone to bed, she'd have put together something tasty for him; she was marvellous at doing that.

'Buggeration!' he swore, scowling at the ceiling. He swore again when his stomach rumbled.

Meg stopped short when she saw Vincent's car parked outside the house. Why had he returned? she wondered, and decided he must have called in to collect some things. Should she go and visit Fee while he got on with it? She didn't really want to speak to him. Or should she go in? After all, she didn't want him taking anything that wasn't his.

Vincent jumped to his feet when Meg entered the kitchen. 'Hello, Meg, it's me.'

'I can see it's you,' she retorted sarcastically, then stared at the huge bunch of flowers lying on the kitchen table.

'Those are for you,' he informed her.

'No, thanks.'

'Oh, come on, Meg, we all make mistakes. And I certainly made one yesterday.'

She frowned. What was all this?

'I've come home,' he stated.

That stunned her. 'You've what?'

'Come home,' he repeated. 'I realized the mistake I'd made, and so here I am. I can't apologize enough. I was stupid beyond belief.'

Meg laid her basket of shopping on the table alongside the flowers. 'And you expect me to take you back again? You must be mad!'

His expression became pained. 'I appreciate how you must feel. I've behaved appallingly.'

'So why aren't you with Rose?' Meg demanded. 'That's where you went, wasn't it?'

Vincent shook his head. 'I stayed the night in a hotel, to think things through.' When he saw Meg's disbelieving look he pulled out his hotel receipt and handed it to her. 'There you are. That's proof.'

Meg gazed at the receipt, then threw it on to the table. 'So what?'

'Rose means nothing to me, I swear.'

'And neither do I apparently.' How she wished Cully was still alive.

He gestured to Cully's chair. 'Sit down, please. Let's talk this over.'

'There's nothing to talk over.'

'Yes, there is, Meg. Please!'

Reluctantly, she found herself settled in the indicated chair. He sat facing her.

'Something went wrong between us,' he began. 'A lot of it my fault, some of it yours. And some of it sheer circumstance. Like your slipped disc, for example. I found that extremely trying.'

'And how do you think I found it!'

'I know, I know,' he soothed, holding his hands up placatingly. 'It was far worse for you than for me. The trouble was, I suppose, that I was selfish, thinking only of my own needs. You must understand how different that side of things is for a man, especially a man such as me—'

'What was required was a little control on your part,' she interjected angrily.

He sighed. 'But it wasn't just that.'

'You never tried to get on with Rory,' she accused.

'True, I grant you. But on the other hand he never tried to get on with me. He never gave me a chance.'

'Did you give him one? Right from the word go you attacked him.'

'You must remember I'm simply not used to children, never having had any of my own. I found it hard.'

'What about Ishbel?' she countered. 'What you tried to do to her is unforgivable.'

'I was desperate, Meg,' he pleaded. 'And fuelled by alcohol, don't forget. You'd been laid up all that time and ... well, I suppose it just got the better of me. I was totally wrong, I admit, but if I hadn't been drinking it would never have happened. I'm sure of it.' Vincent looked contrite. 'Let's start afresh, Meg. I'm willing if you are.'

'Start afresh! After how you've treated me? How many more times can we start afresh?'

'We must try to understand one another better. Understand each other's ways. You were at least partially to blame for how things became.'

'And what about Rose?'

'I'm finished with her. She's gone – forgotten. I'll never see her again.'

'How do I know I can believe you?' Meg asked, her hard stance against him beginning to crumble. He was so plausible. And, she had to admit, perhaps she had been a victim of preconceived ideas, not willing to be compliant to her new partner's obviously very different rhythms and requirements.

Vincent then startled Meg by going down on to his knees and shuffling his way over to her. 'My word of honour, Meg. I'll swear it on a bible if you wish. Only give me the chance to turn over a new leaf, please.'

Doubt assailed her. Maybe she had misjudged him, been more at fault herself than she'd previously realized. And then, very importantly, there was the financial factor to consider. Without Vincent, and with her unable to work, there wasn't any money coming into the house.

Damn! she thought, the remainder of her resistance crumbling. 'All right,' she said slowly. 'We'll give it a go. See how we make out.'

Vincent laid his face in her lap and smiled. He'd won her round. It was, after all, better to have Meg than to have nothing at all.

'You won't regret this, Meg. I promise,' he said, lifting his head to stare at her.

She wasn't so sure.

Chapter Eight

'Engaged!' Meg exclaimed in surprise and delight.

'We wanted you to be the first to know,' Rory grinned.

Mary Louise flashed her diamond ring at Meg. 'What do you think? It's a smasher, isn't it?'

'It should be at the price,' Rory pretended to grumble.

Meg took Mary Louise's hand in her own and studied the ring, which was a rectangular stone surrounded by chips. 'Very nice,' she enthused.

'We're hoping to marry next year, probably in the summer,' Rory said. It was then February 1930.

'That'll give you plenty of time to save up,' Meg commented.

'That's the plan,' Mary Louise smiled.

'And where will you live?'

'A place of our own. I have no intention of starting off married life with my parents, much as I love them,' Mary Louise informed Meg.

Meg nodded her approval.

'A small house or cottage to start with,' Rory declared.

'At least I'm working now, which helps,' Mary Louise said. She'd landed a job in the accounts department at the quarry.

'How's that getting on?' Meg enquired.

'Fine. I'm enjoying it. I'm really no better than an office junior at the moment, but I've been promised more responsibility and more interesting things to do as I learn the ropes.'

'And more money,' Rory added.

'More money as I go along,' Mary Louise countered.

'Well, I hope you're both going to be very happy,' Meg declared, wishing Cully had been there to meet his future daughter-in-law.

Mary Louise grasped Rory's arm and pulled herself close to him. 'We're going to be happy all right. I always knew Rory was the chap for me.'

'She says we're fated,' Rory grinned.

'That's how it is with some people,' Mary Louise said.

Meg thought again of Cully and smiled. 'And you haven't told your parents yet?'

'No. We wanted you to be the first,' Rory answered.

'That was kind of you. I appreciate it.'

On impulse Rory kissed Meg on the cheek. 'I'm doing the right thing, Mum. I have no doubts about that whatever.'

'She's a bonny lass,' Meg smiled.

'Quite beautiful,' Rory enthused, which made Mary Louise blush.

'Stop it, you two. Look what you're doing to me!' she protested.

Rory laughed at her discomfort, thinking how lucky he was to have found such a creature. He felt he'd known Mary Louise all his life, and that nothing had really existed before they met.

Meg had a sudden thought which took all the excitement out of her expression. '*Where* do you plan to have the wedding?'

Rory knew what was bothering her. 'We haven't settled that yet, Mum. But rest assured it won't be Dykes officiating. He's the last person I'd have.'

Meg nodded her relief and approval.

'We'll let you know once we've decided what's what,' Mary Louise said.

'I suppose I'll have to invite Vincent,' Rory stated heavily.

Meg gave him a sympathetic smile. 'He is your stepfather, Rory, and my husband. You can't very well invite me and not him.'

Rory sighed. That was true enough.

'I'll see he's on his best behaviour, particularly towards you. And, for your part, to please me, you try to be civil to him.'

'We came round now because I heard he was away,' Rory said.

'He left yesterday and won't be back for another three days at least.'

'Where has he gone?' Mary Louise enquired politely. She had never met Vincent.

'Up to Inverness-shire. There are some horses coming up for sale that he's interested in.'

'Fascinating job,' Mary Louise commented.

'He enjoys it,' Meg said. 'And he makes a good living out of it, far more than if it was an ordinary nine-to-five.'

'A good living,' Mary Louise repeated quietly, glancing sideways at Rory. That was what she wanted him to earn. But give it time: she'd get him properly organized eventually. She was determined about that.

'Is it going to be a big wedding, then?' Meg asked.

'Huge,' Rory smiled.

'It'll be a wonderful day,' Mary Louise said, her eyes shining at the prospect.

'I can't wait,' Rory told her.

Neither could she – for the day itself or for the honeymoon. One thing was certain: she'd be a virgin on her wedding night. That was how she wanted it, and how it would be. Anyway, the alternative was far too risky. Rowan was a prime example of that.

'A June wedding would be nice,' Meg said, thinking of the weather.

'Or August,' Mary Louise added, for the same reason.

'Whenever, as long as it's you I walk back up the aisle with,' Rory declared.

'How gallant! I never thought he had it in him,' Meg said.

'Oh, he can be very gallant at times,' Mary Louise laughed.

'Obviously a side to him I know nothing about.'

'There's more to me than meets the eye,' Rory joked.

'I'll bet!' Meg replied drily.

'I take it we have your blessing, then?' Mary Louise said to Meg.

'Of course, lass. I couldn't approve more. I just wish I had a little something in with which to toast the occasion, but unfortunately I haven't.'

'Another time,' Mary Louise said.

'Another time,' Meg agreed.

When they were gone Meg sat and had a cry to herself. Rory getting wed! Why, it seemed only yesterday that . . .

Later she wrote to Ishbel and Aunt Dot, telling them the good news.

'There, my wee lass,' smiled Aunt Dot, who was sitting on the floor playing with Jessica.

'My dolly,' said Jessica, waving the doll in question at Aunt Dot.

'And what's her name again?'

'Suzy.'

'That's right. Suzy,' Aunt Dot nodded. She reflected that it was lovely having a child in the house, but so tiring, particularly to someone of her age. Not that she was complaining. She adored looking after Jessica while Ishbel was out at work. How lonely and empty her life had been before they'd come to stay with her. The days had been grey then, stretching endlessly from her getting up in the morning till she went to bed at night. Now her days were filled with colour and joy, and seemed to flash past.

She thought of her husband Ben and how keen he'd been for them to have a family of their own, as indeed had she. But the good Lord had never blessed them, and they'd remained childless. How different things would have been if that hadn't been the case. Although happy enough, the fact they didn't have children had always been a sadness between her and Ben, a sadness Ben had felt more acutely than he'd ever let on.

The front door banged shut, and Dot smiled when Ishbel appeared in the room.

'What are you doing on the floor?' Ishbel asked.

'Jessica and I are having a game.'

300

'With Suzy,' Jessica added.

'The pair of you look like you're enjoying yourselves.'

'Oh, we are,' Aunt Dot replied, hauling herself to her feet. It was easy getting down, not so easy getting back up again. 'How was work?'

'Fine.'

'I'll get started on your tea, then.'

'I'm hungry,' Jessica stated.

Ishbel laughed. 'You're always hungry, poppet. I think you have hollow legs.'

Jessica frowned, trying to understand how she could have hollow legs. They felt solid enough.

'Who'd like some chips?' Aunt Dot asked in an innocent tone, knowing the response she'd get.

'Me!' Jessica squealed, for she adored chips.

'And me,' Ishbel added with a smile.

'Then, chips it is.'

Ishbel picked Jessica up and hugged her close. 'And what sort of day have you had, young lady?'

'We went to the zoo.'

'The zoo!' Ishbel exclaimed.

'It's years since I've been to a zoo, so I decided to give her a treat,' Aunt Dot explained, busy at the sink. 'It was great fun.'

'And what did you see there?' Ishbel asked Jessica.

'Elephants and tigers and giraffes.'

'Well, well, well,' murmured Ishbel. 'Why don't you tell me all about it?'

Which Jessica did while Aunt Dot got on with their tea.

'Hello,' Rory said when Mary Louise answered his knock.

'Come in.'

'Have they gone out?' he queried in a whisper when Mary Louise had shut the door.

'Half an hour since.'

'So we're alone?'

She nodded.

He gathered her into his arms and kissed her deeply,

she eagerly responding. She sighed with contentment and pleasure when their lips finally parted.

'I could do that twenty-four hours a day,' he said.

She laughed. 'That would be spoiling a good thing.'

'And good it certainly is.'

He kissed her again, running his hands up and down her back, then over the swell of her buttocks.

'Enough for now,' she declared, breaking away.

'I never get enough of you.'

'How do you fancy being a chauffeur?' she asked as they entered the sitting-room where a fire was blazing in the grate.

'A chauffeur!'

'It was something I heard at the office today. The Master of Drum was visiting Mr Monteith, and his current chauffeur happened to mention to one of my pals that he's shortly retiring, which means the position will be falling vacant.'

'But I can't drive a car!' Rory protested.

'Surely it's not that different from a motorbike? You could quickly learn.'

Rory thought about that. 'I suppose so. And Fraser's father has a car; he might teach me.'

'There we are, then,' Mary Louise beamed.

'But why a chauffeur? I already have a job.'

'A dead-end job that will never get you anywhere. There are no prospects where you are now; you've told me that yourself.'

'True,' Rory admitted. 'But what prospects are there in being a chauffeur?'

'Well, for a start you'll be working for someone important. The Master of Drum, Mr Archibald Lindsay, is a Liberal MP, and an extremely wealthy man, I understand. Then there's his wife, Celia; she's a very glamorous actress.'

'Actress!' a bemused Rory repeated.

'And, as I say, very glamorous, I'm told. A real beauty.'

'I've never heard of her, though I've heard of him.'

'He's a well-known backbencher with a lot of influence

302

in his party. She's often appeared on the London stage.'

'But I still don't see how being chauffeur to them would advantage me?' Rory queried.

'To begin with, the pay's excellent according to the current chauffeur – more than you're getting now, I would imagine. But the point is it's not the job itself but where it might lead to. It could be a springboard to all sorts.'

'Would I be based locally or would it mean going away for periods?'

'Based locally, I was assured. But that's something you can enquire about at your interview.'

'I don't know,' Rory prevaricated.

Mary Louise gave a sigh of exasperation. 'Don't know what? This kind of opportunity doesn't happen every day. You should grab it before someone else does.'

Rory laughed. 'And how many someone elses are going to be after the position? If it's the plum you claim, they'll be queuing up for it.'

'But if you act quickly you can be first in that queue.'

'A chauffeur,' Rory mused. Now that he came to think about it, he rather liked the idea. A nice big fancy car to drive around in was right up his street.

'The sooner you learn to drive the better,' Mary Louise declared.

'I'll go and see Fraser's dad tomorrow.'

'Why not tonight?'

'Tonight! But ...' He trailed off; there was no reason why he shouldn't go that night.

'I'll come with you,' Mary Louise stated.

'You really are keen on this, aren't you?' he smiled.

'Very.'

'Well, I'm not going round to Fraser's until I get another kiss.'

'Bribery, is it?' she teased.

'And corruption.'

'We'll have less of the corruption if you don't mind.' She slid into his embrace. 'But I've nothing against the bribery.'

'As long as you get your own way, you mean, Duchess?'

She raised an eyebrow.

'I love you.'

He was allowed one kiss at that point and one only. After that they set off for Fraser's where Fraser's dad said he'd be only too happy to teach Rory to drive.

Rory turned his motorbike into the driveway of Drum House, following its snaking, twisting contours until eventually the house stood before him.

He brought his bike to a halt and stared at the building, thinking how magnificent it was. Constructed of grey stone with a slate roof, it had many arched windows and turrets, the overall impression being of a medieval castle.

Now where should he go? Rory wondered as he approached the house. Luckily the problem was solved when he spotted a man polishing a Rolls-Royce.

Rory introduced himself and explained why he was there. The man, as he'd surmised, was the current chauffeur. McIntosh, grizzled and white-haired and looking as though he should have retired long since, directed Rory to the rear of the house and then wished him luck; which Rory thought kind.

'Can I help you?' a fresh-faced housemaid asked as Rory poked his head in through the open doorway.

'I have an interview with the Master of Drum at ten o'clock,' Rory smiled.

'Oh, have you?' She eyed him up and down. 'Here for a job, eh?'

'As chauffeur.'

She sniffed. 'You'd better follow me, then. And make sure you wipe your feet before you go any further!'

The room she conducted him to was small and wood-panelled. It smelled strongly of polish.

He only had to wait a few minutes before a butler appeared. 'Mr Stewart?'

'That's me,' replied Rory, rising to his feet.

'This way, please.'

They walked along a corridor, eventually arriving at an intricately carved door which the butler politely tapped.

'Come in!'

'Mr Stewart, sir,' the butler announced to the man sitting behind a green-leather-topped desk.

The Master of Drum rose and smiled. 'How do you do, Mr Stewart?' he said, extending his hand.

Friendly enough, Rory thought as he shook it. 'I'm fine, sir, thank you very much.'

Rory judged the Master of Drum to be about five feet seven or eight. He was slightly built with thinning hair swept straight back from his forehead. He sported a thick, neatly clipped military-type moustache, while the eyes above the moustache were grey and piercing. The voice was cultured, the product of an English public school.

The Master indicated a chair. 'Please sit down.'

He also sat and regarded Rory thoughtfully across the desk. 'I must say I was surprised to receive your letter regarding a position that hasn't become vacant yet.'

'I hope you didn't think me presumptuous, sir, but I wanted to get in before anyone else.'

'I don't consider it presumptuous at all,' the Master replied. 'Enterprising more like. I thoroughly approve. But tell me, how did you hear that McIntosh would be leaving?'

Rory explained about Mary Louise and how she'd picked up the information after the Master had visited the quarry. The Master nodded as he listened.

'I see,' the Master said when Rory had finished. It was all perfectly straightforward and satisfied his curiosity. 'Have you been driving long?'

'Quite a while now,' Rory replied; which was true, if not the whole truth. He had been driving a motorbike some time.

The Master made a note of that, then went on with further questions. When he had finished, he began describing the job in detail, and explaining what precisely was entailed. He also answered a few questions Rory asked him.

They were nearing the end of the interview when there was a knock on the door.

'Come in!' the Master called out.

The woman who entered the room was younger than the Master and exquisitely beautiful. She had short blonde hair, deep blue eyes and sunken cheeks. There was something ethereal about her that Rory found fascinating. Her hands were long and thin, the nails painted with pale pink varnish.

'Hello, darling,' said the Master, jumping instantly to his feet.

'Burnford said you had someone with you, but I must have a word.'

'Of course.'

She smiled at Rory, who had also stood up; he was quite stunned by her beauty. That certainly hadn't been exaggerated. It wasn't merely a physical beauty, he noted, but something that shone from within.

'Mr Stewart, this is my wife, Mrs Lindsay. Darling, this is Mr Stewart who's applied for McIntosh's job.'

'A pleasure to meet you, Mr Stewart,' she said, shaking hands with Rory. Her hand was cool and so delicate in comparison to Rory's own meaty paw that he was almost scared to exert any pressure whatsoever on it.

'And I'm delighted to meet you, Mrs Lindsay.' He hesitated, then said, 'Is that how I address you?'

'Quite correct,' she said.

'And you call me Mr Lindsay,' added the Master.

Now he knew, Rory thought. He'd been at a loss on either score. 'Would you like me to wait outside while you speak?' he enquired.

Mrs Lindsay gave him a look which said she appreciated his sensitivity and tact. 'That won't be necessary, Mr Stewart, thank you very much.'

She then conferred with her husband over a minor household crisis that had occurred, after which she left them.

'So where were we?' smiled the Master.

Rory reminded him.

* * *

'How did it go?' demanded an anxious Mary Louise.

'All right, I think. They were certainly very good at putting me at my ease.'

'*They?* Are you saying you met *her* as well? The Mistress as well as the Master?'

Rory nodded.

'What was she like? And what was she wearing? Tell me everything about them. I'm dying to know.'

Rory stared at Mary Louise, realizing for the first time that his future wife was a born snob.

'Where would you like me to begin?'

Mary Louise exhaled slowly while she thought. 'With her,' she decided.

From there on Rory had to recount every last detail from the moment he'd turned into the Drum House driveway until he'd left again.

'There's a letter arrived for you,' Fee said to Rory, placing it in front of him at the breakfast-table.

Rory paused to stare at the envelope. His name and address were written in bold purple strokes. He didn't have to open the letter to know who it was from. That was obvious. It was a week to the day since his interview.

'Go on, then, lad,' urged Lex.

Rory picked up the letter, thinking what an expensive envelope it was, not like the cheap ones he used when he wrote a letter.

'It's from the Lindsays,' he said slowly. 'I'm sure I haven't got the job.'

'Well, you won't know that until you read what's inside,' Fee declared, folding her arms over her bosom.

There was a single sheet of paper covered in the same bold purple strokes as the envelope. The signature at the bottom read *Archibald Lindsay, Master of Drum*.

Rory's face lit up in a beaming smile. 'They want me,' he stated.

'There we are!' Lex exclaimed, smiling also, as was Fee.

'When do you start?' Fee demanded.

'In two months' time.'

Fee glanced at the clock. 'You'd better nip down the road and tell Mary Louise before she goes off to work.'

Mary Louise squealed with delight on hearing his good news.

'And here is where the bottles are packed,' Jock Logan, the gaffer, explained to the young man standing beside him.

The young man nodded.

'This is Ishbel Stewart, and the lassie assisting her is Moira Ferguson. Girls, may I introduce Gavin Clarke who's come to work for Blue Bonnet?'

Attractive face, Ishbel thought. 'Hello.'

'Hello,' he replied bashfully.

Moira, who was a lot younger than Ishbel, giggled; which earned her a reproving look from Jock Logan.

'I hope you enjoy working with us, Mr Clarke,' Ishbel said.

'Thank you. I'm sure I will. Everyone I've met so far seems very content.'

Jock's expression showed he was pleased to hear that. 'I do my best to run a happy ship,' he declared. The allusion arose from the fact that he'd once been in the Royal Navy.

'That's how it comes over,' Gavin assured him.

'We'll move on, then,' Jock said, glancing across at a machine filling bottles with golden liquid.

'See you again,' Gavin smiled to Ishbel and Moira, and moved off.

'Not bad,' Moira whispered.

Ishbel thought so, too, watching him walk away. She wondered if he was married, engaged or courting.

Moira heaved the wooden box they'd just filled aside and started on the one below.

'So what do you think of the new fellow?' Sarah Webster demanded. There were eight of them, all females, having their morning tea-break. Ishbel didn't like Sarah, thinking her a foul-mouthed woman.

'Nice eyes,' commented Isa Molloy, biting into a jam sandwich.

'He's the sort I wouldn't mind cuddling up to,' said Betty Hope.

'I could do more than cuddle up to him,' declared Sarah, then made a crude remark which caused Ishbel to blush, others to laugh.

'Fat chance. He has a girlfriend,' stated Ellen Weary.

'How do you know that?' demanded Sarah.

'Because she's a pal of mine. They've been going out together for almost a year now.'

Sarah swore. 'I quite fancied him as well.'

'And you're free,' smiled Olive McGuire.

Sarah glared at Olive. 'What's that supposed to mean?'

'Nothing. Only that you don't currently have a beau.'

Like heck, Ishbel thought. It had been a cutting jibe of which Sarah was well aware.

'Neither do you!' Sarah retorted hotly.

'Oh, yes, I have.'

'Since when?'

'Saturday. We met at the dancing.'

'Huh!' snorted Sarah, clearly not believing her, which incensed Olive.

'His name's Tom and he works in a foundry. We're meeting again this Friday – going to the pictures.'

'Tom?' a still doubting Sarah queried.

'Tillery. Lives in Maryhill.'

Ishbel spotted Gavin talking to some of his new workmates as they were also on their tea-break. He glanced over, saw her looking at him and smiled.

She returned his smile, reflecting again that he had an attractive face.

'So what do you think, Ishbel?'

Ishbel brought her attention back to the crowd to discover that Betty had addressed her. 'Sorry, my mind was wandering. Think about what?'

When Ishbel looked again Gavin had moved away and now wasn't to be seen.

*　　*　　*

'Mrs Lindsay wants you in half an hour,' Burnford the butler informed Rory, who was sitting in the staff kitchen drinking a cup of tea. 'You're to take her to Stirling.'

'Stirling!' Rory exclaimed.

'So have the car out front then,' Burnford added, after which he hurried off.

'Stirling's lovely. I like it there,' commented Mrs Murchie the cook.

'I've never been,' Rory replied. He swallowed what remained of his tea thinking he'd have to consult a map and get himself tidied up.

Half an hour later Celia Lindsay emerged from Drum House to find Rory standing beside the Rolls, ready to open the door for her. She was wearing a black cloth coat with a black fur collar. On her head she sported a cloche hat with a large pin stuck through it. Rory made a note of these details to relate later to Mary Louise, who always wanted to know what Mrs Lindsay had been wearing.

'Good morning, Rory,' Celia Lindsay said, approaching the car.

'Good morning,' he replied.

'Burnford tell you where I want to go?'

'He mentioned Stirling.'

'That's correct. The Floral Gallery in St Mary's Wynd. If you don't know where that is, I'll direct you when we get there.'

'Thank you,' he answered.

She settled into the back seat and immediately lit a cigarette. She smoked incessantly. Rory started the Rolls and they purred away.

They drove for about half an hour in silence, she deep in thought and chain smoking. Every so often Rory checked his rear-view mirror, taking the opportunity also to glance at her.

'How long have you been with us now, Rory?' she asked eventually.

'A fortnight.'

'And you've settled in all right?'

'Fine, thank you,' he smiled.

'Is your room satisfactory?'

'Very.' He had a room at Drum House where he stayed if needed late at night or early in the morning. If not, he went home.

'Good,' she nodded.

She was looking paler than usual, he thought, which somehow made her even more beautiful. The dark smudges under her eyes merely enhanced that beauty.

'We'll have to be back in time for you to pick up Mr Lindsay from the station. He'll be on the four-twenty,' she said.

Rory made a mental note of that.

'He'll be home for the weekend, then it's down to London again. I may or may not go with him. I haven't decided yet.'

'I understand,' Rory said.

The next occasion he glanced in the rear-view mirror he found her staring at him. 'Do you know anything about art, Rory?' she asked.

He grinned. 'Not a thing.'

'Archie's terribly knowledgeable on the subject. I've learnt a lot from him.'

'I've seen some nice pictures round your house.'

'Yes, we have rather a good collection. Modern as well as old masters. That's why I'm going to the Floral Gallery today. I'm hoping to pick up a watercolour for Archie's birthday.'

'Is the gallery holding a special exhibition?' Rory enquired.

'Of local Scottish artists,' she replied, lighting yet another cigarette. 'Some of them I'm familiar with, others are new to me.'

'Well, I hope you're lucky.'

'We'll see,' she smiled.

There was a pause, then Rory said: 'I may not know anything about art but I enjoy looking at pictures when I get the chance. They can be very interesting.'

311

'Glasgow has a marvellous art gallery,' she informed him. 'You should go round it some time.'

'Maybe I will.'

'And of course Edinburgh has several. I adore Edinburgh, don't you?'

'I'm not all that familiar with it,' he confessed. 'I've only ever been a couple of times, and those were quick visits on my bike.'

'Edinburgh's enchanting – quite fairy-taleish, I always think. And has some excellent theatres.'

'Have you performed there?'

'Only in a touring production.' She frowned. 'I can't for the life of me remember what the play was. A new comedy that didn't do all that well.'

Rory was intrigued. 'Have you always been an actress? Again, that's something I know nothing about.'

'Always,' she smiled. 'Since I was eighteen anyway. I was twenty when I first appeared in the West End. That production was a huge success.'

'Sounds exciting,' Rory commented.

'Oh, the theatre's a wonderful life! There's nothing quite like it.'

She was being very chatty and forthcoming, Rory thought, hoping he wasn't doing the wrong thing in answering as he had. He didn't think so; she was the one who'd instigated the conversation after all, and he was thoroughly enjoying it.

'Do you listen to the wireless?' Celia asked.

'Sometimes.'

'They do some marvellous drama on that. Though I have to admit I've never been on the wireless myself.'

'How about films?' Rory queried.

She gave a throaty laugh. 'Oh, a number of those. I've worked with some very big stars. I enjoy filming, though nowhere near as much as live stage. Nothing beats that.'

'Have you anything planned for the near future?'

Her expression clouded over and became sad. 'No,

unfortunately. I've been ill, you see, which has stopped me working of late.'

'I'm sorry,' Rory said softly.

'So am I. But it's only a matter of time before I'm back treading the boards again.'

'I'd like to see that when you do.'

'I'm sure it can be arranged,' she smiled.

'If it was in Scotland, that is. I'm afraid London would be too far away for me.'

'Dear old Shaftesbury Avenue,' Celia sighed, her eyes taking on a reflective look.

She gazed out of the window and again became lost in thought. The next time she spoke was when they arrived in Stirling and she had to give Rory directions.

Vincent stopped his car and stared across the road at Rose's shop. Should he venture in and buy a packet of cigarettes? he wondered. There was nothing wrong in that, and it would be lovely to see her again, to say hello and pass the time of day.

He saw a shape move behind the window. Rose or a customer? He smiled at a memory which flashed through his mind. He missed her a great deal, more than he cared to admit. She'd been such fun, and terrific in bed.

No, he decided, best leave things as they were. She might find his turning up awkward, which would then embarrass him.

He didn't look in the shop window as he drove past, but kept his eyes fixed firmly on the road ahead.

'I didn't know you came this way,' said Gavin Clarke, falling into step beside Ishbel. They were both *en route* home from work.

'Oh, hello!'

'Where do you live?'

She told him the name of her street.

'I'm not far from there. We're almost neighbours.'

'Well, well,' she said.

He had a sudden thought. 'I hope you don't mind me walking with you?'

'Not in the least.'

'Good.' He gave her a broad cheery smile. 'Somebody mentioned you came from the country. Is that right?'

'A village called Glenshields. I'm sure you've never heard of it.'

'I'm Glasgow born and bred myself. The big city is all I know.' He flicked an empty can lying on the pavement with his toe sending it clattering into the gutter. 'Do you miss this Glenshields?'

She nodded.

'So why come here? Or is that personal?'

'No, I came to live with my aunt whose health was poor. She's better now; but, rather than go back, I decided to stay.'

'There's nowhere like Glasgow,' he beamed. 'Best city in Britain, the Empire, the whole world even.'

She laughed. Like all Glaswegians, he was fiercely proud of the place. 'Are you enjoying being at Blue Bonnet?'

'Oh, ay. The pay's good and the conditions aren't too bad. Also the other workers are pleasant enough, which helps.'

'What did you do previously?'

'I was unemployed for a while. But before that I worked in a coalyard. That was a filthy job, and the boss was a swine. He fired me for no reason whatever.'

She pulled a sympathetic face.

'I couldn't live in the country,' he said. 'All that empty space filled with funny smells. Not me at all.'

'You get some funny smells in Glasgow,' she commented drily.

'That's different.'

His expression and protest amused her. 'How so?'

He thought about that and shrugged. 'It just is. Those smells are normal—'

'So are country ones,' she interjected.

314

'I suppose you're right,' he conceded slowly. 'It's just what you're used to.'

'Exactly.'

'Pigs and things.'

She realized she was now being teased. 'Motor cars and dirty bins.'

'Cows and pies.'

'Pies!' she exclaimed.

His eyes twinkled. 'Cow pies. Surely you know what those are?'

He had a lovely sense of humour, she thought, and decided she liked him a lot. Pity he already had a girlfriend.

They continued sparking off one another until they arrived at her street. 'See you tomorrow,' he said.

'No doubt.'

'Till then.'

She walked away, knowing he was standing watching her. She began to hum a jaunty tune that was currently popular. As she turned into her close she glanced back the way she'd come, but by then he'd gone.

Aunt Dot commented on what a happy mood she was in. Ishbel's reply was that she'd had a good day.

Celia entered the Rolls in a cloud of heady perfume, settling back with a contented sigh as Rory closed her door. By the time he took his seat she'd already lit up the inevitable cigarette.

'How was the play?' he asked as they whispered away from the pavement.

'Sheer bliss!' she enthused. 'I've never been a great fan of Shaw's, but that production was magic.'

Shortly after that Rory turned into Princes Street, the castle looming high above them. 'It's a pity Mr Lindsay missed it,' he said.

'Yes, Archie would have adored the evening. But, as you know, he was detained in London. Lloyd George has had another flaming row with MacDonald and threatened to bring down Labour's minority government.'

'And will he?'

'Archie doesn't think so. At least, not yet. But it's certainly on the cards.'

'So there might be another election soon?'

'Within a year, I'd say; but that's only a guess on my part. It would be longer if MacDonald would agree on the electoral reform the Liberals want; but he's being extremely resistant, which is why he and Lloyd George fell out.'

Celia coughed, and reached for the small clutch purse she'd been carrying. She produced a wisp of lace handkerchief and further coughed into that.

Rory stared anxiously at her in the rear-view mirror. Her face was contorted as she continued coughing and spluttering. Celia sucked in a deep breath, then another. 'That's better,' she said, smiling wanly.

'Would you like me to stop? I could maybe get a glass of water from a hotel.'

'No, I'm fine now, Rory. But that's a kind thought.'

She gazed out of the car window. 'Isn't Edinburgh beautiful?'

'Very,' he agreed.

'And that castle. Quite awe-inspiring.'

'Have you ever acted in a Shaw play?' Rory asked.

'Never. I was asked to do *Candida* once, but the dates were moved and they clashed with something else. Perhaps just as well, for I wasn't really all that enthusiastic. My trouble is I don't consider Shaw to be a real playwright, which of course is theatrical heresy. To my mind he's more of a long-winded Irish preacher and pamphleteer.'

She laughed throatily. 'There are people who'd drop a stage weight on my head for saying that.'

'Perhaps I'll get a copy of one of his plays and read it,' Rory mused pensively. 'Just to see what I think.'

'I'll lend you one.'

'Would you?'

'I'd be delighted to. I'll look out something tomorrow.'

'Thank you.'

'You know,' Celia frowned, 'I believe we've got *Arms*

and the Man at home. If we have, you can start on that.'

'So who is your favourite playwright?'

'Ah!' Celia exclaimed, eyes gleaming. 'I have several. Have you ever heard of Pinero?'

Rory shook his head.

'Arthur Wing Pinero. Hardly a major playwright, but I do so love his work.'

From then on, until they turned into Drum House, Celia talked enthusiastically about some of her favourite playwrights.

Meg paused in her ironing, a difficult and painful task for her nowadays, and gently massaged her hands. Her left hand was so bad she couldn't straighten it, and hadn't been able to do so for some while.

She looked over at Vincent asleep in front of the range, the evening paper he'd been reading having slipped down on to his legs. He really was making an effort of late, she thought. If not exactly a reformed character, he was a great improvement on the old Vincent. All she could hope for was that it continued.

She thought of Ishbel, and wondered about writing to suggest that Ishbel and Jessica return home. She decided against that as it could just be too risky. Anyway, as she'd hoped, Ishbel was carving out a nice life for herself in Glasgow.

She must get through and see them soon, Meg thought wistfully. How she missed Ishbel and the baby. And Rowan of course. Never a day went by when she didn't think of Rowan.

She'd put the kettle on and soak her hands in hot water, she thought; that often helped a bit. But she'd finish the ironing first as there wasn't very much left to do.

She glanced again at Vincent who, in sleep, looked almost angelic. Talk about appearances deceiving!

With a snort Vincent came awake to gaze blearily at her. 'Must have dropped off,' he mumbled, his paper falling to the floor to lie in an untidy heap.

'You did.'

He scratched his face. 'Are you hungry?'

'Why, do you want me to make you something?'

He sat up and yawned. 'Tell you what, why don't I nip down the road and buy some fish and chips? A treat for both of us, and will save you having to bother.'

It was always nice to have a meal bought rather than have to make it. 'That would be lovely,' she replied.

'And a few of those big pickled onions? The ones you're daft on.'

Her face lit up. 'Now, *they* would be a treat.'

'I'll get on my way, then.'

Meg smiled when he'd left the room. How thoughtful he was being.

He was definitely making an effort, no doubt about it.

'And Mrs Lindsay really talks to you about plays and things?' Mary Louise queried, slightly incredulous.

'Oh, yes. All the time.'

'I must say I'm surprised, you being an employee.'

Rory nodded his agreement. 'So was I to begin with, but she couldn't be more friendly. In fact there are times when she treats me more like a pal than like the chauffeur.'

'A pal!' repeated a bemused Mary Louise.

'They are Liberals after all, if toffs. Well, he is anyway; I'm not so sure about her background. She speaks well enough, but, of course, she is an actress.'

'You're not saying she's working class like us, are you?'

'It's possible,' Rory shrugged. 'There, again, she could be middle class. No doubt I'll find out eventually.'

He turned to Mary Louise to stare at her. 'Just remember that anything I tell you about them is in strictest confidence. I don't want it repeated to anyone. And that means anyone. It could cost me my job if they found out I'd been gossiping about them. He is an MP, don't forget.'

'No need to worry. I won't open my mouth.'

'Cross your heart and hope to die?'

She laughed. 'Silly bugger. Cross my heart and hope to die.'

'All right, then. I trust you.'

'You'd better. I'm your fiancée.'

'Whose idea it was that I work for the Lindsays. I can't tell you how much I enjoy that job, Mary Louise. It's simply terrific.'

'As is the beautiful Mrs Lindsay?' Mary Louise teased.

'Oh, she is that. I just wish she had better health. Her health is a real worry.'

'What's wrong with her, do you know?'

Rory shook his head. 'She looks consumptive, but I don't think it's that. I'll tell you this, though: I don't think it is helped by those cigarettes. You rarely see her without one in her mouth or hand.'

'I think it a foul habit. Particularly for a woman.'

'It certainly doesn't do Celia any favours.'

Mary Louise came up short. 'Celia, is it? Since when?'

'A little while ago. She told me I could call her that when there's just the two of us together, like in the car. It's strictly Mrs Lindsay at all other times.'

'Very cosy,' Mary Louise commented wryly, in what was almost a sneer.

'Being an actress, I suppose she has a different outlook on things,' Rory explained.

Mary Louise had a sudden appalling thought. 'You don't imagine she fancies you, do you?'

'Don't be ridiculous!' Rory exclaimed, shocked.

'Well, it does happen, you know. A little bit of dallying below stairs. Perhaps her marriage isn't what it should be. I've heard about those public-school boys. He may be married but that doesn't necessarily mean he likes girls. And they haven't a family, have they?'

Rory was outraged. 'It isn't like that at all between us. And I would swear that's the furthest thing from her mind. As for their marriage, I know nothing about that. But I've seen them together, and they seem extremely happy. He dotes on her.'

'It was only a thought,' Mary Louise murmured, seeing how cross and upset he was.

Rory growled dismissively.

'But you must agree, her attitude towards you does seem over-friendly in the circumstances?'

Rory considered that. 'I think she's basically lonely at Drum. Don't forget the Master is away a great deal, and she has been used to a fairly hectic professional and social life.'

'Then, why doesn't she stay in London? You've said they have a house there.'

'In Belgravia,' Rory elaborated. 'I honestly don't know. It's possible Drum is better for her health. London is a smokey, foggy place from what I understand.'

'Talking of houses, doesn't that make you green with jealousy?' Mary Louise declared, pointing at the Monteiths' house. They had been walking and had now stopped again.

'It is very nice,' Rory agreed.

Mary Louise's eyes narrowed. 'I'd give my eye teeth for a house like that.'

'Fat chance of that ever happening,' Rory chuckled.

'Oh, I don't know.'

'Come on, Mary Louise! How could I ever afford such a house? It's way beyond anything I'm likely to achieve. You dream too much, that's your trouble.'

'And yours is you've no ambition.' She paused, then added significantly, 'Yet.'

That irritated him, which showed on his face. 'Perhaps you expect too much,' he muttered.

'And perhaps you don't expect enough of either yourself or life in general.'

'I know my place.'

Now she was cross. 'Place!'

'Yes, place! Station. Where I belong.'

'That's a defeatist attitude.'

'It's realistic, you mean.'

'No, Rory, defeatist. You're clever; I realized that early on. There's no reason why you can't aspire to far more than you've now got, unless you allow your own mind to hold you back. You'll never achieve anything if you don't believe in yourself, and that's a truth.'

He stared again at the Monteiths' house. It was a total nonsense to think he could ever own something like that.

'Anyway, let's change the subject,' Mary Louise suggested tactfully, knowing if they went on as they were the argument would only worsen. 'Tell me again about the dress Mrs Lindsay wore the last time you drove her – the purple one cut low at the bodice.'

Rory sighed. Then he began describing the dress while Mary Louise listened intently.

'How are you tonight, then?' Gavin Clarke asked Ishbel, who'd waited for him. It had become their habit to go home together.

'I've got a bit of a headache.'

'Nothing serious, I hope?' he asked in concern.

'No. Just the weather, I think.'

Gavin glanced skywards. 'It has been an oppressive day.'

'And it seemed extra noisy in the distillery today. Probably my imagination, but that's how it sounded to me.'

He hadn't thought so. 'Possibly the headache had that effect on you.'

'Could be,' she agreed with a smile.

He cleared his throat. 'I was wondering . . . Are you busy this Saturday night?'

She looked at him, puzzled. Now, why had he asked her that? 'No,' she replied slowly.

'Then, how about having a drink with me?'

She halted and gazed at him.

'Or something else if you prefer?'

'What would your girlfriend say?' she asked slowly.

'Not a lot,' he teased, tongue in cheek.

'I certainly would if I was her.'

'Well, she won't. I can assure you.'

'And why not?'

His face cracked and broke into a smile. 'Because she's my ex-girlfriend. We're finished. I gave her the big . . .' He jerked his elbow several times at Ishbel.

'You've broken up?'

'I've just said so, haven't I?'

She tried to mask her elation. 'I don't know,' she prevaricated.

His humour vanished. 'But I thought . . .' He broke off, confused, which was precisely what she'd intended.

'What *did* you think?' she probed.

'That you and I . . . well . . .'

'Well, what?'

'That we liked one another.'

'Of course we do. But that doesn't mean I want to go out with you. My brother had a gerbil once which I liked, but I didn't want to go out with that.'

'Hardly the same thing,' he protested.

She raised an eyebrow.

'Oh, come on, is it?'

'Besides, maybe I'm already going out with someone?'

'You're not. I checked.'

That pleased her. 'Did you now?'

'You haven't been going out with anyone since you joined Blue Bonnet.'

Her pleasure turned to annoyance. There was no need for him to point that out.

'Well, have you?'

She glared at him. 'It could be I don't let those at work know what I get up to. Has that ever crossed your mind, Mr Smart Alec?'

Gavin was taken aback by her sudden antagonism, and at a loss as to how to deal with it. 'I suppose . . . so,' he stuttered, completely thrown.

'H'm!' she exclaimed, and increased her pace.

He hurried to catch up. 'Ishbel?'

'What?' she snapped.

'Does that mean no?'

'No.'

'Then, does it mean yes?'

'No.'

'So what does it mean?' he exclaimed in exasperation.

She stopped and stared at him. 'It means I'm thinking about it.'

He sighed. 'Have you got a boyfriend? If so, I'm sorry for putting my foot in it. I didn't know.'

He'd put his foot in it all right, although not in the way he meant. Idiot! she thought, and softened towards him. He was lovely after all. And hadn't she been wishing all this while that he would ask her out?

'Come on,' she said, and continued walking.

A tram clanked by, and a chap Gavin knew waved to him through a window. He waved back.

'Bobby, a friend of mine,' he explained to Ishbel.

'A drink, you said?'

'Or anything else you'd like,' he answered hopefully.

'Where do you want to meet?'

He couldn't conceal his delight. 'Wherever. I don't mind.'

'Seven-thirty all right?'

He nodded.

'You can pick me up at my place.' She then gave him the address.

'I'll be there.'

They stopped, as they always did, at her street. 'I'll see you tomorrow,' he grinned.

'And Saturday,' she smiled.

'And Saturday,' he confirmed.

She hurried off, dying to tell Aunt Dot she was going out with Gavin whom she'd mentioned on a number of occasions.

'You're early,' Ishbel said.

'Just shows how keen I am.'

'You've certainly got the patter. Come through. I'm not quite ready yet.'

He followed Ishbel into the kitchen where Aunt Dot was washing up, with Jessica on the floor playing with some

323

toys. His face registered surprise when he saw Jessica.

'Gavin, my Aunt Dot whose house this is.'

Aunt Dot dried her hands on her apron. 'Pleased to meet you, son,' she said as they shook hands.

'I'm pleased to meet you.'

'And this is Jessica.'

Gavin squatted. 'Hello, young lady. How are you?'

Jessica giggled, but didn't reply.

'Jessica's my niece,' Ishbel explained.

'Really!'

'Say hello,' Aunt Dot urged.

Jessica giggled again, and covered her face with her hands.

'She's shy because she's not used to men,' Ishbel said. 'Now, if you'll just excuse me for a moment.'

Ishbel was gone for a couple of minutes. When she returned she had her coat on. 'Shall we go?' she smiled.

Outside in the street Ishbel hesitated fractionally, then hooked her arm round Gavin's.

'Gin and orange,' said Gavin, laying the drink in front of her. He was drinking a pint of heavy.

'Busy,' commented Ishbel, glancing about.

'Only to be expected; it's Saturday night. We're lucky to get a table.'

'It's a nice pub.'

'That's why I brought you here. There's very little likelihood of trouble in a pub like this.'

'Have you been here before?'

'A few times.'

She wanted to ask if that had been with his previous girlfriend, but decided not to. It was really none of her business, though she was curious.

'I liked your Aunt Dot and Jessica,' Gavin said.

Ishbel smiled.

'Though I was puzzled about you saying Jessica wasn't used to men. What about her father?'

Ishbel had wondered afterwards why she'd wanted Gavin to call for her at home, and had come to the conclusion she must have wanted him to meet Jessica. 'Her father's dead,' she answered.

'Oh, I am sorry!' Gavin exclaimed softly.

'In fact so's her mother. She's an orphan.'

Gavin's expression became one of sadness combined with pity. 'The wee mite. How awful.'

'Ay,' Ishbel agreed.

'Was he your brother or . . . ?'

'No, Rowan was my sister,' Ishbel interjected, aware of how nervous she'd suddenly become. She didn't like telling lies, but had long since decided it was her only course.

'So how did they die?'

Ishbel took a deep breath. She'd gone over this story so often in her mind she almost believed it herself. 'Influenza. It took them both within days of one another. Rowan's last request was that she wanted me to look after Jessica, which I promised I would do. And I have done ever since.'

'She's now your responsibility?'

'That's right.'

'I see,' Gavin breathed. 'Is your mother still alive?'

'Yes, though bad with arthritis.'

'Surely she would have been a better choice to look after a little girl?'

Ishbel gave him a thin smile. 'The reason my sister asked me to take on Jessica is because she loathed my step-father, who would have been very unsympathetic about the situation. He's not a nice man, I'm afraid.'

'So you got landed.'

'In a manner of speaking, yes. But I've come to love Jessica as my own.'

'I can understand that,' he said. 'She certainly is lovely.'

'Rowan and I were twins.'

'Twins!' he exclaimed.

'So we were even closer than normal sisters.'

'It makes sense now,' he said slowly. 'Though I still think it's hard on you.'

'Hard maybe, but nothing I can't cope with.'

325

'What about the rest of your family? Have you any other brothers or sisters?'

She went on to tell him about Rory and his engagement to Mary Louise.

'And you?' she asked when she'd finished talking about herself.

'I'm an only child.'

She then heard all about his family.

Ishbel lay in bed thinking about the night out she'd had with Gavin; which, as far as she was concerned, had gone extremely well. He was such easy company and a good laugh. She couldn't have enjoyed herself more. Their time together had simply whizzed by.

The only fly in the ointment was the lies she'd told Gavin. She wished she hadn't had to do that. It spoiled things. But what else could she have done? She couldn't tell the truth to every chap she went out with. It would have been both pointless and embarrassing. It would be different, however, when she met someone she was going to marry. He'd have to be told. She wouldn't want any lies or secrets between her and her husband.

But until she met whoever that might be, she rationalized, the story she'd concocted was best all round.

Archie Lindsay glanced at his half-hunter pocket-watch, slipped it back into his waistcoat pocket, then stepped from the car.

'The train's due if it's on time,' he said to Rory, holding open his door. With a quick clearing of his throat he strode off into the station.

Rory wondered yet again who it was they'd come to meet. All he'd been told was it was someone important.

He was about to get behind the wheel when he heard the sound of an approaching train. It then gave a toot on its whistle as it came alongside the platform.

Rory stood to attention beside the passenger door. Man or woman? He had no idea. Someone titled perhaps, he speculated, and smiled to himself. If it was a woman, he'd better ensure he could report back to Mary Louise what she was wearing. And, if she proved to be titled, he'd better be doubly sure he took note of every last detail.

He gazed admiringly at the Rolls, which sparkled and shone. He'd really given it some elbow grease earlier on, to such effect the Master had remarked how excellent the car looked.

He thoroughly enjoyed taking care of the Rolls, treating it with great love and respect and lavishing every attention on it. If the Rolls had been his own, he couldn't have cherished it more.

The Master reappeared with a stocky white-haired man by his side, which was a relief to Rory as he now didn't have to worry about clothes.

Then he saw the man's face, and his jaw fell open.

'Lloyd George!' Fee exclaimed in amazement.

'You could have knocked me over with a feather,' Rory said. 'I was aware Mr Lindsay knew him of course – they're close colleagues – but for him to actually come to Drum and get into a car I was driving was really something.'

'I'll say,' Fee beamed.

Lex harumphed, and settled deeper into his chair. 'The man's a rogue,' he declared.

'Grandpa!'

'Well, he is. A real twister. And there are all these rumours about him and women.'

'But he's an old man,' Rory protested.

A sly knowing look came over Lex's face. 'Not that old apparently, if what we hear is true.'

'I liked him,' Rory stoutly defended.

'Oh, ay,' said Lex. 'The man's a charmer, right enough, renowned for it. But a twister none the less. I've no time for him and his party. They're finished anyway. Their time has come and gone.'

'Do you really think so?' Rory queried. Like many

working-class men, particularly among the Scots, Lex was steeped in politics and political knowledge.

'I do. It's Labour's turn from now on. Oh, they're still in their relative infancy, but they're the party of the future. You mark my words.'

'Mr Lindsay wouldn't agree with you.'

Lex barked out a laugh. 'Of course he wouldn't; he's a Liberal!'

'And an exceptionally nice man,' Rory stated.

Lex shrugged. 'That's as maybe.'

'Anyway, the point is I drove Lloyd George, which is something I'll never forget, and consider an honour, he being an ex-Prime Minister, whatever his political stripe.'

'An honour,' Fee echoed.

Lex grunted, determined to be unimpressed.

'Have you told Mary Louise?' Fee enquired.

Rory nodded.

'And what was her reaction?'

Rory grinned. 'I thought she was going to faint.'

'She's not a Liberal?' Lex demanded.

'Don't be daft, Grandpa. She's Labour same as the rest of us.'

'Just as well,' Lex grumbled. 'Just as well.'

Gray Hamilton prised his eyes open and groaned. What a night ashore that had been! Thank God it was his day for the late shift; it would have been hell having to turn out the way he now felt.

He thought of the brothel he and his mates had gone to, and the female he'd spent a while alone with. She'd been pretty, with a lovely body, but he still felt disgust at what he'd done. The whole episode had somehow been so sordid.

Then his thoughts turned to Rowan, bringing a smile to his lips. He'd been thinking about her more and more of late, wondering how she was, if she was courting, engaged, married. He should have written, he supposed, but letter-writing had never been his forte. His mother was forever complaining about that in her letters to him.

Rowan. He pictured her in his mind. He missed her far more than he'd ever imagined. One thing was certain: when he got home again, he'd seek her out in the hope she wasn't tied up with someone else. It would be his bad luck if she was.

And if she was free ... well, who knew what might happen? He'd love to take up where they'd left off, resume their relationship. And if she agreed to marry him, then he'd give up the sea and travelling, both of which he'd become disenchanted with.

Life with Rowan would be just the ticket. The two of them together, and a family in time.

He smiled again, and began mentally to work out exactly how long it would be, to the nearest day, before he returned to Scotland.

'What about next Saturday night?' Gavin asked Ishbel as they walked hand in hand along the street. Overhead the sky was obscured by cloud and smoke from countless chimneys.

'Fine. Why don't you come to tea?'

He glanced at her. 'I'd like that.'

'Good.'

'And go out afterwards?'

'No, I thought we might stay in for a change.'

'Suits me.'

They turned into her close-mouth, the close itself lit by pale yellow gaslight. As was their custom, they went to the back close where it was dark, a traditional spot for courting couples.

'Ishbel,' he whispered.

'What?'

He smiled in the darkness. 'Nothing. I just like saying your name. Ishbel.'

She sighed when his mouth fell eagerly on hers and he pulled her body tightly against his own. It was the first kiss of many before they eventually, and reluctantly, parted and she went upstairs.

* * *

Gavin sipped his beer and reflected on what a marvellous tea he'd had. Aunt Dot and Ishbel, who'd combined to produce the meal, had certainly pulled out all the stops. The milky rice pudding had been simply scrumptious.

A smiling Aunt Dot entered the room. 'Ishbel won't be long now,' she said. She was putting Jessica to bed.

'There's no hurry,' he replied lazily, basking in the heat washing out from the fire.

'You seemed to enjoy yourself playing with Jessica?'

'I did. I had great fun.'

'And so did she.'

'She particularly liked the choo-choo game.'

'Is that one your parents used to play with you?'

Gavin nodded. 'It was a great favourite of mine.'

'How's that beer? Would you like another screwtop?'

He held up his hand. 'Not for me, Aunt Dot. This is enough.'

'Are you sure?' she urged, mindful of Glasgow hospitality.

'Certain,' he smiled in reply.

Aunt Dot came and sat opposite him. She thoroughly approved of Gavin, thinking he was ever such a nice young man. Ishbel had really fallen on her feet with him, and she hoped the two of them would decide to take matters further. However, it was early days yet.

Ishbel now entered the room. 'You're honoured,' she said to Gavin.

'How do you mean?'

'Jessica wants you to read a story to her. You don't have to if you don't want to, of course.'

'I'd be delighted,' he replied, beaming.

He laid his beer aside and hauled himself upright. 'What's the story?'

'Goldilocks.'

'Right up my street. Lead on.'

Aunt Dot watched them leave the kitchen. They made a lovely couple, she thought.

Vincent was buying a newspaper at the bus station when

he spotted a flustered-looking Rose searching through her copious handbag. 'And a packet of cigarettes, please,' he said to the woman serving him.

When he'd been handed his change he moved off to one side to watch Rose, who seemed to be getting more flustered and anxious by the moment. She finally looked up in exasperation and bit her lip.

'Something wrong, Rose?' he asked, approaching her from behind.

She jumped slightly. 'Oh, it's you, Vincent!' she said in what sounded to him like relief.

'Through in Glasgow for the day,' he informed her, treating her to a flashing smile. 'And you?'

'The same. I had some shopping to do.'

He glanced at the various parcels and paper bags by her feet. 'Which appears to have been successful.'

'It was. Only now I've gone and lost my purse.'

'Oh dear!' he frowned.

'There were only coppers in it, and it isn't an expensive one. Or wasn't, I should say. But, more to the point, it contained my return ticket, which I haven't any money to replace.'

So that was it. 'Lucky I happened along.'

'Can you lend me some cash, Vincent?'

'Better than that. I'll buy you the ticket.'

'No, I couldn't possibly—'

'Yes, you can, and will,' he interjected emphatically. 'It'll be my pleasure to help such a beautiful damsel in distress.'

She blushed, which amused him.

'You stay right here and I'll be back in a jiffy.'

'This really is most kind of you,' she gushed when he returned with her new ticket. 'I don't know what I'd have done if you hadn't popped up out of nowhere.'

'Asked the police to help, I suppose. What else?'

She gave him a smile of appreciation. 'I can always send you the money.'

'Enough, woman!' he rebuked her sternly. Then added

more lightly, 'Just accept the ticket and be done with it, all right?'

'All right.'

He glanced at the board on which the outgoing timetable was posted. 'Another ten minutes yet.' They would both be on the same bus.

'Yes.'

'Can I get you anything for the journey? A magazine? Sweets? A fried-egg sandwich?'

She laughed. 'Fried-egg sandwich! What would you do if I did ask for that?'

'Get it for you, of course. Though we might miss this particular bus in the process.'

'Then, I'll go without.'

'What about the other things?'

She shook her head.

'It's no trouble, honest. Just say.'

'Nothing, Vincent; but thank you for asking. It's very kind of you.'

'That's me,' he declared, flashing her another smile. 'Kindness personified.'

His smile faded, his expression becoming intense. His eyes bored into hers. 'It's good to see you again, Rose. Awfully good.'

'And to see you, Vincent,' she replied softly.

'So how have you been?' he asked when the bus was under way.

'Not too bad. Yourself?'

He shrugged. 'Up and down.'

She thought of a response to that, but restrained herself. 'What about the wife?'

'Meg's more or less the same. Her arthritis has been worse of late unfortunately.'

Rose made a sympathetic face. 'I'm sorry to hear that.'

'It's developed in her left hip, which has been causing her considerable discomfort.'

'Poor woman,' Rose commiserated.

332

'Yes, she hasn't had an easy time of it. But there we are, we all have our cross to bear.'

'Amen,' Rose declared. Then, on a brighter note: 'Fancy bumping into you like that? Amazing.'

'Amazing,' he agreed. 'But tell me, who's looking after the shop?'

'My part-timer. She can now cope with the occasional day – or three-quarters day, I should say – as long as I set everything up in the morning.'

'The shop still doing well?'

'I can't complain. But it is a terrible tie when you're on your own.'

Vincent lit a cigarette. 'Have you heard from Ronnie?' he asked casually.

She shot him a look, then glanced out of the window. 'No.'

That pleased him, though he didn't let it show. 'Have you done something to your hair?' he queried.

She patted the back of her head. 'I had it cut.'

'Suits you.'

'Do you think so?'

'Oh, definitely! Makes you look younger.' That was it, he thought. Give her the old flannel – lots of it.

'Thank you.'

'And I must say you're looking tremendously well.'

'It's nice of you to say so.'

'Nice nothing; it's true.'

She smoothed down the front of her skirt, then flashed him a grateful smile.

They continued chatting until they arrived at the outskirts of Glenshields. 'My stop coming up,' he said.

She was sorry he was getting off; she'd enjoyed their conversation. She'd forgotten how much fun Vincent could be. Or maybe she had simply put it from her mind.

'I . . . go through Penderry occasionally, as you know,' he said slowly. 'I could call in some time, or would you prefer I didn't?'

She hesitated. 'Why not?' she said eventually. 'If you come at the right time, we can have a cup of tea.'

'Sounds great.'

She reached across and laid her hand over his. 'I mean tea and tea only,' she stated quietly.

'I understand.' After all, that was all he wanted.

'Right, then.'

He winked at her, then sauntered up the aisle to disappear down the stairs.

She found it vaguely disturbing that she'd been so pleased to see him; but, then, life had been so deadly dull of late. She spent most nights in by herself with only the wireless for company.

She smiled, already looking forward to his dropping by.

'Oh, hello,' said Gavin as Ishbel emerged from the ladies'. It was their morning break.

'Hello yourself.'

'Listen, how would you like to come to tea with my folks this Saturday? My mum suggested it.'

'Tit for tat, you mean?'

He grinned. 'Something like that.'

'Of course. I'd love to meet your parents.'

'Oooohhhh! The young lovers,' a female voice cooed in a sexy suggestive manner.

Ishbel scowled at Sarah Webster whom she couldn't stand. 'I'll speak to you later,' she said to Gavin.

'Not interrupting, am I?' Sarah smirked, eyeing Gavin in a way that made Ishbel want to slap her silly face.

'Not at all,' Gavin answered.

'So handsome,' Sarah murmured, fluttering her eyelids and swaying her bottom.

Ishbel clenched her fists. 'Goodbye for now,' she said tightly to Gavin, and strode away.

'Bitch!' she hissed to herself.

Rose arched her back and groaned. Her body was covered in sweat, her hair plastered to her head.

Vincent thrust hard and hard again, Rose gradually

being moved up the bed until eventually her head was banging against the padded headboard.

His hands never stopped moving, grasping, squeezing. And all the while he continued to pump into her.

Finally it was over. He stilled with a grunt, closed his eyes, then slowly sank down on to her.

'Jesus,' he whispered.

Rose sucked in a deep breath. How she'd missed that. It had been so long.

'Well?' Vincent demanded hoarsely.

'Well, what?'

'Was it good for you?'

His ego! she remembered. 'Of course it was good, you fool. Couldn't you tell?'

'It was good for me, too.'

He rolled off her and reached for his cigarettes. As he lit up he thought about Meg, and a sense of shame blossomed in him. He'd tried so hard to be good, toe the matrimonial line, but Rose had been a temptation he simply couldn't resist.

'Is there any more of that whisky?' she asked.

'Of course. I'll get you some.'

She regarded his naked body as he got off the bed and walked away. She hadn't meant this to happen. In fact she'd been determined it wouldn't. But he'd turned up with a bottle of whisky, and then been so entertaining and funny. She'd protested when he'd kissed her, but instead of insisting he stop she'd allowed him to do it again. After that, one thing had led to another until they'd ended up in bed making love.

'We've run out of lemonade, so will water do?' he called out to her.

'There's plenty in the shop.'

'I'm not going into the shop like this!'

She could make him dress and go through, but she relented. 'Water will be fine.'

He returned with her glass and handed it to her. 'Cheers!' he toasted, raising his own recharged glass.

'Slainthe.' Rose had a sip, then said; 'Won't Meg worry that you're not home?'

'She's used to my funny hours. She'll merely presume I got held up somewhere. It happens.'

'She's a very understanding wife, it seems to me.'

'I genuinely have the sort of job that means I keep irregular hours,' Vincent explained, trying to conceal his anxiety. 'It's something she's just had to come to terms with. Like a doctor's wife or a vet's.'

Rose pulled the sheets up to her shoulders. She hadn't felt so relaxed, or at peace, in ages. Not since . . . well, the last time they'd made love, for there hadn't been anyone in between.

'Have I blotted my copybook?' he asked.

'How do you mean?'

He patted the bed.

She thought about it. 'I honestly don't know. But what I do know is you're not staying the night.'

'I hadn't intended to,' he replied lightly, which was perfectly true.

She decided to spell things out for him. 'I mean it, Vincent. Not tonight or any other night.'

'Still hoping Ronnie might make a reappearance?'

She blushed.

'But I can come back, visit again?'

She didn't answer.

'Rose?'

She reached out and laid a hand on his thigh. 'I do like you, Vincent. It's just . . .'

'The liking is limited,' he smiled.

'That's one way of putting it.'

'And, if I say the name Ronnie, that's another.'

'Don't be cross, Vincent.'

'I'm not,' he shrugged. 'Disappointed perhaps, but not cross.'

He caressed her sodden hair. 'You like me, but love him, and continue to love him even though he ran off and left you. Know what?'

She looked up at him.

'I don't think you'll ever see him again. That he's gone for ever.'

'Don't say that,' she breathed.

'It's what I genuinely believe. And time will tell whether I'm right or not. But in the mean time there's you and I. The lovely Rose, and Vincent the substitute.'

'Substitute! Hardly that.'

'No?' he replied drily.

She dropped her gaze again. 'Maybe you shouldn't come back.'

He twisted a lock of her hair round his finger. 'I want to. Substitute or not, I want to.'

'As long as you understand my position?'

'I preferred the one you were in a few minutes ago.'

She grinned. 'Don't be filthy.'

'Nothing filthy about it. It was a gorgeous position.'

'You're embarrassing me,' she said, her cheeks reddening.

'Well, I don't mean to.' He gathered her into his arms. 'I may not be staying the night, but that doesn't mean I have to leave right away, does it?'

She could read in his eyes what he had in mind. 'No,' she answered softly.

'Good.'

He finished his drink and laid his glass on the floor. He then indicated she should finish hers.

'I can't be that quick,' she said.

'I know the problem,' he answered drolly, taking her glass and placing it beside his own.

He gently pressed her shoulders, forcing her back on to the bed. His powers of recovery were incredible, she thought, far quicker than Ronnie's had ever been.

She closed her eyes and smiled as he came on top of and straight into her.

'Mum, this is Ishbel Stewart.'

'How do you do?' said Mrs Clarke, a small thin woman with the hint of a squint in one eye.

Ishbel was suddenly reminded of a ferret. The likeness between a ferret and Mrs Clarke was strong.

She was then introduced to Mr Clarke, who seemed amiable enough in a bland way. She quite liked him, she decided, but not his wife who wore her dyed black hair tied back in a bun.

Ishbel glanced from husband to wife, and then to Gavin, wondering who he took after, for he looked like neither his mother nor his father. Thank God, she murmured mentally.

'Let me take your coat,' said Mr Clarke, and stood smiling patiently while she slipped out of it.

She could smell cat, Ishbel thought, having caught a sniff of pungent tom odour. It was stronger still in the sitting-room which they now entered.

'Do you have a sitting-room?' Mrs Clarke enquired.

Ishbel shook her head. 'Just a room and a kitchen, I'm afraid.'

'So where does your aunt sleep?'

'In the kitchen cavity bed.'

'And the ... er ... child?'

'With me in the bedroom.' Ishbel hadn't failed to notice the hesitation or emphasis that had been put on the word 'child'.

'How about some sherry?' Mr Clarke beamed.

'That would be lovely,' Ishbel replied.

'There is also whisky, if you prefer.' He leant forward slightly and rubbed his hands, indicating he was about to make a joke. 'Blue Bonnet of course.'

This was going to be awful, Ishbel thought, praying the time till she could decently leave would zip by. 'Sherry will be fine,' she stated.

'And you, Mother?'

'Sherry,' Mrs Clarke said.

'I'll have whisky,' Gavin informed his father.

A marmalade cat appeared from behind a chair and strolled across the room to disappear out the door.

'Beautiful animal,' Ishbel commented, making conversation.

'Mother's pride and joy, isn't he, dear?' Mr Clarke said.

'He's called Dandy,' stated Mrs Clarke, staring affectionately after the cat.

'Here we are, then,' declared Mr Clarke, giving Ishbel a tiny glass.

She wouldn't have to worry about getting tipsy on this lot, Ishbel thought. She'd never seen a smaller glass! There was hardly enough in it to wet her throat.

'And you come from a village named Glenshields, I understand?' Mrs Clarke said, accepting a similar glass from her husband.

'That's correct.'

'Tell us all about it. And your family.'

There was a strange atmosphere in the room, Ishbel thought as she spoke. *Forbidding* was one word she'd have used to describe it, *disapproving* another. It certainly wasn't friendly.

Mrs Clarke tut-tutted in sympathy when she told her story about Rowan and Will, the fictional name she'd chosen for Rowan's supposed husband.

'How sad,' Mrs Clarke murmured.

'And now you work at Blue Bonnet with Gavin,' Mrs Clarke said when Ishbel finally finished.

'Or he with me as I was there first,' Ishbel smiled back. She watched Mrs Clarke's lips thin and realized she'd said the wrong thing.

Smart-mouthed bitch, Mrs Clarke was thinking, wondering what Gavin saw in Ishbel, who seemed extremely ordinary to her, ugly even, though maybe that was going too far. Whatever, she wasn't a looker as Kate had been. Dear darling Kate whom she missed coming round the house. Kate whom she'd been convinced Gavin was going to marry, and of whom she'd completely approved.

Shortly after that Mrs Clarke disappeared into the kitchen, and then some minutes later they were summoned through for tea.

'I hope you like stew,' Mrs Clarke said to Ishbel once she was seated.

'Stew's lovely.' Well, she hadn't gone to much trouble, Ishbel thought. Surely she could have made a better effort than stew!

Lucky she wasn't a big eater, Ishbel reflected when her plate was placed in front of her. A bird could have eaten this lot and still been hungry.

'Kate adored stew,' Mrs Clarke said when she sat.

'Mum!' Gavin protested.

Mrs Clarke regarded him innocently. 'But surely Ishbel knows about Kate? You must have spoken about her.'

Gavin turned and smiled apologetically at Ishbel. The subject of Kate, despite Ishbel's curiosity, was one he'd studiously avoided.

'And a charming lass she was,' Mrs Clarke continued. 'She and I got on like the proverbial house on fire.'

So that was how it was, Ishbel thought grimly. She forced a smile on to her face. 'You must tell me all about her,' she said to Gavin.

'Another time maybe.'

'She was a secretary,' Mrs Clarke stated. 'A very responsible position. Worked for an insurance company in town.'

'How interesting,' Ishbel commented, still smiling.

'Made good money,' said Mr Clarke, speaking through a mouthful of food.

'Extremely good,' Mrs Clarke qualified.

'Lucky old Kate,' murmured Ishbel.

'They went out together for over a year, you know,' Mrs Clarke went on relentlessly.

'Mum, please!' Gavin pleaded, clearly discomfited.

'That's all right, Gavin,' Ishbel assured him, the smile still stuck on her face.

For the rest of the meal Mrs Clarke spoke about Kate and how wonderful Kate had been.

'I'm sorry about that,' Gavin apologized as they made their way down the stairs.

'Don't worry. I wasn't offended.'

'It was terribly rude, though.'

'Your mother was obviously mad keen on Kate. What happened between you two anyway?'

He shrugged. 'We got on well enough, but deep down weren't really suited. Kate didn't agree with that, but I was certain of it.'

'Do you miss her?'

'No, not really,' he replied, shaking his head. 'At least, not in that way. I miss her as a friend, if you understand, but not as a girlfriend.'

She hooked an arm round his. 'Perhaps your mother will come to think so highly of me in time.'

'Perhaps. I certainly hope so.'

'You don't feel I let you down in any way?'

He stopped to stare at her. 'Let me down how?'

'Kate seems to have been something of a beauty.'

'Don't talk daft, Ishbel. You've nothing to worry about on that score, I promise you.' He went on staring at her. 'You're not jealous, are you?'

'What I'm not is beautiful. My sister Rowan was, but not me.'

'I thought you were twins?'

'We were, but not identical ones.'

He used a finger to trace an imaginary line down her cheek. 'You're beautiful enough for me. And I mean that sincerely. If I wasn't attracted to you, I wouldn't keep going out with you.'

She believed him. 'Let's forget it, eh? And one thing . . .'

'What's that?'

'Not another word about bloody Kate. I've had her up to here for tonight.' And with that Ishbel indicated her throat.

Gavin laughed. 'Not another word.'

When Ishbel arrived home Aunt Dot was still up eagerly awaiting to hear how the evening had gone. Ishbel soon had her laughing about the smelly cat and the size of the meal. She somehow also made her laugh about Kate and how wonderful Mrs Clarke thought her predecessor to be.

*   *   *

341

'Can I help you?' Meg asked the young man with a frown. Where had he got that tan at this time of year? she wondered as it was February 1931.

'Is Rowan at home?'

A cold hand seemed to clutch and squeeze Meg's heart. 'Rowan?'

'I'm an old friend,' he said breezily.

Meg slowly drew in a deep breath which helped calm her. 'You'd better come in,' she said, and stood aside to let him pass.

'I know she works with you,' Gray smiled as Meg shut the door behind him.

He followed her into the kitchen where she told him to sit down while she put the kettle on. 'You can't have heard.'

'Heard what, Mrs Stewart?'

'An old friend, you say. I take it you haven't been in touch for quite some while?'

'No, I've been away at sea.'

Suddenly she knew he was Jessica's father. There was a look about his face which was reflected in Jessica's. There were other similarities also. 'Been to sea?'

'I went off and joined the merchant navy, intent on seeing the world, which I've done. This is my first trip home. I arrived in yesterday afternoon.'

Warm tears oozed from her eyes which she attempted to blink back. 'Am I right in presuming you and Rowan went out together?'

'Yes, we did.' What was wrong with Meg? he wondered. Why on earth was she crying? Had he said or done something? If he had, he couldn't think what.

'I'm sorry to tell you but Rowan's dead,' Meg husked, and cleared her throat.

It took a few seconds for that to register, then his jaw fell open. Dead! Rowan . . . ! It was a joke of some sort; it had to be. 'How?'

'Oh, my God,' he whispered a little later. 'Oh, my God!'

* * *

Ishbel glanced at the clock. 'He should be here at any moment. If he's on time, that is,' she said to Aunt Dot.

Aunt Dot regarded Jessica playing on the floor. 'Jess looks a picture,' she smiled. Jessica had been dressed in her very best clothes for the occasion.

'I'm nervous,' Ishbel confessed, though there was no reason she should be.

'Shall I put the kettle on?'

Ishbel shook her head. 'Wait till he gets here.'

'When are you seeing Gavin again?'

'Friday night. We haven't decided where we're going yet.'

'I really like Gavin. I'm pleased you two are getting on so well.'

Ishbel jumped from her seat the moment the doorbell rang. 'That's him.'

'Then, you'd better let him in.'

Ishbel had a quick peruse in the mirror above the mantelpiece to ensure she looked all right, then hurried off to answer the front door.

'Hello,' said Gray, his face pale and strained.

'Hello.'

'I'm Gray Hamilton.'

'And I'm Ishbel.'

He studied her. 'You're familiar, though I don't believe we met.'

'You're familiar, too.'

'We must have seen one another around,' he said, smiling nervously.

'Must have,' she agreed. 'Come on through.'

Aunt Dot rose when Gray entered the kitchen, but it wasn't her he looked at; rather at Jessica on the floor surrounded by playthings. He swallowed hard.

'I had no idea. None at all,' he said, his eyes glued to Jessica.

'So my mother said in her letter.'

'I would never have . . .' He broke off and shook his head.

'Say hello to Mr Hamilton,' Aunt Dot instructed Jessica, taking her hand and bringing her to her feet.

'Hello,' Jessica murmured shyly.

'Hello,' Gray choked. 'I ... er ... I brought this for you.' And with that he handed her the large parcel he'd been carrying.

Jessica shook with delight. 'A present.'

'For you, Jessica. From me.'

'Mr Hamilton was a friend of your parents,' Ishbel explained.

'I've been away. For a long time,' he said.

'Shall I help you open that?' Aunt Dot offered; then turned to Gray: 'I'm Aunt Dot, by the way.'

Jessica squealed when the teddy bear was revealed, one bigger than herself.

'It's magnificent,' Ishbel smiled.

He shrugged. 'I thought it nice, and that a little girl would like it.'

'Teddy,' Jessica crooned, stroking the bear.

Gray sniffed, finding himself almost overcome with emotion. All during his train journey through to Glasgow he'd been both looking forward to and dreading this meeting. Now it had taken place he was euphoric, all reluctance having completely vanished.

'She's lovely,' he commented, squatting beside Jessica.

'I think so, too,' she agreed, thinking he meant the bear.

'Not him. You, gorgeous. I think you're lovely.'

Jessica giggled, and hid her face behind the bear.

Gray looked up at Ishbel, his eyes sparkling with tears. 'I see Rowan in her, a lot of Rowan, and also ...'

'Her father,' Ishbel interjected smoothly.

He nodded. 'Her father.'

'*Will.*'

'Will,' Gray echoed.

He smoothed down a few stray wisps of Jessica's hair, the colour of which made his heart ache in memory. 'Do you like sweeties?' he asked.

She nodded vigorously.

He produced a half-crown as though by magic and pressed it into her hand. 'That's for you to buy sweeties with. I was going to bring you some, then remembered when I was young I liked to choose them myself, and thought you might be the same.'

She beamed at him.

'Say thank you,' urged Ishbel.

'Thank you, Mr Hamilton.'

'It's my pleasure entirely, Jessica. I can assure you.'

Jessica rushed over to Ishbel. 'Can I go to the shop now, Aunt Ishbel. Please?'

'I'll take her,' Aunt Dot offered.

'Then, I don't see why not.'

Jessica whooped and scampered from the kitchen, Aunt Dot hurrying after her.

Gray turned his attention to Ishbel, his features twisted in anguish. 'I really didn't have any idea. It was all such a shock when your mother told me what had happened.'

Ishbel stared at him grim-faced.

'We only ever . . . once, that is. It never crossed my mind that Rowan might fall pregnant. Stupid, I suppose; and to leave the way I did was selfish on my part. But there we are; I've done a great deal of growing up since then.'

He barked out a laugh. 'The ridiculous thing is I came home fully hoping to pick up with Rowan where I left off – if I was lucky enough to find her unattached, that was.' He paused, then added softly, a catch in his voice; 'I wanted to marry her.'

'Could she have got in touch with you if she'd wanted?' Ishbel queried.

Gray shook his head. 'She didn't have an address, and I never wrote.'

She was angry with him, yet at the same time understood that it had been a combination of unfortunate circumstances that had resulted in Rowan's suicide. Gray wasn't a bad lad; that was evident. In fact he was personable and very likeable.

'No-one knew who the father was, and Rowan would never tell,' Ishbel said.

'And she asked you to look after Jessica?'

Ishbel nodded.

'I'm sure she knew what she was doing.'

'We were twins after all, if not identical twins.'

'I feel so guilty,' he whispered. 'But what occurred was completely unintentional. Except for us sleeping together – we could have avoided that. Except at the time . . .' He sucked in a deep breath. 'We were very fond of one another, but I was more interested in seeing the big wide world than in staying at home and getting tied up. She was most upset by my going away, but did understand.'

He stopped, and stared off into the distance, imagining himself and Rowan together in the Taylors' house at Drumden. 'What a mess,' he sighed.

'You mentioned marrying Rowan. Does that mean you're back for good?'

'I don't know now,' he said, rousing himself. 'I'll have to think it through. But in the light of all this I imagine I'll return to sea. A berth will be easy enough to find.'

Ishbel felt sorry for him. This was a terrible thing for him to carry on his conscience, and he struck her as a man who would do precisely that.

'Would you like a cup of tea?' she asked.

'Please.'

'And something to eat? I have a Dundee cake in.'

He shook his head. 'Just the tea.'

'Jessica's a fine lassie,' he said as Ishbel filled the kettle. 'One to be proud of.'

'Ay.'

'I only wish . . .' He trailed off and smiled thinly. 'The trouble with the past is it can't be altered. No matter how much you'd like it to be, it can't.'

Ishbel agreed softly.

He turned his face away from her so she couldn't see his expression.

Chapter Nine

'So are you still going out with that Ishbel?' Margaret Clarke asked innocently, knowing full well that Gavin was.

Gavin came out of his day-dream to stare quizzically at his mother. 'Yes, of course.'

Margaret slowly shook her head in disapproval.

'There's nothing wrong with her, Mum,' he stated quietly.

Margaret raised an eyebrow. 'Oh, she's pleasant enough, I grant you. But she's not a patch on Kate.'

'Kate and I are finished, through. I wish you'd accept that. Besides, Kate is seeing someone else – a quantity surveyor, I was told.'

'A quantity surveyor,' echoed Bill Clarke, looking impressed.

'I thought it would blow over between you and Ishbel,' Margaret went on.

'Did you?'

'Well, you met her on the rebound from Kate after all. That sort of thing doesn't tend to last.'

'It has in our case. And continues to do so.'

'You like her, then?' Margaret said, almost coyly.

'I'd hardly go out with her if I didn't!'

'You know what I mean. There's like and like.'

'We get on extremely well together. She's a good laugh.'

'A good laugh,' Margaret muttered contemptuously. 'That's hardly a reason to court someone.'

'I think it is. Anyway, there's more to our relationship than that.'

Margaret gazed levelly at her son. 'There is one big drawback with Ishbel which I hope you're taking into account.'

'What's that?'

'The child.'

'She's sweet, Mum. You'd adore her.'

'Sweet, adorable maybe. But she isn't even Ishbel's.'

'It was her sister's wish that Ishbel look after Jessica. What else could Ishbel do?'

'Admirable, of course, on Ishbel's part. However, it means whoever takes her on will be raising a child that doesn't belong to either of them.'

'Ishbel thinks of Jessica as her own.'

'I'm sure, but the fact remains the child isn't hers. What she is is a liability. A mouth to feed, a body to clothe. Have you any idea how expensive that can be?'

'Damned expensive, and I speak from experience,' Bill declared, turning the page of his newspaper.

'A millstone round someone's neck.'

'That's putting it a bit strongly, Mum!' Gavin protested.

'Is it? It may not seem that way to you now. But marriage isn't all beer and skittles, I'll have you know. The rosy feelings you start off with soon fade, which is when resentments can set in. Those are the niggles and upsets that can come between a man and wife.'

'You listen to your mother,' Bill counselled.

'Making a marriage work is hard enough without someone else's child to hamper you,' Margaret went on. 'You say she's sweet and adorable, but what would it be like if you actually were living with her? She might not be so sweet and adorable then.'

'But children . . .'

'You put up with a lot from children because they're your own flesh and blood. All that inconvenience, the annoyances, the frustrations, because they're your own. But it takes a special kind to put up with that from another's child.'

'*I* couldn't do it,' Bill stated.

'Me, neither,' added Margaret, staring hard at Gavin who was now looking extremely thoughtful.

'All I say is this,' Margaret continued. 'Think before you leap. That way you may save yourself regret later, and a life that doesn't turn out as you'd expected.'

'If you take my advice,' said Bill, having been prompted earlier by Margaret, 'you wouldn't land yourself with a problem you don't need. And that child is a problem, believe me.'

'Your dad's talking sense, son. Heed him.'

'Excuse me,' murmured Gavin and, rising, left the room. What they'd said had disturbed him deeply and needed thinking about.

Margaret looked at Bill and smiled. 'He'll come round. You'll see.'

'I hope so, dear, I hope so.'

'What do you think of this photograph?' queried Celia, handing a large eight-by-eight to Rory. 'That's me as Polly Peachum in *The Beggar's Opera* by John Gay.'

Rory studied the photo. It was mid-evening, and Archie was in London. Several days earlier Celia had promised him she'd show him her theatrical memorabilia as he'd expressed a keen interest in seeing them. That was why he was with her in one of the various small sitting-rooms.

'You look terrific,' Rory gasped. 'Very glamorous.'

Celia laughed throatily, thoroughly enjoying herself. She was in her element. 'I wonder . . . ,' she mused, tapping herself with a finger. 'I wonder if I can remember any of Polly's lines.' She smiled at Rory. 'It's been some time.'

'I'd love to hear, if you can,' he encouraged.

Celia furrowed her brow in concentration. 'How about a song?'

'Great!'

She struck a pose, then sang in a husky beguiling voice:

> 'Cease your funning,
> Force or cunning,
> Never shall my heart trepan;
> All these sallies
> Are but malice,
> To seduce my constant man.'

It suddenly hit Rory with a shock who she reminded

him of. Rowan. They didn't look at all alike, other than that they were both blondes, but they had a similar inner quality. There had been things about Celia that had disturbed him in the past, and now he knew why. He and Rowan had been particularly close, and wasn't that how he was coming to be with Celia? They had established a similar type of brother–sister relationship.

Celia's singing interrupted his thoughts, and before long she'd finished, throwing her arms wide and curtsying. Rory clapped enthusiastically.

'You've a marvellous voice,' he said.

'Hardly. But it's strong enough to get by.'

'Well, I think it's brilliant.'

Celia threw back her head and laughed, Rory's praise almost as satisfying as a curtain call. How she missed those. The memory of past first-night applause made her shiver.

'Aah!' she sighed. Then she noticed the peculiar expression on Rory's face. 'What's wrong?' she demanded.

'Nothing.'

'Yes, there is. I can tell.'

She sat beside him on the couch. 'Come on, don't be shy. What's wrong?'

He dropped his gaze, unable to look her straight in the eye. 'It was while you were singing. I suddenly realized who you reminded me of.'

'Who?' she demanded eagerly.

'My sister, Rowan.'

'Rowan! What a charming name. And I remind you of her? Tell me about her.'

Should he or shouldn't he? 'It's not a pretty story,' he eventually confessed.

Celia's gaiety vanished. 'Tell me anyway,' she said in a serious voice.

Her expression became more and more grim as Rory spoke.

'You taste so good,' Gavin murmured to Ishbel as the pair of them were locked together in her back close.

He pecked her on the nose, the cheeks and lastly the chin.

Ishbel made a low noise deep in her throat, then opened her eyes. She pulled him even closer, squeezing him hard against her.

He kissed her again, their tongues darting and entwining. She smiled when his hand came up to rub her breast.

'Enough!' she breathed, pushing him away a little. 'Any more of this and I'll have steam belching from my ears.'

'You mean it isn't already?'

She laughed. 'Oh, Gavin,' she exclaimed softly, and ran a palm over his cheek. 'I'll have to go up in a moment.'

'Stay,' he pleaded.

'It's getting late, and there's work in the morning.'

'Don't remind me!'

'I thought you enjoyed your work?'

'I do, I suppose, but I'd rather lie on in bed than get up.'

Ishbel knew exactly what he meant. There were so many mornings she felt like that, particularly the bitter winter ones.

'I've some news,' Gavin said suddenly. 'Kate got engaged last weekend.'

'To the quantity surveyor?'

Gavin nodded.

She studied him. 'Does that upset you?'

'Not in the least. Maybe Mum will shut up about her now.' They both laughed.

'How would you feel about becoming engaged?' he asked casually.

A tingle ran through her. 'That depends', she demurred, 'on who was doing the asking.'

'And if the right chap asked?'

He had to mean himself, she thought. 'If the right chap asked, I'd say yes.'

She sensed his mood change.

'Ishbel,' he said hesitantly. 'I've been thinking about Jessica. Wouldn't she be better off with your brother Rory and his fiancée when they get married?'

351

'Why would she be better off with them?'

'It just seems to me she might be,' he replied, stumbling over his words.

'What are you driving at, Gavin?'

'She is a big responsibility . . .'

'*My* responsibility,' Ishbel interjected.

He glanced away. He wanted to tell Ishbel exactly what was in his mind, but lacked the courage. 'You wouldn't consider . . . ?'

'No,' she stated emphatically, interrupting a second time. 'Jessica stays with me until she's grown up.'

'She is a beautiful child,' he smiled falsely.

There was a cone of anger in her that he could suggest such a thing, especially as he professed to like the child so much. Then Ishbel clicked that this objection stemmed from Mrs Clarke.

'Go on, spit it out,' she said.

'There's nothing to spit out. I just wondered if you'd ever contemplated putting Jessica with Rory. It would be so much easier for you that way.'

'Forget my promise and feelings for the moment – what about Jessica? Do you think she'd appreciate being sent to another home? I'm all she's known, don't forget. To all intents and purposes, as far as she's concerned, I am her mother. Even if she does call me Aunt Ishbel.'

'I'm sorry. I shouldn't have brought it up,' he apologized.

'No, you shouldn't. I thought more of you than that.'

'It's just . . .' He hesitated. 'Oh, forget it! It's not important.'

He kissed her again, but the magic had gone. What had been an idyllic evening together had suddenly turned sour.

When she repeated that she had to go upstairs he didn't try to talk her into staying on a little longer.

'Good night,' she whispered at the foot of the stairs.

'Good night. See you tomorrow.'

He waved, then walked briskly off into the night.

Ishbel drew in a deep breath and exhaled slowly. If she hadn't realized it before, she now knew Mrs Clarke was her enemy, who, naturally enough, exerted a great deal of influence over Gavin. The evening had also provoked a horrible suspicion that Gavin wasn't the man she'd thought him to be. She hoped she was wrong.

'I tried the factors' offices again today with the same result. Nothing doing,' Mary Louise complained to Rory as they sat staring contemplatively into the fire. They were home alone; her parents had gone out to play rummy.

'If something doesn't come up soon, we won't be able to get married this summer,' she went on.

Rory picked up the poker and stabbed the fire, encouraging flames to break out where previously there had only been a cherry glow.

'Are you listening to me?' she demanded angrily.

He blinked and turned to her. 'Sorry, what were you saying?'

'Only that we probably can't get married this summer.'

'Why not?'

She folded her arms across her bosom and stared at him. 'Haven't you heard one word I've said?'

'I've been thinking. I have a lot on my mind.'

'Oh, have you now?' she exclaimed sarcastically. 'I presume it is important to you that we do get married?'

'Of course, love.'

'Well, then, pay attention.' She paused, then said: 'Are you worried about something at work?'

'Not work exactly. Celia. She's taken ill again. Seriously, I believe.'

Irritation flashed across Mary Louise's face. It seemed to her that all Rory ever talked about nowadays was his precious Celia, to such an extent that it made her want to throw up.

'I knew she shouldn't have gone to London,' Rory went on, 'and told her so. But she'd promised the Master she'd attend an important function at the Liberal Club and was determined to keep her word. She looked dreadfully pale when I saw them off at the station.'

'And what's wrong with her?' Mary Louise demanded tightly.

'The same: general ill health. I just wish she wouldn't smoke those damned cigarettes. I'm sure they don't do her any good.'

'Have you finished?'

Rory frowned. 'Finished? Finished what?'

'Talking about her. Can we talk about us and our problems for a change? We can't land ourselves a house, and without a house there's no wedding.'

'I'm sure something will turn up.'

She could have slapped him for saying that. 'It should be you going round the factors' offices, not me,' she retorted hotly instead.

'I would, but I never get the chance.'

'The Lindsays are away just now. That must mean you have a great deal of free time on your hands?'

'I'm taking this opportunity to do things to the car and also the garage, which is in a terrible state.'

Mary Louise snorted.

'Oh, come on, stop being so miserable.'

'Well, it's always bloody *Celia*!'

'We're good friends, she and I. I like her a lot, and am concerned about her wellbeing.'

He beckoned Mary Louise over, grabbed her when she came to him and swung her on to his knee. 'But it's you I love, Sexy Drawers.'

'My drawers are not sexy!' she protested.

'Then, get some that are.'

He moved his hand up her skirt.

'What are you doing?'

'Feeling your bum. Any objections?'

'Will you stop it?' she said, a twinkle in her eye.

'Nope.'

'But I don't want you doing that.'

'Liar. You'd have jumped off my lap by now if you didn't.' She grinned.

'Now give me a kiss,' he commanded. 'And afterwards

we'll talk about the house and our wedding. All night if you want to.'

'And not another word about Celia?'

'Not another word,' he promised.

'Ishbel loves the child, you say?' Margaret Clarke questioned Gavin.

He sighed in exasperation, knowing he was in for another session regarding Ishbel. 'Very much so.'

'I wonder how that will affect her own children when they come along. I mean, will she favour this Jessica over them?'

'I don't see why she should.'

'Oh, I don't know!' Margaret said slowly. 'The girl is an orphan after all, and there must be a tremendously strong bond between her and Ishbel, especially as Ishbel is her mother's twin. I think it quite possible that Jessica will be favoured over subsequent children.'

'To the detriment of those subsequent children,' Bill added.

'Happens in second marriages,' Margaret went on. She addressed Bill. 'Do you recall Barbara Ferguson whose first man died in a factory accident?'

Bill nodded.

'Well, she had two children by him, and then another by the chap she next married. It was common knowledge that the first two were favoured over the third.'

Seeing Gavin deep in thought, Margaret shut up and left him to his ruminations.

'Are you going out this Friday?' Aunt Dot asked Ishbel.

'I don't know yet. Gavin hasn't walked me home for the past few nights.'

Aunt Dot raised an eyebrow. 'Oh!'

'He may have been doing overtime. Some of the lads have.'

'Hasn't he spoken to you recently at work?'

'I have tried, but he seems to vanish during the breaks.'

Aunt Dot didn't like the sound of that, but refrained from saying anything. Instead she changed the subject.

'Gavin!' Ishbel increased her pace till she was almost running. 'Gavin, wait, will you!'

He reluctantly stopped and turned towards her. 'Hello,' he mumbled when she reached his side.

'How are you?'

'Fine.'

She could sense his unease. 'I haven't spoken to you for days.'

'I've been busy,' he said, lips twitching.

'It's Friday. Are we going out tonight?'

He shifted his weight from one foot to the other. 'I've got something on. Sorry.'

Those feeble words were like a knife thrust into her heart. 'I see. What about tomorrow night?'

He shifted weight again. 'I'm tied up then also.'

She looked into his face and saw a mask hiding his feelings. 'What are you saying, Gavin?' she asked.

He was hating this; it made him feel sick. Coward! he thought. Damned coward! 'Nothing.'

That angered her. 'What do you mean, "nothing"? At least be honest with me. You owe me that.'

He gazed at a chimney-pot which was belching filthy smoke into the grey cloudless sky.

'Well?' she demanded.

He brought his attention back to her. 'It's all getting a bit involved. I think we should go easy for a while.'

'Easy?' she queried slowly.

'You know!'

'No, I don't. Spell it out.'

He felt totally wretched, and not at all sure he was doing the right thing. Yes, he was, he reassured himself. He'd made a decision and would stick by it.

'My mother—'

'Your mother!' Ishbel exploded.

He coloured and looked shamefaced. 'We've talked, she and I.'

'And?' Ishbel's voice was razor-sharp.

'And decided I might be rushing into something I'd later regret.'

The old bitch, Ishbel thought. 'What exactly would you regret?'

He couldn't hold her gaze, and glanced away. 'I did meet you on the rebound after all.'

Suddenly she despised him, contempt welling up inside her. 'The rebound?' she echoed softly. 'I suppose you did.'

'I might be making a mistake. Seeing things as they aren't.'

All she wanted to do was take to her heels and run, to find a quiet secluded place and cry. 'We all make mistakes,' she said bitterly.

'You understand?'

Only too well, she thought, loathing him.

'So I—'

'I think Kate had a lucky escape,' she declared abruptly.

He stared at her, dumbfounded. 'I beg your pardon?'

'I think she had a lucky escape,' Ishbel repeated.

'Why?'

Ishbel laughed, a laugh that rang with a note of hysteria. Without answering his question she strode away, leaving him gazing in puzzlement after her.

'The trouble with hurt is you can't really share it with anyone else,' Aunt Dot said.

Ishbel continued to sob. She was at the kitchen table, her head buried in her hands. 'I did ... honestly ... care for ...' Ishbel couldn't continue, the words choking in her throat.

'He's a bastard,' Aunt Dot declared, harsh words for her.

'No,' said Ishbel. 'He's just weak. Weak and a mother's boy.'

'I really did think he was the chap for you,' Aunt Dot stated.

'So did I.'

'Sodding men. Every last one of them.'

That statement rather shocked Ishbel. 'Not all men surely. What about your husband Ben?'

A strange expression crept across Aunt Dot's face. 'Oh, yes, I loved him all right. Very much so. Except . . . except there was someone else. A friend he had.'

Ishbel was intrigued. This was new. 'A friend?'

'*Lady* friend.'

Ishbel stared at Aunt Dot, disturbed and upset by the pain on her face. 'Lady friend?'

'A woman he was close to.'

'How . . . ?' Ishbel shut up, thinking she was going too far, delving too deep.

'His bit of fluff,' Aunt Dot said sadly. 'I met her once. She wasn't particularly attractive, although she was far younger than me. But Ben liked her; the two of them just seemed to get on.'

'How long did that go on for?' Ishbel asked quietly.

Aunt Dot shrugged. 'To be honest, I don't really know. He'd been seeing her for quite some time before I found out. At least, I think he had. He was very secretive about Julie.'

'And you met her?'

'Just once.'

'Weren't you tempted to scratch her eyes out?'

Aunt Dot laughed cynically. 'Oh, I was that. The way I felt I could have ripped her face to shreds. Instead I simply smiled and said: "How do you do?" '

'If a husband of mine cheated on me, I'd chuck him. No two ways about it, he'd be out the door.'

'You say that now,' Aunt Dot answered, 'but it might not be what you'd do if you loved him. Love makes a person extremely vulnerable and often downright stupid. You put up with things you wouldn't otherwise.'

'You make it sound like a disease,' Ishbel joked.

Aunt Dot barked out a laugh. 'That's precisely what it is. A disease that on one hand can be wonderful, on the other terrible. But I tell you this: despite Julie I wouldn't have missed out on Ben. He may have caused me a great deal of anguish, but he also gave me great joy and pleasure. God bless and keep him.'

Ishbel used her hanky to wipe her nose. She'd stopped crying and, for some reason, felt quite cheered.

'I'll tell you what,' said Aunt Dot. 'Why don't I go out and buy a bottle of sherry? Then the two of us can sit here and drink it.'

'A terrific idea!' Ishbel enthused. 'Only, I'll go and get it.'

'No, me. I insist. And not only a bottle of sherry, but a box of chocolates. I'd buy cakes as well, but the bakery's shut.'

'You buy the sherry and I'll pay for the chocolates. Now, come on, fair's fair.'

'Fair's fair,' Aunt Dot agreed. 'You can pay for those.'

When Aunt Dot had gone Ishbel's thoughts again turned to Gavin. She had liked him so terribly much. Now . . .

'There are always other fish in the sea,' she said aloud. 'Always other fish.'

It was cold comfort.

Rory glanced at his wristwatch to note there were still several minutes to go before the train was due. He was at the station to collect the Lindsays, who were returning from London.

A puff of smoke appeared on the horizon, telling him the train was on time. At least it had stopped raining, he thought with satisfaction, for it had been pouring most of that day.

It would be good to have the Lindsays back, particularly Celia. According to Burnford, who regularly spoke to the Master on the telephone, she had totally recovered from her recent illness. What a worry that had been!

With a hiss and exhalation of steam the train slid alongside the platform, finally coming to a halt with a screech of metal.

'Rory!' shouted the Master, leaning out of a window. 'Quick, I need your help.'

Rory sprinted towards the Master whose expression he could now see was extremely anxious.

'Mrs Lindsay has taken ill again. We'll have to carry her to the Rolls.'

Celia was huddled against a corner of the first-class carriage, her complexion white and mottled, her breathing laboured. 'Can't stand, I'm afraid,' she smiled weakly at Rory.

'Leave this to me,' Rory said to the Master. Gently he scooped Celia into his arms and carried her to the Rolls where he, again gently, settled her in the rear.

The Master appeared with a porter and the luggage, which Rory stowed in the boot. Rory paid off the porter, then hurried round to the side of the car.

'How is she now?' he asked the Master.

'Not good. We must get her home and into bed as soon as possible.'

Rory jumped into the driver's seat and switched on. He drove quickly and smoothly, eventually pulling up outside Drum House where he killed the engine and got out.

'I feel such a fool,' Celia said as Rory again scooped her into his arms.

'Nonsense. Anyone can take ill. It's not your fault.' Turning to the Master, he said, 'If you'll lead on, sir.'

The door was opened for them by one of the maids, and a concerned Burnford bustled up to be told in clipped tones by the Master what had occurred.

'I'll ring the doctor,' Burnford said, and disappeared back into the house.

Celia put an arm round Rory as he carried her upstairs. Beads of perspiration had appeared on her brow and temples. He was certain that if he'd touched her skin he'd have found it to be hot.

Rory entered the Lindsays' bedroom and strode towards the canopied four-poster that dominated the room. The Master pulled the covers aside, and Rory laid Celia on pale-green satin sheets.

'Thank you, Rory,' she whispered.

'I'll be downstairs if you need me further,' he said to the Master.

He left the bedroom, closing the door quietly behind him.

Rory looked up as Burnford came into the servants' kitchen. 'The doctor's with her now,' Burnford announced.

Mrs Murchie, the cook, shook her head in consternation. 'I'll make some broth in case she fancies a bowl of that.'

'It's such a long journey up from London. It must have been too much for her,' commented Burnford, sitting opposite Rory.

'She couldn't have been fully recovered after all,' Rory declared.

'Poor woman,' Mrs Murchie muttered.

Burnford leapt to his feet when the bell from the Lindsays' bedroom rang, and rushed off. He returned a few minutes later to say the Master wanted a word with Rory.

'I want you to drive to Glasgow and get some special medicine,' the doctor informed Rory.

'Of course, sir.'

The doctor handed Rory a prescription. 'You should be able to catch one of the main dispensaries before they close.'

Rory glanced at his wristwatch. 'I'll catch one all right. You can rely on that.'

'Good man,' said the Master.

They were in the corridor outside the bedroom. 'How is she, sir?' Rory enquired of the Master.

The Master's lips thinned. 'Bad, I'm afraid. She's had a relapse.'

Rory swore mentally. 'Is there anything else you want in Glasgow, sir?'

'No, just the medicine.'

'Then, I'll be off.'

Once out of sight of the Master, Rory broke into a run. He didn't bother about his uniform hat, which was in the kitchen, but headed straight for the Rolls.

He drove to Glasgow as if all the Furies in Hell were on his heels.

The Master was surprised to find Rory sitting in the servants' kitchen nursing a cup of tea.

'I thought you would have gone home long ago,' he said, having told Rory earlier that he wouldn't be needed again until the following day.

'I wanted to hang around here, sir,' Rory replied, rising.

The Master smiled in understanding. 'I had a sudden urge for a glass of milk,' he explained.

'I'll get that for you,' Rory offered, and made for the small pantry.

'She's sleeping soundly,' the Master informed Rory when he returned with the milk.

'Good.'

'That medicine you brought has eased her condition considerably.'

'I'm pleased, sir.'

The Master regarded Rory thoughtfully. 'You two have become firm friends, I understand?'

Rory coloured slightly. 'That's correct, sir. I hope you don't think it forward of me.'

'I must admit, I wasn't sure to begin with. It's a bit unusual, to say the least. But, then, Celia is a theatrical, and they do seem to operate outside normal convention.'

The Master hesitated, then said: 'Celia told me about your sister. You have my fullest sympathy.'

Rory dropped his gaze. 'Thank you, sir.'

'I understand that she reminds you of her?'

'She does, sir. It's not Mrs Lindsay's appearance, but a quality she has.'

'Your sister was called Rowan?'

'That's correct, sir.'

'And you have another sister who now lives in Glasgow?'

'Rowan's twin, Ishbel. She's looking after Jessica who's Rowan's daughter.'

362

'I shall be spending several days in Glasgow shortly. That will give you the opportunity to visit them.'

Rory beamed. 'That'll be wonderful, sir. I haven't seen them since they left Glenshields.'

'Then, you write and tell them you'll be popping in soon.'

'Thank you, sir.'

The Master finished his milk and laid the glass aside. 'I'm for bed and I suggest you do the same. You won't help Celia by staying up worrying.'

'No, sir.'

He patted Rory on the arm. 'You're a splendid chap, Rory. I'm pleased we took you on.'

'I love the job, sir, working for you and Mrs Lindsay.'

'How are you getting on with your marriage plans?'

'We're rather stuck there unfortunately. We just can't find a house.'

The Master murmured, scratching his chin. 'A house, eh?'

'There's simply nothing available.'

The Master yawned. 'I'm out on my feet. It's been a long day. See you tomorrow, Rory.'

'Good night, sir.'

'Good night.'

A house, the Master thought as he climbed the stairs. Perhaps he could help.

Rory drove the Rolls off the road to park as close to the lochside as possible. He then opened the rear door so Celia could stare over the loch. This was her first venture out since her relapse.

'Are you warm enough now?' he fussed.

She smoothed the Lindsay tartan rug covering her legs. 'Warm as toast, Rory.'

'What about a cup of coffee from the flask?'

'Later perhaps.'

He frowned when she produced a gold cigarette-case. 'I'm sure you shouldn't,' he admonished.

'I enjoy my cigarettes,' she replied firmly. She lit up

and blew out a stream of smoke. 'Aaahhhh!' she sighed.

He knew better than to argue further; it wouldn't get him anywhere. She was still dreadfully pale, he thought, and needed to regain the weight she'd lost. If only she'd eat more! Mrs Murchie was forever complaining about how little she ate.

'What a beautiful scene,' Celia murmured, gazing out over the loch.

'Ay, it is pretty,' Rory agreed.

'Look, a heron!' she cried in excitement, pointing at the magnificent bird winging its way several feet above the water.

'They're good luck,' Rory said.

'Are they?' she queried, wide-eyed.

'Oh, yes. Very good luck,' he assured her, having just made that up. He knew that Celia, like many actors, was extremely superstitious.

'Can I make a wish on it?'

'I don't see why not.'

She thought for a moment, then nodded her head. 'Done.'

'I hope it comes true,' Rory said softly.

'Shall I tell you what it was?'

'Oh, no!' he exclaimed. 'Then it wouldn't happen.'

'So it stays a secret.'

Celia could only manage a few more moments before she became restless, and so they slowly made their way home.

Ishbel threw open the front door the minute she heard his knock. 'Rory!' she screamed, and fell into his arms.

Emotion welled up inside him. 'God, it's great to see you again, Sis.'

'And you!'

She held him at arm's length and stared at him. 'You look terrific.'

'And so do you.'

She grabbed his hand. 'Now, come on through and meet Aunt Dot. And wait till you see Jessica. She really has grown!'

The reunion was marvellous – one they all thoroughly enjoyed. The only complaint was that it went far too quickly.

Rory poked his head into the sitting-room and grinned at Mary Louise. 'Hello, Duchess. I've got some news.'

'Good news?' she queried hopefully.

'The best.'

He strode over to her, picked her up and whirled her round and round.

'Hey!' she protested, laughing at the same time.

He put her down again and placed his hands on her shoulders. 'What's the very best news I could give you?'

'I don't know.'

'What if I told you we've got a cottage?'

Her face lit up. 'You're not having me on, are you?'

'Nope.'

'But I was at the factors' earlier this week and—'

'The Master,' he interjected. 'The cottage belongs to him. And we're only to pay a nominal rent.'

'Oh, Rory, I couldn't be more delighted,' Mary Louise breathed ecstatically. 'Where is this cottage?'

'Not in Glenshields, but Drumden, which is the next-best thing. It's only a hop, skip and jump away.'

'And we're to pay a *nominal* rent?'

'That's what the Master said. "A token of their appreciation," was how he put it. The cottage does need some work apparently as it's fallen a bit into disrepair, but I said I'd happily take care of that.'

'When can we see it? When can we move in?' Mary Louise demanded eagerly.

'We can see it tonight, but just from the outside, I'm afraid, and we'll be given the key shortly after the Master makes alternative arrangements for the man who's there now. He's a widower in his eighties whom the Master has talked into moving into a home.'

'I'm so excited,' Mary Louise enthused. 'Now we can go ahead and name the day.'

'I've got further news,' Rory smiled. 'The Master has

also increased my wages, again because they're so pleased with me.'

'By how much?'

'A full ten shillings a week.'

Mary Louise exclaimed and clapped her hands. This got better and better.

'I'll tell you what. Why don't we go and have a look at the cottage, then I'll take you to the pub to celebrate?'

'I'll get my coat. But first I must tell Mum.'

Rory sighed with contentment. A cottage and an increase in wages! It had been his lucky day.

Their lucky day, he corrected himself, thinking of Mary Louise.

Ishbel glanced over to where Sarah Webster was deep in conversation with Gavin. It was the afternoon tea-break.

'They've become thick as thieves, those two,' commented Ellen Weary.

Ishbel frowned. 'How do you mean?'

'Don't tell me you don't know,' giggled Olive McGuire.

'Know what?'

'Sarah and Gavin Clarke have started going out together.'

'Sarah and . . . ?' Ishbel stared at her workmates in amazement. 'Since when?'

'A week ago,' stated Ellen.

Ishbel couldn't believe it. What on earth did he see in her. 'I must confess I'm surprised,' she said slowly.

'Sarah practically threw herself at him,' Betty Hope declared.

'He didn't exactly put up a lot of resistance,' Olive commented drily.

Ishbel was furious. Of all people for Gavin to get friendly with, why did it have to be Sarah whom she loathed? Had she intentionally latched on to Gavin because he'd broken with her? For Sarah disliked her as much as she disliked Sarah.

'Good luck to the pair of them,' Ishbel muttered. 'They deserve one another.'

'Sour grapes?' queried Olive mischievously.

'Not at all.'

Ishbel sipped her tea. If Gavin had been there, it would have taken all her willpower not to throw the contents of her cup in his face. She just hoped Sarah didn't start flaunting the relationship; which was precisely what Sarah began doing shortly after that.

Vincent lay staring up at a cloudless duck-blue sky, thinking: This is the life! He and Meg had motored to Loch Thom for a picnic.

He smiled at the memory of a deal he'd pulled off the previous week, one that had proved to be most lucrative. How he had screwed that poor bastard! What a joke. He'd buy himself a new car from the proceeds, he decided: something smart and racy that would make people's heads turn. He'd like that – and so would Rose.

Mind you, he and Rose hadn't been getting on all that well of late. There was nothing he could put his finger on, but it was as though each had lost interest in the other.

He was due to see her later in the week, but now he thought about it he wasn't all that keen. It was all right when they were actually in bed together, but the rest of the time had become a bit of a let-down. Why, the last time he dropped in on her he couldn't wait – after bed, that is – to get away.

The chatter of young female voices made him open his eyes and hoist himself on to an elbow. God, what corkers! he thought as two girls in their late teens strolled by, both sporting swimming costumes.

He gazed at the girls until they vanished, then turned his attention to the lochside. He squinted, the sun shining directly into his face. There was a heat haze over the loch, a haze in which he could make out several shimmering figures, one of which must be Meg who'd gone for a paddle.

He wouldn't mind a beer, he thought, watching one of the sparkling figures begin to wade ashore. He contemplated the beer – they had brought several bottles with them – but didn't make a move towards their hamper, preferring to gaze at the form now emerging from the loch.

It was a woman; he could tell that from the skirt she was holding bunched above her knees. For some reason she fascinated him, though he had no idea why.

The figure, shimmering even more than before, came towards him. It swayed seductively, moving with a languid grace that brought prickles to his skin – skin that suddenly seemed to assume a life of its own, be part of him yet detached at the same time.

Vincent shook his head, then blinked. The sun was getting to him, he thought. He should really move into the shade.

The figure was many different colours now, a kaleido-scope of ever-changing patterns. The face had become a constantly moving liquid mass. Somehow the legs broke free, only to be seen as they were – shapely, very feminine legs, that any woman would have been proud of. The tingling sensation intensified when he imagined touching them, caressing them, running his hands up and down their thighs.

'Vincent?'

The liquid mass solidified into anxious features.

'Meg?

'Are you all right?'

'I ... er ...' He stared at her, and at that moment saw Meg in a completely new light. At that moment he fell madly in love with his own wife.

'I was watching you ... coming from the loch,' he croaked.

'You should have joined me for a paddle; the water's lovely.'

Meg sat, rummaged in a bag to produce a large towel with which she proceeded to dry her legs and feet. While she was doing this Vincent gazed fixedly at her.

'I never noticed before ...' he said, trailing off.

'Noticed what?'

'How very, very attractive you are.'

She stopped and turned to him. 'I beg your pardon?'

'How very, very attractive you are.'

She frowned. 'Are you teasing me?'

'No, I swear.'

He reached for his cigarettes lying close by and lit up. He sucked smoke deep into his lungs, exhaled, then repeated the action. He found himself trembling slightly.

'I think the sun must have got to me,' he stammered.

'You do look a bit flushed.'

He continued to stare at her, thinking it was as though a veil had dropped from his eyes. A feeling of pure love surged within him. He wanted to take Meg into his arms and hold her close, look after her, protect her, cherish her.

Then he remembered a bible story from years previously when he'd attended Sunday school as a boy, a story that brought an understanding smile to his lips.

'Damascus,' he said.

'Damascus!' Whatever was he on about?

'The road to Damascus.'

Meg was lost. The sun really must have got to him to make him behave like this.

'Would you like an ice-cream?' he asked. 'I'll go and get you one.'

'That would be nice.'

He jumped to his feet and smiled at her, not quite believing what he saw or felt. 'The largest cone they do drenched in raspberry topping – how does that sound?'

'Mmm!' she enthused.

'Right.'

He strode away, then halted after a few paces. He turned round again and returned to Meg. 'Forgot something,' he said.

Bending, he kissed her on the mouth. 'That.'

She stared after him in amazement when he strode off a second time.

Meg squirmed with enjoyment. What was happening was so nice!

369

'Are you awake?'

'No.'

Vincent laughed. 'I think you are, Pussy Willow.'

Pussy Willow! She opened her eyes. He'd never called her that before. Then she squirmed again as his hand caressed up the length of her thigh. 'Stop that!'

'Why? You're enjoying it.'

'That doesn't matter. Stop it.'

'I will if you really want me to, but I don't think you do.'

She swung her head round to stare at him, and he responded by flashing her a smile. It was like their courting days all over again, she thought. What a change there had been in him of late. Meg wholeheartedly approved.

'I don't want to, if that's what you're after,' she stated.

'Why not?'

'I don't feel like it.'

'Then, we won't.'

How different to the old Vincent that was! Before he'd have persisted till they'd probably ended up rowing. Now he simply accepted her refusal and left it at that.

'Did you sleep well?' he asked.

'Like the proverbial log.'

'How about a cup of tea?'

'That would be lovely.'

'I'll make it for you. And toast with marmalade?'

'Thank you, Vincent,' she said quietly.

Tenderness came into his eyes as he gazed at her. 'I won't be long,' he declared, and got out of bed.

What a change, she repeated to herself when he'd left the room.

She dozed off, only to wake again with his lips on hers. 'Tea and toast as promised,' he said, laying a tray alongside her.

They chatted away nineteen to the dozen as she ate and he got dressed.

'A surprise!' exclaimed Meg.

'A surprise,' stated Vincent.

'Where?'

'Outside in the hall.'

'Let me have it, then,' she said excitedly. A surprise was the last thing she'd been expecting.

'Close your eyes first.'

'All right, then.' She shut her eyes as instructed, heard him leave the kitchen and swiftly return.

'Hold out your hands.'

She did so, drawing in a sharp breath when a furry object was placed across her outstretched lower arms. Her eyes immediately snapped open.

'A fur coat!' she breathed.

'To replace the one I sold.' He beamed at her. 'This one's also mink, but it's better quality than the other.'

'Oh, Vincent.'

'I thought you'd like it.'

She rubbed a cheek up and down the coat and puffed: 'Gorgeous.'

'Now try it on. Should fit; it's the same size as the last one.'

She quickly slipped into the coat, hugging it tightly to her. The feeling was sensational.

'Well?' he prompted.

'It must have cost . . .'

He wagged a finger at her, indicating she must stop speaking. 'Money's no object where you're concerned, Meg. None at all.'

'Thank you.'

'Do I get a kiss?'

She crossed the few feet between them and kissed him on the lips.

'Happy?'

'Very much so.'

'Then, so am I.'

She went to the mirror above the mantelpiece and gazed at her reflection. 'I just don't know what to say.'

'Then, don't. The look on your face says it all.'

'I'll go and hang it up, shall I?'

'Unless you want to wear it round the house for the rest of the evening?'

'Hardly!'

At the door she halted and turned to him. 'This wasn't necessary, Vincent.'

'It was, to replace the other one.'

'You know what I mean,' she stated softly.

'I know,' he replied, equally softly.

She smiled endearingly at him, then left the room.

It was a smile that meant an enormous amount to Vincent, a man newly in love with his wife.

Another day at Blue Bonnet, Ishbel thought, swinging her legs out of bed. She stretched, before reaching for her clothes.

She frowned as she entered the kitchen; the fire was unlit and Aunt Dot wasn't bustling around as she normally was.

Ishbel went to the cavity bed and peered inside. Aunt Dot was still fast asleep. 'Aunt Dot!' she said, shaking the old woman by the shoulder. 'Aunt Dot!'

Then she noticed there was something strange about Aunt Dot's complexion. It was a bluish white and slightly waxy.

'Aunt ...' The truth hit her with a suddenness that made her suck in a startled breath.

She felt Aunt Dot's forehead, which was stone cold. As she removed her hand Aunt Dot's head lolled sideways.

Aunt Dot was dead.

Chapter Ten

'I'll put the kettle on,' Meg declared, making for the cooker.

'I thought it went well,' Ishbel commented. The pair of them had just returned from the funeral. Jessica was with a neighbour awaiting collection.

'Pity there were so few of us present,' Meg replied.

Ishbel pulled a face. 'She didn't have all that many friends – still alive anyway. I suppose that's what happens when you get to her age. And of course she didn't have any family of her own.'

'So what happens now?'

Ishbel remembered she had some chocolate biscuits in and rose to get them. 'I've already spoken to the factor, who's transferring the house to my name.'

'Who'll look after Jessica while you're at work?'

'The same neighbour who has her now. She's got two small children of her own, which means Jessica will have someone to play with. Jessica likes them all, so there's no worry there.'

'Will you have to pay her?'

'Of course. She's hardly going to do it for free,' Ishbel answered, transferring a number of biscuits on to a plate.

'That means more outlay?'

'Plus the fact I'll be paying the full rent on the house.'

'Will you be able to manage?'

Ishbel shrugged. 'Hopefully. Things are going to be awfully tight, but I should get by.'

'I'd help if only I was working,' Meg declared.

'I know that, Mum, and appreciate the thought.'

Meg stared down in despair at her hands. She could still use them round the house for domestic chores, but sewing remained out of the question.

'I could have a word with Rory.'

'No,' said Ishbel. 'He's soon to be married after all. He'll need every penny he's got.'

'I'll still mention it. He's always been very fond of you.'

'He was more fond of Rowan.'

'Ay, well, there we are.'

Meg opened a cupboard. 'Is this where you keep your caddy?'

Ishbel went to her. 'You sit down, Mum. I'll make it.'

Meg did as she was told. 'You'll be coming to the wedding, I presume?' she asked.

'I should hate to miss it. But I'd prefer not to stay at home.'

'I doubt Vincent would try anything on, but you're probably right. I'm sure Fee will be happy to put up you and Jessica. How long will it be for?'

'Just the night. I'll travel back on the Sunday as I'll have work the next day.'

'That shouldn't be a problem, then. Fee will no doubt give you Rory's room; it will be free then, for he and Mary Louise will be off on honeymoon.'

'Where are they going? Have they decided?'

'Oh, they've decided all right – or, at least, Rory has. But he's not letting on to anyone, least of all Mary Louise. It's to be a surprise.'

'How romantic of him,' Ishbel smiled.

'He has his moments.'

'I'm looking forward to meeting Mary Louise,' Ishbel stated.

'And she's mentioned several times she'd love to meet you. She's naturally very excited about the wedding, and doing up this cottage they're renting. She's there most evenings beavering away like a mad thing. She's got very definite ideas about what she wants and how she wants them.'

'She sounds extremely strong-minded.'

'Oh, she is that,' Meg confirmed. 'But she and Rory seem to get on well enough. I think it'll be a good match.'

Ishbel placed the now-filled teapot on the table alongside

the cups and saucers she'd put out and sat facing her mother. 'I'm glad you could come through for the funeral,' she said.

'It was the least I could do in the circumstances. Aunt Dot was so kind to you and Jessica. And, anyway, it gave me the chance to see the pair of you again.'

Meg gazed at the chocolate biscuits and sighed. 'Temptation,' she muttered.

Ishbel offered her the plate. 'Go on, spoil yourself.'

'I shouldn't really.'

'But you will, as will I.'

Meg crunched into a biscuit and smiled. 'Gorgeous.'

'I adore chocolate.'

'Don't we all?'

They both laughed. 'It's marvellous having you here, Mum. I only wish you could stay.'

Meg considered that, then shook her head. 'I only brought the one change of clothes. Besides, I always feel so uncomfortable in the big city. It's just not for me.'

'And Glasgow's big all right. It frightens me sometimes.'

Meg put a hand over her daughter's. 'You are happy here? At least, that's the impression you've always given.'

'Happy enough, Mum. Though it's going to be lonely without Aunt Dot. I shall miss our chats.'

Meg regarded her daughter thoughtfully, seeing sorrow in her daughter's face which tugged her heartstrings. Ishbel had been given a difficult boat to row right enough. How much easier things would have been for her if she'd been able to stay on in Glenshields, but Vincent had put paid to that.

'Maybe I will stay on a bit,' Meg said slowly. 'I can always wash my smalls at night.'

Ishbel beamed. 'Oh, Mum, that would be marvellous! I can't tell you how pleased I am. I'll have to work of course, but—'

'I'll leave after the weekend. How's that?' Meg interjected.

'Couldn't be better.'

'And while you're at work I'll look after Jessica, which will be a treat for me.'

'I think that calls for another biscuit,' Ishbel proposed.

Meg sighed again. 'How can I resist? They're so lovely!'

Both women reached out to the plate simultaneously.

'There are some things I promised to take to Rory and Mary Louise's this evening and now just don't have the time to do so. Do you think you could take them for me?'

Vincent stared at Meg in surprise.

'I really am up to my eyes in it,' Meg added.

'Me?' Vincent said slowly.

'It's not far. You can be there and back in a jiffy.'

It was several days before the wedding, and Meg was frantically busy with preparations – as, indeed, were Mary Louise and Rory.

'That wasn't what I was thinking about. You know how Rory feels where I'm concerned, and if I was to turn up at his door . . .'

Meg sighed. 'I'm well aware of what he thinks about you. There, again, you have been invited to the wedding.'

'Invited maybe, but only because I'm your husband and it would be a local scandal if I wasn't.'

'None the less, Vincent, I do need this favour, and there's no-one else I can ask.'

Vincent thought about it, then came to his feet. 'I'll deliver whatever it is needs delivering. I only hope I don't get the door slammed in my face, that's all.'

Meg smiled in appreciation. 'Ta, Vincent. I'll get the things together for you.'

Shortly afterwards Vincent found himself striding along the street with a neatly tied parcel under his arm. He wasn't looking forward to this one little bit. The pair of them had not exchanged so much as a single word since that awful night of the incident when Rory had stormed out of the house and gone to live with Fee.

Vincent was on the outskirts of the village when he had a sudden thought which made him halt. Surely this was a golden opportunity to mend fences, to *try* to mend them anyway. Surely it was appropriate timing, which just might find Rory in a receptive mood, with the wedding almost upon them?

Should he make an effort? Vincent wondered. Well, why not? It was long overdue, and a reconciliation would delight Meg.

Swinging on his heel he retraced his steps, heading for the pub where he would buy a peace offering.

'We'll never get ready in time,' Mary Louise was saying to Rory when their bell tinkled.

'I'll answer it,' she said. 'It's probably Meg.'

Vincent was extremely nervous as he heard the approaching footsteps. Then Mary Louise was gaping at him.

'Hello,' he stammered.

'Hello.'

He offered her the parcel. 'Meg asked me to bring this over as promised. She was too busy to do so herself.'

'Thank you,' replied Mary Louise, accepting the parcel.

'Do you think ... ?' Vincent swallowed hard. This was proving even more difficult than he'd anticipated. 'Do you think I could come in and speak to the pair of you? If Rory's at home, that is.'

Rory appeared behind Mary Louise, his brow darkening when he saw who she was with. 'What the hell are you doing here?' he demanded harshly.

'I brought some things from your mum. She asked me,' Vincent explained.

'Well, now you've done so, clear off.'

Vincent took a deep breath to steel himself. 'Rory, can I come in and speak to you? Please?'

Rory marvelled at the cheek of the man. 'On your way!' he snarled.

'Please?' Vincent pleaded. 'For your mother's sake.'

Rory frowned. 'Is something wrong with her?'

'Yes, the estrangement between you and me. It's an ongoing hurt to her. Please, can I come in and say my piece?'

Mary Louise turned to Rory, who had a fixed obstinate

377

look on his face. 'I think you should allow it, Rory,' she stated softly.

He glanced from her back to his step-father. 'I can't really see that you and I have anything to talk about.'

'For your mother's sake, if you love her.'

'Of course I love her!' Rory exploded.

'Then, again, *please*.'

'Where's the harm?' Mary Louise said to Rory.

Rory wavered. This was against all his better instincts.

'I am coming to the wedding after all,' Vincent went on. 'So wouldn't it be better to clear the air if possible?'

Rory had fought against the issue of that invitation, only relenting when Meg had declared that if Vincent wasn't invited, then she wouldn't attend. Vincent didn't know about that.

'All right, I suppose,' Rory conceded through gritted teeth.

'Bless you, lass,' Vincent murmured as he stepped inside.

In the living-room Vincent produced the bottle of whisky he'd bought and set it on the mantelpiece. He then glanced around. 'You've done a fine job of decorating,' he commented.

'There was a lot to do, but we got there in the end,' Mary Louise told him.

'Very tasteful, if I may say so.'

'You wanted to talk?' Rory prompted.

Vincent indicated the whisky. 'That might be easier over a dram?' he suggested.

'A good idea. I'll fetch some glasses,' Mary Louise said, and hurried away.

Vincent stared Rory straight in the eye. 'I know we've fallen out and that it was all my fault. I want to apologize.'

Rory didn't reply.

'I have no excuse for what happened with Ishbel. It was sheer folly on my part.'

'Apart from Ishbel, think of how Mum must have felt.'

'Ay,' Vincent acknowledged as Mary Louise returned with three glasses.

'Have you told Mary Louise about . . . ?' He hesitated, leaving the question open.

'She and I have no secrets from each other.'

Vincent nodded. 'Just as it should be. Start as you intend to go on.'

'Shall I pour?' Mary Louise offered.

'If you would, lass.'

Vincent twisted his hands together. 'It would make your mother very happy if you and I were to forget our differences, Rory. And it seems to me this is the ideal time to do so.'

'You never cared a fig for my mother, so why should you be bothered now about her happiness?' Rory spat.

Vincent dropped his head, not replying for the space of a dozen heartbeats. When he looked up again Rory was startled to see there were tears in his step-father's eyes.

'I know this will be hard for you to believe, Rory, particularly in the light of how matters were between Meg and me when you were at home, but I truly love your mother now. I didn't always, I admit, but I do now. I swear it, and will repeat that oath on a stack of bibles if you want me to.'

How plausible he sounded, Rory thought. And yet . . .

Vincent accepted a dram from Mary Louise with a small nod of thanks. Using his free hand he wiped away his tears.

Doubt began to niggle at Rory. Was Vincent telling the truth? It certainly seemed that way, or else the man was a born actor. There, again, Meg had once mentioned to him that all horse traders were past masters of duplicity. Could this merely be some sort of trick? Then he remembered that Meg had told him on a number of occasions that things had vastly improved between her and Vincent.

'I really do love her Rory. On my life.'

Mary Louise, deeply moved, reached out and touched Vincent's shoulder. 'I believe you,' she declared, gently squeezing his shoulder.

He looked at her in relief. 'And a reconciliation would

be beneficial to you, too. It would mean there wouldn't be any undercurrents on your big day.'

Mary Louise glanced at Rory and raised an eyebrow. Her own feelings on the matter were perfectly clear.

'Let bygones be bygones?' Rory mused.

'That's it, Rory. As I said before, for your mother's sake.'

Rory gazed long and hard at the man he'd hated for so long, and made a decision. As Vincent said, for Meg's sake. But God help Vincent if this was a sham.

'All right, then,' Rory said.

Vincent's face brightened, and Mary Louise smiled. 'Thank you,' Vincent husked.

Rory crossed and picked up the other two drams Mary Louise had poured out, handing her one.

'To a new beginning,' he toasted.

'A new beginning,' Vincent and Mary Louise echoed together.

'You'll have no regrets, Rory, I promise you,' Vincent declared, a catch in his voice. He couldn't wait to get back and tell Meg the news.

Rory hoped he wouldn't.

'The Lindsays are coming over,' Rory whispered to Mary Louise.

A few seconds later the Master and Celia stopped in front of them. 'Congratulations. It was a wonderful wedding,' the Master declared.

'Thank you, sir,' Rory replied.

'And congratulations to you, Mrs Stewart,' smiled Celia. 'Can I say how radiant you look! Quite, quite beautiful.'

'Thank you, Mrs Lindsay,' Mary Louise answered almost bashfully.

'Your dress is magnificent,' the Master said.

'Bought in Edinburgh. We went through especially to choose it.'

Celia nodded. 'Rory told me.'

'It was a tremendous day out. I thoroughly enjoyed myself.'

'Talking of tremendous days,' said the Master affably, 'you've certainly had one for your wedding. Look at that sun; it's positively cracking the sky.'

'We have been fortunate,' Rory agreed.

Mary Louise gazed in admiration at the dress Celia was wearing, thinking how exceptionally pretty it was. It was a blue floral-print cotton dress with a false drape crossover bodice under a delicate lace collar, with five coloured buttons at the side. Each of its long sleeves ended with three more covered buttons.

A waiter appeared carrying a tray of champagne. 'Refills, sir?' he asked Rory.

'Please.'

Empty glasses were placed on the tray, and full ones passed round.

'A toast, if I may,' said the Master. 'To the happy couple!'

'To the happy couple,' Celia echoed.

Mary Louise studied Celia over the rim of her glass as she drank. She admired Celia for her success as an actress and for being the Mistress of Drum. Smiling, she slipped her free arm round Rory's and drew him closer, proclaiming him hers and hers alone, her husband, her property.

She turned her attention to Rory, who was speaking to the Master. 'Perhaps, sir, when we return from our honeymoon, you'd care to call in at the cottage and see what we've done to it?'

'Yes, why not?'

'You could both come.'

'And have afternoon tea?' Mary Louise suggested.

'Afternoon tea would be lovely,' Celia replied.

'Now I think we'd better move on and let your other guests have a chance to talk to you,' the Master declared. 'Thank you both for your present. Mary Louise will be writing to you.'

'I just hope it was to your taste,' Celia said.

'Oh, very much so!' Mary Louise assured her. They had given them a tea service, which was why Mary Louise had suggested afternoon tea as it would give her the opportunity to use it.

'See you when you get back, then. And I'll keep my fingers crossed that this glorious weather continues,' Celia said to Rory, knowing he and Mary Louise would be honeymooning in a small hotel that she had recommended.

Rory watched the Lindsays walk away, thinking how lucky he was to have such people as employers and friends, for that was what they'd both become.

'Isn't she gorgeous?' Ishbel said quietly to Rory and Mary Louise, having come to stand beside them. She was of course referring to Celia.

'Oh, she is that,' Rory smiled in reply.

'Where's Jessica?' Mary Louise asked.

'Mum's taking care of her. Giving me a break.' Jessica had been a bridesmaid, a task she'd performed perfectly and charmingly. Ishbel had been proud of her.

'Enjoying yourself?' Rory enquired.

Ishbel beamed at him. 'I'm having a whale of a time. It's a fabulous "do".'

Mary Louise spotted Vincent in conversation with her father, the pair of them resplendent in morning suits. Earlier Rory had chatted with his step-father, the two of them sharing a joke together. It pleased her enormously, and was a great relief, that there had been a reconciliation between them.

'You're pretty gorgeous yourself,' Rory complimented Ishbel, who had on a pale red dress that she'd been fortunate enough to find in a secondhand-clothes shop.

'Thank you, kind sir. I wouldn't want to let you down.'

'That you'd never do, Ishbel,' he declared softly. Then, with a twinkle in his eye, teased: 'Even if you came in your birthday suit.'

She blushed slightly and laughed. 'Rory!' she protested.

Henry Cameron, Mary Louise's father, strolled over. 'Seen your mum?' he asked Mary Louise.

'Not for a bit.'

'Maybe she's met someone and run off,' Rory teased.

'Peggy!' Henry threw back his head and laughed. 'I shouldn't think so.'

'You never know,' Rory went on, continuing the joke. 'Attractive woman like her. Clearly where Mary Louise gets her looks from.'

Mary Louise smiled to hear that.

A roar went up which claimed their attention. They couldn't make out what had happened. But, whatever, a group of guests huddled together were obviously having good fun.

A little girl called Harriet came skipping up to Meg and Jessica. 'Want to play?' she asked Jessica.

Jessica looked at Meg, who nodded. 'Of course you can, angel. Just don't go somewhere I can't keep an eye on you.'

Jessica and Harriet rushed off and immediately embarked on a chasing game.

'How are you?' Vincent queried of Meg, joining her. 'I've brought you another glass of champagne as I could see your glass was empty.'

'That's kind of you,' she acknowledged, accepting the new glass. He took her empty one and set it on a nearby table.

'It's going well,' he commented.

'Brilliantly so. Mary Louise and Rory must be delighted.' She glanced at her son and newly acquired daughter-in-law. 'They make a perfect couple, wouldn't you say?'

'Perfect,' Vincent agreed.

'And you've spoken to Rory?'

'Made a point of it. He and I had quite a little chin-wag.'

Meg sighed with contentment. 'Thank you for making up with him.'

'It's him you should be thanking for agreeing to make up with me. I was at fault, don't forget.'

Meg again marvelled at the change in Vincent. She felt quite mellow towards him now. Day by day he was regaining her affections.

383

'Cheers!' he said, raising his glass in a toast.

'Cheers.'

He bent towards her and kissed her lightly on the lips.

'Why did you do that?' she questioned in surprise.

'Because I wanted to. You don't object, do you?'

'Not in the least.'

'Good.'

He kissed her a second time. 'Twice for good measure,' he whispered.

A thrill ran through Meg that caused her hand holding the glass to shake. She decided to change the subject.

'I like your sister,' Mary Louise told Rory when Ishbel and Henry had moved on.

'She likes you, too; she mentioned it earlier.'

Mary Louise was pleased as she wanted to find favour with Ishbel. 'And Jessica is lovely.'

Rory's brow creased as he thought of Rowan. He'd have given anything for her to be there that day.

'Rory?' Mary Louise frowned.

He looked at her.

'You suddenly got a most peculiar expression on your face.'

'I was thinking about Rowan,' he explained, his voice tight.

Mary Louise took his hand and squeezed it, which made him smile.

'Thank you,' he said.

'For what?'

'Just being you. I'm a very lucky man.'

'And I'm a lucky woman.'

'Love you.'

'Love you, too.'

He put Rowan from his mind.

Fee and Meg were now standing together, as Vincent had taken himself off to the toilet. 'I think he's a smasher,' Fee said.

'Who?'

Fee nodded to where the Master and Celia were standing with some others. 'The Master of Drum. A real dreamboat.'

384

Meg laughed. 'You shouldn't be saying things like that at your age, Mum.'

'Why ever not? I may be old but my mind is young. And there's nothing wrong with my imagination, I can tell you.'

Meg wasn't sure whether she was shocked or not. 'I must have a word with Ishbel,' she declared, and moved off.

Nothing wrong with her imagination at all, Fee thought, and mentally sighed. She could fantasize, couldn't she? There was no law against it.

Rory reached for another glass of champagne, hesitated, then withdrew his hand. It wouldn't do to let Mary Louise down, not on that night of nights. It would be unforgivable. When he glanced at her she gave him a small nod of approval.

'We can speak to the Lindsays now,' Hugh Monteith whispered to his wife Sybil. He'd been waiting for his opportunity to engage them in conversation.

'Now, you won't go talking business, will you?'

'Me, darling?' That was precisely what he'd intended. There was a matter he wished to pump the Master about.

'Social chit-chat, Hugh, nothing else,' she warned, knowing him only too well.

He'd collar the Master on his own later if that was possible, he thought. 'Nothing else,' he agreed affably.

Sybil hooked an arm round his and together they headed for the Lindsays.

Normally Celia would have been bored by such a gathering. But it gratified her to be there, for Rory's sake and to see how happy he obviously was. She caught his eye, waved to him and blew him a kiss.

Ishbel was chatting to her grandfather Lex when a vision of Gavin and Sarah flashed through her mind. Her spirits fell as she imagined that if things had turned out differently he would have been present with her today. She glanced about, feeling lonely even though she was in the midst of a crowd. The loneliness made her cold inside. Then she spotted Jessica still playing the chasing game, and

385

that brought a smile to her face. She had a lot to be thankful for, she reminded herself.

Everyone, including the Lindsays, applauded when Rory and Mary Louise headed towards the hired car into which their luggage had already been loaded. Mary Louise was wearing a navy blue suit that Celia thought, with her auburn hair, looked very attractive.

Lewd suggestions were called out as Rory assisted Mary Louise into the car, causing Mary Louise to blush. Once inside Rory wound down his window in preparation for the traditional 'scramble' while the children present crowded round.

'Hard up!' someone shouted good-humouredly. 'Hard up!' A customary cry at this point.

Rory saw Celia smiling at him and smiled in return. Then he dug into a trouser pocket for the pile of small change he'd previously placed there.

His hand flashed, and money spun through the air. The children shrieked and yelled, diving this way and that to snatch up what coins they could.

Rory's hand flashed again as he hurled the money as far from the car as possible, then he started up the engine and the car moved off.

'Good luck!'

That and other heartfelt good wishes were shouted. Mary Louise waved to her mother, who was crying unashamedly. Henry, his arm wrapped round Peggy, looked incredibly proud.

'I hope their marriage is as successful as ours has been,' the Master said quietly to Celia.

She gazed at him through shining eyes. 'So do I, Archie.'

He pecked her on the lips, after which they watched the car bearing the newlyweds speed away into the distance.

Chapter Eleven

The only other occupant of the railway carriage, a man who'd got on a number of stops after Ishbel and Jessica, laughed when Jessica made a face at him.

'Don't be rude!' Ishbel admonished the mischievous Jessica, who giggled.

'That's all right,' the man said.

'No, it isn't. She mustn't do things like that.'

Jessica began bouncing up and down on the seat.

'And don't do that, either,' Ishbel chided her, beginning to get cross.

'Tell you what: how about a sweet? Will that get you to sit still?'

Jessica nodded vigorously.

The man produced a bag of toffees. 'With your permission of course?' he checked with Ishbel.

She gestured that he could go ahead and offer the bag. 'Take two,' he instructed a delighted Jessica.

'And you?' he asked Ishbel.

'Thank you.'

He folded over the top of the bag and returned it to his pocket. 'I don't travel by train very often, so I'm rather enjoying this,' he informed Ishbel, making conversation. 'I usually go everywhere by car. But unfortunately it's had to go into the garage for a few days.'

How old? Ishbel wondered. Twenty-five? Somewhere round about that. And quite handsome.

'You're lucky owning a car,' Ishbel commented.

'Oh, it's not mine; it belongs to the company. I'm a commercial traveller.'

A good job, Ishbel thought.

'Have you been on holiday?'

'In a way. I come from a village called Glenshields, and we've been back staying with my brother and his wife.' It was the Glasgow Fair holiday during which Blue Bonnet and most other Glasgow firms shut down.

'I see,' nodded the man.

'We had a smashing time, didn't we, Jessica?'

'Smashing,' Jessica confirmed through a mouthful of toffee.

'Did your husband have to stay at home and work?' the man enquired politely.

'I'm not married.' Then, noting his puzzled expression, said: 'Jessica's my niece whom I've been looking after since her parents died.'

'Oh, I am sorry.'

'It was a tragic thing when it happened. But that's all in the past now, isn't it, pet?'

Jessica nodded.

'Allow me to introduce myself. I'm Peter Lorne,' the man said. Rising, he crossed to Ishbel and extended his hand.

'I'm Ishbel Stewart. And this is Jessica.'

After he'd shaken hands with Ishbel he solemnly shook hands with Jessica. 'Pleased to meet you, young lady.'

She grinned at him, enjoying being treated as an adult.

'So what do you travel for, Mr Lorne?' Ishbel asked.

'Peter, please! I'm a very informal person.'

'Peter, then,' she smiled. 'And I'm Ishbel.'

'Pretty name.'

'Thank you.'

'I travel for a confectionery firm,' he explained. 'So I hope you like the toffee; it's ours.'

'It's tasty,' she assured him.

'And what do *you* think, Jessica?'

'Yum yum!'

Peter laughed. 'I like that. Most descriptive. Yum yum!' he repeated, and laughed again.

'You're not a Glaswegian?' Ishbel said. She'd noticed his accent was softer than the guttural and harsh Glaswegian one.

'No, I'm from Edinburgh.'

'Glasgow's where I now live.'

'Ah! Whereabouts?'

After she'd told him he declared: 'I know the place. There are several shops I visit round there. I like Glasgow and the Glaswegians; they're a friendly people.'

'Extremely,' she agreed.

'And do you like Glasgow, Jessica?' he enquired.

'Yes.'

'Are you at school yet?'

'I start next January.'

'Do you now? I would have thought you were older.'

Jessica loved his flattery, not realizing that's what it was.

'She's looking forward to it, aren't you, Jessica?'

Jessica nodded.

As was she, Ishbel thought, for that would mean she'd stop paying to have Jessica looked after while she was at work. Jess would still have to be cared for between the end of school and her getting home, but that would cost only a fraction of what it had previously.

'My favourite subject was maths,' Peter said to Jessica. 'I was very good at it. You'll have to learn all your times tables, you know. That can be hard, but fun when you've mastered them.'

What a nice chap, Ishbel thought. He was certainly at ease with children. 'Are you married?' she asked, thinking he might have children of his own.

'No,' he smiled. 'That hasn't happened yet. I'm still waiting to meet my lady fair.'

Lady fair! What a lovely expression. So did that mean he wasn't courting, either? She presumed it did. She viewed him with renewed interest.

'Would you like another sweet?' he asked Jessica.

'Please!'

He produced a second bag. 'These are boilings,' he explained, offering the bag to Jessica.

'You'll spoil her!' Ishbel half-heartedly complained.

He pulled the bag back. 'Are you saying she shouldn't?'

'Aunt Ishbel!' Jessica pouted in alarm.

'I can hardly say no now,' Ishbel declared.

'And one for your pocket,' Peter whispered conspiratorially as Jessica delved into the bag, winking at her.

They continued chatting until the train pulled into the station where Peter insisted on helping Ishbel with her two suitcases, dismissing the idea she use a porter.

'Are you taking a taxi?' he asked as they trooped up the platform.

'I'll have to with those cases.'

There was a queue at the taxi rank which they joined. 'It's been a pleasure meeting you,' Peter smiled as they moved rapidly forward.

'And to meet you, Peter.'

'Listen, why don't I drop by and see how you both are next time I'm up your way? I can also bring Jessica some free samples.'

'Oh, yes, please!' exclaimed Jessica.

'It would have to be one evening as I'm at work during the day,' Ishbel said.

'The evening it'll be, then. I'll arrange my calls accordingly.'

Ishbel gave him her address, which he, with a frown, committed to memory. 'I'll write it down later,' he said.

Then it was their turn. He shook hands again with Ishbel and Jessica, after which they climbed into the back of the taxi.

Peter waved to them as they drove off, they waving in reply through the rear window.

Ishbel hoped he'd call on them soon. She'd found his company . . . very pleasurable.

Mary Louise was in the hallway when the letter dropped on to the mat behind the door. Bending, she picked it up and glanced at its front. It was addressed to Rory, the handwriting unmistakably female.

Mary Louise frowned. What woman would be writing to

390

Rory, and why? She sniffed the envelope, but there was no trace of scent.

She regarded the envelope steadily, then looked at the postmark, which told her it came from Glasgow. The penny dropped as she recognized Ishbel's writing.

Oh, well! That explained it, she thought. All quite simple enough. Then doubt assailed her.

She tapped the letter against her thumb and continued staring at it. If she just gave the letter to Rory, he could take it off to work with him and she might never find out its contents. And, if she asked, he could lie.

Lie! That appalled her. Why on earth would he do that? But he might, particularly if there was something going on between him and Ishbel which they didn't want her to know about.

You're being ridiculous! she chided herself. There was no reason why Ishbel shouldn't write to Rory.

Rory. That was what was making her suspicious. Why wasn't it addressed to the pair of them? Why only Rory?

Her intuition told her something *was* going on, that there was a secret from which she was being excluded. Well, she wasn't having that. Making a sudden decision, she hooked a nail under the flap and ripped the envelope open.

There was a single sheet of paper inside which she quickly read, her mouth thinning into a slash before she reached the end. She then read the pertinent bit a second time.

A little later Mary Louise was in the kitchen busying herself with breakfast when Rory joined her. 'Morning, love,' he said, and pecked her on the cheek.

She didn't reply, instead stared icily at him.

'Something wrong?' he asked.

She produced the letter and threw it on to the table.

'When did this arrive?' he demanded harshly when he, too, had read the single sheet of paper.

'Just now.'

'And you opened it.'

She glared defiantly at him. 'I did.'

'But it's addressed to me. Not you and me. Me alone.'

'Which is why I smelled a rat. Justifiably as it turned out.'

Anger flared up in him which he swiftly brought under control. 'And how long have you been opening my mail?'

'Don't be ludicrous. This is the first time.'

'So why this one?'

'I told you. It just didn't make sense that Ishbel was writing to you alone and not to the two of us. So I found out why.'

'And now you know.'

'How much did you give her?' she asked levelly.

'A few quid, that's all.'

'How much *exactly*?' Mary Louise demanded.

'It's none of your business.'

'Of course it damn well is! Your money is mine, and vice versa.'

'I can dispose of what I earn as I see fit.'

She had to bunch up her hands to stop herself from slapping him. How dare he go behind her back like this? 'How much?' she demanded again.

What the hell, he thought. 'Twenty pounds.'

'Twenty . . . ,' Mary Louise spluttered, incensed. 'That's a fortune.'

'Hardly a fortune,' he replied drily.

'Well, I consider it to be. And you just toss it away without a by-your-leave.'

'I didn't toss it away,' he corrected her. 'I gave it to my sister to help her with my niece. Jessica needs new shoes and clothes, which Ishbel simply can't afford.'

Mary Louise glared at him. 'I suppose this isn't the first time you've given her money, either?'

Rory went to the window and stared out. He saw the three of them as children: he, Rowan and Ishbel. They'd been so happy then, a loving close-knit family. Of course they'd had their squabbles, but that was only natural. Now his dad was dead, his mother remarried to someone of whom he was unsure, Rowan a suicide, and Ishbel in Glasgow bringing up Rowan's bastard child. He'd tried to persuade Ishbel to return to Glenshields, but she'd been adamant that she remain in Glasgow. That was where her future was, she'd told him. She and Jessica had their own home there, and she a reasonable job. She'd argued firmly that she was better where she was, difficult as that could be at times.

'Rory?'

He replied without turning round. 'I have been sending her a postal order occasionally. A few pounds here, a few there. I doubt she would have managed otherwise.'

'But what about us?'

'Us?' he repeated slowly, swinging to face Mary Louise. 'Can't you ever think about anyone other than yourself? Ishbel is my sister and was in need. I only did what any decent brother would have done. A small sacrifice compared to the one she's made.'

Mary Louise dropped her gaze, knowing how true that was. 'Perhaps I was a bit hasty,' she muttered. 'It's just . . .'

'What?'

'I don't like the idea of your not having told me, of holding out on me.'

'Can you wonder that I did? I knew full well what your reaction would be. You would have tried to insist I didn't help her, isn't that right?'

'I've been saving so hard, counting every penny,' Mary Louise murmured.

'Very admirable, I'm sure. But what you've been saving has been surplus to our requirements. Ishbel, sadly, isn't in such a fortunate position. She's had her back against the wall since Aunt Dot died. And has she ever complained? Not once, to my knowledge. She's gamely and bravely soldiered on.'

Mary Louise ran a hand through her hair, then pulled her dressing-gown more tightly about her. 'I've got plans, you see,' she whispered.

This was news to him. 'What sort of plans?'

'Well, you're not going to remain a chauffeur for ever, are

393

you? It's a step in the right direction, yes, but not a job for life.'

'What exactly do you have in mind, Mary Louise?' he asked.

'Our own business in time. That's the only way really to get on: be your own boss. You'll never get rich working for wages.'

'And who says I want to be either rich or my own boss?'

'Oh, Rory!' she exclaimed in exasperation. 'You always take such a negative view.'

'But I love my job with the Lindsays. I have absolutely no intention of ever changing it.'

Something of her previous anger returned and a sense of frustration she often felt with regard to Rory. Honestly, he could be his own worst enemy. Thankfully he had her to advise and guide him. 'That's something we can talk about in the future,' she said, not wanting a further confrontation.

'I'll never change my mind about that,' he declared forcefully.

She couldn't help herself. 'What's the big attraction? The job or your darling Celia?'

'Watch your tongue!' he warned. 'I won't hear a word against her.'

'I sometimes think you care more for her than you do for me.'

'That's not true!' he retorted. 'You're my wife whom I love. Celia's my friend. The two relationships are quite different.'

'And is she always going to remain simply your friend? Or will the day come when you'll move on from that?'

'You're making me cross,' he said threateningly. 'There will never be a question of that sort of thing between Celia and me. It will just never arise. She loves the Master, I love you. End of story.'

Mary Louise remained unconvinced. She'd been jealous of Celia Lindsay for some while now, and would continue to be so. Part of the reason was that Celia touched an area within Rory that was beyond her, an area she didn't understand and never would.

Mary Louise sighed. 'Would you like an egg?'

'Boiled or fried?'

'Whichever you prefer.'

'Scrambled,' he stated, feeling, in the circumstances, like being perverse.

She laughed. 'Scrambled it is, then.'

He went to her and took her into his arms. 'We shouldn't fight like this.'

'I know.'

'I did what I thought was right. And what I wanted to do.'

Mary Louise thought of Jessica whose company during the Fair holiday had delighted her. 'I wonder when we'll have children of our own?' she mused.

'They'll come in time. Don't worry about it.'

'Oh, I'm not worried. It would just be nice to get started on a family, that's all. I have plans . . .'

He placed a finger across her mouth, silencing her. 'You and your plans; you always have plans. For this, that and the next thing.'

'Someone has to think ahead,' she mumbled.

'And you've elected yourself?'

She smiled.

'You're a real Bossy Boots, have I ever told you that?'

She removed his finger, and kissed it. 'Why don't I get on with the breakfast? I don't know about you, but I'm starving.'

'Bossy Boots,' he repeated.

And she'd get her own way, she thought. One day they would have their own business and be rich. Her heart was set on it.

'It's you, Peter!' Ishbel exclaimed, her hand going to her hair which she thought must be a bit of a mess. She wished he'd given them some warning of his visit.

'I was in the area and decided to call as I promised I would.'

'Of course. It's lovely to see you again. Come on in.'

'I hope I haven't turned up at an inconvenient time?'

'Not at all. I'm just shortly home from work.' She'd have changed if she'd known he was going to visit, she thought.

'How have you been?' she asked as they entered the kitchen.

'Not bad. And you?'

'Fine.'

'And how's Jess?' he queried when he spotted her.

She squealed. 'Have you brought me more sweets?'

'Jessica!' Ishbel admonished. 'How forward.'

Jessica ran to Peter to stare up at him. 'Have you?'

'Of course. I said I would. And when you get to know me better, as I hope you will, you'll learn I never break my word.'

As I hope you will. Ishbel liked the sound of that. He clearly didn't envisage this as a one-off visit.

He swung his briefcase on to the table.

'Whatever Peter gives you can't be eaten till after tea,' Ishbel declared.

Jessica pouted. 'Aw, Aunt Ishbel, that isn't fair!'

'It's perfectly fair, nor will I change my mind. Not one single solitary sweet till after tea.' To Peter she explained: 'Otherwise she'll scoff the lot and won't eat a crumb of whatever I make.'

'Perhaps I shouldn't give her the sweets, then, until you've finished eating?'

Ishbel was tempted to agree to that as it would mean he would have to stay on, and he hadn't revealed his plans yet. But she decided it would be too hard on Jessica, who'd probably explode with impatience.

'You can give them to her now.'

'Thanks, Aunt Ishbel,' Jessica enthused, eyeing Peter's briefcase, wondering what delectable goodies it contained.

'Right,' said Peter, flicking open his briefcase. 'Let's see what we've got here.' He peered inside.

Jessica began chewing a thumbnail in her excitement.

'Do you like chocolate?' he queried of her.

She nodded.

'That's a pity as I don't have any.'

Her face dropped.

'Or there again ...' After a few seconds' apparent searching in his briefcase he produced a large bar of milk chocolate. 'What's this?'

Jessica clapped her hands in appreciation. 'Yum yum!' she repeated, remembering how well that had gone down on the train – a fact that wasn't lost on either Peter or Ishbel.

Peter handed her the bar of chocolate. 'There you are.'

'Say thank you,' instructed Ishbel.

'Thank you.'

'There's more,' he said, looking back into the briefcase.

Jessica ended up with not only the bar of chocolate but also three half-pound bags of sweets, lime sherbets, assorted jellies and toffees.

'Can I have one now, *pppllleeeaaassse*?' pleaded Jessica, hopping up and down on the spot.

'One won't hurt, surely?' argued Peter, taking up her case.

'But I said ...' Ishbel trailed off, relenting to Jessica's expression and Peter's advocacy. 'All right, but *just* one. Then I'll have the rest, which I'll dole out at appropriate times. I'm not having you making a pig of yourself, young lady, and being sick as a consequence.'

'Sweet or square of chocolate?' Peter asked Jessica.

Her brow furrowed in concentration.

'A toffee would probably last longest,' he pointed out.

That settled it. 'Then, I'll have a toffee.'

'And I'll have the bags and the bar,' declared Ishbel when Jessica had popped a toffee into her mouth. She went over to the mantelpiece and placed them there.

'I've also got something for you,' Peter said to Ishbel, a twinkle in his eye.

'Me!'

Peter produced a large box of chocolates from his briefcase. 'Well, I couldn't just bring treats for Jessica, could I?'

Ishbel accepted the box of very expensive chocolates from him. 'This is very kind of you.'

'Not really. This is a sample. Or I can write it off as such, that is.'

'None the less, thank you.'

It pleased him to see how thrilled she was. 'Well, then,' he said, closing his briefcase.

Ishbel seized her opportunity. The last thing she wanted was for him to leave. 'Are you in a hurry, or have you time for some tea?'

'Tea!'

'I'm not sure what I'm going to cook yet. I have a few things in, though.'

'Tea would be lovely,' he smiled. 'But I'll tell you what, instead of you cooking I'll nip out and get some fish and chips.'

'Oh, I couldn't let you do that!'

'Why not? Is there a chippie close by?'

'Just round the corner,' piped up Jessica, who fancied the idea of fish and chips.

'That's settled, then. I won't be long.'

As soon as he'd gone Ishbel flew through to the bedroom where she hurriedly changed, combed her hair and dabbed on some scent that had belonged to Aunt Dot.

While she was doing this Jessica sneaked a couple more sweets.

'Are you enjoying the picture?' Peter asked Jessica in a whisper, leaning across Ishbel.

Jessica, her eyes remaining glued to the screen, nodded.

'Good,' said Peter. They were at the cinema, his treat, and the main feature was *Dixiana* starring Bebe Daniels and Bert Wheeler.

'I am, too,' whispered Ishbel, smiling at him.

'Better still.'

She flushed slightly on hearing that. It was a Saturday afternoon, and Peter had turned up out of the blue offering to take them to the cinema – an offer they'd both been delighted to accept.

She stopped breathing for a second when his hand

slipped into hers. He squeezed and she squeezed back. Their hands remained entwined until the interval when Peter went up to buy ice-creams. When the lights went down again his hand found its way back into hers.

'Would you like to come up?' Ishbel asked Peter. She and Jessica had just got out of his car.

He pulled a face. 'I'd love to, Ishbel, but I must get home to Edinburgh. I'm going out tonight.' Then, seeing her expression, hurriedly added: 'With my mum and dad. It's a kirk social that I've promised to attend.'

'And you always keep your word,' said Jessica.

'Always!' he laughed.

'Well, thank you again for the pictures. We both thoroughly enjoyed ourselves. Didn't we, Jessica?'

'Thoroughly,' repeated Jessica in a rather grown-up tone.

'We'll do it again some time, eh?'

'That would be lovely,' agreed Ishbel.

'I may be able to drop by next week. How about that?'

'I'll look forward to it.'

'Round about tea-time.'

'This time I'll cook.'

'You're on,' he smiled. 'Goodbye, then.'

'Goodbye, Peter,' Ishbel said.

'Goodbye,' Jessica echoed.

Ishbel watched him drive away, feeling warm inside from the memory of their holding hands. A romance? It seemed to be heading that way. How she wished Aunt Dot was still alive, so she could talk to her about it.

'Why so pensive?' Celia asked Rory, who was taking her to a fête she was opening. The Master had been scheduled to do the honours but at the last moment he'd had to withdraw because of a minor illness and so Celia was taking his place.

Rory glanced in the rear-view mirror to find Celia studying him. Normally they chatted a great deal during their outings together, but that day he'd been quiet since leaving Drum House.

'It's Mary Louise,' he explained.

Celia arched an eyebrow. 'Had a domestic?'

'In a way. She wants me to leave this job eventually and start my own business.'

'I see,' Celia murmured. 'And what do you think about that?'

'I'm not the ambitious type; she is. Extremely so.'

'Did you know that when you married her?'

'Oh, yes! But it's only recently that this "own business" thing has cropped up.'

'Which you're not keen on?'

He gave her a wry smile. 'I might be, in other circumstances. But I genuinely love this particular job and have no desire whatever to do anything else.'

'That's a relief,' Celia sighed, 'although I accept that I'm being selfish. I simply can't imagine you not being our chauffeur. Why, you've almost become family.'

'Don't worry. Mary Louise can put as much pressure on me as she likes; she can't make me do what I don't wish to.'

'Don't be too certain about that,' Celia commented drily. 'Women have their little ways, you know.'

'Whatever, the Duchess won't make me change my mind. I can be just as stubborn as she.'

'Duchess?' This was the first time Celia had heard Rory's nickname for Mary Louise.

He went on to explain why he'd given it to her.

She was absolutely marvellous, Rory thought, listening to Celia speak from the platform. She had a melodic voice, great presence and was at points extremely funny. He could only conclude, as he'd always suspected, she must be devastating on stage.

When she finally finished he led the thunderous applause.

'You're a very good dancer,' Peter complimented Ishbel as they waltzed round the floor. They were in the Plaza ballroom out on Glasgow's south side.

'You're not bad yourself.'

He smiled at her. 'Liar. I've got two left feet.'

'Only two? I thought it was three!' she joked in reply.

'Watch it, you!'

Ishbel glanced round, thinking how gorgeous many of the dresses were – all shapes and colours, with either gold or silver shoes on their feet. She had on a very old pair of silver ones that had belonged to Aunt Dot, who'd luckily been the same size as her. Her dress was a plain black number, nowhere near as glamorous as those around her, but the best she could muster.

'Shall we stay up?' he asked when the dance came to an end.

'What do you want to do?'

'It's what you want to do.'

She laughed. 'Then, let's stay up.'

'Right.'

He reached down and took her hand in his. 'Such a small hand,' he commented.

'But capable.'

'I'm sure,' he said drily.

She turned his hand over and gazed at it. 'And what about yours?'

'Capable also, I hope.'

'I'm sure it is.' She wanted to bring it to her mouth and kiss it, but of course she didn't. 'You've got freckles on the back,' she observed.

'Not too many, though.'

What a silly conversation, she thought; but fun, as being with Peter always was.

'We're off,' he said when the band struck up again.

This was a slow waltz. As they danced she allowed her head to droop on to his shoulder and closed her eyes.

He dropped his head till his chin was nestling in her hair.

'I won't ask you up. It's too late,' Ishbel said. They were standing at the bottom of her stairs.

'No, of course not. Don't want the neighbours talking, do we?'

'How's your hotel by the way?'

He shrugged. 'Like any other commercial hotel. There tends to be a sameness about them.'

'The Plaza was lovely,' she smiled.

'As are you. Lovely as can be.'

She blushed at this compliment.

'As I'm going to be in Glasgow for a couple of days, how about tomorrow night?'

'I won't leave Jessica two nights in a row,' she replied. 'But why don't you come and visit? Come for tea?'

'No. Later. I've got things that will keep me late at work. About half-past seven?'

'We'll expect you, then.'

He put an arm round her waist and drew her to him. For the space of a few moments they stared into one another's eyes, then he bent and kissed her – their first-ever kiss.

He was a far better kisser than Gavin Clarke, she thought later as she went up the stairs. That pleased her enormously.

'I've won! I've won!' shrieked Jessica. She, Ishbel and Peter were playing snakes and ladders.

'So you have,' said Peter, leaning back in his chair.

'And now it's bedtime,' Ishbel told Jessica.

'Aw, Aunt Ishbel, can't I stay up a little while longer? Ppppllleeeeaaasse?'

'No, it's quite late enough.'

'But it's only—'

'I know what time it is,' Ishbel interjected. 'Bedtime. And you look tired. So hop it, young lady! I'll be through in a jiffy.'

'Do I really have to?'

Peter laughed at her persistence.

'Yes, you do,' Ishbel stated firmly.

Jessica rose, said a sulky good night to Peter, then took herself off to the bedroom.

'Would you like a cup of coffee?' Ishbel asked.

Peter shook his head. 'Not for me. Would you like me to go?' he queried hesitantly.

'Not yet. Stay on a bit longer.'

'Good,' he smiled, gathering up the various bits and pieces and putting them back into the snakes-and-ladders box.

'I won't be a moment,' Ishbel said, and followed Jessica through to the bedroom.

While she was gone Peter shovelled more coal on to the fire, then began reading the evening paper he'd brought with him. He was still engrossed in the sports pages when Ishbel returned.

'She's settled down and will be off soon,' Ishbel said.

He laid his paper aside and crooked a finger at her. When she reached him he grasped her by the wrist and drew her on to his lap.

He smoothed down her hair, then placed the tips of his fingers on her cheek. Her eyes were glowing as she gazed at him.

'This is nice,' he murmured.

'Very.'

'Oh, Ishbel,' he sighed, and kissed her.

A kiss that led to another and another and another still.

Ishbel had always disliked Sarah Webster, but she had grown impossible since becoming engaged to Gavin. She now sported a huge ring and was forever flashing it about, particularly when Ishbel was in the vicinity. As for Sarah's conversation, she never failed to mention Gavin.

'It was hilarious!' declared Sarah, slapping her thigh. She was telling the group about a variety show she and Gavin had been to the previous Saturday.

'I must go and see that,' stated Olive McGuire.

'Sounds great,' said Ellen Weary.

Ishbel had a sip of tea and wished Sarah would vanish. She still couldn't get over the fact that Gavin had got engaged to her; she'd thought he'd have had more taste than that. In a way it was rather humiliating to think she'd been replaced by Sarah. They didn't come more common or vulgar than her.

'Penny for them?' Ellen queried of Ishbel.

'What? Oh, I was just thinking.'

'Haven't you got a new boyfriend yet?' Sarah asked innocently, looking as though butter wouldn't melt in her mouth.

Ishbel stared coldly at her. 'I have actually,' she replied.

Sarah's expression became one of disbelief. 'You haven't said?'

'That's right.'

'Since when?' Olive asked.

'A while now.'

'Do tell,' urged Ellen.

Ishbel had purposely kept this information to herself, but decided she'd tell them about Peter – if for no other reason than to retaliate a little against the insufferable Sarah. 'His name's Peter and he's a commercial traveller.'

Ellen's eyes opened wide. 'A commercial traveller!'

'For confectionery.'

'What firm?' demanded Sarah.

Ishbel informed her.

'Commercial travellers earn good money,' commented Isa Molloy.

'Very good money,' Ishbel confirmed, noting that Sarah was now staring daggers, which pleased her.

'And he has a car,' Ishbel added casually.

'A car!' Isa and Betty Hope exclaimed in unison.

'A company car,' Ishbel elaborated.

'Jammy bugger,' declared Ellen jealously.

Ishbel couldn't resist it. 'He and Jessica have become great friends. He thinks the world of her, and she of him,' she said, hoping Sarah would convey that back to Gavin, and Gavin to his rotten parents.

'You sound like you've fallen on your feet,' commented Ellen Weary.

Ishbel smiled enigmatically, knowing it would further annoy Sarah.

'Is it serious?' questioned Betty.

'Might be.'

'And what's he like?' asked Isa.

'Good-looking,' answered Ishbel. 'And twenty-six years old.'

'Where does he live?' queried Sarah through clenched teeth.

'Edinburgh.'

'Edinburgh!' exclaimed Isa, who thought that anyone who came from the capital must be rather posh.

'Newtown,' Ishbel elaborated.

Sickened, Ishbel thought triumphantly, but not letting it show on her face. That's what Sarah was, sickened. So much for Gavin.

A bell rang announcing it was time to return to work. 'Lucky old you,' said Betty, coming to her feet.

'The car's great. When he's in Glasgow we go everywhere in it,' Ishbel declared, rubbing further salt into Sarah's wounds.

Every so often, for the rest of that day, Ishbel would laugh quietly to herself. She hadn't enjoyed anything so much for a long while.

Sarah's expression as she left the group had been priceless.

Ishbel shivered as she hurried through the night. She'd been doing a spot of overtime, needing the money, and was now on her way home to put Jessica to bed.

She glanced up at the sky but couldn't see any stars because of the cloud and smoke – smoke she could actually taste every time she breathed in.

'Hello, hen,' a drunken voice slurred.

There were four of them, all fresh from the pub judging by the state they were in. The speaker leered at Ishbel and belched.

She ignored them, continuing on her way. It was Friday night, pay-night, when lots of working men went straight from work to the boozer where they'd spend a substantial amount of their week's earnings, and later went home to women who cried as a result.

'Nice figure,' another of the men said, the four falling in behind Ishbel.

Fear clutched at her. She didn't like this at all. She walked even faster.

'Give us a kiss, hen. Go on,' a third said, and laughed.

'A kiss! I fancy more than that, Tosh,' the fourth stated.

'Look at those legs!'

'And what an arse. Watch it move.'

Oh my God, she thought, feeling totally vulnerable. She glanced about, but the street was deserted except for her and the four drunks.

'My wife used to have an arse like that once, but she got fat,' the first speaker declared.

'They're lovely at that age. Like cream cake,' number three commented.

Ishbel was now shaking with fear. It was a rough area, but usually safe enough. If only there had been others around!

'Here, stop, you,' the first speaker said, and grabbed Ishbel. She whimpered as he forced her against a tenement wall.

'Pretty, too,' he smiled crookedly. She winced as stale cigarette-smelling breath washed over her.

'Let me go,' she pleaded.

'Oh, ay, sure,' he smirked.

The third speaker, who she now saw had a cast in one eye, reached out and fondled one of her breasts. 'I prefer them with bigger tits myself,' he jibed.

She tried to break free, only to be restrained and pushed back hard against the wall again where the four quickly surrounded her. She opened her mouth to shout for help, but a rough callused hand shut her up.

'I wonder if she's nice and juicy,' the first speaker salaciously mused.

This was a nightmare, Ishbel thought. Surely they wouldn't rape her, not out in the street!

As if reading her mind the second speaker said: 'Drag her into a close.'

They were about to do that when there was the sudden squeal of car brakes. 'Ishbel, is that you?'

She sobbed behind the hand covering her mouth; the voice was Peter's.

Seconds later he was out of his car brandishing the starting-handle. 'Let her go!' Peter commanded harshly.

'Fuck you, Jim!' the third speaker laughed – a laugh that changed to a scream of agony when the starting-handle smashed into his face. He whirled away, blood flying in all directions.

The handle flashed again, and the second speaker fell to the pavement, blood gushing from an ear.

Peter was all set to lay about him further, but the four had had enough. The one on the pavement scrambled to his feet and they ran off, their work-boots clattering as they disappeared into the darkness.

Ishbel sagged with relief, managing to give a small smile of relief when Peter's arm went about her in support.

'Thank God I was passing. I didn't know what was going on, and then I caught a glimpse of your face. I was on my way to your place.'

He helped her over to his car and on to the front passenger-seat. 'I'll soon have you home,' he declared, sliding in beside her.

She was shaking all over. 'If you hadn't turned up when you did . . .' She trailed off, and started to cry.

'There, lass, it's all over now,' Peter crooned, stroking her hair.

She turned to him and fell into his arms where she wept and sobbed against his shoulder.

'Animals,' he muttered angrily. 'That's all the likes of those are – animals.'

'I was so scared.'

'I'm not surprised.'

'I really did think . . . when one of them said drag me into a close.' She shuddered at the memory.

Peter knew exactly what she'd thought.

He waited a few moments till she'd recovered something of her composure, then drove to her house which wasn't far away.

'I'll have to get Jessica,' she said as they climbed the stairs.

'How will you explain the state you're in?'

She shook her head. 'I don't know.'

'Tell you what: say you saw an awful accident in the street which has badly upset you,' he suggested.

'All right.'

He put the kettle on while she retrieved Jessica from the neighbour. When Jessica came in her expression was one of concern.

'Aunt Ishbel saw a terrible accident,' she informed Peter.

He smiled at her. 'Yes, I know.'

Ishbel washed her face at the sink, which made her feel a bit better. She'd stopped shaking, but her hands continued to tremble. When she spoke there was a slight quaver to her voice.

'I wasn't expecting you tonight,' she said to Peter.

'I hadn't planned to be in Glasgow, then something came up which I had to sort out and so here I am.'

'Are you staying overnight?'

'Unfortunately no. But I'll remain with you as long as I can.'

'Thanks,' she smiled in appreciation.

Later, when Jessica was tucked up for the night, Ishbel returned to the kitchen where she went straight into Peter's embrace. There she felt safe and secure and, for the first time since being molested, a little at peace.

'It was horrible,' she husked.

'But all over now, Ishbel. You must try to put it from your mind.'

'You were so brave. There were four of them after all, and only one of you.'

'I never thought of numbers,' he answered truthfully. 'Just the fact you were in trouble and needed my help.'

'They all smelled so foul. Positively reeked.'

He could well imagine.

'Not like you. You smell lovely.'

'Do I?' he smiled.

'Very masculine and clean.'

'You smell rather nice yourself,' he replied, stroking her.

She sighed. 'That's so good.' She snuggled even closer to him, enjoying the feel of his strong hands on her body. How kind and reassuring he could be. And how happy being with him made her.

They chatted for a while, and slowly, gradually he got her to relax. Before leaving he actually succeeded in making her laugh – a real belly laugh in response to a funny story he told her.

They kissed behind the front door, a long lingering kiss that went on and on, neither wanting to end it.

'I'll see you again some time next week,' he promised.

'Thanks again, Peter.'

The house, she thought, felt empty when he'd gone.

'When am I going to meet your family?' Ishbel asked Peter.

'Oh, some time,' he answered vaguely.

'But I'd like to, soon. Have you told your parents about me?'

'Of course.'

'I could come to tea?'

'I'll arrange it, but not now. Mum hasn't been too well recently. She suffers from a bad chest and can be quite poorly at times,' he explained.

'I'm sorry to hear that,' Ishbel sympathized. 'What's wrong exactly?'

'Asthma. There are occasions when she takes to her bed for days on end.'

'Poor woman. And then, I suppose, your dad has to look after her and do the housekeeping?'

'He does, with my help. We both manage.'

'How old are they?'

'What is this, a quiz?' he laughed.

'I'm sorry. It's just that I'm naturally interested.' She

frowned. 'You don't think I'm being nosy, do you?'

'Not really.'

'It's just that you never speak about them all that much.'

He pulled her into his arms and gazed deep into her eyes. 'It's simply that they're boring. When I'm with you I can always think of far more interesting things to talk about than my parents.'

She felt him stir against her, which excited her. More and more she'd been speculating what it would be like to be married to Peter. To go to bed with him at night, wake up with him in the morning. She flushed slightly, thinking about what would have gone on in between.

She closed her eyes when his hand dropped to her bottom and began to caress it. He nuzzled her neck, then gently blew into her ear.

'That's tickly!' she breathed.

'Complaining?'

'No, but it's still tickly.'

She jerked when his tongue probed into the same ear.

'Enough,' she declared, pushing him away.

'Don't you like it?'

'Too much. That's the trouble.'

'Oh, my darling,' he said, hugging her tight.

'You'd better go if you're driving back to Edinburgh,' she told him reluctantly.

He glanced at the clock on the mantelpiece and saw she was right. 'Damn!' he muttered.

She extricated herself and ran her hands through her hair. Her heart was pounding, as his had been.

'I'm becoming extremely fond of you, you know,' he stated.

Fond? That disappointed her. She wished he'd said *love*. Had she fallen in love with him? She believed she had. But maybe it was taking a little longer for him, or perhaps he was being shy, reserved, in declaring himself.

'You're gorgeous,' he said.

'Less of the flattery. Now, be off with you. I've a long day tomorrow.'

'Overtime?'

She nodded. 'Every little helps.'

When he'd left she smiled. What a fortunate train journey that had been. And to think, even if they'd caught the same train but got into different carriages, they'd never have met. Fate, that was it. Their meeting was fate.

'What's wrong with you?' Rory demanded.

Mary Louise glanced up at him, her long face filled with sadness tinged with despair. 'Nothing.'

'Of course there is. Look at you!'

'I said, nothing,' she replied tightly.

'Aren't you well?'

She wished he'd go away. She wanted to be alone with her thoughts and dreams. Normally she enjoyed his company, found solace in his presence, but not at that moment.

'Would you like a cup of tea?'

She shook her head.

'Something else, then?'

She could have screamed. Couldn't he take a hint? 'Why don't you go for a ride on your bike?' she suggested.

'It's raining.' He crossed over to sit on the arm of her chair. 'What is it, love?'

In her mind she could hear a small child laughing, which made her ache inside; a child she could now see clearly with the exception of its face, for where its face should have been was an indistinct blur. Self-pity welled up inside her, bringing a hint of tears to her eyes.

'I'm just being stupid,' she said softly.

'How so?'

'I . . .' She trailed off in what was almost a sob.

'Mary Louise?' He was even more concerned now. This was most unlike her.

Abruptly she rose and went to the window. 'It *is* raining,' she stated, staring out.

'I just said so.'

For some reason that irritated her. 'Can't you find

411

'something to do other than annoying me?' she snapped.

'Am I?'

'Yes.'

'I'm sorry. I didn't mean to.'

'Well, you are.'

He frowned, unaware he'd been doing anything out of the ordinary. On the contrary, it seemed to him he couldn't have been more pleasant or considerate. 'Is something bothering you?'

'Why should it?'

'I don't know. I simply wondered if that's what was wrong?'

She turned to him, realizing he was only trying to help and that she was being unfair. 'I'll tell you what's wrong. I just don't appear to be able to get pregnant; that's what's wrong.'

Now he understood. He should have guessed. He went to her and took her into his arms, she stiff and unyielding from her unhappiness. 'Don't worry, Duchess,' he murmured. 'It'll happen in time. You'll see.'

'Will it? I'm beginning to wonder.'

'I think I know what the problem might be,' he said, a teasing tone creeping into his voice.

'What's that?'

'We're not trying hard enough.'

Despite herself, a small smile curled the corners of her mouth. 'Trust you to put that forward as the answer.'

He nibbled her neck, then lightly kissed her ear, causing her to shiver in his embrace.

'Stop it,' she pleaded without conviction.

He gave a soft laugh and blew into the same ear, knowing how much she liked that.

'Rory!' she protested.

He felt her relax, and her body first pressed, then moulded itself against his. 'I love you,' he whispered.

'Do you?' Now she was teasing.

'With all my heart and soul. What about you?'

She brushed her lips over his. 'You shouldn't have to ask.'

412

'But I enjoy hearing you say it.'

'I love you, too.'

He reached up and smoothed her brow. 'I appreciate how badly you want children, as do I. But we'll just both have to be patient, that's all.'

'I'm not very good at being patient. When I want something I want it now.'

'I know what I want now,' he said suggestively.

'You mean right this minute?'

'Why not?'

'It isn't bedtime yet.'

'Stop being so staid,' he further teased.

'I've never thought of myself as that,' she retorted.

He glanced over at the rug in front of the fire, a sudden thought coming to him. 'Then, you can prove me wrong.'

'How?'

He took her by the hand and led her towards the rug. 'I'll show you.'

When she realized his intention a surge of excitement and sudden desire stabbed through her. She was only too willing to comply.

'I'm all for this trying harder,' she crooned contentedly a little later.

So was he.

'No, Peter, no!' Ishbel husked, disentangling herself. Standing up, she hastily rearranged her clothes. She hadn't intended matters to go that far, but somehow one thing had just naturally led to another, until it had almost been too late.

'What's wrong, Ishbel?' he panted, worked up, and distraught by her refusal.

'I've told you before I won't do *it*. Not before marriage, that is.'

He swore, and adjusted his own dress.

'I'm sorry,' she said.

'Sorry!'

'I know it's my fault, but I'd thought I'd made my position clear.'

'Nothing would happen, Ishbel, I swear. I've got protection on me.'

For some reason that angered her. So he'd come prepared! 'Well, you won't be needing your protection,' she retorted icily.

He went to her and held her in his arms. 'This is silly. We're both grown up. Where's the harm?'

She thought of Rowan. Was that what Gray had said to her – *where's the harm?* Well, look what had happened to Rowan. 'I'm a decent girl,' she said.

'There's no such thing.'

She regarded him in sudden confusion and consternation. 'I beg your pardon?'

'There's no such thing,' he repeated. 'And you're living in a dream world if you believe that.'

'Then, I live in a dream world,' she stated with conviction.

'It happens all the time, Ishbel. Honestly!'

'Not to me, it doesn't. If there's no such thing, then I'm the exception.'

'Exception be blowed!'

How dare he be so presumptuous! And how could he talk such twaddle! Unless he was trying to sweet-talk her into doing something which in her heart of hearts she knew she shouldn't. She pushed him aside and stalked off.

'Ishbel?' he pleaded.

She turned and stared at him, her eyes blazing. Had she misjudged him all this time? Was he only after one thing? 'I think you'd better go.'

Fury flooded his face, brought on by disappointment and the fact he was still fully sexually aroused. 'All right, then, damn you, I will!'

His departure was so abrupt it left her stunned. He stormed from the room, grabbed his hat and coat, then slammed the front door, the ensuing loud bang echoing up and down the stairs.

The bang, she thought a moment later, must have

wakened Jessica. She went through to check, but Jessica remained fast asleep.

She returned to the kitchen where she took several large breaths. No such thing, living in a dream world — what did he take her for, a gullible fool?

The anger suddenly drained from her, leaving her limp and shaking. 'Oh, Peter,' she whispered. Everything had been so rosy, and now this. Had he gone for ever? She simply didn't know. If he'd only been out to seduce her, then he had.

She crossed to a chair and sat down, her thoughts in turmoil. Then the tears came, those and sobs which racked her thin body.

She missed him already. Why had this had to happen? Why?

Curling herself into an embryonic ball, she continued to weep.

Peter stared shamefaced at Ishbel. It was three weeks since he'd gone off, and in the mean time she hadn't heard a word from him. Now he'd suddenly reappeared.

'Can I come in?' he asked.

She wasn't sure what she felt as she had convinced herself by then he'd gone off for good. She stood aside and beckoned him in.

As he walked past her, he handed her a large bunch of hothouse flowers which he was carrying, an expensive item at that time of year. 'A peace offering,' he declared.

She hesitated, then accepted the flowers. 'Thank you,' she answered stiffly.

'Is Jessica in bed?'

'At this time, of course.'

'Of course,' he echoed. 'How have you been?'

She wasn't about to tell him the truth. 'All right.'

'I haven't. I've been awful.'

'Oh?'

She took the flowers to the sink where she began unwrapping them.

'I made a complete and utter fool of myself that night, Ishbel.'

When the flowers were free of their paper she went to the drawer where she kept her scissors.

'Will you accept my apology?'

When she didn't reply, he went on: 'I wanted you so much, that night and others, that I just sort of . . . finally blew my lid, I suppose.'

'Want?' she sneered.

'Yes.'

'And what now? Are you back to try again?'

'I'm back to tell you I love you and to ask you to marry me.'

She went very still, the scissors poised in front of her. 'Marry you?' she replied at last. The words she'd so desperately longed to hear.

'Marry me, if you'll have me.'

She laid the scissors beside the flowers and turned to face him. He was the figure of dejection, looking as wretched as she'd been feeling these last three weeks.

He fumbled in his coat pocket to produce a small box. 'This is also for you.'

She stared at the box, recognizing it as the sort you bought in a jeweller's, which could only contain one thing. She crossed over to him, took the box and opened it. There, nestling in blue velvet, was a single-stoned engagement ring.

'I'm . . .' She shook her head, momentarily lost for words.

'I'm not sure if it'll fit. I didn't know your size. Try it on and see.'

She manoeuvred the ring from its box and slid it on to the appropriate finger, overjoyed to discover it fitted perfectly.

'Well?' he asked.

'It's . . . beautiful.'

'And?'

'Oh, Peter!' She threw her arms round him and kissed him, her heart feeling as though it must surely burst from emotion.

'Does that mean you'll marry me?' he asked quietly when the kiss was over.

'Oh, yes!'

'I do love you, Ishbel.'

'And I love you.'

He gazed at her adoringly. 'I genuinely thought I'd lost you.'

'And I you. I've been so miserable.'

She held the ring out, twisting her hand this way and that so that the stone caught the light and sparked fire.

'It's only a small one, I'm afraid. It was all I could afford.'

'It couldn't be better,' she reassured him.

'It suits you.'

She couldn't wait to show it at work where she hadn't told anyone about her split with Peter. Wouldn't some of them be jealous! For Peter was a prime catch, a definite cut above the lads many of them would eventually wed. But that was beside the point. All that mattered was that Peter was back, and he loved her. His proposal and this ring were irrefutable proof of that.

'We should go out and celebrate,' he said. 'The pubs are still open.'

'But what about Jessica?'

'One of the neighbours?'

'I'll see what I can do. Stay here.'

Ishbel rushed from the room, at that moment considering herself to be the happiest person in the world.

The pub was a typical Glasgow one, filled with heavy smoke and the strong smell of beer. The atmosphere was good-humoured with a hint of underlying violence. The majority of drinkers were men wearing drab coats, scarves and flat caps. A number were already drunk, having loud conversations about football and politics, these being the favourite topics of conversation.

Peter returned from the bar and placed a gin and lime in front of Ishbel. 'It's a double. We're celebrating after all,' he grinned.

She reached out and gently touched his hand, then withdrew it again because of where they were.

He sat and raised his pint of heavy. 'To us!'

'To us,' she echoed.

'It's like sitting inside a chimney here,' she complained, referring to the smoke.

'The pubs round about are all the same.'

'I know.'

She glanced down yet again at her ring, having already looked at it umpteen times since coming into the pub, and a thrill ran through her.

'How do you feel?' he asked.

'Ecstatic.'

'Same here.'

'I'm dying to tell the girls at work and see their faces when I do.'

He studied her, thinking how lovely she was. There was a sultry dark quality about Ishbel that drew him like iron filings to a magnet. He'd met many more attractive females, but there was something about her that excited him, made him want to possess her.

'Now we're engaged, when shall we get married?' she asked.

He gave a low laugh. 'Hold on. One thing at a time. Let's get used to being engaged first. After all, when I came to your house tonight I wasn't at all certain you'd accept me. I haven't even begun to think about a marriage date.'

'This year? Next?' she pressed.

'Next, I imagine. I need time to save up.'

She digested that. She would have preferred that year, but the following would do fine. 'A church wedding, I hope?'

'Of course, Ishbel. I wouldn't dream of anything else. I can just visualize you resplendent in your dress, with me done up like the proverbial dish of fish.'

'And Jessica can be bridesmaid?'

'Naturally.'

She stared into her glass, then up at him. 'Was it because of Jessica that you took so long to propose?'

'Hardly long!' he protested.

'But you hesitated because of her? After all, taking on someone else's child – and in this case she isn't even mine – is a big step.'

'I have to confess it was something I did consider, but I adore Jessica and in the end came to terms with the situation. I'll treat her as though she was my own flesh and blood, I promise.'

'You're a good man, Peter,' she declared softly, and reaching out briefly touched him again.

'I'm not doing this out of goodness, but out of love,' he replied.

That brought a choke to her throat, and almost a tear to her eye. 'Jessica is going to be over the moon when I tell her.'

'Will you do that in the morning?'

'Before she goes to school.'

'How's that going by the way?' It was March, and Jessica had begun school two months previously.

'Couldn't be better. She idolizes her teacher; Miss McFadyen can do no wrong in her eyes.'

'That's the way it should be.'

Ishbel glanced over at the aproned barman collecting empty glasses. He looked vaguely like her dead father, she thought, and a momentary pang of sadness passed through her.

'Will we stay in our house after the wedding?' she queried.

Peter shook his head. 'That's why the wedding has to be next year. I'm based in Edinburgh and have to remain there. You and Jessica will have to move when the time comes.'

'Can't you be transferred to Glasgow?'

'That's impossible, I'm afraid.'

'Then, Edinburgh it will have to be.'

Edinburgh, she thought. It would be an exciting prospect. In a way she'd be sorry to leave Glasgow, which she'd become attached to; but if being married to Peter meant moving to Edinburgh, then that's how it would have to be. Again she experienced a pang of sadness at the thought of leaving Aunt Dot's house, which had become very much her home. But, she reminded herself, she'd be going to a home of her own, one she would create, one that would be a new start in life and not one filled with memories, no matter how happy the memories.

'My family will be beside themselves,' Ishbel declared, thinking she'd write to them all the following evening. They would be delighted for her.

'You must meet them,' she went on.

'We'll arrange it some time.'

'And I must meet your parents. That's overdue.'

He pulled a long face. 'My mother isn't well again. The old complaint. She's laid up at the moment.'

'No matter. I can wait.'

She began contemplating her dress, which she decided she'd make herself, thanks to Meg's training. She'd also make Jessica's bridesmaid's frock. But that was in the future; plenty of time before she need get down to it.

'I'll try to save, too,' she said. 'Though that's going to be hard. Getting by is difficult enough as it is.'

'Don't worry, Ishbel, we'll sort things out. Just leave it all to me.'

'I doubt I'll sleep a wink tonight,' she smiled.

He laughed. 'You'd better, or you won't be ready for work in the morning.'

They continued laying their plans, and he eventually bought another round as they lingered in the pub till closing-time.

'Married!' Jessica squealed.

'And you're to be bridesmaid.'

Jessica clapped her hands in glee. 'Again – and so soon!'

'Now, come on, eat up your porridge before it gets cold.'

'I don't want any more porridge, Aunt Ishbel, I'm too excited.'

Ishbel knew exactly how she felt, for didn't she feel the same way? 'None the less, you need it as it's bitter out. Force yourself if you have to.'

Jessica took a spoonful into her mouth and thought about the stupendous news. 'Peter will be just like a father,' she declared after she'd swallowed.

That touched Ishbel, who was aware from past conversations how desperately Jessica missed having a father, particularly since going to school and meeting lots of other children. 'The next-best thing,' she replied.

Jessica beamed back at her as if Christmas and her birthday had both dawned on the same day.

'Ishbel's got engaged,' Meg breathed as she read the letter that had just arrived from Glasgow.

The piece of sausage stopped halfway to Vincent's mouth. 'Married?'

'To this Peter Lorne she's been going out with,' Meg elaborated, eyes glued to the letter held in front of her.

'That's marvellous!'

'She says the wedding's to be next year. A church affair.'

Vincent, smiling, laid his knife and fork on his plate. 'Well, well,' he murmured.

Meg looked up and sighed. 'What a relief! I can't tell you how pleased I am.'

'I think I can guess.'

'I had hoped when she's written in the past about him. He seems ever such a nice man, and extremely fond of Jessica apparently.'

'A commercial traveller, isn't he?'

Meg nodded.

'She's done all right for herself, then.'

'She says she hopes to bring him here soon to meet the family.'

'Does that include me?' he asked wryly.

Meg gave him a warm smile. 'Of course, Vincent.'

'A church wedding?' he mused. That would cost money, and it was traditionally the bride's father who paid for it. 'You must write back and tell her I'll pick up the tab.' He held up a hand. 'I'll have no arguments about this. After my behaviour towards her I owe her that at least.'

'Oh, Vincent!'

'We'll lay on the very best. Champagne, lots of food, outside caterers, and then there's the question of a honeymoon.'

'You're talking a fortune!' Meg protested.

'So what? I can afford it. And it'll make you happy, right?'

'Right,' she nodded.

'Then, you must write straight away letting her know what's what.'

Meg rose, went to Vincent and put her arms round his neck. 'Thank you, darling.'

'It's my pleasure, I assure you. No expense spared. A present to you as well as to her.'

'I must go and tell Fee and Lex.'

'I'll drop you off there just as soon as I've finished this breakfast.'

'Would you care for more toast? Or another egg perhaps?'

He laughed. 'Neither. Only that you stay like this with your arms round me for a little while longer.'

Bending, she kissed his neck.

Ishbel watched Peter chasing Jessica, eventually catching and whirling her round, causing her to scream with pleasure. It was a Sunday, and Peter had managed to come through for a few hours, so the three of them had decided to go for a walk in the Botanical Gardens.

The air was crisp, breath misting before you when you exhaled. Spring was in the offing; here and there the green shoots of daffodils were showing, promising that winter would soon loosen its icy grip and the growing cycle would once again burst upon a dormant world.

How well they got on together, Ishbel thought with satisfaction. Jessica had been right: Peter would be just like a father to her, the father she so wanted and had never had.

Everything had turned out all right in the end, she reflected, for her and Jess. The darkness of the past had finally been obliterated. A bright shining future lay ahead.

'Come and save me, Aunt Ishbel. Come and save me!' Jessica shouted, face flushed from a combination of the weather and exertion.

Ishbel ran forward to join in the fun.

'You walked out of the loch, and that was it. A thunderbolt struck, and my life changed for ever. I know it may sound improbable, but I swear that was what happened.'

It was a beautiful story, Meg thought, like something out of a fairy-tale or a romance. And yet it had to be true, for hadn't all Vincent's actions since that day borne it out?

'A thunderbolt?' she repeated.

'Zap! Just like that.'

She laughed.

He suddenly frowned. 'You don't think me silly, do you?'

'Not silly at all, Vincent,' she assured him.

'Nothing like that has ever happened to me before. It was as if . . . a miracle had taken place.'

'Such things do happen,' she said slowly. 'Not very often, I think. But they do happen. There, again, maybe they happen more often than I realize.'

He gazed at her, a gaze full of love and affection. 'I want to look after you, take care of you more than anything else in the world,' he declared softly.

She melted inside to hear that.

'I appreciate you don't love me, but perhaps in time . . .' he said, a pleading tone in his voice.

'Love's a funny thing, not always what people believe it to be,' she replied wisely.

'How do you mean?'

'It's not always an unbridled passion, but can be a slow build-up of various feelings and emotions. You used the word "care". Well, caring for someone can become a type of love.'

'I think I understand,' he nodded.

'A caring with depths to it, shall I say?'

'I'll settle for that,' he declared.

'Now,' she said, rising, 'I'm off to bed. I'm so tired I can hardly keep my eyelids open.'

He immediately leapt to his feet. 'You get ready and I'll fill a hot-water bottle for you.'

'For us,' she corrected him. 'For us.'

'For us,' he repeated tenderly.

'Get up,' husked Peter to Ishbel, who was sitting on his lap. She did as instructed to stand frowning at him.

'What's wrong?'

'What do you think! I'm worked up to high doh.'

She sympathized with him, feeling that way herself.

He gazed at her naked bosom, which he'd just been kissing, and groaned.

Ishbel started to put her bra back on, then hesitated. She hated to see Peter in such obvious anguish, feeling sorry for his plight. Weren't they now engaged? she reminded herself. Which meant matters had changed somewhat. Did she have to stick by the strict moral rules she'd set herself, or could she relent?

She considered that, part of her wishing to, another part counselling she should stick to what she'd believed in up until they married. She found herself in a quandary.

Her ring gleamed at her, reminding her of the pledge that now existed between them, and the commitment. Peter wasn't merely a boyfriend, but her fiancé and future husband with whom she'd be spending the rest of her life. Her resistance began to crumble; for, if she was honest, didn't she also want the same thing?

Temptation gnawed at her. If they were careful, she told herself, who would ever know except them? And another year was a long time to keep enduring this, the frustration of stopping when the body was afire and demanding the natural outcome of their – so far – limited lovemaking.

She made a decision – not lightly, but what she considered, in the circumstances, to be the humane one, not just for Peter, but for herself.

'Do you have that protection with you that you mentioned before?' she asked.

Hope dawned in his eyes, and he nodded.

'Then, let's do it properly. No fumbling around on a chair, but in a proper bed.'

He stared at her. 'Are you saying what I think you are?'

She indicated the cavity bed where Aunt Dot had slept after her and Jessica's arrival. 'The only condition I make is that you must be gone before Jessica gets up in the morning.'

He came to his feet and went to her. 'Oh, Ishbel!' he breathed.

As before, his hands were suddenly all over her, touching, caressing, eager.

She kissed him, savouring his taste and smell which excited her so much.

'I'll make down the bed,' she said when the kiss was over.

She found herself trembling as she leant into the cavity. It was too late to back out now, she thought.

When she turned round he was opening his wallet. She averted her eyes, took a deep breath, and began to undress.

Naked, she slipped into bed, gasping at the coldness of the sheets and thankful she'd kept the bed aired. A few moments later he was lying alongside her.

'Put the light out,' she instructed, and smiled when he got out of bed again.

'Peter?' she whispered when he was back once more.

'What?'

'I love you.'

'And I love you, Ishbel. With all my being.'

'Just make sure you use one of those things.'

'Don't worry. I'll be careful as can be.'

He was gentle with her, considerate in the extreme. Momentarily it crossed her mind that he seemed an expert at what he was doing – a thought that fled on wings as sensation took over.

She gasped as he entered her, such an alien yet wonderful thing.

'All right?' he whispered.

'All right,' she whispered in reply.

He began to move.

She listened to his breathing as he slept. So, at long
last, the great mystery had been revealed. She had to
admit it hadn't been as earth-shattering as she'd been led
to expect. The earth hadn't moved. But it had been lovely,
so gorgeously intimate and ultimately satisfying.

How strange, she thought, not to be a virgin any more;
to be a real woman at last. She didn't feel any different,
and yet one thing was certain: she'd never be the same
again. For, once given up, virginity could never be
reclaimed.

Had she done the right thing? She was certain she
had. There were no doubts, not even niggling ones.

She sighed with contentment. She was now Peter's
wife in all but name, and that would happen the following
year.

She imagined herself in white, he in a morning suit. 'Do
you take this man . . . ?' Then there would be the honeymoon. Where would they go? That had yet to be discussed.
And wasn't it marvellous that Vincent would be paying for
everything!

She'd tried to get the date of the wedding brought
forward when she'd received Meg's letter informing her
of Vincent's offer, but Peter had dug in his heels saying
he still needed that amount of time to save for everything
else. It had been a bit of a disappointment, but she was sure
Peter knew best.

Dear Peter, how she loved him. And to think they
were going to spend the rest of their days together. That
prospect filled her with great joy.

They would have children as soon as possible; she was
keen on that. Playmates and companions for Jessica. She
favoured a large family herself, but not too large, something
manageable.

She wondered what Edinburgh would be like, never

having been there. Would the neighbours be friendly? She certainly hoped so.

What sort of a house would they have? One with an inside toilet, she hoped, and maybe even a bathroom! The latter would be nice, and so convenient with a family to bring up.

And what about Peter's mother and father? She was still to meet them. Would they like her and approve? Peter had assured her they would. Still, you never knew.

She remembered with unease her experience with Gavin's parents and could only pray the Lornes were nothing like them.

Peter snorted and shifted position; which made her smile. In her mind's eye she could see them both grown old, surrounded by children and grandchildren. If and when she had a girl, she would call her Rowan, she decided, after her own much-beloved sister whom she still sorely missed.

She smiled again recalling how Peter had asked her why Jessica's surname was Stewart, the same as hers, and her glib reply had been that there were a lot of Stewarts in Glenshields and Jessica's father's surname had happened to coincide with their own. A neat lie, she'd thought, and one she'd been rather proud of.

She'd have to tell Peter the truth about Jessica before she took him to Glenshields, end that little charade as far as he was concerned. She was certain he'd understand her necessity to lie, for Jessica's sake.

Reaching out, she took his hand in hers and clasped it. She was still holding it when she eventually fell asleep.

'I won't be a minute,' said Peter, and got out of his car carrying his briefcase. He disappeared into an adjacent sweet-shop where he had business to conduct.

It was October 1933, and they'd been engaged for six months now. They'd visited Glenshields during the summer where Peter had met Meg and Vincent, Rory and Mary Louise, who still wasn't pregnant.

A party had been given in Peter's honour and a great time had by all. Everyone had declared Peter to be a tremendous chap and Ishbel a lucky lass to land him. The two-day visit had gone off absolutely splendidly.

She was yet to meet his parents, but his mother had been back in hospital and had only recently returned home again. She hoped she'd be invited through to Edinburgh soon.

As these thoughts were going through Ishbel's mind she noticed an envelope lying on the car floor beside her feet. Picking it up, she glanced at its front.

It was a letter addressed to Peter at home; which was the first time she'd learnt his address: 10 India Street.

She opened the glove compartment and put it inside for safe keeping, thinking to mention it to Peter on his return.

As it turned out, he was gone far longer than he'd anticipated, and when he finally did get back to the car, full of apologies for keeping her waiting, she'd forgotten all about the letter.

Ishbel stared out of the carriage window as the train arrived at Edinburgh's Waverley Station. It was a Sunday afternoon, and Ishbel, fed up with never having met Peter's parents, had decided on a surprise visit.

She'd considered bringing Jessica with her, then had changed her mind, thinking that Jess might be too much for the ailing Mrs Lorne to have to contend with. So it had been arranged for Jessica to stay the day with a friend.

Ishbel hadn't seen Peter for over a week as he had been extremely busy at work and not able to manage to come through to Glasgow. She found even such a short spell apart devastating, and couldn't wait to see him again and be introduced, at long last, to his parents.

As the train clanked to a halt, to the accompaniment of loud chuffs and exhalations of steam, she stood and checked her face in the mirror above her seat. Her eyes were bright, her hair well combed, the tiny bit of make-up she was wearing not needing any touching up. She would do, she decided.

She was wearing her Sunday best as she stepped on to

the platform: a navy-blue gabardine suit, a white crêpe de Chine blouse and well-polished dark shoes with half-heels. Her coat was a reasonably fashionable dark one that had recently come back from the cleaner's, while on her head she had a navy-blue cloche hat that matched her outfit. She felt quite the bee's knees, well turned out for a working-class lass.

As she didn't know Edinburgh at all, she would have to take a taxi, for which she'd made provision, believing that Peter would drive her back to the station afterwards.

She knew she was being presumptuous in doing this, but Peter had put her off so many times about meeting his folks that she'd decided the time had come to take the bull by the horns and present herself. She was his fiancée after all!

She made her way to the taxi-rank, waited in the queue, then gave Peter's address to the driver, remembering it from the envelope she'd found in his car.

The taxi took off, and soon they were in Princes Street, the capital's most famous thoroughfare. Ishbel goggled at the shops lining one side, thinking how grand and splendid they looked. And there was the castle overlooking Edinburgh, glowering grimly down. What great and multitudinous events that had witnessed, she thought.

They turned into Newtown, the tall grey buildings towering high overhead. How different the two cities were, she reflected: Glasgow, Scotland's industrial heart; Edinburgh, steeped in history and intrigue.

'Here you are, miss,' the cabbie announced shortly after that, drawing into the kerb.

The tenement they'd stopped outside was graffiti-free and in a rather pleasant road. They were directly outside number ten, the number she'd memorized and given the driver.

'Thank you very much,' she said, standing by the side of the taxi, handing him half a crown. 'Keep threepence for yourself.'

'That's very kind of you, miss.'

She couldn't really afford to give tips, she thought as the taxi sped away. But what could you do? She turned her attention to number ten.

The stairs were grey stone and concave from use. She climbed them, peering at every door she came to until at last she arrived at one with a plate outside bearing the name Lorne.

Taking a deep breath, she reached for the brass bell-pull. A clang reverberated inside the house when she tugged it.

It was mid-afternoon. She had deliberately timed her visit so as not to interfere with Sunday lunch, and to arrive well before tea-time. She presumed she'd be invited to stay for the tea.

The door opened, and a young woman stared quizzically at her. She had long fair hair that fell to her shoulders and was carrying a baby on her hip. She looked tired and drawn, as though finding life extremely hard going.

'Can I help you?' the young woman queried.

Ishbel wondered who she was. Peter was an only child, so it couldn't be his sister. A cousin or neighbour perhaps? 'Is Peter in?'

The young woman frowned. 'Who are you?'

'I know this is a bit of a cheek ...' She trailed off. Maybe she'd come to the wrong door and there was more than one Lorne household up this close. 'Does Peter Lorne live here?'

She nodded.

'I'm Ishbel. Ishbel Stewart, from Glasgow.'

The young woman's frown deepened. 'We don't know any Ishbel from Glasgow. Unless you're something to do with Peter's work?'

'No no,' Ishbel smiled. 'I'm his fiancée.'

The young woman was thunderstruck. 'His what!'

'His fiancée. I've come on a surprise visit to meet his parents.'

'Is this some kind of a joke? For if it is I don't find it funny.' Another youngster toddled into view to clutch at the woman's skirt.

Ishbel was nonplussed by this reception. 'It's no joke,' she assured her. She held up her left hand. 'There's my ring to prove it.'

The young woman swore, which threw Ishbel even more.

'And there are mine,' hissed the young woman, shoving out her own left hand.

Ishbel stared at an engagement ring, far bigger and more expensive than her own, and a wedding ring. 'I don't understand,' she mumbled. What did this mean?

'The bastard isn't home or he could tell you himself. I'm his wife,' the young woman declared.

Ishbel gazed at her in horror. 'Wife!'

'Correct, and have been for the past seven years. And I've got not only two rings but also three children to prove *that*.'

Ishbel literally reeled on the spot. This was a nightmare. She was asleep and—

'So piss off!' the young woman screamed, and slammed the door in Ishbel's face.

Ishbel leant against the nearest wall for support. A wife, three children, married for seven years. 'Oh, my God!' she choked.

She turned and somehow stumbled back down the stairs, hot tears coursing down her cheeks.

There had to be some mistake. Her Peter already married. That couldn't be right.

At the close-mouth she halted and again leant against a wall. Her whole world had just come crashing down about her ears. 'Why?' she whispered. Then loudly repeated: 'Why!'

She gazed up and down the road, thinking wildly that Peter might suddenly appear to offer an explanation. But there was no sign of him.

Married!

For a few horrible moments she thought she was going to be sick, but mercifully she wasn't.

Gathering herself together, she staggered along the pavement in the direction the taxi had come. She was numb, unable to think.

'What a funny-looking woman,' a little boy commented to his playmate as she passed.

Ishbel didn't hear him. She wasn't hearing anything other than that one dreadful word echoing inside her head.

Married.

Chapter Twelve

Ishbel, red-eyed and with a face almost raw from crying, buried her face in the pillow and continued to weep. She was determined to muffle the uncontrollable sobbing that otherwise might have wakened Jessica, asleep in the bedroom.

She would spend the night in the cavity bed with its many marvellous memories, the very bed where she and Peter had so often made love, held one another, whispered endearments into each other's ears, made plans for the future – a future now in ashes.

Why? she raged inwardly. What had been the point of it all? How could he have been so cruel?

She had no answers, only questions and an inconsolable grief. She could remember hardly anything about her journey back from Edinburgh. Somehow she'd got herself to Waverley, aboard a train and then home after the train arrived in Glasgow.

A haze, that's what she'd been in, a dull swirling haze of pain, confusion and bewilderment.

She saw again the young woman's face, Peter's wife, the wife she had hoped to be.

'Why?' she sobbed into the pillow. 'Why?'

The bottle of whisky spun from Ishbel's shaking hands to fall crashing to the floor where it smashed. She stared at it blankly, the third bottle she'd dropped that day.

'What's wrong with you?' Isa Molloy demanded. 'Are you ill?'

Ishbel put a hand to her forehead. When she tried to answer the words stuck in her throat. She should have stayed at home, she told herself. It had been foolish of her to come into Blue Bonnet. She was proving to be worse than useless.

'Do you want to go and sit down?' a concerned Isa further asked.

Ishbel shook her head. That would only make matters worse. At least while she was working it gave her something to try to concentrate on which helped curtail her brooding.

'Well, you'd better watch yourself or you'll have the gaffer down on you like a ton of bricks.'

Ishbel, pale and drawn with circles like bruises under her eyes, got on with the job.

'When's Peter coming again?' Jessica asked. 'I miss him.'

Ishbel turned away so that Jessica wouldn't see her face. She hadn't told Jess yet. She hadn't told anyone. She'd kept the revelation of a fortnight previously to herself.

'I don't know, sweetness.'

'But he hasn't been for ages!' Jessica complained.

'No, he hasn't,' Ishbel agreed, beginning to get slightly irritated. This wasn't the first time Jess had brought up the subject, and on every occasion she did it rankled with her.

'But I want to see him!'

'He must be busy,' Ishbel snapped.

'Not that busy surely?'

'He's an adult with a lot on his plate. Now, don't pester.'

'I'm not pestering, Aunt Ishbel!' Jessica complained, mystified.

'Yes, you are. Now, stop going on.'

'But I—'

Ishbel whirled. 'I said stop it!' she exclaimed angrily.

Jessica's face crumpled. 'I didn't mean to upset you, Aunt Ishbel.'

Ishbel threw the teacloth she was holding on to a chair. 'Well, you have, so please shut up!'

Jessica ran from the room, already crying before she was through the door.

Ishbel came to her senses and stared after Jessica,

appalled. What was she doing? There was no need to take it out on Jessica. She hurried after the child.

She found Jessica in tears. 'I'm sorry, my darling, I really am,' she declared, gathering Jessica into her arms.

'You've been so horrible recently.'

'I know, I know. I'm sorry about that, too.'

'When is he coming back, Aunt Ishbel?'

Ishbel knew she couldn't put the inevitable off any longer. The time had come to tell Jessica and hurt the poor wee mite. How she hated doing it. Damn Peter Lorne! Damn him to hell!

'He won't be coming back, Jess. He and I have broken up, I'm afraid.'

Jessica gazed up at her, eyes wide. 'Not coming back? Not ever?'

'No,' Ishbel confirmed.

'But ... but ...' Jessica began to wail, her feeling of loss profound at the realization she'd lost the substitute father she'd so recently found to replace the real one she'd never known.

'I'm sorry, Jess, truly I am. But there was nothing I could do about it. Please believe me. Nothing.'

Jessica threw her arms round Ishbel and hugged her tight, the pair of them like two lost souls.

Ishbel also began to weep.

Ishbel sat with a cup of tea balanced on her lap gazing at Gavin and Sarah who were soon to be married, laughing and joking intimately in a corner of Blue Bonnet.

If either had noticed Ishbel, he or she would have been startled by the sheer venomous hatred in her stare.

It was too much, Ishbel thought. It was bad enough to lose Peter, find out he was already a married man, and now this!

There was no mistake, she was certain, especially as she was someone who'd never been late or missed a period.

435

Now she'd missed three in a row. She was pregnant; there could be no doubt about it.

She ground her fist into her mouth. She had to do something, because if she didn't they could take her away as they'd done Rowan, commit her to a hellhole of an asylum where she would be in exactly the same boat as her sister had been, the only difference being that Rowan had been under age whereas she was now twenty with her twenty-first birthday only months away.

She whimpered as sheer terror took hold of her. How unfair that this should happen on top of her other agonies.

Peter had always worn protection; she'd insisted on that, and he'd never failed to comply with her wishes. So how had she become pregnant? The only answer was that the protection he'd sworn by wasn't the totally safe one he'd assured her it was.

She pictured Peter, and for the umpteenth time damned him to eternal perdition, more so with this turn of events.

With her other hand she gingerly touched her stomach where a new life had begun and was already taking shape. A baby. Hers and Peter's. A baby she had so wanted, craved, but not like this, not under these circumstances.

She could always go and confront Peter, whom she hadn't seen or heard from since his last visit before that dreadful day in Edinburgh, but what would it achieve? He was hardly going to leave his wife and family for her; if that had been in the offing, he'd have at least contacted her by now. No, she'd been abandoned by him and would now have to sort out this awful matter herself.

Pregnant. The word hammered in her brain. And she an unmarried woman without a man in tow.

She recalled the vision of Rowan last time she'd seen her in Stoneydyke, and shivered. She couldn't let that happen to her. She'd do anything to prevent it.

She forced her fist even deeper into her mouth, making her face ugly and distorted. She whimpered again, an animal-type sound deep in the back of her throat.

She knew what she would do.

Ishbel stood outside the chemist's shop willing herself to enter, embarrassment making her hesitate. There was still one customer in the shop. She would wait until that person left and then pray that no-one came in while she was talking to the chemist. She would simply die with shame if overheard.

Nervously she clutched her handbag to her, her fingers continuously moving over the soft leather that had been a present from Peter. If it hadn't been the only handbag she possessed, she'd have thrown it away along with the other gifts he'd given her.

How could she have got herself into such a position! Sheer madness. But she'd loved Peter and thought he was going to marry her; otherwise she'd never have consented to go to bed with him, not in a thousand years.

What a fool she'd been, what a stupid gullible fool. But how could she have possibly known he was deceiving her? He'd been so plausible. The rage that hadn't left her since Edinburgh erupted again – ongoing rage that fuelled the hate she now felt towards him.

The shop door tinged and a middle-aged matron came out to smile at Ishbel as she passed on her way.

Ishbel took a deep breath. This was something that had to be done, she reminded herself. There was no way round it.

Grim-faced, eyes bulging slightly, she started for the door and went inside.

Ishbel sat slumped in despair. She'd taken the pills the chemist had sold her – Patterson's Female Pills, they were called – following the instructions to the letter, and waited hopefully for them to take their course.

Only nothing had happened. Apart from a slight stomach discomfort there had been no reaction. None at all. And she'd now had to accept that there wasn't going to be any, either. The pills had failed her, just as Peter had done.

*   *   *

The tenement was buried in one of the most evil slums Ishbel had had the misfortune to visit. Close to the docks, it stank of human and animal waste, rotting vegetable materials, cooking odours, unwashed bodies and layer upon layer of filth. Ishbel's nose wrinkled, and the little she'd forced herself to eat earlier rose in her throat. What a ghastly place, she thought, wishing she could have turned tail and fled.

The close-mouth was indescribably dirty with a great dollop of dog excrement lying halfway along its length. Incongruously, in one of the houses a female was singing with the voice of an angel.

The house she was seeking was on the first landing. The door was brown, its paint ancient and cracked. There was no name-plate, which she'd been warned about. Heart hammering nineteen to the dozen, Ishbel forced herself to knock.

The woman who answered was large and jolly. She also looked and smelled as though she hadn't seen hot water and soap in a month of Sundays.

'Yes, dear?' the woman smiled.

'You've been recommended to me,' Ishbel quavered in reply.

The woman, the smile never leaving her face, eyed her up and down. 'Who by?'

'A Mrs McPartland who's a neighbour of mine. Apparently you helped a friend of hers, a Miss Quinn.'

'Oh, ay,' nodded the woman. 'Come away in, then, hen, and let's have a wee chat.'

A greyhound sloped into the hallway, gazed balefully at Ishbel, then slouched off into another room.

'That's Captain,' the woman explained.

There was a stack of unwashed dishes piled high in the kitchen sink, the linoleum underfoot worn in the extreme, while the top of the range was dotted with particles of burnt food.

Ishbel was filled with apprehension as she glanced about. This was simply awful, even more so than her worst fears.

'Now, then, dearie, in trouble, are we?' the woman queried.

Ishbel nodded.

'How far gone are you?'

'Three months.'

The woman regarded her steadily. 'Are you sure about that?'

Ishbel nodded again.

The woman sighed. 'That's not too bad, then. It's the ones who come here when they're a lot more than that I have problems with. You've been wise in consulting me early on. Were you told my price?'

'Five pounds.'

'Ay, that's right.' The woman's tone became steely. 'In advance.'

Ishbel opened her handbag and fished inside. She extracted a large white note which she offered the woman, who plucked it from her.

'Fine, dear,' the woman smiled. 'Now, just follow me and it'll all shortly be over and done with.'

The bedroom the woman led her to was even worse than the kitchen. It was dingy with a distinct smell of damp in the air. The bed was unmade, the sheets and pillowcases grey. Strips of wallpaper had come away from the walls, and there was a yellow stain on what had once been a white ceiling.

'Now, then,' instructed the woman. 'If you'll just take off your skirt and underthings, then lie on the bed, I'll be back in a tick.'

'Oh, God,' Ishbel whispered to herself when the woman was gone. She removed her coat and laid it carefully to one side. Trembling from head to foot, she reached for the fastening on her skirt.

When she was naked to the waist she crossed to the bed and forced herself to lie on it. She couldn't help but wonder if the bed had bugs or fleas. From its appearance anything was possible.

The woman returned carrying, of all things, a knitting

needle. Ishbel had heard they were used for this, but had always thought it some sort of grisly joke. She stared at the long wooden implement in fascinated horror.

'A wee examination first,' the woman declared, setting the knitting needle aside. Coming to the bed she sat beside Ishbel.

'Are you scared?'

'Terrified.'

The woman laughed. 'I'm not surprised. There aren't many who're not. But you're safe with me, lass. What's your name by the by?'

'Ishbel.'

'Pretty. Like yourself.'

That was as insincere a compliment as Ishbel had ever heard. Then she had a close-up look at the woman's hands. The nails were black, the hands themselves far from clean.

'Aren't you going to wash your hands?' Ishbel asked tremulously.

The woman frowned. 'Wash them? What for?'

Her reply boggled Ishbel's imagination. Suddenly she knew she couldn't let those hands touch her down there, and certainly not go inside her. As for a knitting needle . . .

Ishbel pulled herself up, her face a sickly shade of white, her previous trembling now a full-blown shaking. 'I can't go through with it,' she stuttered.

'Eh?'

'I said . . .' Ishbel swung off the bed and hurried to her clothes. 'I can't go through with it. I'm sorry.'

The woman stared at her, perplexed. 'Why not?'

'I just can't, that's all.'

'I'm the best there is.'

Then, heaven help what the worst was like, Ishbel thought, panic beginning to engulf her. Those hands! That needle! Not to mention the woman's fetid breath.

'I'm not giving you your money back!' the woman snapped. 'A bargain was struck and I'm willing to uphold me end of it. No, no, you're not getting your money back, lassie.'

Ishbel didn't care about the money. If she'd had another fiver on her, she'd gladly have paid it just to escape from there.

'That's all right,' she muttered.

The woman exhaled with relief that there wasn't to be an argument. 'Suit yourself.'

Ishbel tugged on her coat, dimly aware she was covered in a cold clammy sweat. 'Thank you anyway,' she said.

The woman rubbed a hand over her chin. 'It's still not too late to change your mind. You might regret this.'

Ishbel knew she wouldn't. Whatever happened, she wouldn't regret it. 'I'll let myself out,' she declared.

She rushed from the room, leaving the woman sitting on the bed gazing after her.

She almost ran up the street in her anxiety to be away from that dreadful creature and house.

On reaching home she stripped and washed herself all over with a flannel. But that didn't wash away her revulsion or the stink of the house and area which continued to cling to her.

'Surprise!' exclaimed a beaming Rory. 'It's me.' Then, on taking in Ishbel's colour, or lack of it, and how pinched her face had become, his beam faded to an expression of concern. 'What's wrong?' he demanded.

'Oh, Rory!' she husked, and fell into his arms. The only person she'd have been more pleased to see was her mother Meg. Tight in his embrace she found badly needed comfort and solace.

He could feel she'd lost weight to the point of scrawniness. Bones protruded where they hadn't before.

'Let's go through and you can tell me all about it,' he said soothingly.

In the kitchen, where the light was better, he was able to verify that she'd indeed lost a great deal of weight, unhealthily so. 'Are you not well, Ishbel?'

She detached herself as Jessica, who'd been playing on the floor, greeted her uncle effusively.

'Hello, my bonny!' he cried in delight, giving her a cuddle.

'Aunt Ishbel's lost her job,' Jessica declared solemnly when the cuddle was over.

'Lost her job!'

'She got the sack.'

Rory glanced over at Ishbel, busy worrying a thumbnail. 'Is this true?'

She nodded. 'I'm afraid so.'

'But how?'

'It's a long story. Jess, will you go and find something to do in the bedroom while I talk to your Uncle Rory?'

'Aw!' Jessica pouted, disappointed at being sent off.

'Please, it's important.'

'We'll speak later,' Rory promised her.

Jessica skipped happily from the room; after which, Ishbel went over and closed the door behind her.

'Now, what the hell's going on?' Rory demanded harshly, not liking the look of his sister one little bit.

'Would you care for a cup of tea? There's still some left, I think.'

'Not now. Maybe later.'

'Then you'd better sit down.'

He noted as he did that there wasn't a fire in the grate despite it being chilly out. Ishbel virtually collapsed into the chair facing him.

'I was fired for falling down on the job,' she explained. 'I went to pieces and kept breaking bottles and doing other things wrong. The gaffer was initially sympathetic but in the end said he had to let me go. It was my own fault.'

'But why?'

'I . . .' She swallowed hard, knowing she was going to have to confide in Rory. 'I'm pregnant.'

His eyes widened. 'By Peter?'

'Of course.' Who else did he think she might be pregnant by? But she didn't take offence, aware it had been a rhetorical question.

'Then, you must get married straight away.'

'I can't,' she stated slowly.

'Why ever not?'

Her voice crackled with emotion when she next spoke. 'Because he already has a wife.'

Rory shot bolt upright. 'What!'

'He already has a wife,' she repeated in a whisper, adding almost as an afterthought; 'And three children.'

'The bastard. The dirty rotten bastard!'

Her sentiments exactly, she thought. She then went on to recount her trip through to Edinburgh and what had occurred there.

When she finished Rory's hands were curled into fists, their knuckles shining white. 'And you had no idea?'

'None at all,' she replied, hysteria in her voice.

Rory leapt to his feet and began to pace up and down. 'I'll go and face him with this. I'll—'

'No,' she interjected. 'Why bother? I don't want any more to do with him. Not now or ever.'

'But, Ishbel . . . ?'

'Leave him be,' she stated firmly. 'And may he burn in hell for what he's done.' She shook her head in bewilderment. 'What I can't understand is why.'

'He seemed such a nice chap, too,' Rory muttered through clenched teeth.

'Do you think he had bigamy in mind?'

Rory barked out a short laugh. 'That's possible. But it's more likely he was simply after a bit on the side.'

Ishbel blanched to hear herself described as that. 'What about the ring? Why should he go to such lengths?'

Rory regarded her shrewdly. 'Did you sleep with him before you got engaged?'

She shook her head.

'There you are, then. The ring was merely a ploy to get you to . . .' He stopped and bit his lip. He felt murderous towards Peter Lorne. If Peter had been present, he'd have knocked him from one end of the room to the other. And it wouldn't have finished there, either. Peter would have been a sorry sight by the time he'd done with him. He'd have pounded the bugger to a bloody pulp.

'Why didn't you write, let us know?' he demanded.

She stared at him, her face tight with strain, tiny beads of perspiration dotting her brow. 'I was too ashamed,' she mumbled.

'Oh, Ishbel!' He breathed. 'None the less, you must go home. Have the baby there.'

'Don't be daft!' she retorted shrilly. 'That's the last thing I can do. You know Glenshields; it would be round the village in no time. I can hear the tongues wagging now. And what about the effect on Mum? She'd never hold her head up again. Rowan was bad enough; this would finish her off.'

'You're right,' Rory said slowly.

'Glenshields is definitely out.'

'There are . . . ways, I believe.'

'Ways? Oh, ay, there are that.' She then told him about the pills she'd taken and her visit to the woman down by the docks.

'I couldn't go through with it, Rory,' she went on. 'You should have seen that place, and her. Even the memory of it makes me want to throw up in revulsion.'

He had a sudden thought, realizing now why she was so thin and pinched. 'How are you managing without a job? When did you last eat?'

'I had some bread and dripping earlier. I'm almost through the money Gray left us, but what little money I've got I've been using to feed Jessica. I'm behind in my rent. I . . .' She trailed off and sobbed.

He immediately went to her and put his arms round her. 'Hush. It's going to be all right now. I'm here.'

'What can you do?' she wailed.

He didn't know, but he'd think of something. 'First thing is to get some decent food inside you. Is there a chippie nearby?'

'A couple of streets away.'

He asked her for precise directions, which she gave him. 'You get that kettle on and I'll be as quick as I can.'

'I feel such a fool!' she further wailed, tears welling up in her eyes.

'Did you really love him?'

'I wouldn't have got engaged or gone to bed with him otherwise,' she protested.

'Then, you've nothing to feel foolish about, I assure you. You acted as a result of your emotions and in good faith. Who can honestly blame you for that? Your only trouble was you picked a wrong 'un to go and fall for.'

'He's certainly that,' she choked.

Rory could well imagine what had gone through Peter's mind. He'd met Ishbel, fancied her, and then strung her along until he'd had his way with her, and kept on having his way. How convenient for him. Perhaps he was having trouble at home with his own wife – that was always a possibility. As for the ring, it was an investment on his part. For wasn't it the custom when an engagement was broken off that the female return the ring? If Peter hadn't planned bigamy, which Rory personally believed to be the case, then no doubt it had been his intention to end the relationship before the proposed marriage.

'I'll be off to the chippie, and we'll talk further when I get back,' Rory declared.

'What am I to do, Rory?'

He didn't know. It needed thinking about. He shook his head in answer to her question. 'I'll be as quick as I can. You must be starving.'

He racked his brains as he waited in the queue. How could he help Ishbel out of the mess she'd landed herself in? When it came his turn he ordered double portions for Ishbel and Jessica. On retracing his steps he stopped off and bought several bottles of stout and another of lemonade.

Jessica, again in the kitchen, clapped her hands in glee when she saw and smelled the newspaper-wrapped parcels Rory was carrying.

'Oh, goody!' Jess exclaimed, hurrying to get plates for this unexpected feast.

Rory, who'd eaten earlier, watched Ishbel wolf down

her meal, hardly able to restrain herself from stuffing the food into her mouth.

He poured her a glass of stout and one for himself, Jessica having already helped herself to some lemonade.

When the meal was over he collected their plates and washed them at the sink. While he was doing this, Ishbel got Jessica ready for bed. Then he had a good half-hour's chat and laugh with Jess, at the end of which Ishbel announced it was the child's bedtime.

Jessica complained vociferously, pleading for more time with her Uncle Rory, but Ishbel was adamant, reminding Jessica she had school in the morning.

Rory gave Jess a good-night kiss, then sat with a glass of stout as Ishbel took her through and tucked her up.

'Does she know anything?' Rory asked on Ishbel's return.

'Only that I've lost my job and have broken up with Peter. She's most upset about the latter as she worshipped him. She thought the sun shone out of his backside.'

Rory's face became even grimmer on hearing that. How could Peter have been so cynical towards Jess? As far as he was concerned, it beggared belief.

Ishbel sat facing Rory, her eyes large and soulful. 'There's another reason why I can't go home to Glenshields.'

'What's that?'

'The minister. Don't forget what he did to Rowan when she fell pregnant. I might not be under age, but my baby would still be illegitimate.'

'I'd kill him first,' Rory breathed in sudden fury. 'If he tried a repetition of what he did before, I swear I'd swing for him.'

'The same thing could happen to me here,' Ishbel continued. 'But I've come to the conclusion it's unlikely. People in this area tend to mind their own business and not interfere.'

Dykes, Rory thought. Another bastard.

Ishbel leant forward and cupped her head in her hands. 'What am I to do?' she asked again.

446

It was a question Rory still didn't have an answer for. Before leaving his sister he gave her all the money he had on him, and promised he'd be back soon with more.

The Rolls-Royce purred through the night, an introspective Rory at the wheel. He'd promised Ishbel money and would keep his word. But that was only a short-term solution as he was only too well aware.

His natural instinct was to send her cash on a weekly basis, but he couldn't spare enough to meet all Ishbel's and Jessica's needs. And what about Mary Louise? He'd have to inform her what he was doing.

He could well imagine the furore that news would cause. Mary Louise would be sympathetic to Ishbel's plight, but when it came to money that was another thing entirely.

Of course Ishbel might get lucky and land herself another job, only that was unlikely with the current unemployment figures being so high. Jobs were at a premium, in Glasgow as elsewhere.

There was always Vincent, mind you. He might be willing to lend a hand, except that would mean telling Meg.

Or did it? It might be that Vincent would keep the secret to himself.

Rory dismissed that idea. Meg was going to have to learn about Ishbel's condition sooner or later. There was going to be a baby after all.

A baby, he mused, thinking that Ishbel wasn't against an abortion in principle. She'd already tried and failed to get rid of it with pills, and then there had been her visit to that ghastly woman down by the docks.

He knew then who he would turn to for advice.

'We'll see you in the morning,' said the Master of Drum, smiling at Rory who'd come to report about the trip to Glasgow where he'd attended to some minor matters for him.

Rory hesitated. 'I appreciate it's late, sir, but can I have a private word?'

'Of course! I'm just about to have a dram. Will you join me?'

'That's very kind of you, sir.'

Celia glanced up from the script she was studying, having detected an odd note in Rory's voice. 'Something amiss, Rory?'

'I'm afraid there is,' Rory replied quietly. 'Which is why I want to ask your advice.'

'What about you, dear?' the Master asked, now standing beside the tantalus.

'A small one with lots of soda.' Celia indicated a pink-covered sofa. 'Come and sit down, Rory.'

When he had done so she queried: 'Is this something personal?'

He nodded.

The Master handed Celia her drink, then gave one to Rory. 'Nothing serious, I trust?'

'That's just it, sir; it is.'

Celia laid her script aside, having already decided to turn it down. Her agent was going to be furious as he badly wanted her to make the film, but she thought the part too short and the writing atrocious.

The Master sat and elegantly crossed his legs. 'Right, we're all ears,' he prompted.

'You know of my sister Ishbel who's in Glasgow?'

'Taking care of your other sister's child,' Celia nodded.

Rory gazed into his glass. 'I hope I'm not being presumptuous . . .'

'Is she in trouble?' Celia interjected.

'Of the worst sort, I'm afraid. She's pregnant.'

The Master's expression became one of faint disapproval. 'I see.'

'But isn't she engaged?' Celia said.

Rory went on to tell them the whole sorry tale, to which they both listened intently.

'The cad!' the Master condemned roundly when Rory finally finished.

'He should have his . . .' Celia stopped herself saying what she thought should be done to Peter, knowing it would have shocked Rory. Perhaps not the sentiment but the fact that it was expressed by a female in her position. She smiled inwardly: Dear chap, he could be so naïve at times, and was a typical product of the class structure.

'The thing is how do I help her resolve the jam she's in?' Rory asked.

'I can understand why she feels she can't return to Glenshields,' the Master declared.

'As for that Dykes. The man's a menace!' Celia added hotly, incensed at what he'd done to Rowan. She considered that entire episode wholly unspeakable.

'Nor can Ishbel come and stay with us as we're so close to Glenshields,' Rory further explained.

'Quite,' the Master muttered understandingly.

'You say she's starving?' Celia frowned.

'You should have seen her. She's always been slim, but there's a big difference between that and how I found her. Her face was like a skull.'

'And you want our advice on the matter,' reflected the Master, more to himself than to Rory.

'I can't come up with the answer, sir. I thought . . . hoped maybe you could between you.'

'It's a poser.'

'No, it's not,' Celia snapped. 'She must have this abortion, which we shall arrange for her.'

'Celia!' the Master exclaimed.

'And why not? We have the contacts.'

'Even so, don't forget who I am. My position. If anything like that was ever to get out . .'

'Archie!' Celia cut in. 'Don't be so selfish.'

'That's the last thing I am.'

'Not in this instance,' she pointed out. 'The poor girl's jobless, pregnant by a bounder she thought she was going to marry, and looking after a small child as it is. Where's your compassion? And you a so-called Liberal!'

'There's nothing "so-called" about it,' he retorted.

449

'That's hardly how your attitude comes over to me.'

'I can't be involved in anything that's against the law. It could cost me my career.'

'Sod your career!'

He stared at her aghast. 'Celia!' he chided.

She was instantly contrite. 'I didn't mean it quite like that,' she said, her tone softening. 'But if we went about this the right way who would ever know? Good God, Archie, it happens all the time in the most proper of circles, as you're well aware.'

He couldn't deny that, knowing it was true. None the less, he was totally against this.

Rory had become nervous during the past few moments. 'I never intended to cause an argument between the pair of you,' he stated hesitantly.

Celia waved a dismissive hand at him, meanwhile puffing a cloud of blue smoke at the ceiling. Her thoughts were racing; she was determined to have her own way.

'I've got an idea,' she said slowly. 'Why doesn't Ishbel come here for some rest and recuperation, and during that time we can discuss the matter further?'

'Drum House isn't that far away from Glenshields. What if word of her condition got out?' Rory queried.

'Is she showing her pregnancy yet?' Celia asked.

Rory shook his head. 'Not as far as I could make out.'

'There we are, then. It can be kept quiet.'

That satisfied Rory, who was now excited at the prospect of Ishbel and Jessica being at Drum House. Then he had another thought. 'The only snag is Jessica's at school.'

'A short spell off won't do her any harm,' Celia countered. 'Archie?'

He knew he was being manipulated, but at the same time felt sorry for Ishbel and genuinely wanted to help her. 'Rory can bring her through, and in the meanwhile I'll sort out her financial obligations,' he answered.

A huge smile lit up Celia's face. 'Thank you, sweetheart.'

'I'll pay back anything you lay out,' Rory promised, thinking Mary Louise would hit the roof when he told her. But damn Mary Louise. Ishbel was his sister after all.

'That's settled, then,' Celia declared with satisfaction.

'When shall I go for her?'

'The sooner the better,' Celia responded. 'You can return and pick her and the child up tomorrow.'

'I can't thank you both enough,' Rory said.

'Nonsense,' retorted the Master, swallowing the remains of his whisky. 'Now, who's for another?'

Over a second dram the details were planned, after which Rory left them to return home as Mary Louise was expecting him.

Celia eyed Archie as she sat at her vanity table brushing her hair. He was standing in the nearby *en suite* bathroom clipping his moustache. She waited patiently until he returned to the bedroom, then said; 'You do realize that if this girl doesn't have an abortion it'll ruin her life?'

Archie stopped and stared at her.

'Just think about it, Archie. Who'll want to take her on with an illegitimate child plus another belonging to her dead sister? No-one, I should imagine.'

He had to admit he hadn't thought it through to that extent.

'And all because of some seducer who led her up the garden path. It's hardly fair, is it?'

Archie climbed into their four-poster bed and pulled the bed clothes up to his chin. Why couldn't Celia see and understand the position *he* was in? He simply couldn't afford to be connected with an abortion, no matter how desirable that abortion might be.

'Archie?'

'You're asking too much of me, Celia.'

'I could arrange it, send her to Harley Street. George Ponsonby would do it for us. He owes you a favour after all. She could be there and back within a week without anyone being the wiser.'

George was in his debt, Archie ruminated, and would

be only too happy to do it for him if approached. Yet still he balked, his career uppermost in his mind. The last thing he wanted was to create a stick that could be used against him.

Celia could easily have gone behind Archie's back about this, but didn't wish to because of his political involvement. If the abortion was done, it had to be with his agreement.

'The girl's only young with everything ahead of her, Archie. It would be cruel to deny her our full assistance.'

'You look very beautiful tonight,' he stated, gazing at her.

She realized he was trying to change the subject. 'You mean I don't normally?' she replied, deciding to tease him.

'Let me rephrase that. Even more beautiful than usual. And that's saying something,' he countered with a small smile.

'You won't flatter me out of this conversation, so don't think you can,' she admonished, jabbing a finger at him.

'I never thought for a moment I could,' he lied drily in reply.

'So what about Ishbel?'

'I'll sleep on it.'

'She needs our help. Rory needs our help,' she reminded him.

'Help is one thing, abortion another.'

'Men!' she exclaimed angrily. 'Their attitude to all sorts of things might be quite different if it was they who got pregnant and had babies.'

'Possibly.'

She knew from the stubborn tone that had crept into his voice that she wasn't going to make any more headway that night. Let him sleep on it as he'd promised; hopefully he'd see matters in a different light come morning.

If not, she'd keep working on him.

'Pregnant!' Mary Louise exclaimed, appalled.

'And starving. She was in a terrible state.'

'How could she be so stupid – after what happened to Rowan.'

'She was in love and believed they were to be married.'

'Even though!'

He glared at Mary Louise, thinking there were times when she exasperated him. He went on to explain tersely about the plan to take Ishbel to Drum House where she was to rest and be built up again. He'd already decided not to mention anything about a possible abortion.

'I'm off to bed,' he announced.

'What about your mother?'

'She's to be told nothing, understand? *Nothing*. At least, for now.'

'Well, I won't let on.'

'You'd better not,' he said threateningly.

'Didn't they have the sense to use french letters?'

'Apparently Peter did, and she still got pregnant. I asked the same question myself.'

'So much for them, then.'

Rory was suddenly extremely weary. It had been a long hard day, emotionally tiring as well as physically exhausting. He was worried sick about Ishbel and the condition in which he'd found her. Thank God he'd dropped by when he had. Who knew what the outcome would have been otherwise?

'Would you like a cup of tea before you turn in?' Mary Louise asked.

He shook his head.

'I shan't be long behind you.'

A little later Mary Louise slipped into bed beside Rory and switched out the light. She lay in the darkness thinking about Ishbel, and the irony of the situation. There was she, desperate to become pregnant and continuing to fail in that respect, while Ishbel had done so even though precautions had been taken.

Mary Louise sighed. There was a great longing inside her for a child, and she knew Rory wanted one as badly as did she. They'd tried, and gone on trying, with no result.

Jealousy nibbled at her. She ached inside. How perverse

the Fates were, bestowing their favours in the wrong direction. Making Ishbel conceive who had no wish for a baby, denying her who did.

When would her turn come? she wondered, closing her eyes and snuggling down. When?

The ache gradually disappeared to be replaced by a feeling of unfulfilment and – strangely, she thought, considering she was lying beside her husband – loneliness.

Rory parked his motorbike by the side of the garage. He hadn't planned a particularly early start as he knew they'd have to wait till Jessica was finished for the day at school before returning to Drum House. He was stretching, having woken stiff that morning, when Celia appeared carrying a wicker hamper basket.

'How are you today?' she smiled in greeting.

'Fine. And you?'

She was about to reply when she was seized by a violent bout of coughing which caused her to double over. Concerned, Rory immediately went to her.

'Never better,' she gasped when the coughing finally subsided.

'You really should see another doctor,' he volunteered.

'Oh, stop talking like an old woman! I'm all right.'

Celia glanced up at the grey heavy sky and frowned. 'There'll be rain before long.'

'Yes, it does look like we're in for a downpour,' Rory agreed. He brought his attention back to the wicker basket. 'What's that for?'

'Lunch. I had Cook put together something nice for us all.'

'Us?' he queried.

'I've decided to come with you to Glasgow.'

This hadn't been part of the previous night's plan. 'I can manage all right by myself, Celia,' he told her.

'I've no doubt you can. But I'm coming anyway, and that's that.'

From the tone she'd used he knew there was no

dissuading her; besides which, he'd enjoy her company. 'Suit yourself.' It suddenly struck him that sounded ungracious, which made him colour slightly. 'I'm sorry. I mean it's very kind of you to take the trouble.'

'Not at all,' she said dismissively. 'While you're helping Ishbel pack what's required, I shall visit the factor's office and sort matters out there.'

'As I said to the Master last night, I'll refund you just as soon as I can arrange to do so.' He and Mary Louise had – by his standards, that is – a sizeable bank account which up until then had remained inviolate. Payments in were made, but to date there had never been a withdrawal. The money they'd saved was earmarked for the business Mary Louise intended to buy one day. The account was in their joint names, needing both signatures for a withdrawal to take place, the latter at Mary Louise's instigation.

Rory stored the hamper in the boot, then opened a rear door for Celia.

'Should I speak to the Master before we leave?' he asked when she was settled.

'No, don't bother. He's busy with a stack of papers that have to be attended to. He has to get through them before returning to London, which he'll be doing at the end of the week.'

The Rolls was leaving the driveway when the first spots of rain spattered against its windscreen.

Celia stared up at the tenement they'd stopped in front of, and couldn't help but think what a contrast it was to Drum House.

Rory retrieved the hamper from the boot and opened up the large golf umbrella kept there, using it to cover Celia during her short walk from the car to the close-mouth. The rain was now bucketing down.

A surprised Ishbel opened the door to their knock; she was not expecting Rory back so soon, and certainly not for Celia to be with him.

'Ishbel, this is Mrs Lindsay, the Mistress of Drum,'

Rory introduced. 'I think you met each other at our wedding.'

'Yes. Hello, how are you?' Ishbel said, wiping her hands on her sides before extending the right one.

There still wasn't a fire in the grate, Rory noted as they entered the kitchen; but, then, he hadn't been able to leave Ishbel all that much cash the previous night.

'We've come to take you and Jessica to Drum House,' he announced.

'My idea,' Celia said. 'Rory has told us about your predicament, and I thought you should come home with us to rest and recuperate.'

'Oh, I couldn't possibly put you to—'

'Of course you can,' Celia interjected firmly. 'In fact I insist.'

'But Jessica—'

'Can have a little while off school. It won't harm her. In fact a sojourn in the country will probably do her the world of good.'

Ishbel was flustered, not knowing what to make of this. It was so unexpected.

'Do you mind if I smoke?'

Ishbel shook her head, and wondered where the solitary ashtray she owned was.

Celia lit up, at the same time surreptitiously glancing round the kitchen. She refocused again on Ishbel, thinking Rory had been right: his sister did look starved, not to mention extremely anxious. Her heart went out to the lass.

'If you tell me the name of your factor, I'll go and settle up with him while Rory helps you pack,' Celia said.

'It's pouring out!' Rory protested. 'I'd better drive you.'

'You remain with Ishbel and I'll drive myself. I'm quite capable, you know, though it isn't something I do all that often.'

Rory was immediately concerned about the car, his pride and joy. He had no idea what Celia's driving was like and

456

would have hated anything to happen to it. 'Are you sure?' he queried.

She pulled a face. 'Quite sure. Now, hand over the keys and I'll be on my way.'

Ishbel gave Celia the name of her factor and his address, with instructions on how to get there.

'Toodle-oo!' Celia said brightly, stubbing out the butt of her cigarette in the ashtray Ishbel had provided.

'Mrs Lindsay is very beautiful,' Ishbel commented when Celia had left them. She sniffed the air appreciatively. 'What gorgeous perfume.'

'Celia's a gem,' Rory nodded.

Ishbel put a hand to her forehead and shivered. 'I'm so cold.'

'Put a jumper on. That'll help,' he suggested. 'Do you have a suitcase?'

'Only the old one I brought from Glenshields.'

'We'll start with that, then.'

He went to her and took her into his arms. 'Are you all right, Sis?'

'I've been sleeping badly and suffering from night sweats. I also have a bit of an upset tum which has been griping me since I got up.'

'Did you have a decent breakfast?'

She smiled at him. 'After dropping Jess off I went to the fishmonger's and bought myself an Arbroath smokey. It was delicious.'

He nodded his approval. 'Celia's brought us lunch in that basket,' he informed her.

'Lunch!'

'All sorts of goodies, I've no doubt. Cook put it together for her.'

'Can I have a peep?'

Rory laughed. 'Help yourself.'

Ishbel crossed to the basket, which Rory had placed on the table, and lifted one section of the double flaps. Her eyes widened at what she saw inside.

Rory joined her. 'Quails eggs, champagne, pâté . . .'

'What's pâté?'

He explained.

'Paste in other words.'

'Not quite, but similar. And far more tasty.'

'God, it looks good. I hope Mrs Lindsay hurries back.'

Rory plucked out a plum and handed it to her. 'Why don't you have that now? I'm sure Celia won't mind.'

'Mmm, scrumptious,' Ishbel muttered as she bit into the fruit.

'Celia told me *en route* that she's ordered a room to be prepared for you. I know the room in question. It's large and light. You'll love it.'

'And Jessica?'

'It's a double bed. The pair of you can share.'

Ishbel stopped eating, and tears filled her eyes. 'Oh, Rory, I can't thank you and Mrs Lindsay enough. I was in such total despair.'

'I know,' he said, putting an arm round her thin bony shoulders, shoulders that now shook in his grasp.

'It's been awful, Rory. First Peter, followed by the pregnancy, then losing my job. There were times when I wasn't sure whether I was coming or going.'

'Well, I'm here now to look after you, to take care of things. It's all going to be all right, I promise you.'

'I keep having nightmares about being locked away as Rowan was . . .'

'That won't happen. Take my word for it.'

'And what's to become of the baby? And me?'

'We'll work something out, you'll see.'

She finished off the plum and laid the stone aside. Having done that, she wrapped her arms round Rory and hugged him tight.

He put a hand in his pocket and pulled out a clean white linen handkerchief. 'Here, use this to wipe away those tears.'

She accepted the hanky and dabbed her eyes. 'I don't know how and when I'll be able to pay back Mrs Lindsay . . .'

'That's my concern,' he told her. 'Mary Louise and I have plenty of money in the bank and can easily afford to meet what you owe. Take it as a gift from me.'

'But what about the rent coming up? I've still no job, remember.'

He stroked her hair, which was dull and lifeless with a great many split ends. 'One thing at a time. For the moment that's my problem.'

'But you and Mary Louise can't—'

He stopped her speaking by laying a finger over her mouth. 'One thing at a time,' he repeated softly.

'Bless you,' she whispered.

'Now, shall we begin the packing?'

Ishbel sniffed, and wiped her nose. 'Come on, then.'

Hand in hand they went through to the bedroom.

Jessica was so excited she couldn't stay still. Going to stay at Drum House! She couldn't think of anything more fabulous.

'Are we all ready, then?' Celia queried.

Ishbel was still satiated from the lunch they'd had earlier, and a little light-headed from the two glasses of champagne she'd drunk.

'Everything that has to be loaded aboard the Rolls has been,' Rory told them.

'Then shall we go?' Celia said.

Ishbel had a last look round, then they all went to the front door, which Ishbel carefully locked behind them. Jessica skipped down the stairs, eager to be in the car and on their way.

The rain had ceased, leaving the streets wet and glistening. It was dark out, as though it was night instead of late afternoon. The sky was black and angry-looking.

'There's more rain to come,' Rory prophesied.

'I'll ride in the front with you,' Celia said to him. 'Ishbel and Jessica can go in the back.'

'Make sure you keep your feet on the floor. We don't want to dirty Mrs Lindsay's leather upholstery,' Ishbel whispered to Jessica.

Jessica nodded; she'd be particularly careful. She wished some of her chums had been around to see her get into such a swanky car, but the street was deserted.

Once ensconced in the rear Ishbel produced Rory's hanky, which he'd told her to hang on to, and wiped a brow that had become clammy with cold sweat. She wasn't feeling at all well, but had put it down to such a large meal after a long period of frugality. She grimaced when her stomach suddenly contracted with a fierce gripping pain.

Celia lit up as Rory drew away from the kerb. She glanced in the rear-view mirror, smiling at the expression on Jessica's face. It was going to be fun having a child round the house, she thought. She'd enjoy that, especially such a nice well-mannered child. She gave Ishbel full marks for the way she had brought up Jessica.

They had just left Glasgow behind them when the rain, as Rory had prophesied, began again, lightly at first, but quickly changing and becoming almost torrential.

Rory leant forward to peer into the darkness, his visibility having been cut dramatically. On the outside of the windscreen the wipers swished efficiently.

'It's certainly wet out there,' Celia commented.

Rory, concentrating on the road ahead, grunted in agreement.

Ishbel gritted her teeth: the pain in her stomach had worsened, while she was also in the middle of experiencing a hot flush. She should never have drunk that champagne, she chided herself, not when she was carrying. But it had been so delicious, as had everything that had come out of the hamper.

'Aunt Ishbel?'

'What, darling?'

'You made a funny sound.'

'Did I?' Ishbel queried, thinking she hadn't been aware of it.

Before Ishbel could explain it a jagged streak of lightning blazed across the sky, followed almost instantly by a loud crack of thunder.

Ishbel jumped, and put a hand to her bosom.

'Storm,' Rory declared.

'And I think it's going to be a bad one,' Celia said, peering up at the sky.

There was another streak of lightning, and then an even bigger one. The thunder that preceded it was deafening.

Jessica cowered against Ishbel, pressing her face into Ishbel's side. 'I'm scared,' she mumbled.

'There's no need to be, Jess. It's only a storm.'

'Don't like storms. They frighten me.'

Using her free hand, the other comforting Jessica, Ishbel groped for her hanky with which she dabbed away the cold sweat that had re-formed on her brow.

'What a night,' Rory grumbled, finding the driving exceptionally hard going.

'I'm sorry.' Ishbel apologized. 'It's because of me you're out in it.'

Rory suddenly swore and swerved the car to the right, praying that he wouldn't go into a skid. His luck was in.

'Bloody cow!' he complained.

'What on earth was that doing on the road?' Celia queried, having seen the Jersey quite distinctly.

'God knows,' Rory muttered. 'It must have broken away from somewhere. It certainly put the wind up me back there.'

A little later a car hissed past in the opposite direction, the first to do so for ages. Rory had already remarked on how little traffic there was.

Ishbel dropped her head and groaned. The gripping pain had been replaced by a red-hot thrust that caused her to wince in agony every time it happened.

'Aunty?' Jessica queried anxiously.

'It's all right, petal. Too much rich food, that's all.' Using her hanky, she wiped a brow that was now awash with sweat.

Celia flicked her cigarette-lighter, lit a cigarette and dragged smoke deep into her lungs. The journey home was going to take for ever at this rate, she thought, for

461

Rory was driving far slower than he would have normally done. But what else could he do?

Flash after flash of lightning pierced the sky, and at one point six flashes spectacularly occurred simultaneously. The accompanying thunder loudly banged and crashed its way across the heavens.

Ishbel knew something was wrong – a conclusion she'd slowly, and unwillingly, arrived at. Should she say something or keep quiet? Keep quiet, she decided. Time enough to speak when they arrived at Drum House, which she fervently hoped would be soon.

'Just listen to that rain,' Rory mused as it drummed against the roof.

'I rather like it,' Celia smiled at him.

'You would!'

She gave a low laugh.

'I suppose you like thunder and lightning, too?'

'No,' she answered truthfully. 'I could do without those, but rain doesn't bother me.'

'This is all a bit of an adventure, eh?' Rory said, not realizing how much of an adventure, in the darker sense, it would transpire to be.

'A bit,' she agreed.

Ishbel gasped as the red-hot thrust became an excruciating hammer-blow that ripped and tore into her belly. Bending over, she clutched herself.

'Oh, my God!' she muttered.

Rory frowned into the rear-view mirror. 'Ishbel, what's wrong?'

Her whole body convulsed as another hammer-blow hit her. As it ebbed away she felt a sticky wetness run down the side of one thigh.

'Rory, can you pull over?' she requested in a tight crackling voice.

'Pull over?'

She glanced at Celia, who'd turned to look at her. 'I think I'm about to ...' She trailed off, not wishing to complete the sentence because Jessica was present.

Celia stared at her blankly.

'I'm bleeding,' Ishbel silently mouthed.

Celia's face fell.

'What's going on?' Rory demanded.

Celia leant across and whispered in his ear. He swore explosively.

A little further up the road Rory spotted a likely parking-spot into which he drove the Rolls.

'Can I change places with you for a short while?' Celia smiled to Jessica.

'Yes, you come and sit here with me,' Rory added.

Celia got out of the car to clamber in beside Ishbel. While, with Rory's help, Jessica squeezed between the two front seats.

'Shall we put the wireless on?' Rory suggested to Jessica, who brightened considerably, thinking that was a terrific idea. He managed to find some light orchestral music.

Ishbel and Celia were conferring together as to what was the best thing to do when Ishbel suddenly rocked back and let out a heart-stopping shriek.

'Aunt Ishbel!' Jessica exclaimed, twisting round in alarm and despair.

'It's no business of yours,' Rory declared, sliding into a position that effectively blocked her view. Reaching out, he turned up the volume of the wireless.

Ishbel shrieked again, incredibly, even louder than before. More wetness flooded out of her.

This was terrible, Celia thought, fussing over Ishbel, giving her what comfort she could.

Jessica began to cry. 'Aunty Ishbel, Aunty Ishbel,' she sobbed.

Celia forced her thoughts to clear. This wasn't a time to panic, but to think. 'Is there a hospital near here?' she asked Rory.

'I'll look.' He swiftly switched on the overhead light and consulted his map.

'There isn't a hospital for miles,' Rory eventually

declared. 'But, to be honest with you, I'm not exactly sure where we are.'

'She needs a doctor,' Celia stated.

Ishbel grabbed Celia's arm and squeezed it hard. 'I . . .' She broke off to shriek yet again, her body lifting right off the seat till she was only supported by the back of her head.

Jessica's sobbing increased.

'Shall we stay here or drive on and try to find help?' Rory husked to Celia.

Celia was gazing at the front of Ishbel's skirt, now stained bright with blood.

'Your upholstery,' Ishbel gurgled.

'Don't worry about that. It's not important. You are.'

Ishbel writhed, her eyes popping. 'I'm so . . . sorry.'

Celia made a decision. 'Drive on,' she instructed Rory. 'We'll turn off at the next signpost and look for a telephone.'

'Right.' He reached up and flicked off the light, then restarted the car.

Lightning flickered and thunder banged as they sped down the road, Rory hunched over the wheel staring intently ahead of him. In the rear seat Ishbel continued to shriek, while beside him Jessica sobbed uncontrollably.

'Here, take this,' Archie said to an ashen distraught Celia.

She accepted the large whisky and soda, and had a sip. She shuddered as the alcohol burnt its way down her throat.

'The poor girl,' Archie muttered, referring to Ishbel. When he thought Celia had regained something of her composure he said; 'Now go on with your story.'

'We never found a telephone. We headed for a village but somehow got lost. Not Rory's fault: the weather was unbelievable. We stopped again, and that was when she lost the baby.'

Archie sucked in a deep breath, then saw off his own drink. He immediately crossed to the tantalus and refilled it.

'It was awful,' Celia went on. 'Particularly with Jessica in the car. Rory did his best, but she became hysterical; she kept asking over and over again if Ishbel was going to die.'

'What do you think brought on the miscarriage?'

'Well, she has been under a tremendous amount of strain lately, including not eating properly. It was Dr Jolly's opinion it was probably a combination of recent events.' Dr Jolly was the local doctor who'd been summoned to Drum House directly after their arrival.

'I wish I'd been here to help,' Archie said sympathetically. He'd been with a constituent advising on certain problems the man was having. He'd returned home shortly after Jolly's departure.

Celia had another sip of whisky; she felt totally drained and somewhat light-headed.

'And now Ishbel's under sedation?'

'That's right. Jolly gave her something fairly strong and stayed with her till she'd dropped off. He said he'd call again first thing tomorrow.'

'And what about the child?'

'Jolly gave her something also, though mild in her case; then Rory took her to his house for Mary Louise to look after. I offered, of course, but he thought she'd be better off with Mary Louise whom she knows.'

'Did she appreciate what had happened?'

'No. The explanation given to her was that Ishbel had suffered a minor haemorrhage. A miscarriage was never mentioned in her hearing. Rory will naturally have informed Mary Louise but doesn't want his mother or step-father knowing the real details.'

'I hope you don't mind me saying, but you look dreadful,' Archie stated.

She gave a hollow laugh. 'I feel dreadful. And no wonder, after that.'

'In such shocking weather, too.'

Celia curled in on herself, the memory of what had occurred earlier horribly vivid in her mind.

465

'At least Ishbel's among relatives and friends now. We'll take care of her,' Archie said.

Celia flashed him a grateful and appreciative smile. 'You are a good man, Archie.'

'Nothing good about it. We'll only be doing the decent thing.'

He paused, then said; 'You know, this could be viewed as a blessing in disguise. Horrendous as it was, over all, in my opinion it was for the best.' For him as well as for Ishbel, he reflected. For her miscarriage let him off the abortion hook. Selfish on his part perhaps, but none the less that was how he felt.

'I only hope Ishbel sees it that way,' Celia murmured.

'I'm sure she will, once she's recovered a little. She did attempt to induce herself with pills after all, and also visited that appalling woman with the same end in mind. It wasn't as if she wanted to keep the baby.'

'True,' Celia agreed. 'But for it to happen like that, in a car with Jessica there . . .' Celia shuddered again.

Archie went to her and put an arm round her shoulders. 'My dearest,' he crooned softly.

'Tonight shook me, Archie; it really did,' she whispered.

'I can imagine.'

'I felt so hopeless. So inadequate.'

'From what you said, you did wonderfully well.'

She gazed up at him and gave him a rueful smile. 'I love you. And I'm sorry I've never been able to give you a child.'

He pecked her on the lips. 'And I love you. We've got each other, and that's enough for me.'

'Funny how a situation like that can put everything in your life into perspective. It's a great leveller.'

'Now, don't get morbid on me. It's all over, finished.'

'She was so worried about the car, which I have to say is a mess. Rory promised to deal with it in the morning, but it could be that the car will have to be reupholstered.'

'If that's the case, then so be it. I shall ensure that I tell her personally that it's not a problem.'

'Thank you, Archie.'

'Now, I think, we should go upstairs. It's been a rather momentous evening for you.'

And for Ishbel, Celia thought.

'She's asleep at last,' Mary Louise announced, entering the room where Rory was anxiously waiting. She was about to close the door behind her, then thought better of it.

'Thank God,' Rory said, concern etched deeply on to his face.

Mary Louise could see how deeply this had affected Rory, and her heart went out to him.

'It was awful, Mary Louise. I can't even begin to tell you how awful.'

'I can imagine,' she sympathized.

'It was so unexpected, and such a shock.' A shudder ran through him.

'Would you like a cup of tea?'

'No, thanks.'

'Something stronger?'

'No. How about yourself?'

'Not for me, either.' She crossed to the mantelpiece and leant against it. This wasn't how she'd envisaged breaking her news to Rory. Perhaps she should leave it till the morning?

Rory also went to the fire and held his hands out against the flames. Despite the heat of the room he was cold.

'I'm absolutely ... devastated by what happened,' Mary Louise stated slowly.

'It was rotten luck.'

Mary Louise didn't agree with that at all. In her opinion, which she shared with the Master, it had been a fortunate occurrence. It was the circumstances she found so dreadful.

'Is Ishbel going to be all right?'

'The doctor was reassuring. But these things can be tricky. We can only hope and pray there aren't any complications.'

'I'm sure there won't be,' Mary Louise said encouragingly, her tone positive.

Rory gave a profound sigh. 'I doubt I'll sleep a wink tonight. How can I after that?'

'Maybe you should have some hot milk?'

'No, honestly. If I tried to get anything down, it would only come back up again.'

She decided then she would tell him her news. It should brighten him a little, lift some of his distress and despondency. 'It hasn't been a totally bad day,' she said softly.

She waited for a reply; but Rory hadn't heard her, lost in his thoughts. 'Rory?'

He roused himself. 'Sorry, did you speak?'

'I said it hasn't been a totally bad day,' she repeated.

'Oh?' his curiosity roused.

She took one of his hands in hers, the hand glowing from its toasting before the fire. 'I'm pregnant. It was confirmed this afternoon.'

It took several moments for that to sink in, then his face lit up. 'There's no doubt?'

'None. I'm definitely pregnant. Well and truly so.'

'Mary Louise, I . . .' He stopped, lost for words.

'Pleased?'

'You know I am. I just wish . . .'

'I know.'

He swept her into his arms, holding her tightly, yet carefully at the same time. 'Duchess,' he breathed.

And with that he kissed her, a kiss full of tenderness and joy. 'I said if we were only patient it would happen,' he husked when the kiss was over.

'And you were right – know-all!'

He laughed, before kissing her again, savouring the sweetness of her lips and mouth, thankful she was his wife and he her husband. As she had said, it hadn't been a totally bad day after all. Catastrophe, followed by elation and sublime happiness.

What a strange old world it was, he reflected as the kiss went on.

'Perhaps you'll sleep now,' she murmured, laying her head against his shoulder.

Which later he did.

'How are you today?' Celia asked Ishbel, who was reclining against a number of plump pillows.

'A lot better, thank you, Mrs Lindsay,' Ishbel responded with a smile.

'The doctor's pleased with your progress. He's allowing you to get up tomorrow, I understand.'

Ishbel nodded. 'How's Jess?

'Having a whale of a time. She and Rory are out having a stroll. He's taken her to the gorilla woods.' That was the name Jessica had given to a nearby wood because she'd thought it so dark and forbidding she'd commented, much to Rory's delight and others he'd told, gorillas must surely live there.

'She'll enjoy that,' Ishbel laughed.

'Quite an imagination, your Jessica,' Celia said, drawing up a chair and sitting beside Ishbel's chair.

'Oh, she has.'

'From her mother?'

'Possibly.'

Celia tactfully didn't pursue that line of conversation. 'The Master and I have been talking and have decided to make you a proposal.'

'A proposal!'

'An idea I came up with actually.' She paused, then said: 'How would you like to come and work for us here at Drum House?'

Ishbel was flabbergasted. 'Doing what?'

'As a housemaid. Sarah, who's been with us for three years, is getting married shortly, which means her position will be falling vacant. It's yours if you wish.'

'But . . . I've no experience as a domestic!'

'The staff will soon train you,' Celia explained.

469

Excitement thrilled through Ishbel. Working at Drum House! 'What about Jessica?'

'There's an excellent local school. And she wouldn't be any trouble round the house. Everyone, including the Master and myself, relishes having her here. She breathes a bit of life into the old place.'

How wonderful it would be for Jessica to live at Drum House, Ishbel thought. All that fresh air and those extensive grounds to play in. It would be a complete change to the soot-laden atmosphere and dirty streets of Glasgow.

Celia stated the wage she was willing to pay. 'That includes all board, of course, for the pair of you,' she spelt out.

'Oh, Mrs Lindsay,' Ishbel breathed. 'This is tremendous.'

'You'll take it, then?'

'Yes, please!'

Celia laughed throatily at her obvious enthusiasm. 'Rory said you'd jump at the chance.'

'And how! When do I start?'

'Not until you're fully recovered. I insist on that. But there's no rush, is there?'

'I was thinking about my house and rent,' Ishbel confessed.

'I've already discussed that with Rory. He'll go through to Glasgow and terminate your agreement with the factor, paying off any balance that's required. At the same time he'll arrange for your clothes and furnishings to be brought here by removers.'

A lump clogged Ishbel's throat. This was the answer to her prayers. Between her miscarriage and this all her difficulties had been resolved. 'I can't thank you enough,' she stuttered.

Celia rose and smoothed down the front of her floral white morning frock. 'Thanks aren't necessary. You'll be a tremendous asset to the household. Neither the Master nor I have any doubts about that. Now I must get on; I have things to do.'

A housemaid at Drum House, Ishbel reflected when

Celia was gone. And Jessica welcomed with open arms!

It was absolutely perfect.

Meg laid the small bunch of flowers on Cully's grave, then stepped back several paces.

It's all turned out well, Cully, she said mentally, addressing her dead husband. Vincent and I are getting on famously of late; we've become quite a couple, unlike the way we were. He just can't do enough for me, literally dances attendance at times. But it's not just that; it's the consideration on his part, and the affection.

Meg sighed. It's not the same as when you were alive, of course; it will never be like that again, and he could certainly never replace you. But I am happy, of a sort, the happiest I've been since you left me.

She thought of Vincent, and smiled. Ever since that day at the loch things had just got better and better between them. And now Ishbel and Jessica were back in the vicinity . . . well, that was simply icing on the cake. If only Rowan could return from the grave.

Ishbel's haemorrhage had worried her, but Ishbel was now as fit as a flea again and settled into her duties at Drum House where she, too, had pronounced herself happy. She'd been over there several times to see them, and they to see her and Vincent.

'Everything's going to be all right from now on,' she said aloud to the grave. 'I'm sure of it.'

In her mind's eye she saw Cully smiling at her, and she smiled in return. He would always be the only man for her, but in the mean time life went on and there was Vincent, of whom she was becoming more and more fond.

I understand, it seemed to her Cully said.

'I knew you would.'

Meg drew in a deep breath and turned away from the graveside. She had some shopping to do and had arranged to call in on Fee for a cup of tea and slice of cake.

She flexed her hands, which weren't too bad that

particular day, nor were her other areas of arthritis.

She walked stiffly away, humming to herself. She'd buy Vincent a treat for his tea, she thought.

Chapter Thirteen

Rory spotted Celia emerging from the train and hurried towards her. When she saw him she smiled broadly and waved.

'Only a small case here. The others are in the luggage-van,' she informed him as he arrived at her side.

Rory dived into the first-class compartment and retrieved the case in question, then together the pair of them made their way along the platform to where the rest of her luggage had been put out and was now being loaded aboard a trolley.

'Everything here?' Rory queried of her.

She cast an eye over the trolley and nodded.

'That's fine, thank you,' Rory said to the hovering guard, who seconds later sent the train on its way.

'It's wonderful being back in Scotland. How I've missed it,' Celia declared as they started towards the exit and the Rolls waiting outside.

'And it's wonderful having you back,' Rory told her truthfully. It was a little over four months since she and the Master had gone to London where the pair of them had been busy ever since.

She looked tired, Rory thought, and extremely pale. All the hard work she'd been involved with recently had clearly taken its toll.

'How's the Minister?' Rory enquired, referring to Archie, who'd become a minister without portfolio in the National Government formed by Stanley Baldwin the previous June. It was a coalition that included four National Liberals.

'Busy, busy, busy,' Celia replied. 'He's run off his feet from first thing in the morning till last thing at night.'

'But is he enjoying it?'

Celia flashed Rory another broad smile. 'Hugely. Loving every moment.'

'That's fine, then. And what about your filming?'

'As you know, I made two films, going straight from one to the other. I found them exhausting, but rewarding at the same time.'

'Did you come across Gracie Fields?' he asked eagerly. He'd read in the newspapers that Gracie had also been filming at Ealing Studios for the same company as Celia.

'I did indeed. We lunched together on several occasions. She's a real sweetie. You couldn't meet a more genuine and charming person. I adored her.'

'I'm a great fan,' Rory confessed.

'I remembered you once mentioning that; which is why I've brought you her autographed photo.'

Rory hesitated in mid-stride, his expression one of disbelief. 'You have?'

Celia laughed. 'I thought you'd appreciate it.'

'Appreciate it! I'm completely bowled over. I'll have Mary Louise buy a silver frame, and we'll display the photograph slap bang on the centre of the mantelpiece.'

'So it won't be missed by anyone visiting?' Celia remarked drily.

'Precisely!'

Arriving at the car, Rory helped Celia inside, then stowed the luggage in the boot, after which he tipped the porter.

'How are Mary Louise and the twins?' Celia enquired as Rory switched on the engine. The twins had been born shortly before Celia and Archie had travelled south. They'd been christened Calum, after Rory's father, and Rowena. Rory had initially intended calling the girl Rowan, then changed his mind thinking the name might be an unlucky one.

'All of them in the pink, the twins thriving beautifully. They're both bonny babies.'

Celia smiled to hear the pride in his voice. 'I'm looking forward to seeing them. And what about Ishbel?'

'Never better.' It was now two years since Ishbel had joined the staff at Drum House.

'And Jessica?'

'Growing all the time. She's shot up quite a bit since you were last here.' Jessica would be eight on her next birthday.

Celia opened the handbag she was carrying and took out her cigarette-case. Her lighter briefly flared.

Rory glanced in the rear-view mirror when she coughed, a hacking cough that came from deep within her chest. He frowned. 'Still got the cough, I see.'

'Now, no lectures, please.'

Eyes sparking with amusement, she inhaled again.

'Can I say something?'

'Would it make any difference if I said you couldn't?' she teased.

He smiled, enjoying the banter between them which he'd sorely missed while she was away. 'You look worn out,' he stated.

'It was a long, tedious and tiring journey.'

'It's more than that,' he went on, glancing again in the rear-view mirror. 'I think you've been working too hard. You must try to get some rest. Can you have some time off before this stage-play?'

Her face lit up. 'You mean *An Ideal Husband* by Oscar Wilde. Well, rehearsals start quite soon. I'm taking the part of Mrs Cheveley, who's a complete bitch. The villainess of the piece. I shall be hoping to upstage the rest of the cast and steal all the notices.'

'You intend doing that?'

'With bells on,' she declared, laughing again.

'I understand there's the possibility of a transfer to the West End.'

'Oh, yes, if we're fortunate,' Celia said softly, puffing on her cigarette, her crimson-painted nails gleaming with reflected light. 'We open at the Lyceum in Edinburgh, followed by an eight-week tour. If all goes well, it'll be Shaftesbury Avenue after that.'

She paused, then added tensely: 'I need that transfer, Rory, to re-establish myself in the position I was in before my health let me down. This won't be a comeback exactly; more of a re-emergence.'

'Then, I wish you all the luck in the world.'

'Thank you,' she smiled and, unseen by Rory, crossed two fingers.

'I expected you home earlier,' Mary Louise commented as Rory shrugged himself out of his coat.

'Celia asked me to stay and go over her lines with her.'

'Did she indeed!'

'I've done it before. You know that.'

Mary Louise shot him a sideways glance, but didn't reply.

'How are the twins?'

'Rowena woke up a little while ago, but she's gone off again.'

'Anything wrong?' he asked in sudden concern.

Mary Louise smiled. He really was the most caring father. He doted on his children, idolized them. But, then, so, too, did she. 'Nothing,' she assured him.

Rory ran a hand over his face; he was dead beat, more than ready for bed. 'I think I'll just go and look in on them,' he declared.

That was precisely what Mary Louise had expected him to say. He always looked in on them first thing when he came home late. 'I'll come with you,' she told him.

The door to the twins' room was ajar. Rory crept in with Mary Louise behind him. Together they stood staring down at the pair of identical cots.

An overwhelming sense of love filled Rory as he gazed at Calum and Rowena, the latter with her thumb in her mouth. A profound feeling of peace descended on him.

'A penny for them?' Mary Louise whispered.

He reached out and took her hand in his, gently squeezing it. 'I was just thinking how fortunate I am. You, and these two – who could ask for more?'

He was a lovely man, she thought. One in a million. She'd been lucky to find him.

'Now, come away before you wake them up,' she said, again in a whisper.

He stayed for a few further seconds, staring at his offspring who were illuminated by the light from the hallway. Then he and Mary Louise tiptoed away.

'You look tired,' she said when they were once more in the kitchen.

'I am.'

'Are you hungry?'

He shook his head.

'A cup of tea?'

'If you have one with me.'

'I will.'

He fell into a chair from where he watched her put on the kettle.

Mary Louise became aware of Rory studying her and blushed slightly, misinterpreting his look. 'I will get my figure back soon, I promise,' she said hesitantly.

'Eh?'

'My figure.' She smoothed down her dress, loathing the bulges she could feel.

'I was just thinking how beautiful you looked,' he declared softly.

'Beautiful!' He must be joking.

'A Mother Earth woman. Very attractive.'

Relief flooded through her with the realization he was being totally sincere. 'Mother Earth or not, I'll get my figure back just as soon as is humanly possible.'

He rose, went to her and wrapped her in his arms. 'Don't worry about that too much, Mary Louise; I'm not. Anyway, you're still feeding. That's bound to keep you plumped up for a bit.'

'But I feel so . . . like a bloody great whale!'

477

He laughed. 'If that's the case, then I must say I like whales. They're very sexy.'

She twisted round to gaze into his face. 'You really mean that?'

'I do.'

'I—'

He stopped her by placing a finger over her mouth. 'I do,' he repeated. Then, removing his finger, kissed her lightly on the lips. 'Now, what about that tea?'

She was spooning tea from the caddy when she heard him, now returned to his chair, mutter something. 'What was that?'

His expression was one of pure innocence. 'I said I'll have to change your nickname.'

'To what?'

A teasing smile lifted the corners of his mouth. 'I rather thought . . . Moby-Dick?'

He roared with laughter, and was still laughing when she pounced on him to beat him over the head with a cushion.

But it had been said in fun, as she well knew.

'The Master wants you to ring him this evening at the Belgravia number,' Burnford said to Rory.

'Me?'

'Those were his instructions. And you're to do so without informing the Mistress.'

'What about?'

Burnford shrugged. 'He didn't take me into his confidence. Merely said that you were to ring.'

'And not tell the Mistress?'

'That's right.'

How odd, Rory thought. 'I'll do it straight away,' he declared, knowing that Celia was in the bath.

'How's Celia?' the Master asked when they'd been connected and brief pleasantries exchanged.

'Tired.'

'How tired, Rory?'

'Fairly, sir. Not that she's complained, but the strain is showing.'

'The travelling?'

'That isn't helping, sir. She could certainly do without it.'

There was a pause, then the Master said: 'I can't manage to make it up; I'm far too busy in the House. But I certainly shall for the opening night; I've promised her that. So I'll tell you what: we'll keep this conversation to ourselves, and I'll ring her later tonight and insist she take a hotel for the remainder of rehearsals. Furthermore, I'd like you to stay at the hotel to keep an eye on her. How do you feel about that?'

Rory was surprised. 'If that's what you wish, sir.'

'I think it for the best. I wanted her to have a rest after those films she did, then this play came up and there was no talking her out of it. She's not a strong woman, Rory, never has been.'

'No, sir,' Rory agreed.

'You have my full authority to bully her if need be. You hear?'

'Yes, sir.'

'But she must ease back a little.'

'I'll ensure she does. You can rely on me, sir.'

Warmth replaced the worry in the Master's voice. 'I know I can, Rory. Where is she now?'

'In her bath, sir.'

'Fine. I'll ring again in about an hour and talk to her then. Meanwhile you'd better hang about so she can speak to you afterwards.'

'I understand, sir.'

'Goodbye.'

'Goodbye, sir.'

Rory hung up, and stared thoughtfully at the telephone. Mary Louise wasn't going to be pleased with this development, but it was unavoidable. She would manage all right while he was away.

He smiled, part of him pleased with what would be more or less a paid holiday, but he'd miss the twins and

Mary Louise. Luckily he knew that she would understand.

Celia was furious and not attempting to hide it. 'The lighting's a mess,' she snapped at Rory, joining him in the stalls. The cast were in the middle of a stagger-through prior to opening the following night.

He didn't reply, but stared concernedly at her.

'The chap on the board is an imbecile. We'll never get it ready in time.'

'Surely that's Jack's problem, not yours. He must be aware if something's wrong.' Jack was the director.

She glared at him. 'Jack's an imbecile as well. I've completely lost confidence in him.'

It was plain to Rory how overwrought Celia was. Nor was she the only one; the rest of the cast were equally keyed up. He wondered if it was always like this before an opening.

'Now, where are my cigarettes?' Celia muttered, rummaging through her handbag.

'Maybe you left them in your dressing-room?'

She swore. 'Must have.'

'I'll go and get them for you.'

'Thank you, Rory.'

He placed a comforting hand on her arm. 'You're going to be superb, Celia, I promise you. You'll knock them for six.'

'I wish we had more rehearsal time.'

'It'll all turn out fine, honest.'

She worried a nail. 'If only I could believe that.' She sighed. 'I'm nothing but a bundle of nerves. God knows what I'll be like tomorrow night. Probably be shaking so badly I won't be able to speak.'

'No, you won't. I'd bet on that.'

She glanced anxiously at the stage where there was yet another halt in the proceedings while Jack and the lighting man were deep in huddled conversation. 'Imbeciles,' she repeated.

'Would you like some coffee to go with the cigarette?'

'Please.'

He was rising when she now reached out and took hold of him. 'You're a darling.'

'Don't worry,' he said with heavy emphasis.

She smiled after him as he hurried off.

Rory stretched out on the bed and put his hands behind his neck. What a day! They hadn't left the theatre till almost midnight, then Celia had asked him to keep her company downstairs while she had a drink – that had become four before he'd finally succeeded in packing her off to her suite. They were due back at the theatre directly after breakfast where, among other things, Celia was having some alteration done to a costume she'd suddenly decided didn't fit properly.

Rory had never heard such moaning and snideness. Every member of the cast was complaining. Henry Agate and Edward Marlowe had fallen out; so, too, had Penelope Brookfield and Florence Fetherston who were playing Lady Chiltern and Lady Markby respectively. At one point Jack had lost his temper and shrieked at the entire cast, which had shocked them into silence for all of two minutes.

'The man's raving,' Edward had confided to Celia, tapping his temple. He'd then given Rory the sort of smile that had promptly made Rory sit down, much to Celia's amusement.

A paid holiday, Rory thought ruefully. That's how he'd imagined this was going to be. He couldn't have been more mistaken. And it would go on for some time yet, because the Master and he had already decided that he'd accompany Celia throughout the tour.

Mary Louise had not been amused by that news. Rory had been able to soften the blow somewhat by informing her that he'd be earning extra money while away, but it had not been easy. He was missing her enormously and was always eager to have news of the twins. Luckily the extra money would go straight into their savings, which had become more or less static since Mary Louise had had to give up work.

He wouldn't have minded a bath, but that meant traipsing down the corridor. Unlike Celia's suite, he thought. All she had to do was drift from one room to another. Still, his own small room wasn't at all bad, though the view of a brick wall left a lot to be desired.

Tomorrow night, opening night, soon to be upon them.

The next thing he knew, it was morning. He'd fallen asleep on top of his bed with his clothes on.

A quick glance at his watch told him it was time to be up and about. If he hurried, he could just fit in that bath he'd been too lazy to have the night before. He grabbed a towel and his sponge-bag and raced off down the corridor, praying the bathroom would be free.

He was lucky. It was.

'How do you feel?'

Celia glanced up at Rory. 'That is a really stupid question.'

He grinned, thinking she was quite right. It was obvious how she felt.

He gazed about her dressing-room, which was festooned with cards and telegrams. Some were jutting out from the edges of her huge make-up mirror, others tin-tacked to the walls. And there were masses of flowers – boxes, baskets and bouquets of them. The dressing-room smelled like a summer garden.

Celia lit a cigarette. 'My stomach's tied in knots,' she confessed.

'Is there anything I can get you?'

Her gaze shifted to the bar Rory had set up in preparation for the visitors they'd have backstage after the show. 'I'd love a gin,' she murmured.

'I doubt that's wise, Celia.'

'Not even a small one?'

'It's up to you of course, but I wouldn't have thought it a good idea.'

She drew deeply on her cigarette. 'I hope Archie made it all right. He wanted to come and see me beforehand, but I said no. Afterwards, I told him; not before.'

'He's bringing a few friends, I understand?'

'He's organized a party of ten.'

Celia glanced up when there was a rap on the door. 'Come in!'

Jack breezed into the room. 'Darling!'

'Jack, dear,' she smiled.

He took her hands and gently raised her to her feet. 'You're going to be sensational tonight, my angel. Quite, quite divine! By the end of the evening you'll have Edinburgh at your feet.'

'Do you really think so?' she murmured coyly.

'In this matter I'm a prophet. Trust me.'

Her eyes, glittering, flicked to Rory, then back to the director. 'Any notes, Jack?'

'None, darling. Just go on there and sweep all before you.' He kissed her on both cheeks. 'See you later.'

'You'll come for a drink?'

'Of course. Wild horses wouldn't keep me away.'

'Fifteen minutes,' the callboy shouted out in the corridor. He then knocked on Celia's door. 'Fifteen minutes, Mrs Lindsay,' he repeated in a deferential manner.

'Right, the two of you shoo. I must get dressed. Send Cathy in to me, will you, Rory?' Cathy was her dresser who'd gone off to do some last-minute pressing.

Jack had left, and Rory was about to follow, when Celia called out. 'Oh, Rory!'

He turned to her.

'Thank you for the flowers.'

He blushed. 'A bit mean by comparison to some you received.'

'They're lovely. And very much appreciated. Thank you again.'

'My pleasure,' he beamed, and left her to it.

'Beginners, please!'

483

The excitement and expectation in the air was incredible, Rory thought. He'd never before experienced anything like it. Camilla the assistant stage manager rushed past muttering to herself. She dived into an open doorway, then reappeared almost immediately to hare back the way she'd come.

'Bloody props man!' she hissed at Rory as she went by. 'Will I do?'

Rory looked round to see Celia, who'd emerged from her dressing-room while Rory's attention was on Camilla.

'I would say so.'

She touched the red wig she was wearing. 'I'm still not a hundred per cent certain about this, but it's too late for a change now.'

Rory agreed.

'I could have got you a seat out front,' she told him.

'I know that. But I'd prefer to watch the show from the wings. That way I'll almost feel as though I'm part of it.'

She smiled in understanding. 'Come on, then. Let's find you a decent spot. And for God's sake keep out of the way when they do the set changes.'

'Don't worry, I've been well warned.'

They went through a door into the wings, which smelled strongly of paint, size, greasepaint and Fuller's Earth. 'Curtain is almost going up,' she whispered to Rory, who nodded.

'If you move about, keep away from the prompt corner,' she further whispered. That was where the deputy stage manager sat running the proceedings.

'House lights out,' the deputy stage manager said quietly.

A nervous Lady Chiltern made a final adjustment to her dress. She was standing on top of a staircase while below her was a brilliantly lighted room full of guests.

Rory glanced over to where Celia was waiting with Lady Markby, the pair of them due to make their entrance together. 'Good luck, Celia,' he whispered to himself.

'Curtain away.'

A round of applause greeted the appearance of the set, which would please the designer.

Mrs Marchmont waited for the applause to start to die down, then came in with the first line. *'Going to the Hartlocks' tonight, Margaret?'*

Lady Basildon replied: *'I suppose so. Are you?'*

Shortly after that Celia and Florence Fetherston made their entrance.

'It seems to be going well,' Celia whispered to Rory.

'Better than well. The audience is lapping it up. You in particular.'

Her face radiated pleasure and self-satisfaction, while renewed confidence bubbled up within her. 'I spotted Archie, so he made it in time. I was ever so worried his train might be late.'

Rory had managed to peep at the audience and had been startled by the black hole that comprised the auditorium. The faces he'd seen had been blurred and shadowy. He assumed it must be different on stage.

'Your call, Mrs Lindsay,' the callboy, who'd sidled up to them, whispered.

'Speak to you again in the interval,' Celia breathed, and took herself off to where she made her next entrance.

'It is love, Robert. Love, and only love. For both of us a new life is beginning.'

As the concluding words of the play were delivered by Lady Chiltern, the curtain began slowly to drop. It was about halfway down when thunderous applause erupted.

The moment the curtain touched the stage the rest of the cast, waiting in the wings, came onstage for the curtain call. When the line-up had been formed the curtain rose again swiftly in complete contrast to its previous descent.

The applause swelled in volume as the cast took their bow, after which the curtain rattled down.

The cast grinned unashamedly at one another, for they knew they had a hit on their hands. On the third curtain call the principals took it in turn to step forward and take individual bows. For Celia's the sound was tumultuous. In a dramatic gesture she blew the audience a kiss, then stepped back into line.

Rory couldn't have been more thrilled by the play's reception, and how Celia appeared to have been singled out. He, too, was clapping loudly, banging his hands together. He sniffed, aware there was more than a hint of tears in his eyes.

Up and down went the curtain, eighteen times in all. Then Rory, as instructed, stole away to be ready for Celia's arrival back in her dressing-room.

It was nearly ten minutes later before Celia turned up, positively glowing with triumph.

'Well?' she demanded.

'It can't fail to be transferred. I'd put a year's wages on it.'

She gave a deep throaty laugh. 'And me?'

'You had me spellbound, Celia. Transfixed. You were simply ... unbelievable.'

'Sweet darling Rory,' she cooed and, crossing to him, pecked him on the cheek.

'You can have that gin now.'

'I want a gallon of the damned stuff!'

'Well, maybe not quite that,' he declared, busying himself at the bar.

There were loud voices in the corridor outside. Actors congratulating one another, members of the audience congratulating them. There was a great deal of laughter overlain with a definite tinge of hysteria.

Celia began to unpin her wig, which she then placed on its block. With a shake of her head she partially released her hair, which had become plastered to her skull.

A breathless Cathy, the dresser, arrived. 'It's pandemonium out there,' she stated.

'I can hear,' Celia told her.

'Will you change now?'

Before Celia could reply there was a rap on the door. 'Are you decent?' the Master enquired, raising his voice to be heard above the hubbub.

'Come in!' Celia cried in reply.

The door was thrown open, and the Master, with others crowding behind him, came striding towards Celia whom he gathered into his arms. They gazed adoringly at one another.

'You were fantastic,' he declared. 'I'm speechless with admiration. Congratulations, my love.'

He kissed her on the lips, a kiss that conveyed the full depth of his feelings to her and those watching.

After that Celia's hand was grabbed and shaken effusively by all those in the Master's party.

Rory was kept busy at the bar pouring drinks as more and more people crowded into the dressing-room till eventually it was completely jam-packed.

'Bertie!' Celia squealed when a tiny man elbowed his way through the throng. It was Bertie Higham, the West End's foremost and most famous producer. His praise was lavish in the extreme. Her eyes opened wide when he actually compared her to the 'Divine Sarah'.

'So what's the verdict, Bertie?' Celia asked breathlessly.

'You must definitely transfer. It would be a catastrophe for you not to. *An Ideal Husband* shall replace my current production at the Queen's.'

'Aaahhh!' Celia breathed.

'A deal has already been struck. All that's needed now is the formality of pen on paper which shall be done tomorrow morning before I return to town.'

Celia grabbed Bertie and gave him a big kiss on the forehead. 'You couldn't have made me happier.'

'And you will make me happy where I appreciate it most. In the pocket,' he riposted, and laughed uproariously.

'What about billing?' Celia queried pragmatically.

'You shall be the star, my darling. Top of the bill, with everyone else below.'

Celia's expression as she heard that was one of pure feline gratification.

She'd achieved what she'd set out to do, Rory thought, having overheard the conversation. She'd upstaged the rest of the cast and, as would transpire, stolen the notices.

'Will you join us for supper?' a flushed and delighted Master asked Bertie. 'We've booked a table.'

'Of course! As long as you're paying,' Bertie joked in reply.

The Master clapped Bertie on the shoulder. 'That I will gladly. Now, and again in London after that opening night.'

'Done,' declared Bertie, shaking hands with the Master.

The Queen's Theatre, Shaftesbury Avenue, in a Bertie Higham presentation, Celia thought with glee.

Rory sat in the Rolls outside the restaurant gazing at the bright lights within and listened to the muted hum of conversation interspersed with the tinkling of glasses. The one note of sadness – as far as he was concerned anyway – was that the play was bound to have a long run in the West End, which would keep Celia away from Drum House for some considerable time. But no matter, he consoled himself, she would be happy.

Celia had certainly been happy during the drive from the theatre, she and the Master sitting in the back, talking and canoodling like a couple of love-birds, which made him smile with pleasure for both of them.

How radiant Celia had looked as the Master assisted her into the car, clad in a sheath of French blue silk that had highlighted her figure.

The world could indeed be a marvellous place, he told himself. And he had been lucky to find this niche in it.

He wondered what Newcastle would be like, as that was the play's first tour-stop.

'Lucky,' he repeated aloud.

'The last performance before London,' Celia said to Rory from behind the screen where she was being dressed by a woman called Pat. During the tour Rory had become more and more involved in Celia's affairs until he was now virtually acting as a sort of manager. He fussed over her the way a mother hen would its only chick.

Rory paused to smile ruefully. 'Life at Drum House is going to seem awfully quiet after all this.'

'At least you'll be home with Mary Louise and the twins. Are they still well?'

'I had another letter this morning. They're fine. But I do miss them.'

Pat dashed out from behind the screen to fetch an article of apparel, then scurried back again.

When she emerged Rory studied Celia whom he thought he'd never seen looking better. Underneath the stage make-up, her skin had a new glow to it, while her eyes were clear and sparkling. Success was certainly having its effect on her well-being.

'Fifteen minutes,' the callboy shouted outside, followed by the usual knock on her door. 'Fifteen minutes, Mrs Lindsay.'

'Pass my cigarette-case, would you, Rory?' Celia requested.

The case was lying on top of her dressing-table. He picked it and her lighter up and passed them to her.

'Damn!' Celia swore on finding the case empty. 'Rory, could you get me a fresh packet from my handbag?'

'There isn't one,' he informed her after looking in the bag.

She pulled a face. 'I must have left it in the hotel. Be a dear and nip over to the pub and buy me another. And hurry, will you! The fifteen's been called.'

'On my way,' he replied.

Backstage once again he tapped on her door. 'Celia?'

There was no reply.

He knocked on the door again, and when there was still no reply he opened it and glanced inside, thinking Celia might have trotted off to the lavatory.

But she hadn't. Pat had gone, and Celia was sitting at her dressing-table with her head resting between her hands.

Asleep! he thought, entering quietly. Amazing when the five must have either just been called or was about to be. He must wake her at once or she'd be 'off'.

He paused to smile down at her. How peaceful she looked, and serene. Even more beautiful than usual. It was a pity to rouse her, but of course he had to. He would insist that she went directly to bed after curtain down, for she was obviously very tired. The part must be taking more out of her than he'd realized.

'Celia?' He reached out and touched her on the shoulder. 'Celia?'

She didn't respond.

She was not only asleep, but soundly so. This time he shook her gently. 'Celia?'

Her body shifted slightly, one arm falling from its position to dangle and sway downwards.

He stared at her in horror. 'Celia!' he croaked, grasping her by the shoulders and shaking her quite roughly. Her body was limp, and somehow strange to the touch. 'Oh, my God!' he muttered, shaking her again.

She slid from her chair, but he succeeded in catching her before she crashed to the floor. Her eyes remained closed, her look of serenity intact.

He knew then, beyond any question of doubt, that she was dead.

'I had considered resigning from the Cabinet and the House but changed my mind when I realized that would only give me more time to brood. I decided the best thing, to keep my sanity, was to continue working,' the Master said to a grim and gaunt-faced Rory, the pair of them out walking at the Master's request.

'Besides,' the Master went on softly, 'I doubt Celia would have approved of my packing it all in.'

'I agree with you,' Rory said.

'Grouse!' the Master exclaimed, pointing with his stick. A brace of birds, disturbed by their presence, raced across the heather.

490

'It was a lovely service,' Rory declared quietly, a catch in his voice. The service had taken place the previous Sunday in the local church, which had been packed out for the occasion.

'So was the one in London,' the Master stated. That one had been held in St Paul's, Covent Garden, known as 'the actors' church'. 'All her chums were there. It was a grand turnout.'

'I'm pleased you scattered her ashes at Drum. I'm sure that's what she would have wanted.'

The Master smiled thinly at Rory. 'That's what I thought, which is why I did it.' He made a sweeping gesture with his stick. 'Although an urban creature, she adored this place. She often told me she found great peace and tranquillity here.'

'A rotten heart-attack,' Rory muttered, shaking his head in bewilderment.

'She was never a well person. I only wish . . .' The Master sucked in a breath. 'I only wish she could have opened in London before it happened. She deserved that.'

Rory murmured his agreement.

The Master resumed walking, and Rory followed suit. 'I suppose the staff are wondering what's going to happen now?'

'They have speculated, sir.'

'Well, I shall inform them later they have nothing to be concerned about. Although I shan't be coming here as often – too many raw and painful memories, I'm afraid – I shall be maintaining a full complement of staff.'

Although Rory had mixed feelings on the subject himself, he was none the less relieved to hear that.

'I have to admit I did think of selling, but it is the ancestral home which I should keep in the family, even though I don't have a direct heir to pass it on to. I had hoped, notwithstanding her career, that one day Celia and I would have a child but . . .' He shrugged. 'It wasn't to be.'

He might marry again some day, in time, when the pain

had subsided, Rory thought. He hoped that would be the case. The Master was too young to go through the rest of his life alone.

The Master swished at a dandelion with his stick, slicing the head from the weed which went spinning away.

'Anyway,' the Master said, 'that brings us to you and the reason for this *tête-à-tête*. Celia was extremely fond of you, as I'm sure you're well aware. Said you were like a brother to her.'

'We did have an affinity,' Rory agreed.

'And you were always very kind to her, providing her with the company and companionship she needed when I wasn't there. Particularly during those last rehearsals and the tour.'

'We got on well together,' Rory said tightly.

'Which is why I wish to make a gesture on her behalf. A thank-you, from her and me.'

'A gesture?' Rory queried.

'She mentioned once that you and your wife hope to set up in business one day. Is that correct?'

'It's our ambition,' Rory admitted, although it was more Mary Louise's than his own. He would have been content to be chauffeur to the Lindsays for the remainder of his working life. But that had changed now that Celia had died. Like the Master, Drum House was full of raw and painful memories for him.

'I want to give you some capital, Rory: a thank-you from Celia and myself,' the Master stated.

'Some capital?' a bemused Rory echoed.

'Yes, I had five thousand pounds in mind.'

Rory stopped and stared in astonishment at the Master. Five thousand pounds! 'I couldn't . . .'

'Oh, yes, you can. For her sake,' the Master interjected.

'But it's so much!'

'I can well afford it, Rory. And your acceptance would please me. So what do you say?'

Rory swallowed hard. 'Thank you, sir. Very much.'

'Good, that's settled, then. When we get back I'll give you a personal cheque which you can lodge with your bank. You do have a bank account?'

'Oh, yes, sir. For our savings.'

The Master gazed off into the distance. 'She was a wonderful woman, Rory. I'm going to miss her dreadfully.'

As was he, Rory thought. As was he.

'Five thousand pounds!' Mary Louise gasped, staring at the cheque Rory had handed her.

'To buy the business we want.'

'I can't believe it.' Mary Louise looked delighted.

'I don't think that's quite the appropriate reaction,' Rory said softly. 'It was Celia's death, after all, that gave us the money.'

'You're right, I know. But it is a dream come true.'

Chapter Fourteen

'There's a Mr Hamilton at the door to see you,' Burnford announced to Ishbel, who'd just entered the servants' kitchen.

She frowned. 'I don't think I know any Mr Hamilton.'

'He asked for you by name.'

She took off her apron, threw it over a chair, smoothed down her hair and went to the door where a man was standing with his back to her. She recognized him the instant he turned round.

'Hello,' said Gray.

It had been a long time since he'd called on them in Glasgow. Four years? No, five. 'How are you?

'Fine.' He shifted nervously. 'And you?'

'Never better. But come in.'

He removed the cap he was wearing, wiped his feet on the mat and stepped inside.

'An old friend who's been away,' Ishbel explained to a hovering and curious Burnford.

She introduced the pair of them, then said she'd put the kettle on. Burnford, thinking they might wish to be alone, excused himself, saying he had things to do.

'Well, this *is* a surprise,' Ishbel stated, laying out cups and saucers. 'How long are you home for?'

'Good this time. I've decided to give up the sea. I got tired of it in the end. It's ashore for me from now on.'

How tanned he was, she thought enviously, and even better-looking than she remembered. He'd aged quite a bit, too; but, then, no doubt so had she. It was five years after all.

'Staying with your folks?' she enquired.

He nodded. 'I hope you don't mind me calling like this. Perhaps I should have written first?'

'No. We're not all that busy nowadays. Not since the Mistress died.'

'I heard about that from my mum. I'm sorry.'

'It was a great loss. Why don't you sit down?'

He did, then glanced around. 'It's a bit different from the last place where I visited you.'

She laughed. Drum House was indeed very different from the tenement in Glasgow.

'How's the old lady? Your Aunt Dot.'

Ishbel's face clouded. 'She's dead, too, I'm afraid.'

'I'm grieved to hear that. I liked her.'

'She was very good to me and Jessica when we needed her. I miss her a lot.'

'But now you're happily settled here?'

'Very happily. As is Jessica.'

He gave her a rather sad smile. 'It was actually about Jessica that I came. I was wondering if I could see her.'

Ishbel picked up the biscuit-tin from the shelf where it lived. 'Of course, though she's at school right now.'

'I realized that. I wanted to speak to you first in case you had objections. She is your daughter now, after all; I wouldn't want to do anything against your wishes.'

She considered that thoughtful of him. 'You're looking very fit,' she commented.

'That's life at sea for you – hard graft, and plenty of it.'

He'd changed, she thought. He'd become more introverted, and the sad smile reflected an inner sadness that hadn't been there previously. 'Did you ever marry?' she asked.

He shook his head. 'What about you?'

'Me, neither.'

He watched her wipe a stray wisp of hair from her forehead. She was fuller in the figure than he recalled, but it suited her.

'Are you working?' she enquired.

'No. I worked for my dad before I went off, but he became ill and sold the business.'

'So what are you looking for?'

'Anything, really. I'm not all that fussed.'

She placed a plate of biscuits in front of them. 'Made those myself.'

He regarded them, thinking they looked delicious.

'Normally Cook makes everything, but she's off on holiday which gave me the chance to dabble.'

'I hope I'm not holding you up?' he queried suddenly in concern.

'Not at all. The Master has only been up once since his wife died, which means there's little to do. Though I'm sure that will be changing shortly. His sister is coming here from Kenya – a spinster, who'll be taking charge of Drum. She's expected in about a fortnight.'

'From Kenya,' Gray mused.

'We're all looking forward to Miss Maisie's arrival. She's a large jolly woman, according to Burnford who's met her. Great fun, he says. So she should liven things up a bit.'

'How is . . . Jessica?' Gray asked quietly.

'You won't recognize her, or hardly anyway. She's shooting up like a weed.'

'I've often thought about her, and wondered how she was getting on.'

'And Rowan?'

Gray's lips thinned. 'I've often thought about her, too. How things might have turned out differently if . . .' He trailed off and shrugged. 'Unfortunately the past can't be rewritten, mistakes undone. All we can do is accept what's happened and go on living as best we can.'

Amen, Ishbel thought, with a lump in her throat.

'So when can I see Jessica?'

'Today, if you like. You can come with me when I collect her from school.'

His face lit up. 'Lovely.'

'How did you get here?' she asked.

'By bicycle. It's outside.'

'We'll go in Rory's car, then. It's an old runabout that he bought a little while ago and taught me to drive.' She glanced at the clock. 'There are a few hours yet before Jessica's due out.'

'I can go away and come back again.'

'There's no need for that. You can sit here until it's time; or go for a walk in the grounds, which are fairly extensive.'

'Then, that's what I'll do,' he said.

'Which will leave me free for the few bits and pieces I have to do.'

They drank their tea and chatted, he recounting various adventures he'd had at sea, describing exotic places he'd been to, all of which she found fascinating.

It was a good day for a stroll, he thought later as he wandered away from the house. He paused for a few seconds when the sun suddenly broke forth, to let the sunshine wash over his face, then he continued on his way.

'You drive well,' Gray commented.

'That's what Rory says; which, coming from him, is praise indeed. Do you drive yourself?'

'I used to, but haven't for years. Still, I suppose I'd quickly pick it up again. Like riding a bike, I'm sure it's something you never forget.'

He glanced sideways at Ishbel, thinking there was an easiness about her that he didn't recall from their previous meeting. There was something about her which made him feel relaxed and cheerful. It was a good feeling.

'Don't forget Jessica believes her father was called Will,' Ishbel reminded him.

'I won't.'

'She's still got that teddy bear you gave her. It's remained a great favourite.'

Gray was delighted to hear that. 'I haven't brought her anything on this occasion, I'm afraid.'

'If you want, we can stop by a shop and you can buy her

a sweet as a special treat. I keep her rationed on that score as I don't wish her teeth to be ruined. But today can be an exception.'

'Then, a sweet it is. And what about you? Do you like chocolates?'

She grinned. 'And how!'

'In which case you'll get a special treat as well.'

'There's no need . . .'

'I know that,' he interjected. 'But let me. In fact I insist.'

In the event he bought her the largest box of chocolates the shop had for sale and Jessica a whole bagful of sweets.

Jessica squealed with pretended fright as Gray whirled her round and round. It was his second visit to Drum House, having arranged with Ishbel to take her and Jessica for a Sunday walk. On his return he was having lunch with the staff which Mrs Murchie, the cook, back from holiday, was preparing. When he finally set Jessica down she went running off to pick some wild flowers she'd spotted.

'She's a terrific child,' he declared to Ishbel.

'Who's certainly taken to you. The pair of you get on like the proverbial house on fire.'

'She's fun.'

'She thinks you're tremendous. Have you known many children?'

He shook his head. 'Only when I was a child myself.'

'Well, none the less, you seem to have an affinity with them.'

Gray was delighted.

'Anything come up on the work front yet?' she enquired.

'Not so far. But I'll keep trying. I'm not in a hurry as I have enough to live on for a while, so there's no pressure from that point of view.'

'I'm surprised you've never married,' he said after they'd walked a short way in silence.

'How so?'

'A good-looking woman like yourself. I'd have imagined suitors would have been queuing up.'

She shrugged. 'I'm only twenty-four – hardly an old maid yet.'

He agreed with a laugh.

'It's quiet living at Drum, without too much chance to socialize. I suppose I could go out more than I do, but I'm happy the way things are. And then there's Jessica, of course. Whoever married me would have to take her on.' She thought of Peter. 'There was someone once, but that fell through.'

'Do you regret it?'

'Him? No, I don't believe I do. It simply wasn't to be, that's all.'

Jessica came charging up with the flowers she'd picked. 'For you, Aunt Ishbel,' she said breathlessly, thrusting them at Ishbel.

'Why, thank you!'

'I've had a thought,' said Gray. 'How about us all going to the pictures next Saturday?'

'Yes, please!' cried Jessica, clapping her hands.

'Ishbel?'

'Why not?' she agreed.

'Then, that's settled. The three of us, together.'

A little further on Jessica slipped her hand in Gray's to walk shyly by his side.

He spun his visit out for as long as he could before eventually taking his leave.

'I heard today there's a garage on the market that might suit us,' Mary Louise said to Rory.

'A garage?'

'Only just been put up for sale. The owner is retiring.'

'Whereabouts is it?' Rory queried with a frown.

'Crossbank.'

'It's not one I've ever used,' Rory reflected.

'But don't you think the idea of a garage is a good one? It would be a perfect business for you.'

Rory agreed. The prospect of owning a garage excited

him; he adored tinkering with cars, and was good at it. He'd become quite a mechanic over the years.

'It certainly wouldn't do any harm to see the place. Give it the once-over,' he declared.

'I'll leave the twins with my mother so we can concentrate on what we're looking at.'

A garage, Rory mused.

'Leave it to me. I'll arrange the appointment,' Mary Louise stated with satisfaction. What she didn't tell Rory was that she already had.

'Another dram, Gray?' Vincent enquired solicitously.

'Only if you're having one.'

Vincent chuckled. 'You've talked me into it.'

Meg gazed at Gray over the rim of her sherry-glass. It had been a shock to learn that he'd started calling at Drum House, thinking he'd quietly disappeared all those years ago. Her reactions were mixed: on the one hand there was Rowan, on the other the personable chap sitting in her kitchen. She wasn't quite sure what to make of it all.

'And what about you, my love?' Vincent asked Meg, whose glass was still half-full.

'I'm fine, thank you.'

'A little top-up wouldn't harm.'

She smiled at him. 'No, I'm all right for the moment.'

'Doesn't she look well?' Vincent beamed at Ishbel, referring to Meg.

Ishbel had to agree that her mother did. *Contented* was the word she'd have used to describe Meg.

'We're going out to play housey-housey next weekend,' Vincent informed them.

'It's a bit of a bother with my legs being so bad, but Vincent's ever so helpful,' Meg said.

'She can run like a cat when she wants to,' Vincent winked at Ishbel.

'At least there he can't cheat, which he does all the time when we play games at home,' Meg went on.

'Cheat! Me!' Vincent protested.

'All the time.'

'Meg, how can you tell such fibs?'

'I'm not.' Then to Gray she added: 'They're mostly in my favour so that I win.'

'Nonsense,' Vincent grinned, shaking his head.

'Once a crook always a crook. It's part of his nature,' Meg said, tongue in cheek.

'I take exception to that.'

'Horse traders are all crooks. You told me so yourself.'

'Then, I'm the exception.'

'Baloney!'

Vincent, flushed from the whisky and banter, laughed. 'She's got such a high opinion of me,' he joked.

'At least he cheats in your favour,' Gray said.

'But I don't want him to. I want to win off my own bat.'

'She's far better at games than she realizes. I don't have to cheat,' Vincent declared airily. He darted forward and kissed Meg on the mouth.

Gray was enjoying this, thinking to himself what a lovely jolly atmosphere there was in the house. It positively exuded happiness.

Meg, eyes twinkling, had a sip of sherry. 'You're a terrible man,' she admonished Vincent.

'Terrible,' he agreed.

'Can I have another cake?' Jessica asked.

'No. Yes,' replied Ishbel and Gray simultaneously.

Jess glanced from one to the other, hesitating because it had been Ishbel who'd said no.

'No,' confirmed Ishbel.

'Oh, go on, let her,' Gray pleaded.

'You'd spoil the child.'

He pulled a face. 'Just the one?'

Ishbel gave a long-drawn-out sigh. 'Honestly, I don't know. You're a dreadful influence, Gray Hamilton.'

'So she can have the cake?'

'*One*, and no more.'

'Thanks,' Gray smiled at Ishbel.

For a moment their eyes locked, then both quickly looked away.

'It's just what we want, don't you agree?' Mary Louise said. She and Rory were on their way back from having viewed the garage at Crossburn.

'I must admit I was impressed.'

'He's let it run down over the last few years, but we can soon rebuild the business. We could pay his price and still have enough left over to refurbish.'

'I am tempted,' Rory mused.

'And as time went by we could extend. It struck me that the area on the side could be turned into a car-hire department. Now, there's something that's going to be very up-and-coming in the future.'

'Car hire?'

'We can start off in a small way and develop from there, eventually adding a new car showroom.'

'Here, hold on!' Rory laughed. 'I think you're beginning to let your imagination run away with you.'

Mary Louise's enthusiasm was infectious, Rory thought, picturing the sort of garage she'd been describing: large, gleaming and very successful.

'I don't know if I'm up to such grandiose schemes,' he prevaricated.

'Of course you are.' With me behind you, she told herself. 'You underestimate your abilities, Rory, always have. You're entirely capable of a lot more than you think. Believe me.'

He was still uncertain.

'Believe me,' she repeated, itching to get home and put some of her ideas on paper, do some costings. One thing was certain: she wouldn't pay the asking price unless absolutely necessary. She'd do her damnedest to knock down Mr Naismith, the owner. But they should move fast, clinch the deal as soon as possible before any other parties became interested.

'We'd be idiots not to buy,' she stated forcibly.

'The garage, yes; but as for the rest . . .'

'Then, we'll buy!' she exclaimed in triumph. That was the first and most important stage; everything else would follow. She'd see to that. Leaning across, she kissed him on the cheek. 'I know we're doing the right thing. I just know it.'

He thought of Drum House. This would mean leaving his job there. It was something he would once have never contemplated, but that was when Celia was alive. It was different now she was dead. Now it would almost be a relief to leave, put it behind him. It was a chapter in his life that was now closed. Better to walk away rather than dwell among memories.

'Car hire,' he muttered. He'd have to look into that, find out just what was what.

'Chauffeur!' Gray exclaimed.

'It was Ishbel who suggested it,' Rory explained.

'You're after work, and it's a good job,' Ishbel said. 'And a lot livelier now that Miss Maisie's here.'

'Mmm!' murmured Gray reflectively. So it had been Ishbel who'd suggested it? That was interesting.

'The pay's good, too,' Rory went on. 'I've certainly never had any complaints about it. The Master is very generous.'

'To all his staff,' Ishbel stated.

'Ishbel says you can drive?'

'But I haven't for years.'

'No matter. I'll take you out and about, give you a chance to get your hand back in.'

'Or I can,' Ishbel added quickly, then blushed.

Rory glanced from one to the other, already having guessed in which way that particular wind was blowing. 'That might be even better as Ishbel will have more opportunity than me,' he stated, lying.

'And it's live-in?'

'If you choose. I've got a lovely room.'

Gray liked that idea. He liked it very much indeed. 'Then, I'm your man,' he declared.

'Right,' Rory enthused. 'You'll naturally have to be interviewed by Miss Maisie, but that will only be a formality with the reference I give you.' Rory rose. 'In fact I'll go and speak to her straight away. I know she's free.'

'Chauffeur,' Gray repeated softly, eyes boring into Ishbel's.

She blushed again.

Gray parked Rory's runabout where the sea was spread before them like a vast bluey-green blanket. His face became strangely blank, his eyes introspective.

'Do you miss it?' Ishbel asked.

He gave her a lopsided smile. 'Not in the least.'

'Good,' she murmured.

Reaching across, he laid a hand over hers, waiting to see if she pulled away, which she didn't.

'We can stop off for a bite on the way home?' he proposed.

'That would be nice.'

He paused, then said: 'Are you sure?'

'Oh, yes.'

Nothing had been said, but they both knew what was intended. His last question hadn't been about food at all, as she was well aware.

As they drove away Ishbel watched the sea until it vanished from sight, then brought her attention back to Gray. 'I'm starving,' she declared.

He laughed. 'Me, too.'

THE END

MAGGIE JORDAN
by Emma Blair

When most of Maggie Jordan's family are killed in a freak flood in the small coastal village of Heymouth, she is forced to find work in one of Glasgow's carpet mills. She becomes engaged to Nevil Sanderson, who suddenly decides he must go to Spain and join the Republicans in their fight against Franco.

Although she struggles on without him, Maggie eventually realizes her place is by his side and journeys to Spain to join him. But the newly promoted Nevil has become distant and ruthless, and is fiercely jealous of her new friendship with American journalist Howard Taft.

Years later, married and with an eight-year-old daughter, Maggie has returned to Glasgow. Astonished when Howard reappears, bringing light and laughter back into her life, she is forced to take decisions – decisions which threaten to destroy even the vibrant and courageous Maggie Jordan.

A Bantam Paperback

0 553 40072 X

SCARLET RIBBONS
by Emma Blair

Sadie Smith can't believe her luck when she is told that soon she will be like all other children *and* her mother buys her a pair of scarlet ribbons. For Sadie, born with a degenerative hip, is unable to walk. When she arrives at Babies Castle, a Dr Barnardo's home, she is so excited that she fails to realize she will never see her beloved family again.

In 1927, once fully cured, Sadie is offered the opportunity of a lifetime: to start a new life in Canada. But when she arrives at the Trikhardts' farm in the heart of Ontario, her new life seems far from perfect. Worked from dawn to dusk, she treasures her scarlet ribbons and seeks solace in her friendship with fellow orphan, cheeky-faced Robbie.

A freak hurricane finally provides Sadie with a lucky escape. From Canadian parlourmaid to pilot in Britain's Air Transport Auxiliary, from office clerk to managing director, Sadie has to draw on all her courage and strength in her determined struggle to find the lasting happiness that had always eluded her as a child.

A Bantam Paperback
0 553 40298 6

THE WATER MEADOWS
by Emma Blair

It is May 1926. Glasgow is crippled by the General Strike and the future looks bleak for John Forsyth. Made redundant from his factory job and with no prospect of employment, he and his family only hold together through the determination of his ambitious wife, Madge. Even though this means a dramatic move to the farthest reaches of England – to Devon.

As the family begin a new life in the village of Atherton, their fortunes change. John works in the copper mine, but unused to the appalling conditions finds solace in the Church and in his secret supply of scrumpy; long-suffering Madge ultimately attains love and happiness where she least expects it; and Graham, their eldest child, soon discovers how thrilling – and lucrative – a smuggler's life can be. However, it is Jennie, the Forsyth's wilful daughter, who faces the greatest challenge of them all. Her dreams take her far beyond Devon's green fields and golden sands, and will bring her both devastating loss and passionate love.

'Another cracking read' *Sunday Post*

A Bantam Paperback
0 553 40372 9

IN SUNSHINE OR IN SHADOW
by Charlotte Bingham

Brougham is an imposing and beautiful house, the stateliest of stately homes, but to Lady Artemis Deverill it brings only sorrow and a lonely, crippled childhood. For Eleanor Milligan, born in downtown Boston of a poor Irish immigrant family, childhood means a continual battle against her bullying brothers and cruel father. When they meet on a liner sailing to Ireland, Artemis and Ellie couldn't have less in common or be more different in looks or temperament. But in spite of this they become friends, and when Ellie's Cousin Rose asks Artemis to stay on at Strand House, County Cork, for a few weeks of an idyllic pre-war summer, Artemis has little difficulty in accepting. It is there that Hugo Tanner meets both girls and is posed a question that will haunt him for the rest of his life.

A Bantam Paperback

0 553 40296 X

NANNY
by Charlotte Bingham

Grace Merrill is born into the middle-class life of provincial Edwardian England, the world of long golden afternoons, and tea on the lawn. In any other society Grace's talent for painting would be a cause for celebration but, in Keston, Art is simply not the done thing. Despite this, Grace is encouraged in her painting, ironically by the very woman who brings about the destruction of her comfortable world.

Grace is forced to enter service as a lower housemaid at the Great House, Keston Hall. That she rises rapidly through the ranks from housemaid to under-nanny, and eventually nanny, is a source of surprise more to herself than it is to those who know her, least of all her employers, the fascinating and idiosyncratic Lord and Lady Lydiard.

Serena Lydiard and Grace become friends and allies, and Grace becomes devoted to the Lydiard children, Henry and Harriet. But it isn't until the favoured visitor, Society painter Brake Merrowby, falls in love with Grace that she begins to understand the kind of commitment that she has been asked to make to children who, while demanding and securing her love, are not actually hers.

In Grace, Charlotte Bingham has created an unforgettable character, a loving soul who cannot bring herself to abandon those who have come to depend on her for that most powerful of emotions, mother love.

A Bantam Paperback

0 553 40496 2

THE FAIRFIELDS CHRONICLES
by Sarah Shears

Set in the heart of the Kent countryside and spanning the period from the turn of the century to the end of the Second World War, Sarah Shears introduces us to the inhabitants of Fairfields Village. As we follow the changing fortunes of the villagers we see how their lives and loves become irrevocably entwined over the years and watch the changing patterns of English country life through the eyes of one of our best loved novelists.

THE VILLAGE
FAMILY FORTUNES
THE YOUNG GENERATION
and now, the long-awaited conclusion:
RETURN TO RUSSETS

Published by Bantam Books

THE SISTERS
by Sarah Shears

For the first time in paperback.

When Amelia Brent's husband dies, a chapter closes in her life and she is forced to acknowledge the far-reaching consequences of widowhood. Required to live in greatly reduced circumstances, Amelia dismisses her household staff and begins to map out the future for her children.

For her two eldest daughters the future holds dramatic change and separation. Ellen, the eldest daughter, dreams of love and romance as the wife of a soldier stationed in India, but all too soon her dreams are shattered by a brutal and traumatic event. For her sister Grace, sent against her wishes to work in London, her future appears to be one of endurance, as she faces the bitter truth that the man she loves belongs to another.

The Sisters is a moving, romantic and richly evocative portrait by the author of *The Fairfields Chronicles*.

A Bantam Paperback

0 553 40582 9

A SELECTION OF FINE NOVELS
AVAILABLE FROM BANTAM BOOKS

THE PRICES SHOWN BELOW WERE CORRECT AT THE TIME OF
GOING TO PRESS. HOWEVER TRANSWORLD PUBLISHERS RESERVE
THE RIGHT TO SHOW NEW RETAIL PRICES ON COVERS WHICH MAY
DIFFER FROM THOSE PREVIOUSLY ADVERTISED IN THE TEXT OR
ELSEWHERE.

All Corgi/Bantam Books are available at your bookshop or newsagent, or can be ordered from the
following address:
Corgi/Bantam Books,
Cash Sales Department,
P.O. Box 11, Falmouth,
Cornwall TR10 9EN

UK and B.F.P.O. customers please send a cheque or postal order (no currency) and allow £1.00
for postage and packing for the first book plus 50p for the second book and 30p for each additional
book ordered up to a maximum charge of £3.00 (7 books plus).

Overseas customers, including Eire, please allow £2.00 for postage and packing for the first book,
£1.00 for the second book, and 30p for each subsequent title ordered.

NAME (Block Letters) ....

ADDRESS ....

....